MW00610536

Cover design by Alejandro Colucci

Map design by Luan Bittencourt

Author photograph by Felipe Koji

Chapter header designs by Claudio Mello

ISBN (ebook): 978-1-957237-00-8

ISBN (Paperback): 978-1-957237-01-5

ISBN (Case Hardback): 978-1-957237-02-2

ISBN (Hardback): 978-1-957237-03-9

This is a work of fiction. All characters, organizations and events in this novel are either products of the author's imagination or are used fictitiously.

A TOUCH OF LIGHT

THE ASHES OF AVARIN: BOOK ONE

THIAGO ABDALLA

THE ALTERIAN PRESS

To Matheus, who, without the need for words, put me on this path, and Erica, who taught me how to enjoy it.

AVARIN

THE ULEAN SEA

DAKHRAN BAY

The Parted Isles

Erez

DAKHRA

THE SKYGATE

The Skygate

THE CLAN LANDS

RONARI

HAGUN

YLTIGG

LOTHRAK

SACANTHA

Pyrran

Dalhold

Pehd

PEHD VALLEY

Farkhul

VIZCARRA

Gheria

Durin

Ratha

ALTERIA

KHET

Halsport

Verneil

Ultenvell

OTHONEA

Talnea

Pelaket

THE BORDERLANDS

THE VISSLANDS

THE CONTINENT OF IMMERIA

LIST OF CHARACTERS, ORGANIZATIONS AND PLACES

The Continent of Immeria

The Domain – Notable characters, organizations and places

OTHONEA – One of the largest and most powerful nations in the Domain.

- **Adrian Pell** – Prince of Othonea.
- **Iridan Pell** – King of Othonea, father to Adrian, Jovu and Ellana Pell.
- **Jovu Pell** – Prince of Othonea. Adrian's brother.
- **Ellana Pell** – Sister to Adrian and Jovu. High priestess of Khet in the Church of the Seraph.
- **Queen Dalenna Pell** – Mother to Adrian, Jovu and Ellana. Deceased.
- **Derren** – Captain of the Othonean army.
- **Old Gera** – Deceased. Took care of Adrian, Jovu and Ellana after their mother died.

KHET – A smaller nation to the north of Othonea. Allied to Dakhra, Othonea's biggest rival nation in the Domain.

- **Henrik Brandt** – King of Khet, Father to Addo
- **Addo Brandt** – Prince of Khet. A coward.
- **Garrick Brandt** – Henrik's brother. Commander of the Khetish armies.
- **Balt Brandt** – Deceased. Garrick's son.
- **Captains Emric, Hart and Nevin** - Captains in the Khetish army aiding the Legion.
- **Raklin** – The cleanser at Ultenvell palace in Khet.
- **Nasir** – A Priest of the Blood found in the Khet.
- **Hyrkil** – Captain of the Khetish guard.

DAKHRA – One of the Domain nations. Othonea's biggest rival.

- **Syvern** – King of Dakhra.
- **Alaya** – Princess of Dakhra and commander of the Dakhran air fleet.
- **Myrra** – Princess of Dakhra, betrothed to Adrian Pell.

SACANTHA – One of the Domain nations. Lynn's home nation

- **Niria** – Queen of Sacantha.
- **Lord Keeper Kerr** – Keeper of the prison of Dalhold.
- **Morna** – A priestess that leads Baywater Temple in Sacantha.
- **Ferrin** – A watcher in the Sacanthan prison of Dalhold.

VIZCARRA – One of the Domain nations. Protects the southern borders of the Domain against possible clan attacks.

- **Rheda** – Queen of Vizcarra.

THE VISSLANDS – One of the Domain nations. Protects the southern borders of the Domain against possible clan attacks.

- **Lesraile** – Queen of the Visslands.
- **Bahar** – Emissary representing the Visslands in the southern clans.
- **Councilor Carswell** – Part of the council under Queen Lesraile. His son is missing in the clanlands.
- **General Misher** – Seen dealing with the Ronar clan.

THE HOLY CHURCH OF THE SERAPH – All Domain nations follow the Church of the Seraph. The religion has declared death as the enemy and it is said that the Seraph's blessings extend the lives of the faithful. The Church is based on four tenets of faith: Breath, Body, Blood and Bone

- **The Seraph** – The goddess who left the land because of all the death. It is the duty of the faithful to prove themselves worthy so that She may return in the Promised Dawn.
- **The High Pontiff** – Supreme leader of the Church.
- **The Priests of the Blood -** Priests trained in elite healing. Represent the Blood.
- **The Sentinels** – An elite force of griffin riders answering to the High Pontiff. The only ones allowed to kill in the Domain outside of battle or prison executions. The Sentinels represent the Breath.
- **Bishops of the Bone** – The tenet of the Church responsible for information and spies. Represents the Bone.
- **High Priests of each nation**: Othonea – Erendal, Dakhra – Harven, Khet – Ellana.
- **Abbot Orwen** – Lynn's old abbot in the house of Farkhul.
- **Abbot Andral** – Standing in for Orwen in the house of Farkhul.
- **Priest Talbot** – A priest in the house of Farkhul.
- **High Priest Lindamm** – The Pontiff's Appointed high priest for the Legion.

THE ORDER OF THE SENTINELS

- **Lynn** – A rogue Sentinel troubled by her past.
- **Vedyr** – Lynn's griffin.
- **Commander Leardin** – Leader of the Sentinels.
- **Olem** – The Sentinel's second in command.
- **Rel** – A Sentinel close to Lynn in the past. Supplied her with ruin-stone.
- **Ildred** – A Sentinel from Lynn's past. Does not forgive her for leaving the order.
- **Thain** – A Sentinel close to Ildred.
- **Sentinels found in Durnn**: Gwyndel, Deria, Cedd, Wyman, Brehnna.
- **Elwin** – A high-ranking Sentinel. Mentor to Lynn.
- **Emida** – Elwin's griffin.

THE CHURCH LEGION – The army of the Church. Reduced to guard the city of Alteria as years of peace prevailed.

- **Burnham** – A drunk leading the Legion in Alteria.
- **Gotzon** – A Legion captain.
- **Iker** – A Legion captain.

THE HAND OF THE SERAPH – A militia formed in Alteria for people to defend themselves where the Legion failed. Led by Commander Ashford.

The Southern Clans – Notable characters, organizations and places

THE FOUR CLANS: RONAR, YLTIGG, HAGUN AND LOTHRAK

THE RONAR – Live close to a volcano. There is a divide between village dwellers and those relegated to the slopes of the volcano, known as Slopers.

- **Nasha** – A hunter for the Ronar. Came from the slopes and proved herself to become part of the clan. Can feel the emotions of others, considers it a curse.
- **Iallo** – A warrior for the Ronar. Does not accept Nasha as Ronar.
- **Mansa** – One of the leaders of the Ronar known as Roots. He is the leader of the hunters. His title is Oringo.
- **Chatta** – Another Root. He is the Warden, leader of the warriors.
- **Tomu** – Chief of the Ronar.
- **Jabillo** – Another Root. Speaker for the Earth. Leads the Speakers: priest-like figures who are spreaders of the tales of the Ronar.
- **Adda** – The Tivezzi, another Root. Responsible for shaping ancestor-stone. Daughter to the Chief.
- **Tedros** – An ancient hero and leader of the clans before they were split into four.
- **Razi** – Adda's son.

THE SLOPERS – Live on the slopes of the volcano. Slopers are not considered part of the Ronar until proven.

- **Shai** – Daughter to Ife, a Sloper close to Nasha. Struggles to get supplies from the village.
- **Ife** – Deceased. One of Nasha's closest friends when she lived in the slopes.
- **Uvo** – Shai's brother.
- **Landi** – Shai's mother.
- **Devu** – Bahar's son (the emissary of the Visslands). An initiate drafted for the proving.
- **Berg** – An initiate drafted for the proving.
- **Verena** - An initiate drafted for the proving.
- **Zima** - An initiate drafted for the proving.
- **Leku** – Leader of the Zaruni, a militia that dubs itself the protectors of the slopes.

The Continent of Azur

A nation-continent of copper sands. The capital city of Dar Drezji is where the Xakhar rules with the support of the ten consuls, each represented by a noble family.

- **The Xakhar** – Ruler of Azur.
- **Kahlia** – Princess of Azur daughter of the Xakhar.
- **Niilar** – Prince of Azur son of the Xakhar.

PROLOGUE

The dead shall not be mourned or remembered, for death is the enemy and will only drive the Seraph away. To keep death in our hearts is to delay Her return in the Promised Dawn.

— *The Book of the Blood*

F ather's officers shuffled around the map on the council room table, pointing out routes and offering suggestions, each one more certain than the last about the location of the missing airship. Half a dozen voices, all arguing over whose unsuitable excuse would be brought to the king. Adrian stood by the window with his back to them, gaze set on the palace grounds, mind set on his brother.

Jovu would've had theories of his own, no doubt, and the officers would likely have followed them. It should have been him standing in the room instead of Adrian—Father would certainly say so—but everything had changed when Jovu died, and Adrian was all that was left.

None mentioned the dead prince, of course. They'd never risk falling out of the Church's grace by speaking of the dead. But that didn't stop the questions in Adrian's mind.

Why had Father sent Jovu into the clanlands in the first place? Why had the Pontiff not preserved Jovu's body to be brought back in the Promised Dawn? They'd followed the Church of the Seraph, lived for hundreds of years off what the Pontiff called Her blessings, but how much was each year worth if Jovu's name couldn't ever be spoken again?

Adrian let out a long breath and turned to look at the officers, still arguing around the map of the Domain. He'd never even believed in the blessings, and he was sure his years came from the power of his family's blood, not some misguided notion that the Seraph found them worthy. Yet Father seemed to have a different opinion, and it was strong enough to sacrifice the memory of his eldest son.

He left the men to argue in the room and paced down the corridor until he reached the open doors of the reflection hall. Myrra sat on a low stone bench in the center of the rectangular chamber, head bowed, hands on her lap, while priests tended to scriptures and images of griffin riders carved into the walls. They brushed off motes of dust that drifted in the rays of sunlight streaming in from the openings above.

Adrian watched her for a while. Silent. Holding back any expression that could alert the priests to his true feelings about Jovu. One of the clergymen lingered on him—his eyes inviting Adrian into the chamber, perhaps—but he managed nothing other than a frown in return. His own eyes were still dry from the lack of sleep, his throat still tight from strangling down the tears he could not show.

He shifted his feet, and the clinking of his sword caught Myrra's attention. She rose and walked towards him with a solemn aspect of her own, while Adrian forced a steady gaze into his eyes and a weak smile onto his lips—his best attempt at masking the ache tearing at his chest.

She stepped into the corridor and tilted her head while pulling him away from the sight of the priests.

"You don't have to put on that face with me," she said in a gentle voice.

Adrian's mouth twisted, and he closed his eyes, trying to keep back the pain that was seeping through. She stepped up and kissed him lightly on the lips.

"I'll always be here for you," she said, then gave him a smile, much warmer than his own. It was veiled by the waves of her auburn hair but touched her leaf-green eyes and was as soft as the lines of her face. He held her gaze for a while, hoping he could forget all of it, wake up from whatever madness had fallen upon them.

"He shouldn't have gone," Adrian said.

"You shouldn't dwell on this, Adrian. We should look ahead."

"He attacked the clans, Myrra!" Adrian started moving down the hallway, struggling to keep his voice down, and she followed. "Jovu had been the leader of the Othonean armies for over a hundred years. He never attacked the clans. Not even the Pontiff would have ordered it."

"Wasn't he expanding the Domain?"

Adrian shook his head. "No. I . . . heard things after he left. One of Father's generals grumbling to his captains about being left behind. Jovu was looking for something. Something my father trusted no one else to look for."

"In the clanlands? What could have been so important outside the Domain?"

"I'm not sure, but he was willing to sacrifice Jovu for whatever it was he was after."

Myrra frowned. "You shouldn't think like that. You'll need your father to get through this, and he'll turn to you now. Maybe you can ask him about it."

"I doubt he'd trust me. I'll never be Jovu."

"You can be better."

Adrian scoffed, eyes trained on the corridor ahead. "I love you, but not even you believe that."

"I don't remember you provoking the slaughter of entire

19

villages. Would you attack the clans knowing they'd strike back? Even if your father ordered it?"

"I . . . I don't know."

"I know you wouldn't."

They started making their way down a stairwell towards the King's Temple, Adrian's gut clenching with every step closer to Father.

"You're stronger than you think, and your father knows it too. Why don't you talk to him about Khet?"

"He'd never listen to me, and he'd never trust Khet. Jovu tried."

"Jovu didn't know them as you do." She lowered her voice to a whisper. "Khet has been a foothold for Dakhra for too long. Every step your father takes is with one eye over his shoulder. If you could remove the threat from his back . . ."

"You talk like you're not a Dakhran princess."

"I'm your wife-to-be, and that is stronger than any title."

Adrian gave her a true smile this time. He knew she was right.

The circumstances of his brother's death were still too shadowed for Adrian to accept, and, even if he asked, no one would ever talk about it. He was the one who needed to understand what his brother had died for, no matter how grim the notion of getting close to Father. Maybe removing a thorn from the old king's side could soften him enough to make the ordeal bearable.

Adrian narrowed his eyes at Myrra. She didn't smile, but the triumph was plain on her face by the time they reached the bottom of the steps and paced into the chamber before the closed temple doors.

Dignitaries representing the five other nations of the Domain stood in private groups, but Adrian's gaze was fixed on his father. The king's short, sandy-blond hair mirrored Adrian's in all but length, as did the thin shape of his eyes. He'd always wondered if it made the old man proud, seeing parts of himself in his son, but wasn't sure he'd care for the answer. Father was flanked by a handful of priests and a lightly bearded man with shoulder-length tawny hair in a silver cloak that fell off the shoulders of his glinting armor.

A stacked circle of crescent moons emblazoned on his chest showed the Sign of the Breath. A Sentinel.

The man tried to stay in the shadows, but Adrian caught more than one uneasy glimpse shooting towards the Sentinel. Most kept their distance; others looked anxiously at Father, but he did not look back.

It was only a moment before a man in the silver-and-white robes of the Church parted the temple doors and turned towards Father.

"They are ready for the cleansing, King Iridan."

Cleansing. Adrian balked at the word. He could still remember the day Jovu took him to the palace Cleansers. It was the day Old Gera died, and Adrian couldn't accept how no one would speak her name. She'd raised them after they lost Mother and had been as important to Adrian as any person he'd known, but much like today, after life left her, it was as if she'd never existed. Adrian tried asking Father, yet things had never been the same between them without Mother. The old man demanded too much of his children with hardly any explanation, and, unlike Jovu or Ellana, Adrian was never short of questions.

Father hated the questions. He turned Adrian away, as always, and it was Jovu who took him to see the old woman burned into indistinguishable ash along with the rest of the piled, unworthy bodies of the dead.

Father strode into the temple and the procession slowly filed after him, filling the space of the circular cloister along the edges of the open-roofed temple. Adrian waited for another moment in the entrance hall. He could never have imagined he'd see Jovu burn, and it was impossible to think of his brother as unworthy. Impossible to accept that a private . . . *cleansing* was all he'd get. It was more than Old Gera had gotten, but it still wasn't enough.

He breathed in, held the air for a moment, then blew it out and walked into the temple with Myrra by his side.

Blood-red Othonean banners hung between cloister pillars, and short steps descended into a wide circular patio where Jovu's body lay on a pyre. The setting sun splayed across the Seraph's scriptures carved through the temple walls, projecting the words in orange-yellow light on the shaded temple ground.

A shadow moved over the gathered dignitaries—a winged outline, gliding over the opening—and looks shot up towards the massive griffin circling above. Adrian had seen the beasts on the ground once. They stood three men tall and two men wide, but this one seemed even larger with its spread wings. None lingered on the Sentinel's beast for long, though. No one was ever comfortable around the Church's elite, and there was always a haze surrounding their mounts, something in the way their silver eyes locked onto your own.

Adrian's gaze drifted down to his brother's body, lying motionless on the pyre. His neatly combed long black hair and clean face almost made him look as if he were asleep, if not for the paleness of his skin. It churned Adrian's stomach, and he had to press his teeth and swallow hard to keep his expression under control.

He glanced at the gathered dignitaries, but none seemed focused on him. They were here only as witnesses, an assurance that Othonea was doing its part in cleansing the unworthy from the Seraph's Domain.

A priest strode to the center and stopped beside Jovu, flaming torch in hand. Father paused but did not hesitate for long before descending the steps, taking the torch and putting it to the bottom of Jovu's pyre—eyes still devoid of pain.

Myrra brushed a warm hand against his. "Now is the time. Stand by your father."

Adrian nodded, sucked in a breath, held it for a moment, then blew it out, just like she'd taught him. It loosened the knot in his stomach, and he stepped towards the pyre.

Father did not move as Adrian approached, his empty gaze fixed on the flames. Even now, he still had eyes only for Jovu, it seemed.

"Your sister should be here." Father's voice was solid as winter ice, no wavering, not even now that they could not be heard.

"Ellana is a high priestess, Father. Her family is the Church."

"Blood still holds ties. You'll learn that soon enough, boy, and she'll learn to respect all I've given you."

"I am your blood, and I am here at your side."

"With Dakhran blood at yours."

"Myrra's ties are with me, with Othonea." Adrian paused, but the question had already risen to his lips. "Why did you send Jovu into the clanlands? What were you after?"

"Always asking questions, yet you still do nothing to deserve the answers." Father shook his head, his eyes focused ahead. The finality in his tone was the same Adrian had heard since childhood. He'd get nothing from the old man. Not today.

Adrian looked back at the pyre. The smoke made his eyes water and his nostrils burn. He would have taken anything at that moment to be convinced it wasn't true, but each burning breath reminded him of the reality that nothing had been enough. Neither Jovu's deeds, nor his faith, nor his belief in the Seraph's blessings had protected him. The thought that someone like his brother had put so much faith in the blessings set a fire in Adrian's veins. Maybe Jovu should have asked a few more questions himself. Still, the Church had some truth. Adrian had never believed in the blessings, but he'd never denied the Promised Dawn. The day the Seraph would return, raising the worthy, whose bodies had been preserved by the Pontiff. There was enough evidence in the texts, and Father had taken them to see the original scriptures in Alteria after Mother's body was embalmed.

Maybe some small measure of hope that Jovu might still follow Mother's path had lingered before, but that hope had crumbled and was swirling away like Jovu's ashes. The Seraph would have no body to bring Jovu back. Adrian's brother was truly gone.

Adrian turned back towards the gathered witnesses, blinking hard—they were breaking away, their duty done now that Jovu had been burned.

Hypocrites. They wore the mask of piousness, but it was nothing more than fear of losing their so-called blessings. They'd be struggling just the same if their brothers were lying on the pyre.

Adrian stood beside Father with his back to Jovu. The old man had his eyes on the pyre, but the words still seemed stuck in Adrian's throat. He closed his eyes and repeated the ritual Myrra had taught him—breathing in deep, letting the burning air swirl in his chest, then blowing out. She was right. He had to get close to Father to find out what Jovu had been after.

"We should talk soon, Father. I . . . might have a solution to some of our problems with Dakhra."

Father did not turn to him and gave no indication he'd heard the words, but Adrian knew the man well enough. There would be no answer now. Adrian walked away, incapable of bearing the ashen scent or the lightheadedness that always came while standing beside his father any longer.

Myrra waited for him in the raised cloister, and Adrian lingered beside her, not wanting to face the stares that would fall upon him now that Jovu was gone. They stayed there until the temple was devoid of witnesses and all that remained were the priests collecting Jovu's ashes to be scattered over the Ulean Sea and taken away from the Domain.

Not even his ashes are good enough for their precious Domain.

Adrian moved close to Myrra, but a hand touched his shoulder from behind. He turned to find Derren looking at him, a heavy beard giving his somber expression even more weight. The captain of his father's army was said to have been with Jovu when it happened, but Adrian doubted they'd discuss it; the living should not dwell on the dead, and there was too much faith in the old captain's heart for that. Derren moved aside, and Father stood there, regarding Adrian with placid, ice-blue eyes.

"Let us talk, then." He stepped past them and into one of the many doors that led into a private reflection chamber, one of many constructed around the covered walkway of the temple.

Adrian hesitated, and his stomach coiled into a knot again, tighter than before, but he could not refuse his father's sudden invitation.

"You are stronger than you think," Myrra whispered as she, too, stepped past him and into the chamber. Adrian breathed deep, then followed.

The room was cramped, lit only by candlelight that illuminated a carved depiction of the Seraph on the far wall: Her flowing hair framed sharp features with a squared-off jaw and eyes that were as empty as Father's had been—no irises or pupils carved into them. Three pairs of wings extended from her back, the white veins in the ruin-stone flickering with the dancing candle flame.

Adrian and Myrra sat on wooden benches to one side, while Father took the bench facing them on the other. He frowned at Myrra, likely preferring not to have her there, but Adrian ignored the expression.

"I'd expected some more—"

"Things are never as we expect, boy. Speak."

Adrian regarded his father for a long moment before doing so. "You and Syvern have been at each other's throats for years."

The king's gaze flicked to Myrra at the mention of her father, but her own gaze remained collectedly calm.

"Yet Khet has never let you focus," Adrian said, trying to regain the old man's attention. "Their ports are a doorway for Dakhran troops, one you must always keep your eye on. You've tried things your way, but they don't seem to be working." The words tasted treacherous. He wasn't used to criticizing his father's strategies or his brother's execution of them, and doing so after seeing Jovu burn only made it worse. "We should propose an alliance."

Father let out a sharp laugh. "The wolf does not ally himself with the crows. He takes what is his and leaves them the scraps. An alliance presumes trust." His gaze slid to Myrra again. "Maybe if King Henrik had a daughter, we could consider marriage. It would bring more than your current . . . situation."

Myrra's stare remained as composed as the king's had during Jovu's burning. "Your discomfort is well noted, King Iridan, yet not even Jovu held the respect Adrian does among the Khetish court."

The king's eyes narrowed at the sound of Jovu's name, but Adrian gave him no time to steer the conversation away.

"King Henrik listens to his son, and Addo will listen to me," Adrian said. "Would it not be better to have them on our side? Mitigate Dakhra's presence so close to Othonea? We'd control the Ulean Sea, know if Syvern tried to send airships over it. You wouldn't have to rely on men like the ones you trapped me in that council room with."

Father's eyes darted between them, his brow knotting into the slightest of frowns. Maybe it was the mention of the airships, maybe he was recalling the incompetence of his officers, or maybe he saw the sense in what Adrian was proposing. Whatever it was, he seemed to be entertaining the proposition. "We've tried talking to them before. Henrik is a snake."

"I'm sure he'd say the same about you, Father, and I was never part of those conversations."

"Indeed, you were not." Father's tone was laced with disapproval, but after a long moment, he grunted and stood. "I will consider your request." The door opened, and the king paused on the way out, looking back at Adrian. "The Pontiff has sent me a Sentinel, thinks it will help keep me safe." He snorted. "You should have him. Elwin, I think he was called."

Father walked off, making his way past Derren and back into the palace. The captain looked back at Adrian, nodded, then followed the king.

Adrian let out a heavy breath, ignoring the underlying slight in his father's offer of the Sentinel. He'd listened. He'd shown his usual resistance, but Adrian had sat through enough audiences to know that he would at least consider the idea, and that was the first step in uncovering what Jovu had died for.

He turned to Myrra, who had a hopeful glint in her eye. It still hurt not having Jovu. It still felt wrong stepping into the void left by his brother, but he had her, and she was all he needed to keep going.

Adrian smiled. "I don't know what I'd do without you."

CHAPTER ONE

The Seraph blesses Her favored with endless years. Life is the reward for the faithful who keep death's influence at bay. To forget the unworthy is to forever cleanse the memory of the enemy from the Domain. It is the only true path to the Promised Dawn.

— The Book of the Body

The last shadows of night still clung to Ultenvell's empty streets, draping them in an eerie half-light as Adrian rode past the gates into the Khetish capital.

There had been attacks of late—crazed fanatics, taken by some kind of battle-fever, was all that had reached Adrian's ears—but Father's orders were to come alone, and so he had. He might have questioned them another time, but not today.

Adrian kept his wits about him and his hand close to his sword on the way to the palace gates, but he noticed little more than anxious eyes peeking occasionally through cracks. He dismounted at the edge of the square before the palace, looking up at the domed building while soldiers milled about one task or another through the square. He stepped up the pathway flanked by towering statues of the old kings of Khet and up to the guards at the gate, who recognized his attire, if not his face, and stood to attention. Adrian checked the terms he'd folded in a pocket close to his chest, then produced the Othonean royal seal. The guard's eyes widened.

"Lor—ehrm—Prince . . ." He slammed a fist against his chest and began falling to his knees, but Adrian shot out a hand to stop him.

"No need to alert the people to my presence, soldier. Lead on."

Adrian kept his eyes down as the guards led him through the main hall, but his mind was unconsciously taking in the details, picking up all the lines that Myrra had always loved to point out: moss-green marble intertwined with dark ruin-stone, the gray streaked with white veins that shone when touched by the pale light trickling in through slits that had been cut into the walls on every side. The perfect balance of bright and shadow, she'd called it, yet the halls were darker today. The cold gloom and lukewarm glow were enveloped in a musty smell, like an old memory that might have been pleasant once but was now too tainted to keep.

"I . . . served under you at Sacantha, sir." The guard's nervous voice pulled Adrian's eyes towards him. "Finest commander I've ever had, sir. They never stood a chance, sir."

Adrian's ribs tightened. It was Jovu who'd commanded the Domain armies at Sacantha. He couldn't begrudge the recognition, though. He'd felt the same about his brother, as had Father, and Adrian was sure some in the Domain hardly knew the king had another son. He gave the man a weak smile but no answer.

The guard breathed in and puffed out his cheeks a few times, maybe trying to understand if he had given offense, but when he was about to speak again, his companion halted abruptly before the throne room and slammed the butt of his spear on the ground, silencing his fumbling counterpart before any more damage could be done. They ushered Adrian through, then closed the screeching stone doors behind them.

The throne room was a richer, more illuminated extension of

the main hall. The mossy motif of the previous chamber now joined a lighter palette of the Khetish colors, with gold-leaf designs adding to the green and gray, glinting in the light coming from the enormous windows on either side.

Henrik Brandt lounged on the throne atop deep-green gold-trimmed cushions. It was easily the most spectacular part of the room, with jade, gold, and ruin-stone wrought into a perfectly flowing whole. Brandt was a tall man, slightly built, with sharp eyes that did not linger on Adrian, instead focusing on the wine in his hand. His brother, Lord Garrick, was as tall as Henrik, with twice the bulk and a scar going down the side of his face. He stood beside the throne but did not wear the customary armor that identified him as commander of the Khetish troops, and he stared straight ahead, his face a blank mask.

Ashamed of his defeat, perhaps?

Addo stood at the bottom of the steps. His balding head was bowed, and his narrow, twitchy eyes jumped from his father and uncle to Adrian. He wore an odd smile, as if he were unsure whether to be encouraging, apologetic, or pleading.

Adrian paused before them. He didn't kneel.

"So . . ." Lord Henrik's languid speech was as infuriating as it had ever been. "Iridan could not usurp me himself. . . . He's sent his pup."

He'd kept his own Khetish guard in the room—two standing between Adrian and the throne, others lining the walls—and seemed comfortable enough in his defiance to sneer when he realized Adrian's knees would not be touching the ground.

"Henrik Brandt." Adrian cleared his throat. "I am here to deliver terms of surrender to the province—"

"Nation! Have some respect, boy!" His voice rose to a piercing shrill, and he spat the last word like his wine had gone sour.

A flush crept up Adrian's neck, his face hot, his arms light, almost numb, ready to lunge at the man. Adrian glared at him, but Father's words drifted into his mind: "Do not dawdle. Get them to Alteria to sign the terms."

He swallowed. *Yes, Father.*

"You and your guard are to vacate the palace imm——"

"Your brother had respect. He'd at least have the decency to kneel before a king. He's dead now. If he's the unworthy one, where does that leave you?" He was slurring each word out like he couldn't even be bothered to move his lips enough to form them. "Ah, . . . still reeling over your dead Dakhran bitch, I see. Would you like her bones to chew on, little pup?"

"You will not talk about her!" Adrian bellowed, his pounding heart a deafening roar in his ears. He took a step forward, every muscle on edge, begging him to pull steel. He could almost hear the sweet scrape of sword against scabbard, like a lover's whisper, Myrra's whisper. *Do it.*

His hand twitched, and he took another step forward, but Brandt only smiled.

"Come on, then," Brandt said.

The words sliced through Adrian like a shard of ice. He'd seen this before. Jovu had used the same words with him dozens of times in sparring, and Adrian had fallen for them every time. Charged in, only to leave himself open to his brother's counterattack.

Remember why you are here. You need Father. Jovu and Myrra cannot have died for nothing.

His eyes settled on Lord Henrik, thoughts cooling. The bastard wanted this, wanted Adrian to strike. Dead nobility during the negotiation of terms? That would certainly rile up the people in revolt against their invaders. But he couldn't be sacrificing himself. He'd never give up his own life.

Who, then?

Adrian regarded the other faces. The guards were as stiff as the marble pillars, and Addo's odd, apologetic smile hadn't changed— aimed at his father, then his uncle. Garrick still stood beside the throne wearing the same blank expression: too blank, almost pale . . . and no armor. That's the thing about sacrifice. It always looks good when it isn't your own. The ones paying the price, however, are easy to spot.

Adrian looked back to Addo, understanding what his smile was apologizing for. He'd always been a coward. Always let others pay the price. Garrick was the one taking the fall, but not even Addo looked comfortable with it.

Seems like not all blood holds the same ties, Father.

"Lord Garrick," Adrian said. The man almost jumped at the sound of his name. "How old was your pup when he died? As a pious man, you undoubtedly spare him little thought. Do you even remember how Balt died? Something to do with fighting in his cousin's stead, I believe?"

The man's eyes jumped to Addo, then moved towards Adrian, seething like burning coals. Adrian pressed on, one hand still on the hilt of his sword, the other with his palm out towards Garrick.

"Your brother's the one serving up the bones of the dead for us to chew on. Tell me, Lord Garrick, how does it feel knowing yours are the bones he is offering to keep that pretty chair of his?"

The heat from Garrick's eyes was seeping out into his reddening face, while Henrik was gaining a bit of a pale countenance himself.

"So this is how Othonea negotiates terms?" Henrik said. "With lies and scheming?"

A convincing argument. Not nearly as effective without his dead brother sprawled out before him.

"Why don't we make this simple, Lord Garrick? The terms for Khet stand. You will be annexed as a province of Othonea, paying tribute to the king and tithes to the Church. I'm certain we can come to an agreement on the amount. The more personal terms I have to offer, however, are——"

A sudden scraping of steel was the only indication before Garrick's dagger plunged into the side of his brother's neck. A precise stab, quickly in, quickly out, no feeling in it.

Blood gushed out onto the throne, staining the cushions and spreading around Henrik, who grabbed at the wound as he stumbled to the floor, words choked in a pathetic wheeze. He twisted and coughed at the foot of the throne as if there something he could do to prevent his fate, but the blood ran down the steps all the same and pooled at Adrian's feet. It was a deep Othonean red. Fitting to seal the deal.

Addo gave out a whimper, looking at the guards and pointing at his uncle, but received only a silencing glare from Garrick in return. The guards had their weapons up, seemingly confused by the meaning of this unexpected sacrifice.

"Governor Garrick has acted to protect Othonea and the Church from the vile traitors who would seek to upset the peace in this holy Domain. I do hope your weapons are raised in salute." Adrian shot them a hard stare.

The Seraph would have probably frowned upon Garrick. The Pontiff would have condemned his actions as delaying the Promised Dawn. But Garrick's survival seemed to have won out over his piety. Strange how Adrian had found that to be the case with most men.

The weapons went down, one by one, back to their original positions, and all eyes fell on Garrick, siting upon the throne over the bloody corpse at his feet. His posture was stiff, with his bulk taking up more of the throne than his brother ever had. The scar on his face seemed to waver, but his gaze was set unflinchingly on Adrian.

"We accept your terms, Prince Adrian. Please send my apologies to your father on behalf of my family."

Adrian nodded. Always easier when pride was left out of politics. "I will need you to accompany me to Alteria for the signing of the papers before the Pontiff."

"Addo will go." He shot his nephew the same glare he'd given Adrian a moment ago. "You understand if I am wary of leaving Khet unprotected from the snakes spreading poison in the hearts of its people, yes?"

Adrian studied Garrick, then Addo, who averted his eyes.

"Very well," Adrian said. "And my sister?"

"In her chambers, Prince Adrian."

Adrian nodded again, then turned back towards the heavy doors and showed himself out, leaving bloody smears behind in his footsteps.

Adrian drew in a cold breath, closed his eyes, and let it swirl in his chest. He used to love this. It used to calm him every time Myrra made him do it, make him ready for anything. Now all it did was burn his lungs as he raised an uncertain hand to his sister's door.

He blew out, then knocked, and a moment later Ellana was looking at him placidly, likely hiding her underlying dread at the recent happenings in Khet. The room was dark but tidy. A steaming teacup sat on a small, round table close to the balcony, but the curtains leading out were drawn. Adrian paced towards them and reached out.

"Don't." Ellana moved to stand behind the table, while Adrian looked out over the busy palace square through the light curtains.

"What? I know there've been attacks, but you're the high priestess, Ellana."

"I'm just an Othonean, now." She left the "princess" unspoken, hadn't let herself be called one since joining the clergy. "Father just couldn't let me have this, could he?"

She spoke as if the occupation of Khet was a slight targeted at her, somehow. Maybe a bit of princess lingered within her after all.

"Did you expect him to sit idle while Dakhra handed them over?"

"Isn't that the point of the Domain, brother? The smaller nations are supposed to be safe from occupation. Othonea has overstepped."

"Not when they're letting princesses die in their own palaces." Henrik was supposed to keep Myrra safe. He'd failed. Adrian would not absolve Khet, even if it had been Elwin—that blasted Sentinel Father had assigned to them—who'd killed her. He searched his sister's eyes, gauging the terrain. "The Pontiff didn't seem too upset when he urged Khet to call for terms."

"What choice did he have? You'd have a bloodbath *inside* the Domain?" She looked away. "I thought I was out of Father's reach here. Enough that he'd forget about me. Feels like a foolish hope now."

"Whatever your qualms with Father or his with your Church, I doubt this was aimed at you, Ellana."

"My Church?" Ellana curled her lip. "Makes no difference where he was aiming. I was respected here, loved even. Now I'm just another invader."

"Blood holds ties, sister, more than any—"

"Oh, please! I never thought you'd be one to fall for his preaching. The only blood that holds us is the Seraph's. Should be, anyway. But Father always finds a way to twist the scriptures."

Adrian frowned for just a moment, then swallowed, unable to decide if the truth in his sister's words stung more than standing by Father's decisions.

Ellana moved around the table, tea still untouched, gazing into what Adrian hoped were his emotionless eyes. She was his sister, but she was also a high priestess. Adrian could not show how he felt about Myrra. He'd need to convince the Pontiff of her worthiness first.

"We must all accept the Seraph's judgment, Adrian, hard as it may seem." Ellana put a hand over his own and kept her gaze on him, probably recognizing his failed attempt at controlling his expression. She bore what looked like a practiced expression of her own, with welcoming eyes and a soft curve to her lips. It was probably the same she used to comfort her faithful, but Adrian found himself drawn to it all the same.

"Father twists us all to his will, little brother. Be wary of him and trust the Faith. It is the only path forward." Ellana removed her hand from his and looked out the balcony's still-drawn curtains. She might have been right, but there was little to gain by antagonizing Father.

He is all I have left. Blood holds ties.

Adrian sighed, then forced a smile, the thought of Myrra still preventing him from making it sincere. "I'll see you in Alteria, then?"

Ellana paused, then nodded and returned his smile with what seemed like genuine warmth. He knew the look. It reminded him of the days when no politics or religious institutions were pulling them apart, but those days were gone: he could see the lack of trust bleeding through the cracks in her stare like a bridge ending midway over the growing chasm between them.

He stepped out of the room, already knowing where his legs would take him. Myrra had been killed within these walls—the Cleansers would have her. Adrian tried another breath like Myrra had taught him, but there was no relent. He needed more. He needed her back.

There might be nothing left but blood, and Father still didn't trust him enough to tell him what Jovu was chasing in the clanlands, but Adrian was not his father. He would not let Myrra burn.

CHAPTER TWO

All life that is wasted must be taken, the essence returned to the Silent Earth.

— *Ronar clan saying*

"We should keep going," Nasha said. "Their tracks are still clear."

She stood at the edge of the tree line, frowning back at the three Ronar clansmen in the clearing, but Iallo only itched at the back of the stubble that covered his head and looked away, while Embe was already starting the fire.

"Can't track in the dark," Embe said.

His pack was on the ground beside his heavy axe and a belt filled with throwing knives, and his heavily bearded face was turned towards the firewood. He was blowing embers into life, while Jima, the only hunter other than her, was squinting unhelpfully at the ground, trying to make out the tracks. Nasha shook her head with gritted teeth.

Sending a one-striped hunter was bad enough, but she'd never understand why Mansa would send warriors as well, especially these two. Iallo and Embe might be happy with what they had. They'd been born in the village—born Ronar—and hadn't needed to claw their way from the Slopes into the clan, but Nasha couldn't afford their laxness. She'd seen their looks, their hushed words the whole way.

All they see is a Sloper, no matter how many stripes I've earned.

She turned to Iallo. He was leading them. He needed to see the sense in it. "We can't stop, Iallo. The Hagun rarely leave their lands, and we've barely circled the Great Mountain. If they're this close to the village, the clan could be in danger."

"We don't even know if they're Hagun—"

"Saw 'em with my own eyes," Jima said. "Long hair, pale skin, and all."

Iallo frowned at him. "And how many of your hunter's stripes does it take to be sure?"

Jima's eyes darted to the single dark scar line on the inside of his forearm, then away at the darkness.

"That many crossing the border would be a declaration of war. Why not attack the village? Why stumble through the wilds towards the Domain?" Iallo said.

"Besides, those Hagun skins would light up in the dark." Embe looked up from the fire and shot them a lopsided grin. "Whoever they are, they're heading away from Ronar land. Looks like things will resolve themselves soon enough."

"Those were not Mansa's orders," Nasha said. "The Roots—"

"The Oringo isn't here, the other Roots aren't here, and I'm in charge," Iallo said.

He turned away again, and a spike of irritation poked at Nasha's ribs. She wasn't sure if it was her own or if it came from one of the warriors, but the familiar tingle of rising emotion was already running across her skin, and that was warning enough. She couldn't keep pressing Iallo—couldn't risk losing herself to her curse.

She turned her back to them, closed her eyes, and emptied her thoughts, pushing the moment away so that their emotions would not gain control, just like Mansa had taught her. The effort drained her strength, and her body felt heavier, but she anchored herself in the blackness and did not open her eyes until her heart had become comfortably cold and dead to all feeling.

Nasha blew out a long breath. Mansa had helped her find a sliver of control over her curse, but it was a constant strain, and sweat was already beading on her brow. She stepped back and sat against a tree a few feet away from her fellow clansmen.

"How about a story?" Embe said. The flame was lit, and her most recent kill was on the spit and turning over the fire. "Tedros slaying the Earth-Breakers and uniting the Ronar?"

Nasha looked away. She'd always hated the stories, the Tedros ones most of all. No one is like that: no one does those things. Not alone. She focused, trying to suppress the emotions around her, but her mind was spouting unbidden questions.

What would happen if they knew about her curse? She wasn't an Earth-Breaker—those were long gone—but would they see it that way? What would they do? What could she do to them? Couldn't really kill them. They were Ronar. But so was she. Would they see her that way if they knew?

She chuckled. Damn stories had already made her thoughts wander.

"I say something funny, tracker?"

"Oh, come, Embe, you know me well enough to use my name. And I'm a hunter, thrice-striped." She displayed the three scars on the inside of her forearm, along with an emotionless smile.

"You shouldn't mock Tedros. He is beloved by the Great Mountain," Jima said.

"He's a story, dead as any Sloper taken by the fire in that mountain," Nasha said.

Embe was shaking his head, and Iallo frowned at her, probably offended by the comparison of the clans' greatest hero with a Sloper.

"We're all talking about him, aren't we? Seems pretty alive to me," Iallo said.

39

Jima nodded. "So is the mountain. You shouldn't mock Zala's fire, either."

"Zala's dead too, Jima."

"Yet the dead goddess's hands still move within the Earth," Embe said.

The prodding in Nasha's ribs was growing stronger, but it was clear now the irritation was her own. She stepped up to the fire, took a piece of the spitted meat, and moved away.

"Where're you going?" Iallo asked.

"Anywhere away from"—she gestured towards them—"this."

Someplace where your emotions aren't trying to drown me.

"Don't get yourself killed. We still got tracking to do," Jima said.

"If I do, maybe Embe can tell a story about me and you'll find your way."

She took a bite, let the flavor sink in, and walked into the cover of the citrus trees, releasing her concentration against their emotion with a long sigh when she was deep enough. No one would come this far out at night, and unless the Hagun invaders had turned back, she was alone with only her own emotions to deal with.

If any Hagun *had* turned back, though, she'd have to fight. . . . Burning wood and a sharp metallic taste rode her tongue, tainting the flavor of the meat. She couldn't fight, not with her curse. That's why she became a hunter. Keeping her defenses up would exhaust her, and she'd be overwhelmed, absorb the emotions all around, mix them with her own, and be controlled by whichever won the constant battle within her. No telling if she'd ever come back to herself from the chaos. She'd barely managed last time.

It won't happen again. I'm not the monster, no matter what the tales say.

Nasha swallowed hard and tried another bite, but the taste was soured by the persistent burning on her tongue, as if she were chewing the meat into bitter ash. She spit it out and threw what remained into the trees, the prodding in her ribs growing stronger still. It had been too long since she'd had a proper bite of game: she always relinquished her kills to the village, and even in the village, the food wasn't much better, not for a three-striped hunter.

Nasha shook her head, trying to put her thoughts into place, and forced her gaze towards the Great Mountain. It was a black stain on the night-blue sky. The obsidian that covered it formed darker patches, and the peak emanated an acrid, smoky scent that mixed with the citrus wafting from the trees. Not pleasant, but sharp enough to ground Nasha in the memories of her hunts among the citrus trees and cut away her wayward thoughts and rising anxiousness. At least she could still count on the dead goddess for the fumes. She breathed out and focused her mind, but something hit her senses. Nasha's hands went to her knives, and she prayed absentmindedly to the Silent Earth for it not to be Hagun.

She concentrated on the citrus and the thickness of the fumes, ready to suppress incoming emotion, but what hit her was different, hollow. Nasha followed the feeling, hurrying through the tightening trees with the Great Mountain on one side, a sheer drop on the other. The trees became sparse as she reached the edge of the cliff, but the feeling of emptiness only grew stronger. Her feet were on the ground, but this was like standing over an abyss. Nothing around her. No pressure, no emotion trying to break through. Strangely liberating. Peaceful, even.

And then she saw it: a small light in an alcove at the base of the mountain.

Nasha edged towards it down a jagged path, sharp obsidian jutting out, becoming larger and denser as she drew closer, sticking out from the rock face around the shallow cave like the Great Mountain's own blackened forest, glimmering in the moonlight. What trees were left here had changed. Their trunks were cracked and seemed to be crumbling in places, and the ground had a gray tinge to it, ashen all around. The normally vivid green of the citrus leaves had turned brownish yellow—most of them fallen—the characteristic aroma replaced by a sour decay that brought the back of her hand to her mouth.

The mountain rumbled and stones shifted above the alcove. Nasha hesitated. She knew this land better than any Ronar and had seen her share of rockslides rushing down the mountainside, but the gleam on dark Ronar skin from within the alcove pushed her on.

A man was slumped against the wall inside, his skin charred in

41

places, resembling the patches of obsidian along the Great Mountain. He sat before a fire in a pool of blood, breath rasping and weak. Nasha stepped inside, and her gut jumped when his face came into view. Chatta, the Warden of the Ronar.

"Hun . . ." The word died on his frail breath.

Her instincts told her to raise her defenses, but there was still nothing to suppress, and it felt like Zala herself was draining Nasha's own emotions into the Earth, numbing her mind.

She looked down at the ashen earth around Chatta. Maybe it wasn't so silent after all. Had it done this to him? The wounds certainly weren't the Earth's doing. A run-in with the Hagun, then? How many had there been to leave him like this?

There were long slashes across his chest, viciously thin and deep. Almost like cuts from . . . Ronar blades? Couldn't be. Ronar would never turn on one another, let alone a Root of the clan. His own blades used against him, then?

The blood oozed thick and dark, red so deep it shone black in the night. Maybe not even red, now that she inspected him closer. Nasha took another few tentative steps, one hand close to her obsidian hunter's knife, breath held in her chest.

Chatta's eyes jumped around as if unsure of where or who he was. They flashed towards her hands, and Nasha looked down. She'd taken her knife out. Instinct, really—hadn't even noticed—but her eyes lingered on the blade.

A Warden in his state could not do his part for the clan. If there were a Proving, they'd lose the ancestor-stone necessary to ward the village so that Zala could not spread her corrupted fingers through it. Nasha had never seen Zala's corruption, but if this was what it looked like, what she needed to do was clear.

Nasha's held breath burned in her chest, her body hot as the heart of the Great Mountain. Whatever had spread through him, he was too far gone. His veins were black with it, forming dark braids of twisting lines all over his face.

All life that is wasted must be taken.

Mansa had told her that enough times, and Chatta would not recover from this. It was the right thing to do. These were the moments others—those village-born like Iallo—balked at, the ones that had given her the stripes cut into her arm: the moments she proved herself willing to do what was necessary for the clan, truly Ronar, no matter where she'd come from.

Nasha's grip tightened on her knife.

Chatta was shaking his head, the obvious threat filling him with vigor. "I can help—"

His words slid out through his slashed neck, burbling away with the blood. He couldn't help her or the Ronar. Couldn't even help himself. She'd need to get proof back to Mansa—

Another wave of emotion prickled on her skin. Fleeting, but enough to indicate people were approaching. She pressed her back to the inside of the alcove and peeked around. Iallo led the way, Embe and Jima behind him.

Her heart raced, and the questions reared up again. What would they do to her? What should she do to them?

Nasha looked down at her bloody hands. A mercy killing for the good of the clan. But would they see it that way? A Sloper killing a Root? No. It didn't matter where she'd come from. She was Ronar.

I did the right thing.

Still, how many times had doing the right thing proven more important than how other people chose to see her? Would they see through her Sloper origins? All the rumors that had sprouted from her own Proving?

Nasha's hands were answering the question for her. They pulled out her hunter's axe, still bloody from cutting up her latest prey, and hacked away at the dead Warden's head. Iallo was at least ten strides off and moving slowly down the obsidian-littered path, but that still did not give her much time. Her breath puffed as she detached the head from the body, then bundled it into her pack. She could have hacked at the face to obscure it, but she'd need it as proof for Mansa.

She brushed dirty hands on her vest to mask the pattern of spotted blood, then used Chatta's own vest and linen trousers to wipe her arms and face. Not all of it, but enough to seem like she'd only searched the body and not hacked off its head. She peeked around the corner again. Iallo had spotted the blood coming from the cave and was easing towards it.

"Spread out," he whispered. "Might be them."

No more hiding now. She pushed the bundled head deep into a crag at the far end of the cave, snuffed out the fire, and stepped out. "No need, Iallo. Only me." She moved around the obsidian-covered rock face that surrounded the entrance of the alcove, muscles tight, wary of the shifting stones above.

"Did you find them?" Jima asked.

"No. He wasn't Hagun."

Nasha moved out of the way, and Iallo's eyes narrowed at the sight of the body. "He was Ronar?"

"Dead when I found him, taken by the corruption."

Embe strode towards the body, Jima at his side. Iallo edged closer but seemed wary to give his back to Nasha. His gaze flicked over her. "And the blood on you?"

Nasha frowned and took a step back, trying to pull their attention away from the cave. Maybe they'd turn away from the body if they thought she might run. "There's something different in his veins. Had to be sure he was dead." She wiped her hands on her vest again, but Iallo didn't seem convinced. He was about to say something when Jima's gasp cut him off.

Nasha worked around a trapped breath of her own as Jima stepped out, holding Chatta's severed head.

"Is that . . . Chatta?" Iallo asked. Jima slowly nodded and Iallo rounded on Nasha. "You did this? You killed him?"

"He was bleeding out, weak. Look at his face!"

Embe drew his heavy axe, iron scraping. "Dirty Sloper. I knew we could never trust you."

Jima was standing close to Nasha, seemingly unsure if he should draw or step between them.

"The Speaker said the words. I'm Ronar, same as you." Nasha's voice was steady, sharp as the obsidian all around them. "All life that is wasted must be taken."

"Not the life of a Root!" Iallo bellowed. "He was going to . . ."

The warrior glared at her. "Would you have done the same to Mansa?"

"He was as good as dead, Iallo. It had to be done!"

"That is not your decision to make, Sloper!" Embe said.

That word again. She glared at Embe, squeezing the grip of her knife. She was Ronar, but in their eyes, she was nothing more than a mongrel from the Slopes, and no number of stripes would change that. She ran her tongue across the back of her teeth, her muscles quivering, but what caught her attention was Iallo's glinting obsidian spear-tip. His knuckles were white around the haft, his feet shifting towards her.

Embe inched closer, and Nasha could see the intent in his eyes— might have felt it if the emotion had not been drained away. He was about to strike.

Nasha moved towards Embe, turning sideways to Iallo, bloody knife still in one hand, the other with her palm out. "I'm not a traitor, I'm—"

She rammed her shoulder into Iallo, sending him sprawling to the ground, then kicked Embe back into one of the spikes. He slammed into it, obsidian piercing his back and showering them with dust and loose pebbles from above. Embe's cry of pain rose into an anguished howl as she stabbed him in the gut and opened him up to the chest. The life bled out of him and he fell silent, but obsidian scraped on leather behind her: Jima had finally decided to draw his own weapon. Nasha pulled out a throwing knife from Embe's belt and turned in a swift motion, driving it into Jima's eye and kicking him away.

Her mind was firing, warning her. She shouldn't be fighting. She should be focusing her thoughts on something that would anchor her against the emotions that would surely come crashing through any moment now. But something was still dulling them, allowing her to retain her strength. She ignored the warning and drew her other weapon—the defensive parry knife—then stepped onto the ledge. Only Iallo left.

He glowered at her with rage-filled eyes as Nasha paced around him, knives up. The long parry knife—sharp-tipped and lined with

ridges on both its obsidian edges to catch and turn weapons away—
was held before her, while her hunter's knife was held back,
obscured by Nasha's sideways stance so Iallo would not see the strike
coming. She wasn't the monster and wasn't going to let them
slaughter her like one.

"Traitor," he spat. "Always knew there was something wrong
with you."

"Oh, you have no idea."

She lunged with her hunter's knife, trying to catch him off-
guard, but Iallo was more alert than she'd thought. He batted away
her strike with the butt-end of his spear and followed through, spinning it so that the tip opened a shallow gash along the length of her
forearm. Nasha stumbled back but regained her balance and
pushed forward on the balls of her feet. She stabbed at his gut with
the parry knife, then slashed at his neck with the other, but Iallo
sidestepped and almost skewered her with a counterstrike to her
ribs, forcing Nasha into an awkward roll to avoid it.

"I'm not one of your marks. You can't take me," he said.

Nasha ignored him. She'd made her choice. Running was no
longer an option. She encircled him with her knives raised until he
had his back to the ledge, while she had her back to the obsidian
she'd spitted Embe on.

Iallo grinned, but Nasha was done with words. She leaped
forward with all her strength and thrust out her striking blade, but
he was still too fast. He evaded the knife and drove a knee into her
stomach, then grabbed her by the scruff of the neck and flung her
back, aiming to throw her against the rock. Nasha spun enough to
miss it, falling breathless to the ground. Her knives clattered away,
obsidian gleaming black and red on the ashen earth. Iallo was
standing over her in a heartbeat, hands digging into the short braids
of her hair and pulling back her head. He drew his face near to
hers, ash puffing up around them.

"Go ahead. Call out. See if any of your Sloper friends hear
you."

Nasha struggled, but he had enough leverage to keep her
pinned. He slammed her forehead into the ashen ground, then

pulled her back again. She let her head slacken and her gaze fall. That seemed to give Iallo enough confidence to press his face closer, his grip loosening. "They'll reward me for this, maybe even make me Warden in—"

Nasha snapped her head around and bit down on his ear. He screamed in shock and pain, letting go. She scrambled up, using the moment of surprise to shove him against the obsidian-covered stone beside the alcove, then drove her shoulder into his back. Iallo slammed against the sharp rock, missing the spikes, but the obsidian still cut deep lines into his face. The Great Mountain rumbled with the impact, and Nasha pulled Iallo back and slammed again.

Iallo was the better fighter, but she knew this land better than any Ronar, and the Mountain's rumbling voice was clear. She slammed his face against the cliff once more, then scrambled back as the rocks above them loosened and rolled down, burying the warrior between obsidian and stone.

Nasha stood over the stones, panting out the pain in her slashed arm, watching for movement under the boulders, but movement came from behind her instead. Jima was crawling away, knife still in his eye. Nasha picked up her knives, strode to his side, and squatted beside him.

"P-Please. Just let me go. I'll never come back to Ronar land. I'll—"

Nasha sunk her knife into the back of his skull as painlessly as she could. She wasn't the monster, and he was a hunter like her. Well, not exactly like her. He only had one stripe. . . . And that was why she could not keep him alive.

"You've seen too much. Can't have you trying to use this to pull me down, get another stripe."

Nasha got to her feet, gut clenched, muscles still shaking with the thrill of battle. She hadn't fought like this since her own Proving, and she almost expected to be overwhelmed by some lingering rage or fear her curse had not picked up on, but all that surrounded her was silence, and her mind was still her own.

Her gaze moved back to the alcove where Chatta's body lay.

47

The Hagun invaders would have to wait. She needed to get back to the village.

Still, she could use this. Mansa should know the truth, but there was no sense wasting three Ronar lives if she couldn't make things better for herself. She looked down at the three stripes carved into her arm again. A fourth would look good there. Maybe even Chief Tomu would take notice and give her a chance to talk to the Tivezzi. Nasha was sure she could convince the Tivezzi to read the stones and reveal the path to the First Tree. She could be rid of her curse. She could be in control.

Nasha pulled her thoughts back into focus, gritted her teeth, then picked up Chatta's head and secured it tightly in her hunter's pack. She wondered if any of this would be worthy of the tales. Were they ever this bloody? Sure weren't told that way.

Made her hate them even more.

CHAPTER THREE

Her church reflects the four aspects of life: The Bishops of the Bone bring knowledge to her people. The Sentinels of the Breath protect them from bearing the taint of death. And the Priests of the Blood zeal for the health of the Body, composed by the faithful throughout Her Domain.

— The Book of the Blood

A patch of sunlight filtered through the window of Lynn's cell to cut away the dark. Not only the sun—that mark in the sky had been shining for days now. Small but bright, like a star had envied the sun and carried on into day. Lynn stood by the window, squinting down at the execution yard through the shadowy lines of the window bars across her face, repeating the thought she'd been trying to convince herself of.

This is a win. This is a win.

Lynn willed the words through the roil of her thoughts, but they arrived quieter than a whisper, shredded into broken echoes by the sharp laughter of the voices in her mind.

Repeating it did nothing to change the sour taste at the back of her throat, and the looks on the gaunt faces of the three men about to be hanged didn't help much either. They'd be joining the laughter in her mind soon enough, but there was no blackness around their eyes, at least, no sign of the Madness. Funny how she always checked, even after all these years.

You ended it. It's gone.

Eager eyes and screaming voices rained on the men staring into the eyes of death through the nooses before them. Spectators clambered onto boxes and carts, jostling for a better view of other men's failures, likely hoping they'd be enough for them to forget their own. Two nooses swung empty in the wind. Were those saved lives enough for Lynn to forget her own failures? Her voices sneered the question away. It was never enough.

Lynn shook her head as the crowd jeered on, so sure of their worthiness, so oblivious of how easily any of them could be standing beneath the gallows.

She wrestled with her tightening chest, trying to keep her heart still and her mind silent. Perhaps she should have been content with the ones she'd saved; perhaps the Seraph wasn't half as hard as Lynn had been on herself lately. But if the Seraph had been trying to speak to Lynn, Her voice was not loud enough to be heard over the ones in Lynn's head.

The jailer's steps creaked along the boards beneath the gallows, and the crowd quieted in anticipation, their anxiousness hanging in the air like the noxious vapor of some Dakhran potion. For a religion focused on life, its faithful sure enjoyed the ending of it.

Lynn turned away, put her back to the window, and slid onto the rough ruin-stone slab beneath it, the soft white glow of the veins in the stone pulsing against her face.

Coward! Alren screamed at her. *You've failed them as well.*

She almost regretted having locked herself in here sometimes—and choosing a cell with a window overlooking the execution yard had certainly been a mistake—but if death was going to hound her, better to keep what she could by her side. She'd done enough outside, and Leardin and the Sentinels would never find her here.

Besides, prisons were the only place death was accepted in the Domain—other than at the hands of a Sentinel—and the only place she could keep doing the Seraph's work. Not all prisoners deserved death, and Lynn would not let the enemy take worthy lives.

"Oy! Get up!" the watcher outside her cell said.

Lynn pushed short dirty-blond hair out of her face and regarded him with sharp brown eyes but no words.

He had a bandaged nose and stood with a spear in hand, wearing the expression of a man facing down enemy ranks on a battlefield instead of a woman behind bars.

"Get up and watch. Don't make me come in there."

Lynn spat on the ground. "Don't make me break your nose again. Hasn't even healed yet."

The man brandished his spear as though having it would change the outcome this time. "You follow the Lord Keeper's orders, or those bodies won't be the only ones swingin'. Won't be quiet neither!"

It's never quiet in here. Dentos's voice, maybe? Or Roki's. The others sniggered behind them in the depths of her mind.

Lynn sighed. Lord Keeper Kerr hated her, hated having to negotiate the executions. Bad for business: less of a show. He was hanging those he deemed unworthy, after all. She'd given him little choice, though. No one denied a Sentinel, and the fear was plain on his face once she let the silver flash in her eyes. She was glad to still command that fear, even if no true Sentinel would carry the voices of the dead in their mind or dwell on them like she did.

She looked over the watcher but didn't move. He stepped closer to the bars.

"I said, get up."

"Keep talking. At least I won't have to sit through the jailer's damned speech again," Lynn said.

The guard gave another motivated step towards her cell, fumbling for his keys. "I'll show you talk! I'll sh—"

He was hit over the head from the shadows and crumpled to the ground. A slender shadow took the keys, stepped slowly over him, and opened Lynn's cell door.

Rella came into the light wearing dirty rags and a dirty grin that showed through the half of her face that wasn't covered by greasy black hair. Two men stepped in behind her: Bac, a towering man with enough fur to be mistaken for a bear; and Gaire, a shorter, balder man with more fingers than teeth and a vicious look in his one good eye. Gaire and Rella stepped closer to Lynn, each holding a rust-spotted, sharp length of metal.

"Hello again," Rella said. "You've considered?"

Lynn was on her feet, ready, the familiar heat flushing through her. She spat on the ground once more. "And here I was, thinking that watcher was the biggest idiot mucking about these cells. Seems like you've outdone him."

Rella shook her head, clicking her tongue. "Wrong answer."

Gaire lunged at her with an outstretched arm, blade glinting in a tight grip, but Lynn jumped to the side, already focusing on the cell door. She couldn't fight all three of them, not in here. She darted towards the exit, but Bac was stepping back so that his considerable bulk blocked the door. Lynn didn't slow down. She sunk a fist into Bac's gut, then spun around him as he doubled over, and darted out the cell. She missed the shadow lurking outside, though, and a massive hand enveloped her head from behind and pushed it sideways into the iron bars while twisting her arm behind her back. Cold metal rammed into the side of her face, peppering it with rust and taking what vision she might have had.

Her ears rang, Rella's voice distant.

"Dangerous thing," she whispered, covering Lynn in rancid-fish breath, "sending all your friends away."

We're always here.

Always.

"Time's up, Mistress." Rella spat the last word, raising her voice and flicking drops of her foul-smelling saliva into Lynn's ear. "I don't care how many times you have to fuck the Lord Keeper, you're getting us out of here. Today."

Lynn blinked the flecks of rust out. Bac had taken hold of her free arm from inside her cell and pulled it in up to the shoulder. Gaire was beside him, still inside the cell, but with the point of his knife at her throat, while Rella had hers pricking Lynn's side.

"Looks like we ain't that dim, eh?" a deep voice said behind her. Pert, probably.

Lynn grunted and tried to struggle but was held tight. "Yo—on't —want—" Lynn said through pressed cheeks, trying not to taste the rust.

"Couldn't quite get that. Come closer," Rella said.

Pert pushed her against the bars, and her ears pulsed, burning hot. The heat that had flushed through her now fueled her anger.

She didn't want to give herself away by the flash of silver in her eyes. But even as her heart argued against it, she was already closing her eyes and reaching out for Vedyr.

She channeled her anger towards Vedyr and the burning in her ears reached her eyes. Her mind was filled with a calming clarity, and Vedyr's strength flowed into her like a wave that made her muscles brim with power.

Lynn moved in a blur. She pulled her arm away from Bac's grip like it was nothing, too fast for Gaire to react before Bac fell backwards, opening his arms for balance and taking Gaire down with him—and the knife away from Lynn's neck. Lynn's other arm was still held behind her back, but her free hand had already gripped Rella's wrist and pulled the woman's knife away. She fueled more of her anger towards Vedyr, the fire in her chest dwindling as she exchanged it for the calm confidence of his strength. It was the last she'd get—her anger was spent—but it was enough. With all her power, she threw her head back from the bars and into Pert's chin, launching him into the bars of the cells behind them. The metal bent with a strained creak as Pert crashed into them.

Lynn let go of the Bond and fixed Rella with a callous stare, knowing the traces of silver in her eyes were gone, her Sentinel identity safe. To Rella, it must have all happened in a blink of an eye, and she was still blinking repeatedly, trying to make sense of it. The men inside Lynn's cell were staring at her as well, Pert's unconscious body under the disfigured bars seemingly removing any inclination for them to move.

"W-what are you?" Rella stuttered.

Alren had three different answers in her mind—all of them involving cowardice and none recognizing her as a Sentinel—but Lynn had her own answer.

Lynn drove her fist into the woman's gut, then kicked out her knee, twisting it at an awkward angle that made it crunch. Rella doubled over, screaming almost as loud as the crowd, if less enthusiastically. Her knife slid away, her hands flying to her knee.

Lynn picked up the knife and the keys. She shut Bac and Gaire inside her cell, then came back and kneeled beside Rella. Lynn was calm now, her movements slow and deliberate. She grasped the woman's hair with one hand while holding the improvised knife at her throat with the other. There was a snap of wood, and the crowd outside erupted in celebration. First one gone. Death was among them, and its call was almost as clear as the voices in her head.

Do it. Cut her. She deserves it.

A chill crept up the back of her neck, threatening to move down her arms and take hold of her hands. Lynn breathed in and out, in and out. Slowly. Until she had exhaled death's words from her mind.

Her limbs felt heavy, Vedyr's power replaced by the pounding headache that followed the use of her Sentinel Bond. Lynn looked back at Rella.

"The next time you think jumping me might be a good idea, remember how this went."

She nicked the flesh under the blade, and blood slowly welled from Rella's neck, dribbling onto the white-pulsing ruin-stone. The woman whimpered, still taking hard breaths.

"I really am the mistress here, and every breath you take from this moment until your last comes at my mercy."

"Don't matter what you are, you won't kill me," Rella said between gasps. "I seen how you run from the dead. . . . Can't even watch, ach, the hangin'." Her words were laced with pain, but her pride was still intact.

"Oh, I won't kill you, but eventually . . ." The distant voice of the jailer, a second snap, and a mad cheer from the crowd. "He will." Rella's eyes widened. "And it'll be a lot more painful than this until he gets to it."

She dropped the woman back on the floor and stood over the strewn-out bodies.

Deep breaths.

Lynn's hand dug into the pocket of her breeches and closed around her Sentinel coin, carved to resemble the stacked circle of crescents that formed the Sign of the Breath. She inhaled once more, and the musty smell of damp stone brought just enough comfort to dull the throbbing in her skull. She couldn't blame them for trying. She'd seen the shadow of death twist even the best of men, but their desperate attempts would not save them. The Seraph was the only one who could do that.

Rella was blubbering in pain, but still alive. All of them were. Lynn lingered on the solace that she had not delivered these lives into the hands of death. That and the empty nooses would have to be enough for now, at least until she could pry more lives away from Kerr's fat fingers.

Still won't be enough. You were always Elwin's weakest, Cara said.

Lynn's heart wrenched as Elwin's face drifted into her mind, but not even her old mentor could make up for her mistakes or break death's footsteps, always following in her own.

The last snap sounded to a deafening cheer, and Lynn headed down the corridor, still breathing deep. The Church might accept the executions, but there had been enough death around her. She wouldn't stand by and watch people cheering it on.

A watcher rounded the corner as she moved away. He had short-cropped hair, lanky arms, and a face marked with lines from constant smiling. He was one of the few who were glad to have her and was the reason she'd hid herself at Dalhold, even if he did not know it.

"Hey!" he called out, scrambling for his weapon.

"No need to get excited, Ferrin," Lynn said. "It's been dealt with."

Ferrin stepped closer and grinned, showing the lines around his eyes and mouth. "Always could count on you." He looked around, then back at Lynn, still smiling. "Guess that's why they call you Mistress, eh?"

"You know it isn't." She didn't return the smile.

"Right." His tone darkened. "Kerr wants you."

"So soon? Why's that bastard so intent on all this killing?"

Ferrin shrugged.

Little time to prepare, but looked like she'd have to make the best of it.

"Lead the way."

Lord Keeper Kerr's office was in the east corner of the prison, as far from the execution yard as Lynn could get, yet the noise of the crowd still followed her. She focused on following Ferrin through the wide corridors of the guard wing while trying to decide which prisoners Kerr would more likely let walk. Maybe judging them herself made her no better than the Lord Keeper, but she'd been in the prison long enough to know the worthy ones, and her judgment was all they had. Even the risk of being wrong about some was preferable to letting them all hang. It might not be much, but it was her best attempt at atonement for the lives she'd taken.

Ferrin left her at the base of the steps to Kerr's office and smiled, but, as if remembering he wasn't supposed to, gave her a curt nod and a grunt before leaving. All Lynn could do was shake her head. Some men just weren't cut out for certain things. How had he ended up in here?

You know exactly how. Alren's words were sharp in her mind, cutting through the rumble of the distant crowd.

Lynn didn't answer him. She climbed up the steps and rapped on the door, wrangling her mind away from her voices.

"Enter," Kerr's puffy voice came from inside.

The chamber was a stark contrast to the cells. It was one of the newer constructions, made from Dakhran basalt, which was lighter and much softer than the ruin-stone that housed the prisoners.

The Lord Keeper stood looking out one of the glass-paned windows, hands behind his back and a pipe dancing along his teeth. He was a rotund man, with a drooping mustache and sausages for fingers. His desk sat between them, too large for the room by half, with stacks of rolled parchment on one side, quill and ink on the other. The usual list of names did not sit upon it, though, and he kept his back turned, muttering something under his breath.

Lynn frowned. The man had never been able to mask his fear. It was what allowed her to stay here unperturbed—and why he hadn't disclosed to the Church he had a wayward Sentinel hiding in his prisons. She'd always been careful not to reveal too much or push him too hard; too much fear made men unpredictable.

Something was different today, though. Wrong.

"The list?" Lynn asked.

"How long has it been? Since you broke into my cells?"

"Is this reminiscing part of your demands, or is it just a slow day, Lord Keeper?"

He let out a sharp breath that could have been a muffled laugh. "You always did have a tongue on you."

Lynn stepped forward, scowl deepening and thoughts on Vedyr, hoping the silver flash in her eyes would help Kerr find his fear. But Kerr did not turn towards her, and he didn't seem to be hiding his fear: he was absent of it.

"What's this about?" she tried again, keeping her voice as imposing as she could.

"One would think you'd at least learn patience in those cells. But then again, you're not actually trapped in there, are you?" He looked off into the afternoon sky and took a long pull on his pipe, then blew smoke slowly from his nostrils. "What I could never understand is why of all places, would you pick Dalhold?"

"I can make things a lot harder than having you draw out a list of names."

Kerr finally turned to her with steady eyes and a slight grin. "The papers will be here shortly." He turned back to the window and brought the pipe to his lips, still mumbling inaudibly around it.

Lynn gripped the chair before her and pulled it to the side, muscles tensing. If the man had lost his respect for her, she'd need to remind him of her power. She reached out for Vedyr—

The door opened and a Priestess of the Blood stepped in. She was clad in the white-and-silver robes of the Church, with a white shawl over her head and a pendant around her neck—a thin line of metal woven around ruin-stone. The stone traced the shape of a drop with the ends curled outwards to form handle-like shapes instead of meeting at the top. The Sign of the Blood, as most priests wore. But unlike most priests, she also wore a small piece of bone in the shape of a sharp-edged eye suspended in the drop: the Sign of the Bone.

Lynn's anger turned to ice in her veins and ran all under her skin at the sight of the priestess. Was this the Lord Keeper's play? No, it couldn't be. He'd never reach out to the Church.

"Ah, here we are." Kerr turned so fast he almost stumbled onto his desk. "You have it?"

"I do." The priestess's voice was soft and unamused.

Kerr snapped his round fingers repeatedly and stretched out an open palm, but the priestess brushed past him with the expression of one avoiding an inconveniently placed pile of excrement and sat smoothly in the chair beside the one Lynn was standing behind.

Oh, not a play, then. Another player, perhaps?

The woman fixed her small blue eyes on Lynn. They almost reminded her of Alren.

"So, you're the one?" A shadow of a smile touched the side of the priestess's lips, and there seemed to be a note of kindness in her voice now.

Lynn hesitated, gaze flicking to the Sign of the Bone, then back to the priestess's eyes. "I don't think so." Lynn couldn't quite smile back.

"Oh, I think you are." She leaned in close, and Lynn's head pounded with her beating heart. Had Commander Leardin found her?

The priestess jerked her head towards the increasingly impatient Kerr. "I don't know how you've convinced him, but I do appreciate the help."

"Help?"

"I assure you, the lives he's been sending us are being put to good use. Most of them have become acolytes in the cathedral, some even attempting to take up the cloth." She studied Lynn with cool eyes. "What are you detained for?"

The pressure in Lynn's head eased a little. If she thought Lynn was detained, Kerr hadn't had the guts to tell the priestess who Lynn really was. No Sentinels on her trail.

"I . . ." The words seemed to have stumbled out of her mind, unable to find their way back to her mouth.

"No matter," said the Lord Keeper. "Shall we get on with it?"

The priestess gave a slow nod. "Your past is your own, I suppose. I am absolutely certain, however, that you will greatly appreciate what we have prepared in return for your help."

A shiver ran through Lynn, and the pounding in her head returned. An absolute degree of certainty is always a dangerous thing. The priestess reached inside her robe, then produced a neatly rolled piece of parchment with an unbroken seal of the Sign of the Blood, and Kerr's eyes lit up at the sight of it.

Shit. She hadn't thought he had it in him.

Lynn had been taking this piece by piece, counting the lives she'd kept away from the noose, building up to each negotiation, each execution. But he'd been playing the long game.

Keepers couldn't pardon the detained. The only way Kerr could free up space was by executing them once they ran out of usefulness, guilty or not. Pardons only came from the Church, and even those needed to be signed by high clergy. But no priest would complain about the prison unofficially sending new acolytes their way, and that had been the best use Lynn could think of for those she'd saved. Yet Kerr's relationship with the Church was so broken that she'd always assumed he'd been letting the prisoners out the back door. There was a time she'd even thought he'd been killing them privately, just out of spite.

That would have been bad enough, but this . . .

He'd kept his word and reached out to the Church. He hadn't told the priestess Lynn was a Sentinel, but there was no list because he'd gotten her pardoned. There wouldn't be one ever again.

He'd won.

"I . . . . Surely . . . there are many more deserving than myself."

"None in here," said the priestess. "You are fortunate. The Church does not take pardons lightly. We have had an eye on you for some time now."

Some time? What had they seen?

The priestess broke the seal and unfurled the scroll. Maybe she expected some show of gratitude, but all she got was Lynn's disbelieving stare and slack mouth.

The woman placed the parchment on the table before Kerr, but he barely looked down before reciting, "You have been deemed worthy by the Holy Church of the Seraph and are granted freedom in Her Domain. May She watch over and guide your steps so that death may never find you."

So that's what he was mumbling out the window. Bastard.

He cracked a smile through his thin lips and handed Lynn the pardon.

"By the Breath and the Body, the Blood and the Bone, the Holy Church of the Seraph hereby recognizes your worthiness and your freedom," the priestess said, and turned towards Kerr. "I hope we can count on your continued collaboration, Lord Keeper." She didn't wait for an answer and walked away.

Lynn would have held her breath if she'd been able to draw one. Whatever safety she thought she had gained, whatever steps to redeem herself, were now withering away as quickly as the smile falling off Kerr's face in the priestess's wake.

She racked her mind for a way to stay but found little else than the usual accusing voices.

Kerr sunk his brow and his mouth twisted like he'd bitten something sour he couldn't wait to spit out. He raised a stubby finger towards the door. "Get. Out."

Lynn stepped towards him, fists clenched, hoping to impose the usual fear commanded by a Sentinel. "This isn't over."

Kerr smirked and opened his arms. "What are you going to do?

Hit me?" He shook his head. "You can't afford that, can you? You've been hiding. And now they have their eye on you. Tread carefully, Sentinel."

Lynn flung the chair at the wall and Kerr flinched as it shattered, but she breathed deep and diffused her anger into a glower before walking out and slamming the door behind her. Her path of atonement had been a shaky one, but having it pulled out from under her tasted bitter just the same. The voices were as loud as ever.

You are weaker than death. You do not deserve the title of Sentinel.

She stomped down the stairs, thinking about her old mentor again. She'd gotten comfortable. Underestimated her opponent.

Elwin would be ashamed. He'd taught her better.

CHAPTER FOUR

I mourned him. Don't we all? We put on our masks for the Church, but our hearts are hidden deep within our chests. Their beats are their own, and they cannot be betrayed. I took Her blessing with a steady gaze and an aching heart, and now the Seraph has forsaken me to unworthiness.

— Ramblings of a dying man

Ultenvell Palace had always been cold, but Adrian was ablaze with every descending step. Sweat twisted a prickling path down his back that made the tunic cling to his skin.

"Through here, my lord."

The guard led him through a small chamber to large stone doors, hallways leading into darkness on either side. He pushed open the doors and stepped into an unassuming chapel. It was nothing like the intricately wrought chambers of the palace. Older, and colorless but for the green-and-gold embroidered cloth covering the altar and the Ever-Tree standing behind it in usual oranges and pinks and yellows.

A man stood halfway through a door beside the tree. He had a hooked nose and a thin neck but wore more ruin-stone than was in the chapel itself: pendants of each of the four Signs of the Seraph, and a dozen others in shapes Adrian didn't recognize. Sparse white hair touched his shoulders, and a smile touched his lips.

"Yes?"

"The Cleansers," Adrian said through tight lips.

"Only one." The man bowed his head and stepped towards them, his pendants rattling softly as he walked.

The guard that had led Adrian stepped forward. "Cleanser Raklin, this is Prince Adrian Pell of Othonea. Governor Garrick has accepted the terms. You are to attend to—"

"Governor . . . Garrick?"

"Lord Henrik is dead." Adrian did his best to keep his tone level. Jovu had always been the one to speak in situations like this. "Yet you will find Othonea to be a most generous nation to the loyal servants of the Seraph."

The priest held Adrian's gaze for a moment, then bowed his head. "My place is to serve, my lord."

Adrian nodded. "The Dakhran princess. Lady Myrra."

"The body?"

". . . Yes."

"My lord, no one is to see a body before the Alterian priests arrive, especially one in this . . . circumstance."

"Wait outside." Adrian shot a look at the guard, and the man saluted, then left without complaint. He turned back to Raklin. "I understand your reservations, but this is Othonea now. Surely having friends closer to home would be a lot more profitable?"

"I do not seek profit, my lord. Only to set my faithful on the true path. I cannot—"

Adrian put a hand on his shoulder. "Keep the body veiled if you must." He'd be too nervous to look at her face, anyway. "All I ask is that she is kept unburnt."

"Unburnt?"

"I understand the blood of the Ever-Tree can keep a body whole?"

"Only those given the Pontiff's blessing can be kept for the Promised Dawn, my lord." Raklin clutched one of his pendants like he was reciting some holy text. He might have been. Adrian probably wouldn't know the difference.

He pressed the man's shoulder a little tighter. "You let me worry about the Pontiff. How does Royal Abbot sound? You'll answer directly to High Priest Erendal."

Raklin shook his head, ruin-stone clinking around his thin neck.

"A title changes nothing, my lord. But . . . these attacks in Khet. They are calling it a battle-fever, but it has nothing to do with war. It is spreading among people who have never even seen a blade. Ultenvell is untouched for now, but it is a taint I fear will require Priests of the Blood, maybe even Sentinels." He regarded Adrian through narrowing eyes. "Can you get me those, or is your father the one I should be talking to?"

The mention of Sentinels had Adrian fighting a scowl. That bastard had been meant to protect her, but the reports said Elwin had struck the blow himself. It didn't matter if he was a Sentinel— how powerful or how feared. Adrian would have his head.

Just one more reason I need Father's resources.

The priest held Adrian's gaze for another moment, then seemed to take his silence for an answer and began to move away.

"Wait." Even leagues away, Father's shadow was still making him swallow his pride. "I doubt the Sentinels would get involved, but I can take you to my father. He'll be in Alteria to sign the treaty before the Pontiff. We'll need a priest to sign it, too."

Raklin stopped. "And is your sister not enough?"

"She is my sister, no matter her oaths to the Church. A priest with no blood ties would be . . . cleaner."

Ellana would have to forgive him. She was still alive, but this was Myrra's only chance.

The priest stood silent, back still turned to Adrian. "You'll support me before him? Amend the treaty so that the Pontiff sends us Priests of the Blood?"

Won't change much. "I will."

Raklin searched Adrian's eyes for the truth, then slowly nodded.

"I will embalm and keep her in the cleansing room until we return."
He bowed his head. "And Royal Abbot will do fine, my prince."

Adrian exhaled silently, the pressure lifting off his shoulders.

"But I must warn you," Raklin continued. "King Syvern has
asked for her body to be returned to Dakhra."

"King Iridan is the only ruler you should worry about now."

Raklin studied Adrian for another few breaths, then put a hand
into his robe and pulled out a small circular object. For a moment,
Adrian thought he was about to put another pendant around his
neck.

"She wore this. I was keeping it for the Alterian priests, but . . ."

He held a medallion of the Bone in his hands. *Her* medallion of
the Bone—white-veined ruin-stone forming a sharp circle around a
sculpted bone eye. Adrian fought down memories of all the times
she'd tried to bring him to read the sacred texts, but they burned
with a cold flame in his heart.

He took the medallion, nodded, then paced back towards the
doors, pausing before them and pressing his eyes shut to force the
wetness out of them. Not enough for tears. Father would be proud.

"I'll bring you back," he whispered.

Adrian grasped the medallion tight, then threw open the doors
and followed the guard back up, sweat going cold on his skin.

They rode for the eastern gate, Raklin regarding Adrian, Addo ahead
of them, looking warily at those in the crowd who'd ventured too
close to the guards surrounding them, as if they might suddenly mob
them and take his horse. Addo had always been kept too far from the
people for his own good, but there was a certain disquiet among the
crowd. Maybe it was the rumors of the frenzy Raklin had mentioned,
or maybe Adrian was letting his own discomfort of riding to meet
Father take control. The thought of Father sent barbs up the back of
his neck, and Adrian refocused his attention on the road ahead.

"Something on your mind, Prince Adrian?" Raklin regarded

Adrian from atop his horse, the clop of hooves on stone mingling with the clacking of his stone charms.

"Too much is on my mind, Raklin. Nothing worth talking about."

"There is always solace in words. Maybe you just haven't been offered the right ones."

Adrian grunted. He might never have been offered the right words, but he doubted a priest of the Seraph would have them. Raklin did not press him, and they rode on. Their horses had just cantered past the eastern gate when Adrian heard the screaming. His thoughts jumped back to the attacks Raklin had talked about, but they'd been contained in the outer Khetish cities. Ultenvell was too heavily guarded. It would be madness to attack the Othonean guard here. Guards ran past them nonetheless, joining others at the side of the road.

Adrian rushed his mare through close-packed timber-and-lime-wash houses and reined up to an alleyway where the Othonean soldiers had gathered, Raklin close behind, Addo hanging back, still a coward when the action started.

Two slashed bodies lay bleeding and unmoving at the mouth of the narrow passageway, a third further in with a man standing over it with his back pressed against the wall. Only fragments were visible through the amassed guard, but the cornered man's movements seemed to have a strange cadence. His head darted unnaturally from side to side, like he did not recognize where he was or what these men around him meant, clearly taken by what the soldiers had called a battle-fever.

The guards closed in, blades flashing in the afternoon sun.

"Stop!" Raklin yelled, but Adrian doubted they would have, even if he had given the command.

They stabbed and slashed at the man, then left his bleeding body behind and rushed up the street towards an injured guard leaning against one of the buildings. They did not recognize Adrian, barely looking at him as they tended to the deep gash that had gone through the plate protecting their companion's chest.

"We should go," Adrian said. He shot a look at Raklin, who seemed on the verge of charging at the guards himself.

Raklin glared at him. "These men do not judge the worthy, do not decide who lives or dies on a whim."

"Your words won't change their minds. There is nothing we can do here."

Raklin stared at the guards for a long moment, then begrudgingly turned his horse back, hands moving to the Signs around his neck once more, murmuring under his breath as they moved away.

It took them a little over two weeks to reach Alteria, and the city was an altogether different sight than the Khetish capital. Massive stone buildings and solid brick housing towered around them, but Adrian's focus was on Myrra's medallion, sitting in the palm of his hand. He closed his fingers around it and forced himself to remember her smile again. The vision was fading, had been for a while.

Adrian looked up. They were drawing close to the cathedral. Squared-off towers with dark-tiled roofs and stained-glass windows rose to four times the height of the houses leading up to them. The towers were linked by halls that sprawled across the horizon, making it impossible to look at anything else. They'd caught up to the Othonean delegation, but Adrian and his men hung back, away from Ellana's sight. This was not the place to discuss Raklin's presence. Derren was ahead of the delegation, shouting at—

A bolt whistled past and into the side of his sister's carriage with a heavy thud, bringing Adrian's mind to life in an instant. He wheeled his mare around, opening his mouth to deliver orders, but they were surrounded by unmoving shadows—there was nowhere to direct the guards to.

Derren seemed to have a better idea of where the attack had come from, though. "To the left!" the captain bellowed, brandishing his drawn sword, and three of the mounted guard galloped off.

The delegation clattered ahead at double the speed, and Adrian followed close this time, but they drew to a halt, with hooves and wheels screeching on the cobbles. A crowd of people and guards were blocking the road, some curious and others with all kinds of improvised weapons, looking around at the rooftops and in alleys. They looked like militiamen, but that couldn't be. The Legion had always kept the peace in Alteria.

Derren had dismounted and was gesturing wildly at one of the Church's Legion officers—in the Alterian white-and-silver uniform —while soldiers pushed people out of the way to inspect shaded gaps between the buildings a few strides to their left. They managed to thin out the crowd enough for Adrian to have a clear view of the shadow that leaped out a window. It fell with its arms outstretched and sharp nails gleaming in the sunlight, and people started to scream even before it landed onto the Legion guard.

It tore into the officer's chest, his pained shrieks lasting for only a moment before the creature pulled back its claw and ripped the guard's throat. Ribbons of blood flew onto the cobbles, and screams spread like fire through the streets as people rushed away, pulling others who'd barely seen what happened into their stampede.

The creature seemed like a frenzied animal with a savage blood-lust, skittering at sharp angles. It pounced from the dying Legion officer to another who was caught between raising his spear and fleeing. Teeth sunk deep into the sentry's face, and the man's screams joined the growing desperation of the crowd in a mad cacophony of cries, clattering weapons, and trampled bodies.

Adrian drew his sword, a rush of heat washing over him. The hiss of steel sharpened his thoughts, and he ran forward, sword point held before him, Raklin following in his wake until they stood before the creature.

Othonean guards and militiamen were both trying to reach the attacker, while Alterians were running the other way in fear. All of them adding to the chaos until they were tangled in a bewildered mass—an impenetrable barrier between Adrian and the delegation.

Adrian saw the beast clearly now. Not a beast: a man. His rags were covered in crimson, as was his face, and his elongated nails dripped with the remains of his victims. He darted his head from side to side, snarling, his jerking movements reminding Adrian of

69

the fevered man in Ultenvell. The attacker's bloodshot eyes jumped among the disarray until they found Adrian's glinting steel and Raklin's ruin-stone pendants.

He charged at Raklin with a raw howl, claws ready to open his gut, but Adrian pushed the priest out of the way and took the brunt of the strike, sharp nails tearing at his chain mail and scraping his flesh. The man was on him then, slashing wildly with his claws. Adrian bent away from a swipe at his neck, then raised his sword, deflecting the claws by a finger's breadth. He punched the man's side with his free hand to push him back, but his enemy showed no pain and raked at Adrian's chest instead of moving away. Adrian's armor held the claws away from his skin, but the beast barreled into him, taking them both to the ground.

Adrian grasped his sword with his back to the cobbles, one hand on the blade, the other on the pommel, raising it to avoid the frantic snapping of the lunatic's jaws. The sharp steel of Adrian's blade cut into his palm, but he pushed it up and tore a gash on the side of his opponent's face, then booted the man off him.

Adrian scrambled to his feet, trying to ignore the stinging in his hand. He feinted low, then raised his blade high and sliced down. The sword bit into his opponent's shoulder, but there was still no show of pain, and the madman clutched the blade with both hands, then wrenched it free of Adrian's grasp and flung it away with a raw-throated growl. Adrian stepped back, weaponless but for the dagger in his belt as the man paced around him like a predator sensing the kill. He steeled himself and retook his stance, defiant. Fear was as great a killer as any weapon.

His opponent lunged, no technique in his frenzied state, yet dangerous all the same. Adrian evaded the first strike, but the beast turned with a vicious uppercut. Adrian put his shoulder forward, and the claws slashed through his chain mail and up his arm, but he spun, jerking his head out of the way and drawing his dagger. He sunk it deep into the man's spine, then pushed him to the ground and pinned him with his boot.

Adrian gave the writhing beast no time to react. He bent down, pulled out the dagger, and plunged it into the creature's brain with a roar. It slid in past the hilt, spraying blood onto Adrian and the stones beneath.

Adrian's chest heaved in and out, each breath bringing the stench of death along with the metallic taste on his blood-spattered tongue. His arm was burning under the torn chain mail, rivulets of red flowing. It almost made him forget the cut in his hand.

Raklin was on the ground murmuring a prayer, his hands moving along his pendants while blood oozed from a shallow cut in his side. Adrian stepped towards him, but the priest shook his head. "I am fine."

His eyes did not reflect his words, but the concern didn't look to be for the wound alone. Seemed like whatever afflicted the people of Khet was spreading, and much faster than they'd expected. It had reached Alteria before them.

That would explain the militiamen.

Derren had finally passed through the crowd and was unfazed by the viscera on the stones, but his face was still concerned. "Have you ever seen anything like this?"

Adrian considered whether explaining what was happening in Ultenvell would help, but he shook his head. "He seemed to feel no pain. I'll have to ask my father."

"Not the Pontiff?"

Adrian shook his head again. He'd promised to take Raklin before Father, and frenzied attackers in Khet and now Alteria was too much of a coincidence. "I'm seeing my father first."

"He'd much prefer the blood red to the road brown, I'd wager." Derren smiled, but his expression quickly faded at the sight of Ellana.

She wasn't looking at him, though. Her eyes were focused on Raklin. "What are you doing here, Cleanser?" she asked, tone almost as sharp as Father's.

"We'll talk about it later, Ellana," Adrian said. "Now is not the time."

She looked between them, face darkening, then turned to Derren.

"Captain?"

"A madman, your holiness, not a direct attack, it seems."

"And that?" She pointed at the bolt sticking out of the carriage, her voice cold and commanding. More princess than priestess.

"Wayward bolt, Prin—erhm . . . High Priestess. Some farmer on edge. Thought having a weapon and no training would somehow make him safer. He has been properly dealt with."

Ellana paused at the tip of the pool of blood, far enough not to soil her robes. At least one of them would be presentable. "Send word to the Legion, Captain. The Pontiff must be informed."

Derren shot Adrian a look but knew better than to ask for permission, even if Ellana no longer held the power to officially command him. The captain bowed, mounted his horse, and galloped towards the cathedral.

Ellana looked Adrian over, lingering on his bloody shoulder. "You're bleeding," she said before turning on her heel and stepping back into the carriage.

The coldness in her voice was palpable. Father would be proud.

CHAPTER FIVE

The Earth-Breakers wove their spells, syphoning all that was alive around them, but Tedros was strong and cut the monsters down. Their essence was given back to the Earth, and from that life returned, the First Tree was born.

— *Tales of the Ronar*

Rain had been her only companion on the road towards the Ronar village. The water had found its way into her hunter's pack, and Chatta's swelling head weighed on her shoulder. Nasha peeked inside. The brown skin had gone pale with death, but the corruption still showed, black lines weaving along ashen patches of skin. She let out a misty breath, hoping the state of the Warden's head would be proof enough of her intentions to protect the strength of the clan.

In and out, quick and quiet. Find Mansa. He'll know how to go about things.

A simple enough plan.

Nasha's skin tingled under the rain, the cold seeming to seep into her gut. The smell of charred wood pressed at her again, but nothing was burning, and she struggled to push it away. The crowds in the village would drain enough of her strength. Her own emotions had to be kept under control.

I did the right thing.

The village sat at the base of the Great Mountain, with the Slopes and their ever-growing population looming above it. Huts made from mud and scraps of wood sprawled as high and wide as the steepness would allow. They stood in a chaotic lattice over the unstable mountainside, which threatened them with deadly promises of earth sliding underfoot or fire flowing from above.

It had been a while since the Great Mountain had raged, spewing its burning insides down the slope, and that seemed to be enough to make the Slopers confident—the incline was as crowded with buildings as Nasha had ever seen it. Their population had probably reached half that of the village, thousands bustling about despite the overhanging drab. The houses had spread down the mountain as well. Shelters of broken and rough-cut wood had been built almost up to the ancestor-stone wards around the ditch that surrounded the village. Even the ditches—meant to divert the mountain's fire and earth away from the village—had people living in them.

They mock the Earth and I'm the one who ends up cursed by it.

Nasha gritted her teeth. The Earth would collect its due soon enough. The Slopers wouldn't have much choice then. They'd either join the gangs who commanded the slopes—the Zaruni—to participate in village raids, or beg at the village gates and farms for food . . . or for a Proving. They always asked for Provings, even if Nasha hardly ever saw them put in the work to survive one. It was their own fault. *She'd* left the Slopes, and none of them had her curse.

Nasha set her jaw and plowed on. She'd have to take the Market Gate. It was more crowded than the Root Gate, but a three-striped hunter would have enough trouble getting through the latter without being questioned, and the Warden's severed head certainly wouldn't help matters. Nasha moved towards the gate, almost giving in to the anxiousness trying to take hold of her. Maybe it would bring a sliver of warmth against the rain. She caught herself and pulled up the stinging scent of the fumes to focus her mind into emptiness, then displayed her stripes to the warriors at the Market Gate, keeping her pack firmly shut.

Even with the rain, people still crowded the streets. They flooded the market and unwittingly assaulted her with the thrills and frustrations of their haggling. It brought up the first of the warning signs of her curse, which manifested as an intense prickling on her skin, like tiny knives poking but not breaking skin. Nasha immediately felt the drain of pushing back against the emotions. Every step became heavier, rain and mud clinging to her squelching boots.

It was only the first sign—far from the intense brightness that had taken over her vision and near-suffocation she'd felt right before breaking in her Proving—but it was enough for her to veer away towards Old Kolg's hut.

The man had always treated her with respect, and she'd spent enough time around him to know the pattern of his emotion. Never too cheery, but hardly ever pushed to anger, either. He was always steady, stable as ancestor-stone, and one of the havens Nasha had adopted to get through the crowds. There were others, each familiar enough to act as an anchor so she wouldn't lose herself in the roil of the village, but Kolg rarely left his home.

Nasha latched onto the old man's wafting calm. It was like holding onto a rope that she could follow across an angry river, and she was soon at the back end of the village, heading through the Mountain Gate and over the flat bridge towards the Slopes. The pathway that bridged the ditch was five strides wide and twenty strides long. It was filled with Ronar and Slopers, but none even glanced at the long drop to either side.

Nasha crossed it quickly and paused beside the ancestor-stone wards. There were Slopers all around them, asking for favors of the Silent Earth and running their hands over the runes that had been inscribed into the stones. The wards were a source of protection to make sure that, even asleep in the Earth, Zala's wild power would not touch the village. No one had ever really told her what that power was, but Chatta's rotting head in her pack seemed like proof enough. Even so, Nasha did not dare get close enough to touch them. Ancestor-stone was bad enough, but the wards had been augmented by the Tivezzi and her stone-shapers and seemed to be receptacles of emotion. Touching them would pull Nasha into a vortex no anchor could save her from.

Nasha breathed deep—trying to keep focus on Kolg's waning emotion as she distanced herself from his hut—then made her way up the Slopes.

The foothills had also grown denser, homes forming tight, winding passages the Slopers used for streets, some barely wide enough for two abreast, but she'd come through here enough to know the way.

Mansa's hall stood on a slight outcropping. It had straighter walls than the other buildings and thick timbers rising from a stone foundation that made it stand out from the uneven wooden boards of the rickety houses below. He was the only Root that kept one of his halls outside the village. He always had an eye out for opportunity, even among the Slopers. Nasha moved quickly through and turned the final corner—but froze as if the mud at her feet had hardened into stone.

A score of steps led up to the front doors, and a mass of Slopers had gathered around them like crows around a carcass, with more than a dozen hunters struggling to keep them back. There could only be one reason for this. There'd be a Proving soon.

The Slopers were clamoring, pleading, all of them hoping to get a word with Mansa, convince him why their sons and daughters would be the best choice for the Proving. Their commotion was picking up, and so was the rain, but Nasha's focus was on the quieter voices of men dressed in sturdy leather vests and club-like lengths of wood, who ambled among the mass. Zaruni. The self-proclaimed protectors of the Slopes.

The village had tried getting rid of them, but they'd only lost warriors doing so. The Zaruni were too firmly entrenched: they knew the twisting maze among the houses like no other. And the lack of Ronar support in the Slopes meant the Zaruni were usually the only promise the Slopers had of a more comfortable, if more dangerous, life. They offered wealth and protection, and the Slopers protected them in return. Nothing was ever free, though. The riches promised by the Zaruni had to be taken from the village, and the Slopers were always the ones paying the price. Arrested by the Ronar in village raids if they joined the Zaruni, taken as slaves by Domain hunting parties that prowled ancestor-stone dig sites if they did not.

What Nasha heard now was new, though. The Zaruni weren't recruiting more for their raids; they seemed to be intent on inciting discontent among all the Slopers. Whispers of "The slopes are strong" and "Justice for the slopes" were more prevalent the closer Nasha got to the hall.

Mansa will need to know the unrest is not just because of the Proving.

Nasha's body was reacting to the crowd. The prickling on her skin had been joined by shallow breaths and blurring at the edge of her vision. She stepped back. No attempt to blank out her thoughts would work to quiet her curse against this crowd. She needed an anchor. That was a problem. She'd spent most of her time in the village and had anchors through the paths she was used to taking, but there were none in the Slopes she could trust for that. Well, . . . almost none.

Her feet didn't move, but her blurred vision darted frantically from face to face. Shai wouldn't be among those shouting to be proven—not for herself, anyway—but if her brother had come, she'd be close by. Nasha circled the hall, the anxiousness from every frustrated call at Mansa's door pressing against her. No sign of Shai.

She took another deep breath. If the girl wasn't here, the back entrance was Nasha's only chance. There was no clear path in sight, but it was looking like she'd have to fight through all the same. Nasha grasped at wisps of the memory of Old Kolg's calm, trying to keep hold of the encircling, stable sensation, then stepped forward. It was like walking against crashing waves, each one larger, breaking heavier onto her. Nasha gritted her teeth, her jaw hurting from the constant pressing. Another step—

"Nasha?"

Nasha spun round to find Shai standing under an awning in one of the rough buildings. She focused on the girl as if she were being carried by a current and Shai was the last boulder before a sheer drop. Shai wasn't as stable as Kolg, but Nasha had learned to recognize the hopeful anticipation with which she was normally greeted. There was a hint of apprehensiveness riding it now, but the pattern was familiar.

"Where's your haul?" Shai asked.

Nasha took another step away from the crowd, fighting against her own cold apprehension crawling up her spine. With all that had happened, she'd forgotten about getting Shai the food she'd promised.

"I don't have it, Shai. I'm sorry."

"What do you mean? Did you sell it all in the village?"

"No. There was nothing to sell."

A spike in Shai's emotion shot through Nasha, and she pulled back reflexively, but that only threw her into the chaos of the crowd again. She refocused on Shai, trying to make her next words as soft as she could—she couldn't afford to anger the girl, not while she was this exposed. She'd be overwhelmed in a heartbeat.

"Look, Shai, something's happened. I don't have much time. I'll get your meat as soon as this is over."

"And what should I do until then? Starve? Beg Sika to sell to me —Ife's daughter? She wouldn't sell me scraps even before my father was killed."

"I know the merchants won't sell to you, and I know the promise I made your father. Nothing will change that."

"I can't live on promises, Nasha. His weren't enough to feed Uvo or my mother, and neither are yours. I'm not him, no matter what they say about me. I won't steal from the village. I'm not involving myself with those Zaruni bastards."

Ife had taught her that, at least. Nasha looked back at the crowd, the pressure closing in on her. "Why don't you try the Proving? Uvo seems intent on it."

Shai let out a dry laugh "I'd rather be free."

Nasha had no time to argue, but there was that nagging feeling at the back of her mind again. She'd left the Slopes, but it seemed like her past wouldn't let her go. She could cut ties, leave Shai, Uvo, and Landi to fend for themselves, but she'd promised Ife, and she wasn't the monster.

"I'll go through the market on my way back, Shai—see what I can get from Sika."

Just the thought of the market set Nasha on edge. She could almost feel the pull of the effort it would take, but Shai relaxed a touch, and that was all Nasha needed.

Shai's familiar shots of anxious hope brought back the feeling of Nasha's hours spent talking with Ife about how they'd break free from the Slopes and join the Ronar. It was a good memory, strong enough that the blurring faded from her vision. Nasha nodded to Shai, then turned back and skirted the crowd. She rushed past a few of them, flashed her stripes to the hunter keeping the people at bay, and dashed up the back steps.

The hall was far enough from the crowd that the pressure was reduced to a dull drumming on her senses, but her muscles were spent, and she was still nowhere near comfortable.

Voices came from inside. Nasha pushed the doors open and was greeted by the heat from the firepit at the center of the small hall. Mansa sat on a low wooden bench, talking to a man with squared features, dressed in a Domain-styled tunic and breeches rather than a clan vest. Bahar, the emissary from the Visslands. He stood in stark contrast to Mansa, his skin pale where Mansa's was dark, his hair shaggy where Mansa had always kept a neatly trimmed beard and closely attended, short coils of hair.

Mansa looked up at her with a smile.

"Have you come to plead your case for the Proving, Sloper?"

Bahar got up, also smiling. "You wouldn't be mad enough to come to him for a chance, would you?"

Mansa laughed almost as warmly as the fire. "Sit, heat your bones, but not too close. You smell of wet dog."

Nasha smirked, then sat beside her Root. He wrinkled his nose, then stretched out a hand, and they clasped forearms.

Bahar sat back down, looking to Mansa. "I could use her, Oringo."

"For what?" Nasha asked.

"Missing noble boy, Councilor Carswell's son. Whole council's on edge."

"You wouldn't be here if they suspected the Ronar. What do they want from us?"

"Oh! They'd scour the place, take some of your ruin—ahm—ancestor-stone back with them. I, on the other hand, wish to maintain my son's home intact."

"Self-interest is always the most trustworthy of motives," Mansa said.

"That it is," Bahar answered. "But what really convinced them was the gold. Expensive thing, wars."

"Wise men," Nasha said.

"That they are. Was hoping to put together a scouting party: a few hunters, maybe a few warriors, set out to find the boy."

"You'll have to talk to Chatta about the warriors, but I'll get you the hunters." Mansa said.

Bahar rose and bowed his head to Mansa. "Generous as always, Oringo. I'll let you two talk." He turned to Nasha. "Wait for you outside?"

Nasha nodded. She might need a familiar face to get back through the crowd, even if not familiar enough to be an anchor. She waited for his footsteps to recede before turning back to Mansa.

"Loves using my title, that one. Where's Jima?" Mansa asked.

"Dead. Along with the others."

Mansa frowned at her. "Hagun?"

"Me."

Mansa's frown deepened. "You know I like you, Nasha, but this is not something I can overlook."

Nasha opened the bag weighing on her shoulder and pulled out Chatta's severed head. Mansa grimaced but did not shy away.

"All life that is wasted must be taken. That is the Ronar way," Nasha said.

"It is."

"He was on some kind of ashen ground, dead all around. Even . . . even the emotion. It had to be done, Mansa. The corruption is clear in his veins, as if Zala had claimed him. He was gone."

Mansa regarded the dead Warden's head for a while. "And the others?"

"They couldn't see what I was doing for the clan, the danger a weakened Warden would pose. They attacked me." Nasha took a breath. "I fought back. They were weak, and I returned their essences to the Earth."

Mansa's eyes were on the flames of the firepit.

"This ashen ground. That's how you managed to fight them?"

Nasha nodded. "I did this for the clan, Mansa. I . . . didn't know about the Proving."

"No one does, officially. But nothing stirs the masses like Domain generals sniffing after ancestor-stone in the Chief's Hall. Like we haven't given the Domain enough already."

Nasha shrugged, releasing some of the tension in her shoulders. "Keeps them off our backs, though."

"Only until they come searching for more." Mansa worked his jaw. "I'll tell them about Chatta. We should keep the others between us, though. When they ask, you were ambushed by Hagun."

"You think that'll work?"

"Worst thing that can happen is they ask me to send a larger party after the Hagun, but they don't seem to be anywhere close. Or . . . you know, you could tell the truth." Mansa smiled. "Do you have more heads in there?"

Nasha shook her head and looked down, eyes moving to her forearm, where her stripes were carved.

Mansa seemed to have caught the motion and put a hand on her shoulder. "We'll talk about your position if all goes well. What-ever the Chief's decision, you did the right thing."

Nasha's chest relaxed, and the warmth of the fire bled through, calming her for the first time since she'd laid eyes on the village.

"Thank you," she said, already rising, but paused before leaving. "Should we be worried about the Slopers? There were whispers for more than a favored eye in the draft. Zaruni were prowling the crowd."

Mansa clicked his tongue. "The Domain's been taking more Slopers close to the borderlands, and Zaruni weapon-thieves were killed yesterday, pushed into the fire of the Great Mountain. You know how Jabillo loves his theatrics." He shook his head. "We're keeping an eye on them. Adda has taken notice this time, at least, and wants her stone-shapers to widen the placement of the wards, expand the village as a statement to the Zaruni. That would require clearing part of the Slopes, though, and we know how that's bound to turn out. . . . We'll pull through. We always do."

"I'll leave you to fend off the crowd, then."

Mansa laughed again, and Nasha made her way back to where Bahar was waiting.

They walked up the Slopes to avoid the raucous mass, then back down towards Nasha's home, which was in one of the less crowded parts of the village. A frown crept onto Nasha's brow, deepening the valley across her forehead.

"Didn't get what you expected from Mansa?" Bahar said.

"I'm not sure what I expected, but it seems I can't get it from him. Just hate waiting for the Chief."

"Want me to put in a good word? I'll need to know more, though." He smiled at her, and Nasha mirrored him.

"If Mansa fails, I'll come to you," she said. The smile slid off her face. "Did the Visslands really send someone to talk to the Chief?"

"General Misher," he said. "But I can never understand why you people associate us with your Provings. Never really understood how you live among death so comfortably, either."

"The Earth has only so much life to give, and Zala is a selfish mistress."

"Ah, your 'dead' goddess."

"That's why we need the Earth alive. To keep her that way."

Bahar kept shaking his head. Even after all these years and a son among the Ronar, his Domain beliefs still got the better of him. Nasha could never understand them. They were what had forced him to bring Devu to the Ronar as a babe and subject him to a life on the Slopes—all because his mother had died while birthing him, as if that cursed the boy somehow. But returning life to the Earth was not a curse, and Nasha doubted these Domain folk knew what a true curse, like hers, really was.

Bahar pulled open the door to Nasha's house—sturdily built out of stone, nothing like those on the Slopes—and ushered her in.

"How's Devu?" Nasha asked.

"Oh, he's fine. I'm the one who's nervous about this ritual of death you people insist on. Really, Nasha, does it have to be—"

Shouting drowned out whatever complaint he had about their customs, and splashing footfalls sounded all around them. Nasha strode out and was met by a string of armed warriors.

"What's going on?" she asked.

Speaker Jabillo, another of the Roots, stepped out from behind one of the warriors. He had lithe arms and a sharp nose, and his voice had always been brittle, despite his title. There was a battered man beside him, hair stubbly and face bloodied, but still recognizable.

Iallo.

Each raindrop became a shard of ice, cutting deep into her skin, and that taste of burning wood mingled with a touch of iron—almost like blood—was on her tongue again. How? He couldn't be alive. He'd been buried!

"It's her!" Iallo said, raising a trembling finger.

Bahar was beside Nasha, raising his voice in the authoritative tone of a Domain officer. "Whatever he's accusing her of, Jabillo, she is a friend. I am a representative of the Domain. You'd do well to—"

"Enough of that, Bahar. Quiet, or you'll join her."

Nasha's gaze was darting around, and she was already straining to suppress the nervousness surrounding her, but the warning signs were racing towards a breaking point—her vision blurring, her ears ringing. Nasha stepped forward. Maybe the signs weren't a bad thing this time. Maybe this was what she needed to break through and make a run for it. Bahar touched her arm lightly, stopping Nasha before she could take another step forward.

"I'll fix this," he whispered.

Nasha paused, looking among them.

In and out, quick as quiet. A simple enough plan. Strange how those were always the easiest to complicate themselves. Nasha closed her eyes and dug up the memory of Ife that Shai had helped her find. It gave her a measure of control.

"Get Mansa," she said, then lowered her arms and let them bind her wrists and pull her away.

Jabillo led them along the sodden roads of the village, Iallo and a handful of warriors close behind, one of them pulling at a rope attached to her bound wrists. Nasha clamped her jaw tight, trying to remember the scent of citrus and fumes that had anchored her a few days ago, but she could smell nothing beyond the rain and muddy earth.

She was past the blurred vision, and the high-pitched ringing in her ears was increasing. Nasha's heart beat faster. These were the later, more dangerous signs. The world would start to grow brighter next, then she'd have trouble breathing, and then . . .

She looked up to the Great Mountain, trying to anchor herself in the scent of the fumes that had always been around her on the Slopes, but the press of men, horses, and onlookers became heavier as she neared the Chief's Hall, and every raindrop was a drum beating on her skin. She squeezed her eyes shut, focusing on the darkness, on nothing. Almost there, almost—

A heavily armored man strode past, followed by at least a dozen other soldiers, splashing through puddles. Domain folk, all with the triple waterfall of the Visslands embroidered on their chests, pale skin contrasting with the Ronar around them. General Misher, probably.

Part of her mind wondered what the Domain was doing here in these numbers if Bahar was already leading the search effort for the Carswell boy, but the thought dissolved into the rain as Jabillo pushed open the heavy darkwood doors of Tomu's great hall.

The ringing in her ears stopped, and the warm mahogany and burning hearth would have been almost comforting if she hadn't known what she was walking into. She was pushed through an entry hall, her wrists scraping against the coarse rope, her whole body exhausted as if she'd just sprinted up the Great Mountain, and her skin still prickling with her curse's warning.

The hall had a huge relief of the First Tree embedded in raw ancestor-stone across one of the walls, blue veins pulsing, mingling with the firelight and incessant pattering of the rain on the window ledge. There was a table full of what looked like the remains of a feast on the opposite wall, or maybe the beginning of one. More meat than she even knew how to name, and enough flagons of drink for what seemed to be the entire clan. Nasha's stomach grumbled, but her captors pulled her forward to stand on heavy legs before the Chief.

Chief Tomu sat in his high-backed chair, bearded face resting on a steeple-fingered hand that pushed into the wiry hair that fell to his shoulders. He was half-covered in shadow. The other half was filled with reflected flames dancing across his skin. His daughter, Adda—the Tivezzi, the Stone-Shaper—sat to his right, sharp features and thin lips turned towards Nasha, hair tied in an elaborate bun at the top of her head.

Tomu's gaze moved towards Nasha, then fell on Jabillo.

"What?" he grumbled in a deep voice that scraped like stones tumbling down a mountainside.

Jabillo stepped forward, bowing his head. "It is told in all the Tales that the Ronar will never turn on each other—"

"Get on with it, Jabillo, I've had enough preaching for one day." His eyes flitted to the door where the Domain general had passed them.

"We have a traitor among the—"

The doors to the hall burst open, and Mansa marched in with a bag under his arm, Bahar in tow. Mansa paused beside Nasha, opened the bag, and rolled Chatta's head towards Tomu. "The Warden is dead."

Speaker Jabillo gasped. The Chief and the Tivezzi remained silent. All of them regarded the severed head for a long moment.

"Hagun?" Adda asked, the full weight of her gaze sending cracks through Nasha's will. She couldn't break in here, not now. But the ringing that had left her ears was returning now. Louder.

"She did it!" Iallo burst out. "Filthy Sloper killed Embe and Jima. Tried to kill me, too!"

Tomu looked at Nasha. She raised her bound arms and displayed her stripes.

"I'm no Sloper—I'm Ronar! And he was withering away! Everything around him was. Look at the corruption in his veins, on his skin. We don't know what it is. I couldn't risk bringing him back. Not alive."

Jabillo was still frowning at the head, seemingly taking in the blackened veins on Chatta's brown-gray skin for the first time. Whatever this corruption was, not even the Roots seemed to know about it.

"And these others?" Adda asked, her father still silent.

"Nasha is a trusted hunter," Mansa said. "She came to me with this as soon as she returned to the village. She acted in the interest of the Ronar."

"That was not her decision to make," Jabillo said. "Not when it involved the Warden, and the others were not affected."

"They attacked me! What I did was for the clan, Speaker. You must see this!"

Jabillo looked towards Chatta's head, then back at Nasha. "I think I've seen enough."

Tomu was shaking his head. He shifted in his seat, and every gaze in the room fell upon him. "Do you know how a new Warden is chosen, hunter?"

Nasha swallowed hard. Mansa had always been practical. He'd taught her what she needed to know, but he'd never delved into old rituals—those had always been reserved for the Roots. She'd always assumed the Chief would simply appoint one.

Nasha shook her head.

"We do things the old way. The right way. A true Warden must be chosen by the Earth, and for that, the Roots have their own kind of trial."

Jabillo glared at her, his anger rising within Nasha, fighting against her attempts to swallow it back down. Numbness spread through her. Her vision was brightening, and her muscles trembled with the strain of keeping herself stable.

Mansa seemed to have noticed. He stepped forward and put a hand on the exposed skin of her shoulder. He'd never been a strong anchor. Even through all their training, Nasha had gotten little stability from him. But his touch was like a fresh breath now, and the thought of their training sessions helped remind Nasha that she had gotten through worse. She held on, looking up at the Chief.

Tomu let out a long sigh. "I've sent runners to the Yltigg with a message to accept their challenge. There will be a Proving in three weeks."

"W-without a Warden?" Jabillo blurted out.

Tomu nodded. His mouth twisted, and he looked at Nasha. "You can see how your actions have caused us trouble, yes? An accepted Proving without a Warden is forfeit."

Nasha's words stumbled, and cold gripped her throat. The panic taking over her was surely her own. "I-I didn't . . ."

"This is not a simple matter," Tomu said. "Your intent was clear, but you have put the clan at risk with your brashness. I will not make the same mistake." He looked to Jabillo. "Keep her bound to the post. We will hold a trial when your fires have cooled."

Nasha's eyes went wide. If it weren't for Mansa standing beside her, she'd probably have cracked already. "Chief, the post—"

"Would you rather I strike you down right now, hunter?" Tomu said, and a spiking irritation stabbed at Nasha. She fell silent.

Adda still had a curious look in her eyes, but none contested the Chief.

The cold spread through Nasha, running all along her skin, her head light, as if none of this was true. She'd come to the village expecting another stripe, a chance to show her worth to the Ronar, perhaps find a path to the First Tree and rid herself of her curse. But being bound to the post was as good as removing the three stripes she'd fought hard to earn. She pressed her teeth together, trying to think of a way out of this madness. It couldn't be real.

Tomu's voice brought reality crashing down on her, though, and no one—neither Bahar nor Mansa—could stop it.

"Take her away."

CHAPTER SIX

To control the enemy's weapon is to diminish its power. Only the truly faithful are worthy of bearing the burden of death so that others may be spared the weight. These are the Sentinels, who watch over the people of the Seraph's Domain.

— The Book of the Breath

Ferrin was waiting at the gate. No smile this time.

"I'm . . . erm . . ." He looked like he had something caught in his throat. "Happy," he blurted out. "So happy for you, Lynn."

"Don't be."

Lynn still had a sour taste in her mouth. She eyed the watcher, but Ferrin looked down. He'd never been good at meeting people's eyes, Lynn's least of all.

"Sorry to be the one to lead you." A contrite smile was trying to make its way onto his face now, as if it were the only expression he owned and he was attempting to work it in favor of the current mood. "I walked a few of yours out, you know. Most couldn't even look back. Never thought I'd lose you, though."

Lynn knotted her brow, unsure if she even knew how to smile anymore. She'd always imagined it would be Leardin or one of her fellow Sentinels finally catching up to her, or the gallows. Death had always been close. Why not take her for its own? Maybe it would soon enough. There was little she could do on the outside without drawing Leardin's eye, and he would not be inclined to mercy if he found her.

Ferrin was looking straight ahead at the iron gate, perhaps purposefully avoiding her gaze.

"You're too good a man to be a watcher, Ferrin," she said, then tried a calming breath, but there was no stony prison damp—only dry freedom. She squinted, shielding her eyes from the evening sun, and walked away from Dalhold.

She crossed the bridge that connected the prison to the rest of Pyrran, followed by the smell of rotting fish from the market that had been set up for the execution. The roads she'd traveled day after day growing up in the city seemed foreign now, and even if she had a path to follow, she wasn't sure she'd know how to find it.

The city was emptier than normal, but her mind was full of broken ideas and discarded possibilities, struggling through the voices to decide what to do next.

Kerr would certainly ramp up the executions with her gone. Maybe they were her path back into Dalhold. She'd sneak in during the next one, make her way up to the cells. . . . No. There was no way back, not with a Church pardon. It would raise enough suspicion for the priestess to wonder. Besides, she doubted she'd be able to hold any leverage over Kerr.

Lynn let her legs guide her while her mind faltered. The sea was drawing near. The wind had picked up through the twisting alleyways and was clawing at her with cutting determination, like knives raking against her bones. It took her attention away from the voices, at least, but it also carried voices of its own, along with the smell of saltwater and the sound of waves lapping at the stones of the pier. Lynn turned towards the source, and more voices rode the wind, louder this time, drawing closer. She hesitated. Maybe there were worthy lives at risk, but she also couldn't risk being found by her old companions.

Coward!

That was Alren's favorite word. Lynn couldn't quite argue.

She stepped back, but the voices were now followed by desperate footfalls heading her way. People burst out screaming from one of the side streets, eyes maddened by fear, legs carrying them past without a second glance.

Lynn looked to the sky and let them run around her, half-wishing she had Vedyr.

What are you expecting? Him to fly down? They all laughed.

She strode towards the alley, avoiding the rampaging Pyrranese. They'd always been accustomed to the protection of the palace and their closeness to the queen. It hadn't ever taken much to set the people off. Whatever had happened probably wasn't much—

Her mind went blank. Houses rose around a narrow street that was empty but for the bodies: half a dozen covered the flagstones in blood, mangled as if they'd been mauled. A girl stood close to one of the buildings, shaking and covered in blood. Lynn stepped slowly towards her, but the girl remained still, giving no acknowledgement of Lynn's presence.

Lynn stole a glance at the bodies as she moved. She'd seen men butchered this way only once before, and the memory was sharp and cold like a shard of ice. No. It wasn't the Madness. It couldn't be. She'd killed them all. She'd ended it.

Her eyes locked onto the girl. Lynn bounded forward and grasped her shoulders, almost lifting her off the ground. The girl quivered in shock, but Lynn ignored her and hastily rubbed away the blood around the girl's eyes, breath held in her lungs.

They were clear, no darkness around them. Of course not. She'd killed it.

The girl was looking at Lynn like she was mad herself, snapping Lynn's thoughts back into the present. She released, letting the girl fall to the ground with a squeal. The girl scrambled away, forced herself clumsily to her feet, and bolted off. Lynn did not follow. She closed her eyes for a long moment and took a few more shallow breaths that filled her with the stench of death, stronger even than the fish from the execution market. It brought back the faces from her past: all those she'd never see again but was cursed to hear in her mind.

A true Sentinel would not risk letting her go, Dentos said. *A true Sentinel has command over death.*

No. There were no signs. To command death is to know when to use it.

She made herself look over the bodies again. The girl might not be tainted, but whatever did this could not be ignored. She'd done her work in the prison, but if death was going to follow her, she'd have to find another way to keep it at bay. The Seraph had not spoken to Lynn, but maybe this was Her sign that there was still work to do. She had to find the source of this.

Lynn looked up at the mark in the sky.

I will follow Your will. I will prove myself worthy of my title.

She ignored the laughs.

The attacks grew in the weeks that followed. The Pyrranese were becoming nervous, and Kerr's watchers seemed to have been brought in to help the city watchmen. They did what they could to keep the carnage out of sight, leaving little behind for Lynn to go on. She tried preventing the attacks, but Pyrran was large and the guardsmen seemed intent on cleaning up before Lynn could get anything from the scene. All she found were bloody, empty streets, devoid of even dead bodies.

Today would be different, though. The streets were filled with more and more watchmen in the days leading up to Spring Reflection, and now that the day had come, the city was flooded with faithful—too many for the watch to focus on much else. If there was something to be found, it would be today.

Lynn watched from a backstreet as the trickle of people widened, filling the High Bridge and changing the streets into streams that flowed towards the cathedral. Her eyes lingered on the building. It was barely large enough to be considered a cathedral, but Sacantha itself was a small nation, and its people had always seemed content with what they had. She'd been as well, until death found her.

She stepped out and walked with her head down among the meandering devoted until she stood before the cathedral doors. She'd always been fond of the doors as a child but saw now they were ugly things, a mockery of flint with only a light touch of ruin-stone. Nothing compared to the doors of the cathedrals in Alteria.

Was that how Elwin would see her if they met after years apart? A shadow of a true Sentinel?

I've saved lives. The priestess will tend to them at the temple.

Roki laughed at her. *That changes nothing.*

Lynn grabbed the Sentinel coin she'd strung around her neck and stepped away from the drifting throng. She circled around the cathedral, thoughts moving back to Elwin. He'd probably laugh and tell her there was too much to learn for her to worry about the past. That was what he'd told her when he took her in, laughing when, even as a child, she warned him she'd bring death into his home.

"It's already here," he had said.

She'd left even her own father behind. She'd loved him too much to bear bringing more death upon her family, but Elwin hadn't cared. Too much still to learn.

Lynn kept moving around the cathedral and away from the crowd, then stopped a few steps away under the domed shadow of the tower, straining to hear movement in the city beyond. Her gaze fell on the cathedral wall and the sacred texts chiseled through it so the words would be projected in light inside. She knew what they said. Elwin had brought her there every day.

"To control the enemy's weapon is to diminish its hold over the faithful."

At first, she hated reciting words she didn't understand or believe. But he'd taught her their true meaning; he'd shown her the power of the Breath.

"The true test is not only to bring death when needed," he'd said, "but to have the faith to not dwell on it once you are done. That is what makes a true Sentinel."

Lynn had believed him. Believed she could fight death with its own means and move on. And for a while, she did. She controlled it, smote the unworthy, and protected her own.

And then the Madness took those closest to her and forced her to kill her own. And now death would never let her go.

The memory lit a fire in her, and her body tensed with the images of the faces she'd killed. She let the anger flow, let her muscles become tense with it.

What difference does it make? Your anger won't bring us back, Cara said.

Lynn didn't answer. She moved away from the richer part of town that surrounded the cathedral, and upwards to where the houses clumped together and the streets began to narrow. She found a lower house with enough cracks in the brick to fix her feet into, then propelled herself upward. The anger still burned in her as she stood on the ledge and looked over the city, muscles rigid, but eyes moving across the streets. Guards patrolled in the distance, yet all seemed calm around her. She moved along the rooftops, carefully avoiding the patrols, keeping low—

Darting shadows caught her eye. They weren't far, and she didn't think or look down. Lynn looked up instead and reached for Vedyr. She fed him her pent-up anger, and the burning in her gut moved to her eyes as she dove into the Bond. The fire that had burned in her spread through her veins, and she dashed across the roofs with powerful leaps, the stone fracturing under the impact of her feet as she vaulted multiple houses at a time.

The air rushing in her ears turned into screams from people fleeing one of the streets below. Men and women lay bleeding on the ground, but there was no sign of an attacker. Lynn checked the surrounding streets.

Nothing.

You've failed again, Dentos said, but his voice was distant, filtered away through the Bond. She hadn't failed yet. The bodies were still on the ground.

A thrill ran through her, and she jumped down, focusing Vedyr's strength on her lower limbs and landing with a crack on the stone. Her anger was burning away, and the Bond dug into her, danger-ously close to pulling at the parts that made her mind whole. If she kept at it, she'd lose herself, piece by piece, until she became no more than an empty husk.

Can't hollow out now.

She released the Bond, thanking Vedyr and praying to the Seraph that she wouldn't need it anytime soon. Even if she had more anger, Vedyr was too distant, and it was taking its toll: her head pounded with the aftereffect of the Bond, and Lynn instinc-tively began to recite the names. Elwin had always told her she needed a tether—something that, as long as she could remember, was enough to make sure that she was not losing parts of her mind, drawing close to hollowing out.

Alren, Roki, Cara, Dentos. Their names had not been her tether when they were alive, but there was nothing clearer in her mind now than the names of those she'd killed.

Lynn pushed through her throbbing thoughts and checked the bodies. None moved. Their chests were ripped open, and their eyes were pale and empty, but there was no blackness around them. No Madness.

"Help . . ." The voice was weak, more a gasp than a word, but Lynn dashed towards it and was beside the man in an instant.

He held his hand to his gut, trying to keep the blood in as it flowed between his fingers. A knife lay on the ground beside him, discarded on a tattered cloak.

"Hold on," Lynn said.

She took the man's knife, cut a rag from one of the dead bodies, and bound it tight around his torso and stomach. "Who did this?"

The man coughed blood, shaking his head. "I . . . didn't see. He moved too fast."

"A man, then? Did you not catch a glimpse? Anything?"

Another fit of coughing and more blood. Lynn grimaced. She hated seeing death do its work, but this man still was not in its clutches. She could help him—

Heavy footfalls sounded from behind, and Lynn knew her time

was up. Her chest tightened, the anger rising again. If the man had nothing for her, maybe the guards would. She took his discarded knife, wrapped it in his cloak, and stepped back.

"They'll help you," she said.

He gave Lynn a glazed stare, eyes blinking ponderously, but she had no more time to tend to him. She darted away, climbing up onto the roof again, and lay still, chest pressed onto a low parapet.

The guards wore the uniform of the city watch, one of them slender with a full beard, the other bald with a long scar atop his head. They checked the bodies but found only the man Lynn had talked to alive. The bald man kneeled beside him, while the other kept watch. He tried exchanging words with the man, but a group of approaching figures caught his attention—all of them dressed in silver and white. Church guard.

"You Kerr's men?" one of them asked the watchmen.

They nodded.

"You know how this goes, then."

The bearded man looked confused, but the one with the scar on his pate pushed his companion's spear down and pulled him away. Two of the Church guard rounded up the dead bodies, while the rest of them blocked the entrance. Lynn looked for a healer but didn't recognize one.

Her gaze returned to the guard captain who'd sent Kerr's men away. He was on his haunches beside the wounded man; he hushed a few words, then steel flashed, and the injured man fell back, throat slit.

Another life you could not save, Roki said.

Lynn gripped the edge of the parapet, knuckles white. Even if she could take these men, she'd make too much of a show, and she'd probably have to kill them. She wouldn't add to the count of the dead. There'd been enough for one day.

Still, it didn't take a Sentinel to know that the man could have been saved. That his life was taken by the Church guard only fanned the flames in Lynn's stomach.

We've seen this only once before, Alren said. *You know what it is.*

No. She'd checked. These people didn't have the Madness.

Besides, no one knew about the Madness. They'd contained it, not wanting to create a panic among the ranks of the Church. The Pontiff had been told, but Lynn doubted whatever was happening here had reached him. What was the Church doing, then? What were they so afraid of?

The guard blocking the entrance made way, and a small cart was pulled inside. They loaded the bodies onto it, covering the pale faces on the back of the cart with a thick oilcloth, then hurried out.

Lynn stayed there for a while, waiting to be sure they had left.

Coward, Alren said.

He might have been right again, but sometimes, being a coward was necessary to prevent a worse fate than wounded pride.

She'd found a path, at least. If the Church was trying to cover something up, she had to dig into it, and the leader had mentioned Lord Keeper Kerr. Delving into the Church guard would be dangerous, but if Kerr was involved, maybe one of his watchers could help.

She needed to find Ferrin.

CHAPTER SEVEN

Even after the creation of the Domain, Othonea and Dakhra still held their differences. The scars of past wars were too stark a reminder for true friendship to evolve.

After the nations pledged themselves to the Church, they agreed to not mention those lost in war, but one wonders if they were truly forgotten.

— *Histories of the Domain*

The House of the Seraph stood watchful over the city of Alteria, its towers casting claw-like shadows that raked the faithful into a smothering embrace. Adrian and Raklin strode towards the cathedral through considerably emptier streets, but the guards around them still glared away those who strayed too close to their group. Monuments of the Seraph flanked their path, two on each side: towering behemoths of polished ruin-stone shining silver, with white veins flowing through Her three pairs of outstretched wings. Each statue held a sign high—the Breath, the Body, the Blood, and the Bone.

Adrian was a blemish on the gleaming pathway, tarnishing the immaculate cobbles with his dripping blood and road dust. Fitting, really. He'd always been out of place here, but even more now without Myrra or Jovu.

He looked up, shielding his eyes with his uninjured arm. Dakhran airships floated above, indicating King Syvern's arrival, but Adrian's gaze was pulled towards the mark hanging in the sky, a ball of light like a watchful eye, piercing bright even during the day. It shone off the Signs of the Seraph and onto the massive slabs of veined ruin-stone that formed the cathedral doors. They were at least five strides wide and ten strides high and carved with scriptures from top to bottom.

The doors were closed today, whether because of the attack or some other occasion, Adrian could not tell. His boots were mud-caked and bloody, but he didn't bother cleaning them before climbing the steps.

"You are dismissed," he told the guards, then pushed open the doors, leaving a smear of blood where his hand touched the stone. A shade of Othonean red to offset the Alterian silvery-white.

The walls of the empty reflection hall rose to twice the height of the doors, with the traditional carving of the Seraph's scriptures through the stone so that the words were written in sunlight on the smooth stone floor.

Raklin stood silent while Adrian regarded the texts, the monotone of the various tutor-priests of his childhood droning in his mind: man had tainted the Seraph's perfect world with death, driving Her away, and now had to prove their faith, remove the unworthy, cleanse Immeria, and expand Her Domain so that She may return, bringing the Promised Dawn.

Adrian had never put much stock in the Faith, but Myrra had started to change that. Maybe that was why he kept the hope that the Seraph would bring her back in the Promised Dawn, or maybe he couldn't bring himself to bear the alternative. Still, it was not faith or blessings that extended his life while commoners and lesser noble families could barely reach half his current years. Father had lived for centuries. Adrian and Jovu had been alive for almost two, and Father handpicked the nobles surrounding him, somehow recognizing the same power of his own blood in theirs. Blessings were not responsible for their years: their blood was, even if Adrian hated to admit the connection to Father.

Adrian pulled himself away from the texts, the slow dripping of his blood echoing across the chamber. Raklin shuffled behind, still silent, but had a scowl on his face and a hand pressed to the shallow wound along his ribs. Some men just could not take pain, it seemed.

Adrian pushed past the gloomy reflection hall until they came to a circular room with an opening in its domelike ceiling above a huge Ever-Tree. Beams of light cut through its boughs, highlighting its yellows and reds and oranges and reflecting off the pool of sap that surrounded the tree. Adrian's gaze followed a petal floating down towards his bloody palm, brow furrowing as it drifted closer.

"W-what is the meaning of this?" A priest with a wrinkled face was looking them up and down from mud-caked boots to the trail of blood in their wake.

Adrian crushed the petal in his fist. "I thought these weren't supposed to fall."

The priest's eyes went wide at the sight of the discarded colors floating in the pool at the foot of the tree, seemingly unable to decide between Adrian's state and the petals falling in every color of sunlight.

Adrian lifted his arm. He wasn't Jovu. He'd have to tidy up before seeing Father. "The Priests of the Blood?"

The priest's words were still failing him, but he seemed to have decided to focus on the tree. He pointed a trembling finger at the passage behind him without moving his eyes.

Adrian gave him an appreciative nod and left the gawping man behind.

The Priests of the Blood had done what they could. The stitches had stemmed the bleeding, and they assured Adrian their blessings would accelerate the closing of the wound, but the pain was still lancing through his arm and creeping up his neck. Raklin didn't look like he was doing much better. His wound had been shallow, but his face was still contorted in pain, skin pale.

They paused at the king's door, where two guards stood on either side.

"Wait here," Adrian said. "I will send for you when we are ready."

Raklin frowned at him. "Khet suffers under his rule. I—"

"You will have your time, Raklin. Do not complicate matters." Adrian grimaced at the pain rushing up his arm. "Please."

Raklin blew out a frustrated breath and curled his lip but gave him a begrudged nod. Adrian took a breath of his own, then signaled the guard to announce him.

Father's rooms were humble compared to the grandeur of the rest of the cathedral, but they were by no means modest. The bed alone could fit the entire Othonean delegation, and the cloth of gold covering it would probably fetch enough to feed them.

Father stood by the window, looking out through the silver-lined curtains, which let in a fraction of light that splayed onto the king's clean-shaven face and made his short, sandy-blond hair look almost white. His hands moved over the interwoven circles of the Sign of the Body in his ruin-stone pendant.

Adrian narrowed his eyes as he entered the chamber. He felt his head go light as he stepped close to Father, but it was probably just his wounded arm taking his strength—that and not having Myrra to help him talk to the old man. He blinked hard to keep his focus and stepped forward.

Derren stood by the desk, quill in hand. He acknowledged Adrian with a half-smile, and Adrian gave him a nod, then kneeled before Father, looking down so he could wince unnoticed at the pain.

"I've received word," Father said, still looking out the curtains. "You've made quite the entrance."

"A madman, Father. Nothing the Legion guard wouldn't have handled." Adrian stood.

Father scoffed. "The Legion. The Legion is nothing. Derren tells me it ravaged two of them before you took it down. With a dagger?"

His father turned to Adrian with a glint in his eye and the wisp of a smile on his lips. It settled Adrian's heart a touch. His father's approval was hard to come by, and it almost reminded Adrian of when he had a haven in Myrra. More than that, it was a clear step closer to the old man's trust and finding out what he'd sent Jovu after.

"I'd lost my sword," Adrian said.

Derren nodded, and the king chuckled.

"Did you bring the Khetish boy?" his father asked.

"He's been shown to his rooms," Adrian said.

"And you are convinced he will sign?"

"He will."

"Good, we'll get your sister—"

"Has Ellana been here to see you?"

His father frowned, eyes returning to their usual coldness. "I think you know the answer to that well enough."

"Then what makes you certain she will sign the terms?"

Father studied him for a long moment. "You have another solution?"

Adrian bit down on the numbness riding his tongue. Myrra had always given him words to convince the king. Now his own seemed almost too poor to speak.

"I've brought a priest. One who has agreed to sign if you listen to his request . . . and make him Royal Abbot."

"So this is what it's come to? The ruler of the most powerful nation in the Domain listening to the requests of strangers."

Adrian gritted his teeth. "It's less than what Ellana will ask for, . . . Father."

I'm sorry, Ellana.

The king turned towards the window once more, moving his head in the subtlest of acknowledgements. "Maybe you are correct, but her I know. I can deal with what I know."

"He is our best chance. All he wishes is to be heard. By you, the

Pontiff, perhaps. I'm not asking for promises. Listen to him, remain silent if you must."

Father did not react for a long while, then moved away from the window and sat at his desk. He fixed his cold stare on Adrian. "Send him in."

Adrian signaled to the guard, and a moment later, Raklin was escorted into the room. He fell to his knees before the king, but Father did not linger.

"I understand you have something to ask of me?" His tone was one Adrian had heard so many times: one that set men to stuttering, forgetting what it was they had come for.

Raklin stood, regarding his new king with steady eyes. "Khet suffers under the heavy boot of your army, King Iridan. Your soldiers have taken Ultenvell but have not tended to its people. They die on the streets, ignored, pushed to the sewers and left to die like rats."

Father sighed. "I did not ask you for a story, priest. What is your request?"

"We need healers—Priests of the Blood. And we need your soldiers to let us heal in peace."

"I am not the Pontiff. I do not have a sortie of Priests of the Blood. You are asking for help from the wrong man."

Raklin paused, but he still seemed firm in his conviction. "If years of whispered rumors are to be believed, you are the closest man to him in the Domain—"

"You assume too much from whispers, priest." Father always sounded irritated in moments like this, but linking him with the Pontiff seemed to sharpen the sentiment.

"He will respect your power, if not your friendship," Raklin said. "All I ask is that you support me in my claim to amend the treaty. There is little to be lost on your end."

Father ran a hand along his smooth jawline, and Adrian watched him with a frown and held breath. He needed Raklin. If he let this slip away, Myrra would soon follow. "Raklin speaks the truth, Father. There is little risk."

His father set heavy eyes on Adrian once more. "There is *always* a risk, boy. Always." His gaze moved back to Raklin. "I must consider. Sign the treaty, show faith in your new nation, and my consideration may be greatly swayed."

Raklin seemed to be building up to a protest, but Adrian caught his eye and shook his head slightly. The priest seemed to be too bogged down by his ideals to understand the politics of kings. This was as close to agreement as he would get.

Raklin looked at Father for another moment. "I will sign your terms before the Pontiff." He bowed his head, wisps of white hair floating around his balding head, pendants rattling around his neck, then turned and left the room.

Father watched him for a while, then turned to Adrian. "Now . . ." The king stretched out his hand, and Derren delivered the parchment he'd been writing on when Adrian entered the room. "Let us hope you can resolve this next matter as well."

Adrian's chest puffed up a fraction. Was this what Jovu felt like with Father?

"I have been in contact with the Xakhar in Dar Drezji. It seems like the situation among the families is at a low point."

Azuri fighting amongst themselves to fail at usurping their ruler. What else is new?

"Yes, Father." He'd said those words countless times, but they did not taste as bitter now.

"It seems like they are in need of allies, and you are in need of a new bride." He frowned out the window. "I have sent word. The Xakhar is a proud man, but even he knows better than to turn us away."

Adrian struggled to keep his face blank, his father's words souring in the pit of his stomach. He might never have been a man of the Church, but he could understand faith, and all of his faith was Myrra's. He would not betray her. She wasn't gone. "Father, surely . . . . They're heathens, death worshipers. The Pontiff would—"

"The Pontiff would not matter." His father had a smile on his lips, as if they had just shared a private joke.

Adrian grimaced again. Nothing to do with the pain this time.

Azur was as large a continent as Immeria, but the Azuri considered themselves one nation. Marrying the princess would, in time, make Adrian Xakhar and give him command of an army as large as all the armies in the Domain combined. None in all of Avarin could stand up to an army like that.

A pious man might have said it was faith that united the Domain—but Adrian knew better. The rulers only put up with each other out of necessity, both for protection against the Azuri and for the Pontiff's promise of the Seraph's blessings. Othonea and Dakhra might be two snarling dogs, but they had never bitten each other, not with the wolf looming overseas.

If Father managed to make an ally out of the wolf, or, even better, make his own son the wolf, he'd be powerful enough to need no more than a snarl to command the other rulers of the Domain, even the Pontiff. It still didn't explain what Father had sacrificed Jovu for, but if Adrian had learned something about Father, it was that he had a plan for every piece on the board. He was offering Adrian the chance for a kingdom of his own, and maybe that would be necessary to gain his trust, but . . . no. The pain in his arm was nothing compared to the thought of betraying Myrra. He couldn't do it. Wouldn't do it. He'd bring her back.

"We will send your ship out from Khet. You can head back there as soon as we are done with this gathering."

Adrian looked once more into his father's eyes. A twinkle of satisfaction, maybe even pride, was reflected within them. It was a look he'd so often given Jovu. There was nothing to gain from antagonizing Father now.

I won't do it. You do not command me.

Adrian bowed his head. "Yes . . . Father."

Adrian's footfalls echoed in the corridor leading to the gathering room. The walls went up as far as he could see, the details chiseled at the top impossible to make out. Alcoves lined both sides, with statues of the worthy standing in most of them and an Ever-Tree sculpted into the stone behind, white veins in the silvery ruin-stone giving each recess a soft glow. Only a few stood empty. Too few. Adrian paused before one of the openings, and his mother's sculpted face looked down on him.

What had it taken to get her here? A different time when the king and Pontiff were still on better terms, perhaps? Or had it always been politics? Maybe his father had done nothing, and Mother was here out of her own worthy actions in life. Adrian scoffed at that. More likely her tithes.

His eyes drifted towards one of the empty niches, trying to imagine a statue of Myrra—remembered in worthiness by the Church, body preserved to be brought back by the Seraph in the Promised Dawn. He couldn't. He could hardly get a sharp image of her in his mind.

Adrian dug his fingers into a pouch on his belt and pulled out Myrra's amulet. He placed it around his neck, hiding it under his tunic, and closed his eyes, grasping at the image of her in his self-produced darkness.

I will not lose you.

He moved on, out of the corridor and into a wide hall leading towards the gathering chamber. Silver silks lined with white draped the walls on either side, and a massive carving of the Seraph was chiseled above the passage into the chamber. He'd arrived early, hoping to get a word in with the Pontiff. A moment alone would be invaluable for his efforts with Myrra, and he was sure he'd need all the help he could get.

"Magnificent, is it not?" The doors had opened silently, and the High Pontiff of the Domain stood before Adrian with a gentle gaze.

Adrian's eyes snapped away from the carving to meet the old man's cool pools of green, framed by sleek silver hair.

"High Pontiff, an honor to be in your presence."

He hadn't been around the man much, but he'd found flattery was never a bad course of action around men in power, especially ones who'd lived this long. Adrian started to kneel, but the Pontiff held him up with a tender touch.

"No need, my boy. We all bow to the Seraph, and Her alone. I am merely the bridge that seeks to bring us closer to Her splendor."

He led the way into the chamber while Adrian mentally rehearsed the words—

Adrian looked inside the room, and his legs stopped moving. His sister sat at the table, accompanied by the high priests of every nation.

The Pontiff turned to Adrian with a bemused stare, but Adrian's words were already stumbling from his lips. "I . . . had hoped for a word in private . . ."

"Don't we all, my boy? Yet times are trying, I'm afraid. There were Church matters to resolve before our esteemed rulers grace us with their presence."

He kept walking, and Adrian strained to keep his dashed hopes off his face. The priests were all looking at him, except for Ellana, who hadn't had Adrian's success in managing her expression and had a dour aspect painted on her.

"You've played quite the hero since your arrival, I'm told."

"A reaction, High Pontiff—nothing worthy of note."

"Certainly worthy, my boy, certainly worthy." He gave Adrian a smile. Something familiar in it, like Ellana's own practiced expressions, but smoother—real, perhaps. He took a seat and gestured. "Please sit, Prince Adrian. The rulers should—"

The door burst open, and King Syvern strode in with Alaya at his side. They both gave the room haughty stares, Alaya reserving an especially glacial one for Adrian. Her eyes were nothing like Myrra's, but both shared their father's auburn curls.

"High Pontiff." Syvern didn't look at the clergyman and walked past without any further acknowledgment.

The high priest of Dakhra—Adrian could hardly remember their names, they changed so often—managed only a contrite smile and fearful eyes, trying to hide behind the frayed hair that fell over them while he regarded the Pontiff.

The Pontiff ignored the lack of proper reverence and watched, still seated, as the Queens of Sacantha, Vizcarra, and the Visslands followed into the room and sat beside their respective high clergy.

Adrian let himself into one of Othonea's chairs beside High Priest Erendal. The other stood empty beside him.

The rulers murmured with their high priests while they waited for King Iridan, but Syvern was eyeing Adrian all the time, tapping a thumb on the table. He finally puffed out a breath and looked at the Dakhran high priest. The man cleared his throat before standing with an uncertain glance towards the Pontiff.

"D-Dakhra would like to—"

"Where is she?" Alaya said through gritted teeth, pointedly staring at Adrian. Alaya had always had a fire to her, but the outburst took him by surprise. Whatever her feelings about Myrra, showing them before the Pontiff was a quick path to falling out with the Church.

Adrian swallowed the sour taste of unwanted yet necessary words. "That is not the matter of this gathering, Alaya. Othonea—"

Alaya was on her feet, pointing a finger at Adrian. "You were to bring her back here for a private burning. Where is she?" she shouted across the table.

Myrra's amulet grew heavier around Adrian's neck. All he wanted was to scream back at Alaya, curse her lack of faith in her sister, in him. Myrra wasn't gone. She was waiting. And he wouldn't let her burn.

The Dakhran high priest was still standing. "The dead should not be dwelled upon, my princess, especially—"

"Quiet, Harven," Syvern said. "Myrra was worthier than any of you. It seems your Sentinels do not have the clear judgment you thought they did, High Pontiff. The Church should—"

"I'm sure I can decide what the Church—and my Sentinels— should or should not do, King Syvern." A shroud of silence fell over the room as the Pontiff, still seated, delivered the words without raising his voice.

Adrian gripped the side of the chair, gaze moving from the Pontiff to the Dakhran King. This was as much Syvern's fault as any other. If he hadn't marched his armies into Khet, Father wouldn't have reacted. Adrian wouldn't have been forced to leave, wouldn't have been forced to count on Elwin—that damned Sentinel his father had offered him—for Myrra's protection. But it had been done, and pressuring the Pontiff before the rulers of the Domain was no way to gain his approval. Syvern might think himself strong enough to pressure the Pontiff, maybe even get a few other rulers behind him, but this was a dangerous gamble. Especially since Alaya had made the mistake of bringing up Myrra.

"The judgment of the Seraph will not be questioned in my presence, and the dead shall not be mentioned," the Pontiff said. "Prince Adrian is right. There are larger matters at hand."

A flicker of hope welled in Adrian's heart. It was a simple concurrence by the Pontiff, but it was a lot more than what he'd given the Dakhrans.

"Priestess Ellana brings word that Khet is ready to accept Othonea's terms of peace," the Pontiff continued.

Adrian tensed, eyes jumping to his sister: "priestess," not "high priestess." She didn't look at him. Her expression was blank now, her eyes straight ahead.

"Khet will now be under High Priest Erendal. Priestess Ellana will continue to serve the Church in a different capacity once she has signed the terms. Does the gathering hold any objection?"

Adrian kept his eyes on Ellana, but she made a point of not looking at him. Maybe Father had targeted her after all.

"Sacantha grieves the Church's loss of such an . . . accomplished high priestess but is confident she will continue to serve the Faith with the same light," Queen Niria said.

She didn't look too grieved, and her words were far from an objection. None of the other rulers had any complaints, either. Adrian looked among them, and one by one, their gazes, including Ellana's now, moved towards him.

A flush crawled up his neck, his face hot. He could object, but this was clearly the Pontiff's will. A challenge would do him no favors for Myrra's sake, especially given how her family had just treated the man. His sister would have to understand.

I'm sorry Ellana.

"Othon—"

"Othonea does not object." Adrian did not need to look to know the cold, detached tone of his father's voice. Adrian knew he'd come, and he doubted Father's tardiness was involuntary.

Ellana glared at Father, but he brushed past her, Addo and Raklin pacing behind him, ruin-stone pendants clattering as usual around Raklin's neck. His movements were different, cloddish. It might have been the wound, or maybe awe at standing before the Pontiff.

"The terms have been agreed upon." Father walked up to the Pontiff and placed the terms before him, then urged Addo forward.

The Pontiff glanced over the parchment before looking at Addo. "You are in accordance, Lord Brandt?"

Addo nodded slowly without meeting the Pontiff's eyes. "I am, High Pontiff." He picked up the quill and scribbled at the bottom.

The Pontiff studied Addo for a moment, then looked to Ellana. "Priestess Ellana?" he asked.

"The Priestess will not be representing Khet, High Pontiff," Father said. "This is Abbot Raklin. Lord Brandt has vested Khet's representation of the Faith in him. He has served in Ultenvell Palace for years and can—"

"He is a Cleanser, not an abbot!" Ellana shrieked. "You do not decide who represents the nation you invaded. You do not—"

"Oh, I've decided nothing, my dear." Father pointed a look at Addo.

"It is Khet's wish that Abbot Raklin represent the Faith, High Pontiff," Addo said in a numb tone.

The Pontiff's placid eyes regarded them for a moment, then turned to Ellana. "Have you read the terms, Priestess?"

Ellana took a deep breath, eyes locked on Father. "No."

"And you?" he asked Raklin.

"I . . . am an abbot, Your Grace, recently elevated—"

"The terms," the Pontiff said, tone wavering with the slightest touch of impatience. "Have you read them?"

"I-I have . . . ahm . . . Your Grace." Raklin cleared his throat. "I am in agreement, but before I sign, I would appreciate the opportunity to raise the issue of the state Khet's faithful find themselves in. They suffer from the battle, many taken by a maddening fever, not unlike what we found when entering Alteria." He flashed a look to Adrian, then returned to the Pontiff. "A few Priests of the Blood would be of great help in resolving the matter. And it would show the benevolence of the Seraph in these changing times for Khet— help boost faith in the future. A small contingent would do, High Pontiff, only enough to quell the affliction, guarantee the protection of the worthy."

It was a well-delivered speech. Clearly practiced, with truthful, sensible arguments. But Adrian had learned long ago that the politics of kings were never rooted in sensible arguments.

"There have been attacks in Sacantha as well," Queen Niria said. "Yours is not the only plight the Church must look to, Abbot."

The Pontiff looked around the room. He did not seem surprised by the mention of the frenzy, but Adrian had hardly ever seen the man surprised. There *was* something behind his eyes, though. Maybe not fully at ease, but it did not leak into his words.

"In this, I am afraid I must agree with the queen. The Church will look to protect the Seraph's people throughout the Domain, but we cannot favor one nation over another, no matter how small the contingent. But I am sure I can count on your formal agreement to the terms while the Church considers, yes?" The Pontiff held out the quill.

Raklin hesitated. He looked to Father for support, but Adrian could see the hope draining from Raklin's eyes as he slowly realized his defeat. If he did not sign, the rulers of the Domain would see him standing against the Pontiff, and no man would ever want that, especially a man of the Faith. He gave one last look to Father, but there was no reaction.

Guess that's what happens when sheep come to dine with wolves.

Raklin took the quill with a shaky hand and signed the terms, then shot a look at Adrian that was clear enough. They'd have words after this.

Syvern scoffed quietly, and Alaya still had a glare in her eyes.

"This is not enough," Syvern said. "Othonea has taken one of the sovereign nations of the Domain. What prevents them from threatening another?"

"You've been trying to steer Khet behind my back for years, Syvern. There will be no threats, as long as we are not threatened ourselves," Father said.

Syvern rose, face reddening. "You waged war inside the Domain! Brought death into our—"

"Enough." The High Pontiff rose, and the room fell silent once more.

He retook his seat and showed a hint of a frown for the first time. "Syvern has a point. Othonea's army has grown, and these attacks are not limited to Khet. They have taxed the Legion. People are starting to take matters into their own hands. Militia. The Seraph's Hand, they call themselves, thinking they can solve this—and using the Seraph's own name, no less. A show of faith from Othonea would go a long way to resolving this, Iridan."

"That can be arranged, but a sizeable contingent must remain. Othonea has its own borders to tend to and its own issues to resolve."

"Men alone will not get you out of this, Iridan," Syvern said. "We need a show of faith in the Domain."

Father chuckled. "Like what?"

"The Khetish ports would do. Leave them accessible and tax-free: a gateway for trade to benefit all the Domain."

"You've gone mad, Syvern! Where were the other nations when you were maneuvering troops through Khet behind my back? The men are concession enough. The ports remain closed."

"Then Vizcarra would have no choice but to agree with King Syvern and fight to liberate the nation of Khet," Queen Rheda said.

"You'd wage war over ports, Rheda?"

"Not ports, Iridan. Principle."

Adrian looked from the Pontiff to Raklin to Father, heart beating faster. More fighting would jeopardize Myrra's body. The Pontiff's focus needed to be on Adrian, not another war. He stood. He needed to step forward, just like Jovu would have.

"Maybe there is another way for Othonea to show good faith," he said. All eyes were on Adrian again, but he had to do something.

For Othonea, for Myrra. "These attacks threaten all our nations. Let me lead the charge against them."

The Pontiff mulled over the words, seeming as if he'd just tasted wine and was still unsure if he enjoyed it.

"The Legion could use a Light," he finally said. "We would rebuild it—start in Alteria, then move throughout the Domain to end these attacks."

Some of the queens talked among themselves, while Syvern kept his stare fixed on Father. Adrian's offer had not been what they wanted. It would not favor their trade or reduce Othonea's mercantile power, but if the attacks had already reached Alteria from Khet in two weeks—and had been reported in Sacantha as well—then what Adrian proposed had to strike close to home, and if it was principle Rheda was after, then protecting her people had to be worth more than a favorable tax deal.

"I suppose it will have to do," Queen Lesraile of the Visslands said. "It is better than war."

Queen Niria was nodding beside her. "Sacantha has enough expenses, and we do not wish to bring more death to the Domain."

Queen Rheda looked at Syvern, then back at her fellow rulers. "Peace then, and a symbol for the Domain to fight the rising threat."

Syvern and Father eyed each other. The other nations had agreed, but Dakhra and Othonea could still pull the Domain into chaos if they wished.

Father rose, chair scraping. "Better than war."

Syvern nodded to him, eyes narrowing with the slightest twitch. "Better than war."

Alaya seemed restless beside him, but Syvern laid a hand on hers, and she seemed to swallow down whatever she'd wanted to say.

Father left without a second glance, and the room got to its feet and slowly trickled out. Adrian held his breath. He hadn't thought the Pontiff would make him Light of the Legion, but he couldn't back out now, even if this meant cutting ties with his family and serving the Church. Come to think of it, maybe that was the convincing factor that had gotten the rulers onboard. He'd have to find a way to keep all that he'd built up with Father, though. There was more than just Jovu's death at stake. Myrra still had a chance.

The Pontiff was still seated, and he waited until they were alone in the room before speaking again. "It takes a bold man to cut ties with his family and become a symbol for the people," the Pontiff said. "The Seraph will surely appreciate the gesture."

Adrian struggled against the inclination to scoff at the words. He doubted the Seraph wanted him for a champion.

"These militias," the Pontiff continued. "I won't have men preaching twisted ideas, thinking they can besmirch the name of the Church. Take care of them." He locked his gaze on Adrian. "Thoroughly. Show Alteria you can be a beacon for the Faith, as you say, and then we can discuss whatever it was you had in mind, yes?"

Adrian nodded, the flicker inside him catching in his veins, spreading the warmth of renewed hope for Myrra.

"Yes, High Pontiff."

CHAPTER EIGHT

Before Tedros returned to the Earth, he left runes inscribed above the Chief's Hall that would echo through generations. The inscribed words were his final gift of knowledge to the Ronar: Weakness is a corruption of its own.

— *Tales of the Ronar*

I t had rained all day: a mocking drizzle that insisted on keeping most of the village indoors. The ancestor-stone post Nasha was chained to had little cover, nothing more than a light rag making a bad excuse for an awning that was too soon soaked and dripping. The showers had moved on, at least, and the setting sun was trying to peek through the pall of clouds covering the sky, but there was still that incessant tap of water accompanied by the low humming of the man sharing the post with her.

He sat huddled under the wet fabric, leaning on the blue-veined post. The veins weren't pulsing, but Nasha still knew better than to touch it. Even chained to the post, she couldn't afford to lose control. Whatever her current state, she still hadn't been judged.

I can turn this around. I can find the First Tree myself if need be.

Nasha's jaw ached. She was gritting her teeth again, and the man's humming had brought back the prodding in her ribs.

"Could you stop?"

The man looked up at her with confusion in his eyes. "Me?"

"Humming," Nasha snapped. "The water tap is bad enough."

"Was I?" He chuckled. "Don't even notice it anymore." He broke her a smile as if they were sharing a meal instead of captivity.

She sighed and tried moving further away from the man, but the chain around her ankle was taut, and he was still well within earshot. Nasha sat in the mud and started putting her mind to cooking up some kind of defense for the trial, but all she could muster was the will to keep down the rage when she thought of Iallo.

He'd been born in the village and never needed a Proving—never needed to ask for almost anything.

He should be the one on trial. They would have killed me, and the clan would have been in danger. Even more than now.

Maybe she was still paying for her own past actions. Mansa had put to rest most of the rumors about her a few years after the Proving, but there was still often a sideways glance, a suspicious word uttered behind her back. There would always be tales about the initiate who killed her own in the Proving, even if some who told them did not know it was Nasha they were talking about. Rotting Earth, she hated tales.

Nasha pushed the thoughts away. Reminiscing would do nothing. She needed to find a way out of this.

"Must have really set them off to be out here," the man said.

Nasha's eyes snapped back to him. "A mistake. It'll be cleared up soon."

"Aren't they all?" He chuckled again. "Right till the moment Zala's earth-crusted hands pull you down."

"You lost your will to live, old man? I could send you to the Earth myself. Maybe they'll let me go if I do."

"Oh, my will is strong, but you're not a killer, if you're to be believed. All a mistake." He showed her a gap-filled grin, and it spiked the poking in her ribs, setting fire to Nasha's veins. She stepped towards him, hardly noticing the movement.

"Not so big of a mistake, perhaps?" His smile widened.

Nasha closed her eyes and breathed out the irritation. It sent an ache through her already tired muscles, but she pressed her teeth together until her hands fell back down.

"Least you're smart about it. Nothing to gain by killing me, is there?"

"They put you here as punishment for the rest?" Nasha said.

"Hah! No, I'm here 'cause I remind them too much of things they'd rather pretend didn't exist." That rotten smile again. "Tomu won't kill me, though. They need people like me." He paused, studying her through matted strands of wet hair. "You think they need you?"

That was enough. The man had been bound too long. Or maybe the ancestor-stone did have the power to affect others beyond her. Whatever it was, he was cracked.

Nasha turned away, but the question still hung over her head. *Did* they need her? Mansa did—he had to. She was a hunter, thrice striped, no matter what they accused her of. All she'd done was for the Ronar, for Mansa. Besides, he knew about her curse and saw it as a boon. No other hunter had that.

But something was pulling at the back of her mind.

What if he doesn't need you? What if he can't convince them? What if he doesn't want to?

She shot a sharp look at the man, who'd resumed his humming, and shook her head. She needed more time, and her companion wasn't making it easy to focus. Her eyes darted around the outskirts of the village, dreading the moment a shadow might move towards her, a sound might break the stillness of what was now the rapidly cooling night. Her breaths were strangled—coming out in small, anxious puffs of mist—and her stomach was arguing with her thoughts.

The bowl of stew and rainwater that had been left beside her would have been bad enough in the lukewarm state it was brought in, but cold and thinned by rain was too much, even with her stomach trying fiercely to convince her of the idea.

Nasha chuckled to herself. She'd been thinking of meat a day ago, trying to climb another rung on the ladder, and now she couldn't even get a decent bowl of stew. The ladder was looking pretty bare. Her stomach grumbled again, and her gaze fell on the bowl. If it was to be death, better that it be with a full stomach. She reached out. Couldn't taste worse than the bitterness already on her tongue.

"You never answered the question."

Nasha kept her back to the man, turning only her head sideways. "What?"

"Do they need you? Really need you, as more than a piece in their game?"

"Doesn't look like it."

"Then how do you make them?"

Nasha turned to him. His smile was wide as ever, but she didn't feel so irked by it this time.

"Good luck," he said. "Name's Hemlicht, by the way. Since you're not killing me, might as well know." He held her eyes for another moment, then curled on the ground into a lump that was soon snoring softly.

She still had no idea what he meant, and by the time an uncertain attempt at an answer had floated to her mind, the sun was rising, and shadowy outlines were making their way towards her.

Nasha did not resist the men who dragged her away from the post. A small part of her still fought the prospect of being paraded before the entire village as a traitor without having been judged, but struggling would only use valuable energy. Energy she'd need if she was to hold back her curse.

Ronar flooded her path, and a thousand stabs cut into her, some tiny—the curiosity of passersby who didn't really care—others stronger, almost intent on breaking her down and engulfing her in their accusations. The warning signs were clear, but she had nowhere to run. All she could do was try to reach out to her anchors among the village—Old Kolg, Tanner Hilka, maybe even Shai if she'd made the trek down from the Slopes. How long would Nasha last against the tide of emotion? A dozen long breaths, perhaps?

She took the first one, taking in the fumes that increased as she shuffled towards the Great Mountain where the trail would be held, and began to count.

One . . .

Her head was pointed towards the ground, pressure mounting in her chest. The scent helped a little. But the warriors were walking slowly before her, letting the moment sink in.

Iallo was leading them, head held high, chest puffed out, maybe already imagining himself in Chatta's place. Nasha could barely take a step without wincing, and the vise of emotion pressed down on her with the thickening crowd.

Two . . .

She stopped, jaw clenched, hands curled into fists and half expecting a shove, but it seemed Iallo was content to let her wallow in her disgrace. The stares were getting heavier, the prickling sensation rising on her skin, her heart starting to race and breaths coming quick and shallow. She had to move. . . . But what if she didn't? She'd put together a plan—or at least the intention of one—but would it be enough? Her curse wouldn't save her, but it had never failed to take hold if she let it. There was no way of knowing *what* would take hold, but the relief of the pressure alone might be worth it.

How would they feel, she wondered, if the Sloper scum they were looking down on suddenly rose? Nothing new. She'd done it before, seeing their disbelief with every new stripe. Perhaps a few deaths were a worthy price to see that look on their faces again.

Three . . .

Nasha uncurled the fingers of one hand.

How many would die? Maybe none—maybe she'd just run, taken by the crowd's fear. Or she might kill them all.

Would the Earth thank me for that? Lift my curse?

One hand open, she fell to one knee and steadied herself with a palm on the ground. The fumes still filled her lungs, but the taste of unbridled freedom was sweet in her mouth, pushing the tartness of the smoke away.

Four . . .

Both hands on the ground. Nasha raised her trembling face to look at Iallo, a smile almost touching her lips. He stepped towards her, maybe sensing something was wrong.

"Get up! Move!"

The warriors leaned down to grab her, but she struggled now, the chinks in her will letting emotion in as she shifted her focus away from it. What trickled in empowered her. She had no control over it, but her muscles brimmed with strength, and she shrugged the men off. Fear spread in Iallo's eyes, and a murmur rose in the crowd, sending waves of excitement and apprehension towards her. More warriors bore down on her, and she writhed again but couldn't get loose.

Time to let go.

Fiv—

Nasha's vision went white, and her ears were filled with a distant ringing. She stumbled and blinked, but when the world came back into view, it was blurred and streaked with red from the blood flowing down her brow. Her mind flashed, and she was somewhere else. Blood-soaked hands. Heavy breaths. Screaming. The smell of burning wood riding the smoke that filled her lungs, thick enough in her mouth to taste. Bodies were laid out, their smell even stronger than the taste in her mouth. But it was wrong, bitter, almost like the fumes.

The fumes always did it.

Nasha fell back into herself, memories still shattered in the fog of her past, her vision cut short by the bitter scent of the Mountain. She closed her eyes and strained to blank her thoughts. Her energy trickled away, but she rode the scent of the fumes until they snapped her out of the anger that had threatened to take hold. She couldn't kill them all. She was still Ronar. She wasn't the monster.

She set her jaw and looked at the warrior with a bloody axe

shaft in his hand. It was still raised, and it was her blood on the shaft.

Nasha breathed deep and got up with an effort, looked away, and moved on.

Stupid! Stop wasting your strength!

Six . . .

Iallo stood by as she went past, eyes narrowed, still full of trepidation. She didn't challenge him, just kept moving.

The mass of Ronar and Slopers grew thicker as she neared the Great Mountain. Nasha scanned their faces, some eyes sharp and disapproving, but others seeming softer, almost . . . pitying? Something had shifted in the surrounding emotions, like the Slopers recognized one of their own. They *were* pitying her. It made Nasha's fire rise. She would not be a symbol for the Slopers or the discontent brewing among them. She was Ronar. She'd prove it.

Seven . . .

Her vision blurred at the edges again.

The warriors pushed her forward into an open patch of earth to stand before the Roots. They stood on a natural formation of raised stone, looking over the population of the village. Tomu, somber in his high-backed chair, Jabillo in his ceremonial robes, Adda in her stone carapace of an expression, an empty Warden's chair, and Mansa beside it, sitting stiff in the Oringo's chair—a far cry from his normal posture. Bahar stood to the side with disbelief in his eyes.

Nasha sighed, pushing out whatever dregs of hope might have been at the bottom of her stomach. Whatever argument they'd tried hadn't worked; she'd have to fend for herself.

Iallo put a heavy hand on Nasha's shoulders, bringing her down to her knees, and suddenly, her heart was pounding, as if she was taking in the full meaning of her situation for the first time. The morning air held a chill, but the Earth was hot beneath her knees, its fire hungering for her life.

"Clanfolk of the Ronar," Jabillo said. "The Warden is dead."

Eight . . .

Nasha barely heard the words: her heart was beating faster and faster, and the ringing was rising in her ears as the crowd finally began to chatter between themselves. It was time to prove herself, show them she was more than just a Sloper with a past shrouded in rumors.

"This hunter has returned him to the Earth along with two other Ronar and attempted to kill the third." Jabillo gestured towards Iallo. "The Ronar do not shy away from their duty to the Earth. It must be fed life to keep Zala asleep in it, but that is a fate reserved for the weak. And those who are Ronar have been proven strong." He shot a look around, maybe eyeing the Slopers. "The judgment of their lives was not hers to make."

There were murmurs around her, and Nasha dug her fingers into the earth, straining to hold back the barrage that stabbed at her senses. He was wrong. They were weak.

Nine . . .

None of her anchors seemed to be among the crowd.

"What I did, I did for the Ronar," Nasha said. "A weak Warden is a danger to the clan. It might not have been my judgment to make, but Iallo and the others made their own judgment when they attacked me."

"No Warden poses an even greater danger, especially with the Proving that is to come," Jabillo answered. "I am the Speaker for the Earth, and I can sense it recoiling at the taste of Ronar blood." He turned his back to Nasha and looked towards the Chief.

"Chief. The consequence for betrayal has always been clear, and necessary to keep the Ronar united."

Another murmur from the crowd, but Nasha was focused on the unheard murmur of their emotions. They drained into her, and she looked around to confirm the sentiment. It was plain on the faces of the Slopers: some were shaking their heads, and others had creased brows and offended stares. They did not agree with the Speaker.

Nasha struggled against the notion. She was Ronar. She would not be a symbol for the Slopers or the Zaruni, but her words were falling short. Nasha clenched her jaw again, trying to latch onto the fumes. She couldn't keep this up. She was Ronar, but if they insisted on seeing her only as a Sloper, maybe that was her way out. Her plan had been to fight Iallo and prove his weakness before the whole clan. What she hadn't figured out was how they'd let her do that. But now the path was clear.

Nasha stood and looked straight into Tomu's eyes.

"You're only doing this because I came from the Slopes. You can't take it that one of us has risen so far."

More than a murmur now, even a call of agreement or two. Nasha kept her eyes locked on Tomu's cold stare.

Ten . . . The ringing in her ears grew louder.

"I can show you my worth. Yes, I killed the others, and that only shows my strength. They were not corrupted like Chatta, but weakness is a corruption of its own"—Nasha pointed at Iallo—"and he is the weakest of them all."

She still wasn't sure how she'd beat Iallo, but if it was to be death, better that it be on her feet.

Nasha breathed in the fumes, even got a whiff of citrus. It brought a shred of remembrance from her hunts and the freedom of the empty wilds, enough for her to focus for a moment and hold back the next count.

The crowd had risen with her, shouts of "Let her show you" and "The Slopes are strong" ringing out—the same words the Zaruni had whispered. It felt wrong. She was still Ronar. . . .

Adda stepped past Jabillo. Her expression was still hard as stone, and her presence commanded the silence of the gathering. She descended the steps until she stood on level ground with them and looked over the crowd before letting her gaze rest on Nasha.

"You speak the truth, hunter. Weakness is a corruption of its own."

Nasha frowned at the Tivezzi. Those were part of the words of induction into the clan, but she hadn't expected them to have such effect.

"You will let me fight him, then?" Nasha asked.

A flicker of hope mingled with the familiar scent of burning wood and blood—the scent of her fear—took over her.

I couldn't beat him in the wilds. What will I do while having to fend off the pressure from the crowd?

"No." Adda ignored the protests. "But I will not ignore your pledge."

She turned to Tomu. "Chief. Father. We have a Proving and little time to argue over a Warden. Those on the Slopes have voiced their grievances, and I propose we listen. Let them have a Root amongst us. Let us see if she can prove the truth in her words. Let us elevate Nasha from hunter to Warden of the Ronar."

Silence. No cheer, no objection, only steady eyes regarding Tomu as he sat silent in his chair. The shock from the onlookers swirled on Nasha's skin like the water of an icy river, but not even Jabillo, who presided over the event, dared interrupt Tomu's pondering. But Nasha's heart was battering her chest like some wild beast desperate for escape—so loud in her ears, she feared Tomu would hear it.

Cold rivulets of sweat streaked down her back while the clan waited on their Chief's consideration. Nasha pressed back against their mounting pressure on her senses.

Eleven . . . This was taking too long. Her focus on the fumes was not enough. Her head was a stone on her shoulders, and the fire in her gut was spreading, urging her to move, to fight, to kill.

Tomu let out a slow breath and moved his head slightly. "I agree."

The noises in the crowd rose at that. Some—likely the village-born hoping to see another Sloper burn—cried out in outrage, but they were overwhelmed by the Slopers, who clapped each other on the shoulders and cheered like they'd won some great victory. Probably Zaruni, thinking they could use her. Iallo shot a seething look towards Nasha and stormed off, disappearing in the dissatisfied part of the crowd.

Nasha looked among the Roots, still in disbelief. She was alive, was her first thought—still alive. But soon it was overwhelmed by the clawing at her chest. She was Warden. They'd eventually expect her to lead initiates in the arena. To fight. She could barely hold herself together standing before the clan. How would she fight in a Proving?

She'd promised never to let it happen again, never to lose

126

herself to the killing as she'd done in her own Proving. She'd barely escaped that—barely found herself again. She couldn't imagine how she'd do it now.

Nasha looked to Adda, who had the same hard stare and a hint of a smile, and the expression filled her with understanding.

She was still a pawn being used by a Root to quell the unrest among the Slopers. Her hopes of being recognized by the Tivezzi and shown the path to the First Tree to rid herself of her curse seemed suddenly foolish. The unattainable dream of a child, of a Sloper who did not understand the workings of the village Roots. The thought almost made her sick, almost finally split her, but Tomu's outstretched arm pulled her attention away. He had hard eyes on her, and his mouth was pressed tight.

Nasha clasped his forearm with her own, trembling. He nodded, then walked back towards the village. The crowd broke after him, and Nasha stumbled aimlessly, unable to focus.

Twelve . . . Her vision had gone bright, and her chest was moving, but she didn't seem able to draw a breath.

Some of the Roots lingered, most wearing masks for expressions, but Mansa had cracked a wide smile and was nodding towards her from his chair.

He frowned when he saw her face, though, and the smile turned into widening eyes. Nasha stumbled, pushing her way through the mingling mass and the chaos of her mind. Hard breaths, strength whittling away—

Strong hands gripped her shoulder, and Nasha barely recognized Mansa dragging her away from the chaos, away from the unwitting, relentless assault that put all of them in danger.

He pulled her far from the Slopes and the village and into the tree line. She could breathe again but could hardly walk. Nasha steadied herself under a tree for a moment, but her body gave way, and she collapsed. She wasn't the monster, but she wasn't sure what she'd become now. It only filled her with fear, and the scent of burning wood and the taste of blood flooded into her before she passed out.

CHAPTER NINE

Death does not deserve our tears. We do not value its work with our mourning or wasted breath.

— *The Book of the Breath*

Lynn approached Dalhold under the cover of night. Moonlight glinted off the moat surrounding the prison, with watchers patrolling the obscured path around it, two standing guard at the bridge. Lynn stayed to the shadows, hoping for Ferrin to be among the watchers. Her eyes jumped among them but found no sign of his lanky arms or even a flash of a smile.

She sighed. *Never the easy way.*

There'd be no way through the bridge, no easy climb up the walls this time. Kerr had taken precautions, but it seemed he had little notion of what a Sentinel could do, even without a mount.

Lynn stepped deeper into the shadowed street and let the voices flood her mind. Their endless supply of rage engulfed her, and each accusation brought back images of what she'd done: hunting them down, killing them one by one, all in the name of the Church, all in the name of the Seraph's Domain.

Your Madness was my fault.

She accepted it, let herself be swallowed by the memory and let the anger grow hot and sear through her veins until it was strong enough to reach Vedyr once more, even if he was still distant, their Bond tenuous. Her mind reacted, pulsing to warn her of the threshold she should not cross. Lynn closed her eyes.

Alren, Roki, Cara, Dentos. I can control it. I won't hollow out.

Strength flooded into her, and her eyes burned. She knew they'd be glowing like pools of silver in the darkness, so she lifted her cowl—the one she'd taken from the injured man in the alley—and moved fast. She leaped onto the roof of the building before her, sending fragments flying from the fractured stone where she fell, then moved along it towards the prison. She scanned a few more of the watchers before settling on the one patrolling her side of the wall. He had a familiar gait, almost relaxed. Too relaxed. Ferrin.

She gauged the gap before her between the roof and the prison wall. Ten, maybe twelve strides. Could she make that jump?

You've done enough. Leave him alone! Alren screamed.

Lynn channeled his anger towards Vedyr and took a few steps back, then sprinted forward, putting all of his strength into her jump. She felt the stone crack as she pushed off, but the rush in her gut was only fleeting before she flew with arms open wide over the gap and landed on a low turret only a short way above Ferrin's path.

She tried to land as silently as she could, but the enhanced strength from her Bond made the stone break as she landed. Enough noise for Ferrin to whirl round, eyes wildly searching the darkness.

"Don't call out. It's me," Lynn hushed. She cut off her Bond and the burning in her eyes faded, but it wasn't only her head that hurt this time. Vedyr felt further away than he'd been before, and the Bond had drained her more than she'd expected.

Alren, Roki, Cara, . . . Dentos. The last one took a little longer, but her mind was still whole.

Ferrin squinted up, knuckles white around his spear. "Lynn? How did you—"

"Keep your voice down! And turn around, or every watcher who's ever dreamed about killing me will be here in a breath."

Ferrin looked at her for another moment, then turned. "What are you doing here? You were pardoned."

"I . . . need your help."

It felt strange, asking for help, knowing she could be pulling him closer to death, always waiting on her shoulder.

Selfish bitch, Roki said, but Lynn focused on Ferrin. This was the Seraph's work. A Sentinel's work.

"These attacks," Lynn went on. "You've seen the bodies?"

Ferrin shuddered. "I've seen the blood, but not the bodies."

"Two of Kerr's men found the last one. One of them was bald, had a scar running across his head."

Ferrin nodded. "Teague, one of the city patrolmen. What do you need from him?"

"The Church guard arrived. He seemed to know what to do, like Kerr had given him orders."

"Hasn't given me any, and I doubt I can get anything from Teague. He's Kerr's man through and through, but I could try, maybe in a few days . . . or I could talk to Morna."

"Morna?"

Ferrin didn't turn. He had one hand on the battlements and was looking out over the moat. "My sister," he said. "The priestess who pardoned you."

Lynn tensed, her tired muscles sending waves of pain through her. She was unable to keep the ice out of her tone. "Were you the one who sent for her?"

"No." He shook his head. "You seemed like you knew what you were doing here well enough."

Lynn let out a breath. It would be easy to be angry at Ferrin, to give her an excuse that Alren's accusations were wrong, but she'd never taken the easy way.

"She's the priestess at Baywater Temple. Whatever you're looking for, I can talk to her and have you two meet."

"I need to talk to her tonight, before there are more attacks." She needed to stop them. She'd let one kind of madness spread already.

"You'll find her at the temple. . . . She seemed fond enough of you. Shouldn't be too hard to get what you need." He turned slightly and shot her an uncertain look. "Care telling me what this is about?"

"I'm not sure yet. Better if you know only when I do."

Ferrin nodded again. "Fair enough. You know your way out, or should I raise an alarm on the other side of the wall?"

"No need. I can manage."

"Good. Kerr would chew me out if I raised another one of those." He smiled at her, but there was still too much weighing Lynn down for her to return it.

"You're too good a man to be a watcher, Ferrin." She walked to the other side of the turret, her instincts driving her towards Vedyr, but her anger was gone, and the Bond had taken enough out of her already. She relied on her own strength instead, using the crags in the turret to make her way down.

Lynn frowned at the mark in the sky, a pale circle of light like a second moon shining behind the blue-gray cloud cover. She'd heard people calling it the Seraph's eye but didn't care to imagine what the Seraph would think of what She'd see. The mark seemed to be growing, though, as if Her eye was eager to take in more and more.

Are you really watching?

She lowered her head and walked on along the cobbled path on the edge of the water, closing her eyes to silence the turmoil in her mind. The smell of salt drifted on the wind, picked up from the waves crashing on the rocks below. For a moment, she could almost convince herself things were right, that death wasn't hounding her, that the only voice in her head was her own, but lying to herself did little to help.

All you are is a bringer of death, Dentos said, but Lynn focused on the scent coming from the sea and plowed onward.

Baywater Temple was a shadow slashed in the night. A vaulted roof supported by columns let in the cold moonlight, almost like the bars in her old cell. Lynn stepped off the road, staying to the shadows, and approached the temple with wary steps, but something stopped her.

There was no sound, no movement in or out, and the scent of salt was tainted by the metallic smell of blood. Her eyes darted among the columns.

There was nothing.

The temple had no walls or places for her to hide in case of an attack, and the thought that Lynn might have to kill again sent a chill up the tense muscles on the back of her neck.

Coward, Alren whispered. *Always choosing the easy way.*

Lynn almost laughed. There was never anything easy about killing, and the bitter taste of it was always on her tongue. She spat onto the cobbles and stepped inside.

The blood was the least of it. There were pieces of flesh, hair, and bone scattered all around the vast space of the temple. Sparse pillars extended into the far end of the temple, twenty strides away or more, but the darkness wasn't enough to hide the splattered remnants of bodies that had been slammed into the pillars. Lynn's throat went dry, a prickling numbness spreading through it and down to the pit of her stomach. Most of the remains were unrecognizable, but a few of the faces she'd fought to keep away from Kerr's noose were clear, disfigured and locked in silent screams, with frozen eyes gazing at the face of death. All her work was laid out bare in guts and shattered bones on the white-veined ruin-stone of the temple floor.

The smell that had assaulted Lynn outside was a gruesome concoction on her tongue now. She tried to cough it out, but the dryness in her throat only brought up repugnant bile, and she vomited to the side. All the steps she thought she'd taken towards redemption had led nowhere. The lives she'd wrangled away from the noose were now gone. Wrecked and scattered before her.

She breathed deep and rasped out what she could, frustration rising as she tried to regain a semblance of control. She could not yield to death, not now. Maybe Morna had gotten away—maybe she wasn't here.

Fool. Always hoping. Always failing, Cara said.

Lynn looked around the shadows of the temple, searching for a sign of movement, of life, but there was still nothing. A single beam of silvery light through the center of the roof illuminated the Ever-Tree and the small pool before it. Lynn crept towards the tree, eyes still searching the shadows, gut sinking with every intake of the scent of death.

She inched into the light, circling the pool of sap at the base of the tree, turning over remains with her feet—

A branch cracked, and a shadow flew at her from the boughs. Lynn whirled away and pressed her back against the Ever-Tree. She grasped behind for her weapon, but all she found was air. Old habits. Her hand moved to her belt, and she pulled out the knife she'd taken from the man killed by the Church guard. It would have to do.

The attacker was small. It lingered in the shadows for a moment, then crept, beastlike, into the light. The girl she had seen covered in blood days before stared at her, teeth bared, hair falling over her face.

This is your fault, Dentos said.

Lynn saw the accusation reflected in the girl's eyes, bloodshot with a frayed, hungry stare and a blackness tainting the surrounding skin. The familiarity of it made Lynn's stomach clench. It was a sight she'd hoped was lost in her past, but the icy fingers running all over her skin were all too present.

"No!" Lynn stepped forward, raising her knife.

The girl prowled on her hands and feet, circling at the edge of sight. Lynn kept her gaze on the girl, inching her feet around the trunk with her back still pressed to the Ever-Tree. The girl's eyes shone in the dark: the eyes of the Madness.

No—I killed it. It's gone.

We're never gone, they said.

Never quiet.

Always here.

Lynn tried to muster her anger, still circling away from the girl. It hadn't been long since she'd reached for the Bond, and her body complained at the attempt.

Nothing happened.

Lynn gritted her teeth and reached harder.

I won't hollow out, Vedyr. Come to me. I can bear your strength.

Still nothing: only a deep emptiness. Vedyr was either unwilling or too far. She was truly alone.

The girl launched off the edge with absurd speed, and Lynn barely jerked her head away from the hungry claws. They ripped strands of her dirty-blond hair and raked at the tree, sinking sharp nails into the deep grooves of the undying, iron-hard bark.

The girl's hand was caught. Lynn stepped in beside the girl and stabbed deep into her ribs, but there was no reaction. No show of pain. Lynn went for another strike, but her opponent wrenched her claws out of the tree and turned on her, snarling. She pounced, but Lynn rolled sideways on the ground, and the girl skid past. Lynn sprang to her feet, but the girl had already turned and charged again. Faster, this time.

Lynn swiped her blade, steering the claws away from her face, but the knife clattered out of her hand. She kicked her attacker away, aiming to grab her knife, but the girl closed in and slashed again. Lynn shifted her shoulder backwards to evade the claws, but the girl's head rammed into her jaw. It sent Lynn reeling, back slamming into the Ever-Tree, then falling to the ground, and rolling away.

The girl was on her in a heartbeat, teeth bared, jaws snapping. Lynn held her back with a knee to the chest and one arm, punching desperately with the other at the wound in the girl's ribs, but there was still no reaction. The girl pressed down, and Lynn used the movement to hook her leg between the girl's own, grab her by the shoulders, and launch her overhead. The girl smashed head-first into the Ever-Tree and crumpled onto the ground.

Lynn bound towards her, grabbed the girl's hair, and slammed her face into the tree.

The wood was hard as iron, but the monstrosity didn't flinch. She turned her head towards Lynn and showed all of her teeth in a guttural growl. Lynn pulled her head back and drove it into the wood again. The girl tried to wriggle free, but Lynn had her held tight.

She slammed again and again and again, flooded with familiar sensations: control, anticipation, the knowledge she held life in her hands. The girl did not scream or moan, but bones are brittle, and death does not require pain.

Solve this before she can spread more death.

Lynn could already feel the embrace: death's arms holding her.

Welcome back. I've missed you.

She smashed the head harder. The girl's eyes closed and her mouth went limp.

One death will avoid dozens of others.

She has killed in the house of the Seraph.

Lynn slammed the head again and looked down. The girl's mangled face looked almost like the bodies that had been ripped apart around her. It was the face of death, looking deep into Lynn, eager for the final blow. It snapped Lynn back into reality with an icy wave of dread, and she let the girl go, backing away with hard breaths. Revulsion gnawed at her chest for almost giving in, and she felt like vomiting again.

She went to her knees in the blood around the tree—part from the girl, part from the victims. Not only the clergy but all the lives she'd saved from the prison: they'd all been sent here. None of it seemed to matter now. She'd known, really. Hadn't wanted to admit it, but it couldn't have been anything else. The girl did not feel pain, and she was taken by a speed Lynn had not seen in the afflicted before, but it was the Madness.

What had she missed? Had the signs changed? Had the Madness been growing stronger all this time?

I killed it. I killed it!

You only killed us.

The pain in her chest welled up, and tears streamed silently down her face. She kneeled in the beam of light, surrounded by all the lives she'd fought for, but she was guilty and alone.

Falling petals from the Ever-Tree pulled her eyes up, and she regarded them with a salty taste in her mouth as they settled around the bodies. Even the tree had gone mad, it seemed. Their petals shouldn't fall. They were eternal.

Lynn remained on her knees for a long time. Part of her was wary of the girl, but neither of them moved.

I should search for Morna.

The thought was clear, but her body did not obey.

Perhaps she should stay here and join the dead. It would be easier. Maybe it would be the right thing to do. The world did not need her, the Seraph certainly did not need her, and whatever work Lynn had thought she'd done in Her name had just been mercilessly undone by the girl she let go a few days ago. Her chest was so tight it hurt to breathe. The Madness had returned. The accusations in her mind were all true. She'd killed them for nothing. She'd failed.

Lynn looked towards the pool. The sap was dark, corrupted, but it would be easy to slip in and never come out. Maybe that was what the Seraph wanted. She raised a foot, then the other. She stood, took one step, then another, and peered into the dark liquid, teetering on the edge.

"Hey!"

She tore her eyes away from the dark sap. A silhouette was edging closer, a shadow but for the flash of steel and fearful eyes. Even without the smile, Ferrin was easily recognizable.

He lowered his lanky arms when he saw her. "Lynn? What . . . how did this happen? Where's Morna?"

Lynn's eyes were still wet, and her lips were sealed as if by some Dakhran binding agent. There was no strength left for words.

Ferrin paused, recognizing the pain in her eyes. "Is she . . . ?"

Lynn shook her head. "I don't know."

Ferrin looked around, eyes never focusing on one spot for too long, then looked back at Lynn, hesitant. "Are you alright?"

Was she? Lynn wasn't sure what that even meant anymore, couldn't even remember the last time someone had asked her that. She closed her eyes, retreating to the only place in her mind where she'd ever felt something close to right, where the words of Elwin's lessons rang clear.

Death does not deserve our tears. We do not value its work with our mourning or wasted breath.

It wasn't enough to settle her heart, but the sound of Elwin's voice brought her a shred of sanity. Enough for Lynn to move away from the pool.

"I'm fine." She wiped her face, replacing drying tears with smudges of blood. "Let's find her."

They walked silently in the darkness, neither likely believing life could have endured through the slaughter, neither daring to say it out loud.

Morna was splayed out at the altar, unmoving, body ripped apart like the others, but enough of her face preserved to be recognized.

"No . . . no, no, no." Ferrin broke down beside her, grasping at the dead body.

He moaned, unconcerned by the Seraph's judgment. The sound reminded Lynn of the war, the Madness. She pulled him away while he struggled against her in a pointless effort to hold his sister.

Ferrin slammed his fists into the ground beside Morna, shaking his head. "I can't lose you too."

Lynn's stomach clenched, and Alren's voice was already roaring in her mind. Lynn had never known he had a sister: she'd thought it was only him and Ferrin.

Tell him what you did to me. Tell him why he has no one left.

"Why would She take her? She was devoted, faithful. She . . ."

Ferrin broke down into uncontrolled sobs, and Lynn kneeled beside him, a hand on his back, but little in the way of words to comfort him. A chill wind blew through the open temple, biting at

Lynn's skin. It ruffled the petals of the Ever-Tree, and more drifted down, coming to rest on the girl's crumpled body beneath.

The right thing would be to kill her. That would be what Elwin would tell her to do as a Sentinel. But that was what the voices were telling her as well, and no matter how hard Lynn willed the thought forward, her hands would not move. Maybe she really was a coward.

Tell him, Alren spat.

She turned back to the watcher. "Ferrin . . . I—"

There was movement behind, and Lynn jumped to her feet, swiveling round. The girl was shambling towards them. Lynn grabbed at her belt for her knife, but she'd left it under the tree.

She steeled herself, ready to fight the girl off, but the Madness worked its way through what was left of her life. The girl fell to the ground, screaming, clutching at her head, finally showing pain.

Ferrin darted for his sword, but the girl had stopped moving, her eyes as vacant as those of the rest of the dead.

He screamed at the corpse and slashed at it all the same, again and again.

Lynn had seen this before. No matter men's faith, no matter what promise their lives still held, death could twist them until they inevitably followed the same path as those they'd lost. She couldn't let that happen. Not to him.

"Ferrin!" Lynn's tone was hard enough to give the watcher pause.

He turned to her, eyes still carried by rage.

"She's gone. It's done."

He shook his head. "It's not done. It can't be done." He kicked at the girl's body again. "I don't care about what Morna preached, what the Faith says. This isn't the Seraph's work."

"Maybe not, but it isn't the girl's fault." *It wasn't Alren's fault either.*

"Not her fault? Look around, Lynn! They've been mauled, like the attacks in the city! How can a girl even do that alone?"

"The strength came from something else. . . . An infection, a—" Lynn bit down on the word, reluctant, but there was nothing else to call it. "A Madness. She was stronger than most, but she isn't the one who attacked the people in the city."

Ferrin rounded on her, finding an outlet in her words to vent his rage. "How do you know that?"

"Because I found a survivor. Got to him before Teague did. He didn't see much, but he knew his attacker was a man."

"And where is he?"

"The Church guard got there before I could learn more. They killed him."

Ferrin blinked, some of the fire going out of him. "They . . . that makes no sense. The Church guard don't kill faithful."

"They do if someone tells them to."

Ferrin shook his head. "How does that help Morna? Why should I care about some crazy conspiracy you've cooked up?"

Lynn set hard eyes on him. She wasn't used to being talked to this way, but he didn't know she was a Sentinel. "What this girl had, this Madness, it isn't new, but she didn't have it a few days ago. Maybe you shouldn't care. The pain won't stop, and we won't find the man who did the killings in the city—it's too far spread for that —but we might find a way to fight it."

"What does that give me?"

"Hope? Peace? A legacy for Morna? Who knows what the Promised Dawn will bring, but you'll be a lot lighter on the road to it knowing you've helped fight whatever killed your sister against the Seraph's will."

Ferrin studied her for a long moment, eyes moving among the dead, tearing when they lingered on his sister. "How do we go about it?"

Lynn hesitated. She'd fought the Madness, but it had risen again, stronger than ever. She needed a new way, a better way. Her first thought was to find Elwin, but he was still Leardin's right hand, and Lynn doubted even he'd be able to protect her.

Her thoughts pushed her past her mentor. Farkhul was close enough, and if Elwin couldn't help, maybe the abbot who'd anointed her could.

"I know an abbot in the House of Farkhul. If the Church guard are involved, he'll know what to do."

It was thin, and Ferrin knew it, but it was better than the emptiness she imagined was filling his heart.

"I'll get a cart and horses." He left her in the dark temple with no parting smile this time.

Lynn watched him go until his footfalls drifted away and the only sound left was the rumbling of waves through the open space around her. She closed her eyes and took a deep breath. She'd kept strong for Ferrin, but her memories were gnawing at her now. The Madness was back. All that she'd done, all that she'd sacrificed . . .

No.

She wouldn't let herself follow her woe. That was the edge she'd just pulled Ferrin away from. Lynn looked at the lacerated corpses around her. She'd been struggling to make up for her past, but none of it had gotten her any closer. Not really.

She had a chance now. If she did things differently this time, maybe she'd end the Madness for good and protect the Domain. Maybe she'd find her redemption. The voices laughed at her, but they were drowned out by the sound of the waves and Lynn's echoing footsteps as she walked out of the temple after Ferrin.

CHAPTER TEN

Other nations tried, but none could truly replicate the feats of alchemy and engineering of the Dakhran airships. To this day, Dakhra remains the only nation with an air fleet, and they are keen on using it to look down on others as an alleged symbol of their superiority.

— *Othonean teachings of the histories of the Domain*

Adrian knew he'd be summoned, but he hadn't expected it so soon. That knot in his stomach was coiling up again, and his throat was so tight he feared he wouldn't be able to breathe, let alone speak with his father. Yet here he was, standing at the door, signaling for Derren to announce him.

Father sat at a table on the balcony, legs crossed, looking out over the city. Alteria seemed to have quieted since Adrian's run-in with the frenzied man. It had only been a day, but the story of the slaughtered Legion soldiers had already spread, and that seemed to be enough for people to prefer the safety of their homes to the danger of the streets. Adrian would need to head to the barracks, put things in order. After he'd dealt with Father, of course. The sun fell onto the balcony where the king sat, but Adrian had seen enough in the gathering room to know no warmth would be coming from the old man.

"What are you playing at, boy?" He barely gave Adrian time to approach, and his tone was no invitation for Adrian to take a seat.

"I did what was needed for Othonea, Father. Jovu would have—"

"You do not decide for Othonea. I am Othonea. Do not dare undermine me ever again, especially before that—" He composed himself. "Especially before the Pontiff."

Adrian stepped out onto the balcony. "Would you rather have another war?"

"Do not assume to know my desires. Your shortsightedness blinds you to the larger concerns of our nation."

Yes, Father. The thought came unbidden, like a practiced form in a sword drill. Adrian's heart protested, knowing he'd say it like he always had.

He opened his mouth, but something stopped him: something in the way his father's tone was pushing Adrian away, the way he didn't care to even look at Adrian. Adrian had been agreeing like a loyal servant, trying to gain Father's trust—as he'd always thought Jovu had done—but what had that gotten him? A servant's treatment. Maybe Ellana was right. He could no longer be his father's dog.

He frowned and let a touch of coldness into his own tone. "What else do you want from me, Father? Jovu is ash, yet you cling to him like the fires that burned him away." His words tasted like ash themselves, but Adrian pressed on. "I'm here fighting for Othonea by your side, yet you won't even tell me what Jovu died fighting for. He's gone, but I'm here!"

Father turned to him, and his tone was collected now but still dagger-sharp. "Your brother earned his army. He followed my will while all you did was demand answers you did not deserve. Then you ran off with that . . ." His father looked away, breathed out, and smoothed the silk of his tunic. "Jovu would not have done this. He knew blood holds ties. If you want to learn what we were truly fighting for, you need to earn that knowledge, like he did, and that is not done by abandoning your family so the Pontiff can use you to strike at me. It is not done by putting yourself willingly into his hands." Father gazed back on Adrian, for just a moment. "As if your sister was not enough . . . . This so-called Legion is nothing!"

No. He wouldn't take it. This was his Legion now. Adrian strode to his father's side and placed a heavy hand on the table.

"I'll show you what nothing looks like."

He did not wait for an answer or to be excused. He marched towards the door, pausing with a hand on the handle. "I'm taking Derren."

Father scoffed. "That has always been your problem. You focus on the lambs when you could stand with the wolves."

Adrian shut the door behind him and strode into the hallway.

"You heard that?"

Derren twisted his mouth. "A little. He does it out of love, you know? Ellana has left him. You're the only one he has left."

"He's got quite a way of showing it." Adrian let out a long breath. "Doesn't matter, though. We have work to do."

"We?"

"I'm appointing you general. You're helping me build this Legion."

Derren puffed out his cheeks. "Adrian . . . I . . . your father."

"He will find a new captain of the guard. You've been following him around long enough."

"I'm not sure—"

"You remember your oath to my mother, yes?"

Derren's eyes darkened. "I have failed in that."

"Not entirely. Ellana is safe, and you can make sure I am, too. I need someone I can count on."

Derren puffed his cheeks again, then blew out. "Would you leave me be if I declined?"

"No."

"Don't really think that gives me a choice then, eh?" He chuckled. "Very well."

"Good. Get ready and meet me at the Legion barracks. Let's see what the Pontiff has pulled us into."

Derren set off, and Adrian made his way through the long hallways of the church-palace, then down the steps towards the main cathedral. It was still closed to visitors, but Raklin walked among the texts projected on the ground. The sun was setting, and the scriptures carried an orange glow, but the reflection hall was gloomy where the words did not touch the stone.

Adrian paused beside the abbot, who was surveying one of the passages.

"You lied to me," Raklin said.

"How so?"

"You did not stand beside me. Did not help me convince the Pontiff."

"Would it have mattered?"

Raklin frowned, and Adrian could see his jaw muscles working. "You can make it matter now. You have the Legion. March it to Khet."

"I will." Adrian took a deep breath. "But I can't do that now."

"What could be more urgent than the preservation of your loved one?"

Adrian narrowed his eyes at Raklin, but the abbot's gaze remained trained ahead. The threat was obvious, though, and his words sharp enough for Adrian to recognize the truth in it. He could not anger the man any further, even if his gall made Adrian want to strike him down. "The Pontiff would not allow me to—"

"The Light controls the Legion. You do not follow the Pontiff's orders."

Adrian shook his head. "That is why you failed, Raklin. Every man follows the Pontiff's orders."

Raklin held Adrian's gaze. There was something different about him. The dark circles under his eyes betrayed his lack of sleep, but it was something else, as if some kind of fire had been blown out from within. Even the ruin-stone pendants seemed to weigh heavier on his neck.

"Then the Domain is doomed," he breathed.

Adrian put a hand on the man's shoulder. He couldn't lose the abbot. Myrra was still under his care.

"You are a loyal servant of the Faith, Raklin. Do not let a setback lead you astray. The Legion will come to your aid, but I need it to be ready first. I cannot sneak off in the dead of night. We would be no help to Khet. Have faith, Abbot. Keep to our agreement, and we will soon cleanse Khet together."

Adrian had never spoken much to religious men. All he could hope was that Raklin believed his words more than he did.

"Coming here was a mistake," Raklin said.

He left Adrian in the darkening cathedral with only hope as assurance of their arrangement. The abbot had put his faith in words on the way to Alteria, but Adrian knew words would not change much now, even if he could have found the right ones. Maybe it would have been easier if he'd left it to faith, but he'd never been one for that. All that was left now was to build his army before Raklin could find an alternative.

Adrian stepped out of the cathedral, heading towards the Legion barracks through empty streets, mind working to settle his thoughts all the while.

He paused before the gates of the barracks, and soon Derren was rounding the corner in a mail shirt and an old expression Adrian hadn't seen in a while. It stirred something within him. He hadn't realized how much he missed the purposeful look in the old captain's eyes.

Father sucks the life out of us all.

The gates to the barracks were closed, and there were no guards watching it.

"Slow day?" Derren asked.

"Or a busy one."

The gate's hinges creaked open, and they stepped into a vast courtyard that once might have been a training ground but was now abandoned to the weeds. A tower rose behind the long building at the far end, a wafting smell of cooked meat the only indication of life within. Adrian shot a look towards Derren, who shook his head and trudged on.

The guard in the main hall looked as surprised as if the Seraph Herself had just walked in. "Y-You're not supposed to be here. Legion only!" He straightened his back, gaining confidence with every word.

"Where is your captain?" Derren asked.

"The commander is a busy man, and you are not allowed entry into these barracks!" He put a hand on his sword.

Derren chuckled, giving Adrian a sideways glance. "Do you think he knows how to use that?"

"He'd have to finish waking up first." Adrian produced the parchment signed by the Pontiff and rulers of the Domain.

"The Pontiff will have sent word," Derren said. "This is your new commander, the Light of the Legion."

The man looked between them for a moment, face slowly changing into a smile, then burst out laughing.

"Oh, you're good!" The guard walked through one of the side doors, still laughing. "Light of the Legion, Burnham? How much did you pay these oafs?"

Adrian and Derren stepped into the office, unsmiling. A man sat at the desk piled with stacks of disorganized papers, yet he seemed to care much more for the bottle in his hand. He raised an eyebrow at the laughing guard.

"You'll have to talk to the Pontiff about that one, Brent."

"Oh, come, Commander, no use keeping it up. I've—"

The man in the chair turned serious eyes on Brent, and the guard's laughter shriveled away into an awkward choke. "Y-You're serious?"

"Pontiff seems to be . . ."

The guard blanched, turning towards Adrian again. "I . . . . My lord, . . . ah—"

"Leave us," Derren growled, and the guard scurried off.

Adrian shut the door behind them.

"You've been informed, then?" Adrian said.

Burnham took a swig of his bottle and grunted.

"Why are there no guards at the gate?" Derren asked.

"Do you see much to protect . . . ahm?"

"General," Derren snapped. "And this is Commander Adrian Pell, the Light of the Legion. You will be following his orders now, Captain. How are your men posted?"

Burnham tilted his head towards Adrian as if they'd just been acquainted at a party instead of a messy command chamber. He spread out his hands before the papers on his desk, bottle still in hand. "There are mounting grievances, and the men are spread thin throughout the city. We've been focusing on the area around the cathedral, but the attacks are rising in the outer quarters. The men have surrounded and closed off the East Row, but there's no telling where they'll pop up next."

He picked up one of the papers on the desk. "Here, a request for help from the Bracken Quarter. Who's to say if it's true? I'd wait for more before jumping into *that* hole." He tipped the bottle again, took a long gulp, and smiled at them.

Derren reached over the table and snatched the bottle out of Burnham's hand. He pointed a finger at the man's face, but Adrian stepped between them. He knew what Derren was doing. The general had done it with Jovu a thousand times to cast him in a better light.

"What information have you gathered on the militia?" Adrian asked.

Burnham frowned at Derren, then his eyes searched the clutter on his desk again. "All this. Feel free to look over it. We've gone from two to three men in the patrol groups. Can't cover the entire city anymore. Way I see it, the more people fighting these madmen, the better."

"The Pontiff has a different notion. How fast can you recall your men?"

"Recall them?" Burnham let out a sharp laugh. "You'd have an easier time convincing your father to dine with King Syvern, Lord Light. There is no recalling them. The people would tear down the barracks themselves to get my men back on the streets. We'd need guards at the gate then!"

"What are you doing here, then?" Derren asked.

"Commanding!" Burnham spread a toothy smile. "Guess that's your job now."

Adrian sighed. "And how big is the current contingent?"

Burnham shrugged. "Two hundred, maybe three."

"And the militia?"

"Oh, the Hand has gathered at least five hundred men. They grow by the day."

"Have you not tried recruiting these men before the militia get to them?" Derren asked.

"Oh, we've tried, but they don't trust us—think we're here only for the rich, won't protect their families."

"And is that true?" Derren asked.

"Doesn't matter, does it? We don't get the men either way. Maybe your father could help, Lord Light. His resources—"

"King Iridan is not part of the Legion. I'll not have you mention him again." He glanced at Derren, then back at the captain. "We'll have the room, Burnham. General Derren will summon you when needed."

Burnham got to his feet and gave an exaggerated bow. "Lord Light."

He shuffled around the table, eye on his bottle, but Derren glared him out of the room.

Adrian let himself down in the commander's chair and looked over the stacks of parchment on the desk—some splattered with wine, others barely touched. He blew out a breath, shaking his head.

"No wonder the people are arming themselves," Adrian said. "Two hundred men . . ." His father's words stabbed at his thoughts.

The Legion is nothing.

"Whatever the Pontiff's tools to keep the rulers in line, it seems the threat of an army is not one of them," Derren said. "Want me to pressure the drunkard? Get the men here?"

"No, he might be right on that account. He's a drunk, but he needs to keep things as quiet as he can if he wants to drink in peace."

Adrian racked his mind, trying to come up with something, anything, to solve the matter quickly enough. Raklin's patience would run out soon, and then he'd look for new allies. Myrra had little time.

His thoughts drifted back to the attack when they entered the city and the bolt striking his sister's carriage.

"When we arrived, you said you tracked down the man who shot the bolt."

Derren nodded. "The boy was jumping at every shadow. This Seraph's Hand might have numbers, but they're disorganized bastards."

"Might be, but there has to be some coordination at the top. I'll look over the papers. You dig up what you can on them. I want to be there the next time they're recruiting."

"Changing sides already?" Derren smiled at him.

"I need to get close, see how they work."

"And then?"

"I'll think of something."

"You don't think they'll recognize you?"

Adrian shook his head. "I'm not Jovu. Time I used that to my advantage."

Adrian had tried to bring the Legion to resemble a cohesive force, but it had been two weeks and he'd barely managed to get through the mess Burnham had left him in the commander's office. Not to mention the new grievances that came in every day.

Word had spread among the men and people of Alteria about a new commander, but the madmen attacks were rising, and people had openly turned to the Hand for help wherever Derren could not deploy enough men. The militia numbers had been affected as well, though. The madmen were never taken down without felling at least a few, and the Hand seemed to have lost enough that Derren had finally heard whispers of recruitment.

Night had fallen, and Adrian padded his way through the shadowy streets of the Bracken Quarter. They had a permanent scent of feces, and the houses were cluttered in an impossible jumble, their walls stained so long with city dirt that the whitewash had almost turned black. He was alone, much to Derren's disagreement, but the general had already begun to make an image for himself in the city, and Adrian could not risk the recognition.

A single torch lit a warehouse doorway at the edge of a narrow street. Two men stood beneath it, checking those who entered. Adrian had dressed appropriately in a torn shirt and a threadbare cowl, which he now lifted over his head. He'd been forced to leave his sword behind as well. The lack of its familiar weight was like losing a limb, but Myrra's amulet was still heavy around his neck.

I'm coming, Myrra.

Adrian watched the warehouse for a moment. Derren hadn't managed to uncover much about the militia leaders, probably wouldn't from the outside. Adrian needed to join them himself, get a face or a name to help him bring them down. He latched onto a group heading for the door, hoping to pass unnoticed, but one of the sentries put a grubby hand on his chest.

"Haven't seen you around, friend."

"I'm new."

"New can be good. Or bad. You know what this is?"

"World's gone to shit, looks like." The smell was confirmation enough. "This is where I was told to go if I want to make it better."

The man nodded. "The Seraph's Hand will pull us through."

"Aye," Adrian said. "The Hand will pull us through."

The guard looked at him another moment, trying to commit his face to memory, perhaps, then let him pass.

The warehouse was warm, the walls lined with torches. A ragged, eager-looking crowd was being held back by a line of men in mismatched, boiled-leather armor. They kept the people pent up near the entrance, blocking their way to the raised platform at the far end. The Bracken Quarter had been hit hard with the attacks lately, and the fear was visible. Adrian paced through groups with guarded postures, their gazes jumping around the room, wary for signs of frenzied attackers.

The people quieted down as a man stepped onto the platform, surrounded by guards that looked more the part than the ones keeping back the crowd. They formed a line at the back of the raised platform, and the man they'd been surrounding stepped forward.

"Welcome, faithful." He paused, looking over the gathering and bringing two hands towards his chest. "Times are dark. The nations of the Domain have forgotten us! The Church does what it can, but the kings and queens have gutted our Legion, and the people are left to fend for themselves."

The people around him nodded along, seemingly in need of little convincing.

"Yet the Seraph still blesses Her people and extends Her hand. Alteria is in need of defenders. Your families are in need of defenders!" The crowd rumbled in agreement, and the recruiter let the mood rise before going on. "The Hand will provide the tools to those who can prove their faith. Step forward if you think yourself worthy enough of the Seraph's name, and rest assured, the Hand will look out for you."

Adrian frowned. He'd expected at least a veiled attack against the Pontiff, or even the Legion, but as he chewed on the thought, men and women began to move forward, unwittingly pushing him towards the line of guards. They were screaming at the recruiter, promising their devotion to the cause, proclaiming they could be trusted. Some even produced tools and waved them around as if they were blades, but there were no proper weapons on display. None seemed to have the coin for those. Some were let in, others turned away, and all Adrian could do was grit his teeth as more people tried to push past him.

This was why he'd rarely delved into religious matters. This man wasn't a priest, yet fear had these people begging for a blade and a chance at their own death, and it was being fed to them under the guise of safety and the blessings of the Seraph. Still, if this was the way in, so be it. Myrra was waiting. Adrian swallowed his pride, then edged his way forward through the crowd as best he could.

"That is enough," the recruiter said from atop the platform.

The panic rose. The tightly packed people all moved forward, threatening to crush Adrian now in mindless desperation.

"Please! My son is sick!"

"I have three daughters!"

"I'll pay, please, I'll pay!"

Adrian's gut tightened, and the heat grew around him. Getting close to the militia leaders would take long enough. He couldn't wait for another one of these: he had to get in.

He shoved his way past, shoulder down, moving people out of the way until he reached the line of militiamen pushing back. They had an amalgamation of improvised weapons, and the occasional glint of steel kept the mass alert but still pushing forward.

A man tried to break through the guard line but was battered on the head and taken away, and the idea fell into place, then. There was a faster route to the top than the cautious anonymity of making his way up the ranks. Derren had been worried they'd recognize him, but maybe that was what Adrian needed. All he needed was some attention on himself.

Adrian let out a howl, then slammed his shoulder into the militiaman before him. The man pushed back, but the fear was plain in his eyes. These were not seasoned men.

Adrian went for the guard again, and the man raised a blade to fend him off, but Adrian moved under it and sunk his fist into the man's stomach, then barreled into him, wrenching the blade from his grasp. He rose with blade in hand, hood still up, ready to fend off more attackers, but the recruiter raised a hand. The guards that had surrounded the recruiter moved to encircle Adrian. The line had closed behind and more blades had been drawn, dissuading any who might have been inspired by Adrian's display. Adrian removed his hood and looked straight at the recruiter. This path was faster, but the look of the men surrounding him sent a shiver through Adrian. They had death in their eyes. The recruiter smiled down, giving Adrian little time to regret his decision.

"Take him."

The militia fell onto him—too many to fight off—but his instincts had him trying. He attempted a stab but was hit by a spear butt from behind and fell to the ground. A man pinned him with a knee and held his head to the ground. After a moment, all Adrian could hear were slow footsteps approaching. The recruiter kneeled beside Adrian and spoke softly in his ear.

"A pleasure to have you among us, Lord Light. A shame you think so little of our brotherhood that you would consider yourself unrecognizable, but Commander Ashford will be pleased to see you, I am sure."

The spear shaft hit Adrian again, and the world fell into blackness.

Adrian blinked, trying to make sense of the foggy forms. He was seated with his hands bound, unable to move much other than his eyelids, so he pressed them again until an image sharpened before him.

"Welcome, Lord Light." The man's voice was thick, the accent distinctly Sacanthan. "I hear the High Pontiff has a desire for my head. Have you been the one sent to take it?"

Adrian coughed the dryness from his throat. "Commander Ashford, I assume?"

The commander nodded. He had a tangle of wild, dirty-blond hair that extended to his shoulders and brushed his armor as he moved his head.

"I'm glad I could get your attention." Adrian stifled the growing anxiousness in his chest and tried to remain steady. He raised his bound hands. "Is this really necessary?"

"Take it as a compliment. You have earned those."

"The burden of notoriety."

Ashford laughed a deep laugh and signaled past Adrian. Feet shuffled behind him, and a door closed. They were alone.

Adrian tilted his head slightly. "You are not Alterian."

"No."

"And not a commoner, either."

"The questions that need answering are my own, Lord Light. Why were you trying to join my army?"

"I wanted to talk."

155

"Hah! Quite the way of getting an invitation. Still, you have not put yourself in the most favorable of positions to negotiate." His gaze flicked to Adrian's bound hands, then back to his eyes.

"This?" Adrian raised his arms, then let them fall back into his lap. "What are you going to do? Send a letter to the Pontiff threatening to kill me? Bargain for my life? He won't pay very well, I assure you."

"And your father?"

It was Adrian's turn to laugh. "Even less."

"I do not wish to kill you, but you are not doing a very good job of defending your life."

"Well, you just said you won't kill me."

"I said no such thing. Sometimes we are forced to take action, especially in times like these."

Adrian regarded the man for a while, but Ashford's eyes gave little away. "Do you really think you'll start a new church? Challenge the Pontiff?"

Ashford let out his deep laugh once more. "No wonder the Legion cannot protect the people. You do not know even who to fight. I never wished to challenge the Pontiff."

"Your recruiter spoke like a priest."

"And did you hear him attack the Pontiff? The Church?"

Adrian shook his head slowly, and Ashford smiled at him.

If he's not trying to fight the Church . . .

"You're trying to get noticed."

"In that, we are the same. These attacks are only rising. People are desperate. I am doing my part for the Domain."

"No. You wouldn't put your men on the front lines if that were true. You're highborn. No nobleman wades among the common folk like this, not if you had your blessings. What you do isn't for them. It's for you. You seek the grace you've lost." The commander remained silent, and Adrian pressed on. "Yet you have not sought an audience with the Pontiff. Either you are afraid or"—Adrian lowered his voice to a whisper—"you've been exiled."

Ashford did not laugh this time, and Adrian knew he'd struck deeper with his words than he would have with any sword. "So, what?" Adrian continued. "Now you offer my life in return for a word with him?"

"He has much to gain from me. I have over five hundred faithful."

"And you think it's faith that has them following you?"

Ashford narrowed his eyes, but the side of Adrian's lips rose into a slight grin as the obvious idea fell into place.

"Join me," Adrian said. "I need the men. You need the blessings."

"And what prevents the Pontiff from taking my head?"

"I do. You'll be one of my captains, answering to the Legion. The Pontiff would take care of the expenses of the additional men."

"If he has the money to pay more men, why hasn't he already done so?"

"He may be the most powerful man in the Domain, but he doesn't have free rein over the rulers of all five nations. The Legion has always been enough to protect Alteria, and that was what it has been limited to. Things have changed now. But still . . . people are scared, and their faith in the Seraph does not extend to the Legion. I'll need your help on that, too. Your recruiter seemed convincing enough."

Ashford was silent for a long time, eyes searching Adrian's face. He itched at his beard once more. "General, not captain. I answer only to you, and you make sure my name is mentioned when we've cleared this scourge from the city. I want to talk to the Pontiff, too. Personally."

Adrian ran his tongue over the back of his teeth. "You'll talk to him once we've cleared the city." He raised his bound fists. "Now, if you haven't changed your mind about killing me . . ."

Ashford drew a short blade and stepped closer, then cut the rope binding Adrian's wrists.

"As you command, Lord Light."

CHAPTER ELEVEN

The knowledge of the path to the First Tree was Tedros's greatest secret. When he was gone, Twezzi Udda shaped the knowledge into ancestor-stone, to be recalled only through ritual, then quickly forgotten.

— *Tales of the Ronar*

Nasha strained to keep her eyes open through the ache pressing behind them. She'd never held on for that long, and every muscle seemed keen to remind her of it. The room was foreign, but its size and the softness of the bed told her she'd been taken to the Chief's Hall. Sunlight glinted through the window beside her, colors reflecting off droplets left behind by the recent rains.

"That was close."

Nasha's head swiveled round, sending lashes of pain through her bones. Mansa was smiling at her, but all she managed was a wince.

"You brought me here?"

Mansa's smile widened. "You're one of us now, . . . Warden."

Nasha's insides flared at the word. She'd almost forgotten. "They don't really expect me to . . . ?"

"They do. As do I."

"I can't fight. That's why you made me a hunter. That's why I stay away from the village. Do you want a slaughter like at my Proving? We won't be able to hide it from Tomu again. There are enough rumors about what I did. He won't take the risk, not with me as the—" Nasha coughed, words stuck in her throat. "As the Warden."

"The Lothrak were never good opponents, anyway."

"Mansa! I'm serious!"

Mansa raised an eyebrow at her. "Were you not seeking more stripes?"

"To rid myself of this curse, not to become Warden!"

"You'll control it, like you did last time. We found ways to get you through the village, did we not? Old Kolg, Tanner Hilka?"

Nasha shook her head. "This is nothing like that. . . . Do you think Adda can get me to the Tree?"

Mansa gave a sharp laugh. "Don't you think you're in deep enough with her? She stood for you, put you in this position. She'll want something in return."

"I . . . I never even asked for this!"

"And when has that ever changed anything?" Mansa's expression grew somber for the first time.

"I won't let her use me."

"Let's hope so. Tomu's gathering the Roots tonight."

"Tonight? Have the Yltigg set the date?"

"You should focus on the draft first. We're using ancestor-stone."

"What?!" Nasha almost screamed.

"It's part of the assurance. Tomu can't have heirs to the Earth-Breakers as Roots. As you said, he can't take the risk."

"I'm not an Earth-Breaker, Mansa! I'm not the—"

"I know. I'm the one who's kept your gift a secret, remember?"

Nasha was still shaking her head, thoughts racing. "I can't," she said. "I can't control the curse. It hasn't gotten any better."

"You'll have—we'll have to find a way. Focus on me. You'll be close enough for me to anchor you through it. We'll get through the draft, then I'll get hunters to help you train the initiates while we work things out. I can send warriors, too, if you're feeling up to it."

"Don't the warriors answer to the Warden?"

"Tomu has them answering to me for now."

Nasha looked at the gleaming drops clinging to the windowsill. *He gave me the title, but not his trust. Can't say I blame him.*

Her chest tightened, and her breaths seemed trapped in it. "The Roots. They're just going to find a use for me before I'm killed, aren't they? Just another rung on their ladder."

"You're a Root now, too."

"What does that change? I'm just here to appease the Slopers. Whatever Tomu throws me into, he won't be able to use a dead Root, and that's what'll happen. Either that or . . ." The memories of wrecked bodies flooded her mind again, and the burning taste stuck in her throat.

"I'm still here, Nasha. Like always. We'll find a way to use your gift."

Nasha scoffed and looked away. "It's a curse, not a gift."

"Focus on me," he repeated. "We'll find a way."

He stood and squeezed her arm before leaving, but Nasha kept her seething stare on the ground, heat roiling inside her chest.

"Shit," she said. Then louder, screaming it and slamming a fist into the wall beside her. The wood cracked under it, as did her will, weakening her and making her whole body ache again.

Nasha took deep breaths, blowing out the anger.

Get a hold of yourself. There's enough in the world trying to break you.

She pressed her teeth tight. That had always been her way, stumbling blindly into another pit just as she climbed out of the last one. All for another stripe, another rung. She'd reached the top now, but it already felt like she was sliding back down.

Still, if I can get through this . . .

Nasha got up and paced down to the common hall to find some meat. The anger still burned in her stomach, but she might as well enjoy what she could.

The Roots had gathered around the firepit behind the Chief's Hall. Nasha stepped slowly towards them, encircled by a breeze that set fallen leaves to flight and twisted the light on their faces. They were all looking at the ancestor-stone basin resting over a plinth: the Cradle.

Her eyes lingered on the blue-veined basin; it was filled with smaller, smoother stones, their veins white instead of blue in their polished state. Nasha's every instinct recoiled at the memory of touching ancestor-stone, but she stepped closer to join the Roots. There was no greeting, only the rustling of the wind and Jabillo's shuffling feet.

Just get through this. Then you can talk to Adda about the First Tree.

"Let us begin, then," the Speaker said. "The Proving shall be held in the Yltigg peaks. It is the Warden's job to defend the Cradle. Five shall be chosen to enter the Ronar clan. Five—"

"She knows how it works, Jabillo. Get on with it," Tomu said.

Jabillo seemed to struggle with his expression, maybe trying to keep it steady for the Chief, but he nodded, dug into a pouch, then sprinkled some kind of dust over the pit, and the fire danced with renewed hunger.

"Who among you has chosen an initiate to be delivered to the Warden?"

Adda stepped forward. "I have."

"Very well."

Jabillo produced a short knife from his belt, and Adda stretched out her hand. He cut a thin line in her palm and handed her one of the smooth, unmarked ancestor-stones.

Adda closed her bloody hand around it, and Nasha's eyes widened, her heart beating like a mad horse's hooves. Touching the ancestor-stone was bad enough. She could not imagine what would happen if it touched her blood. Nasha struggled to keep the nervousness down, but she was still spent from the trial.

She looked at Mansa, and he held her gaze: steady, focused, trying to be the pillar she would need to stabilize herself. How could he think she'd be able to get through this? Focusing on him would never be enough against the ancestor-stone touching her blood.

I'm dead. We're all dead if I touch that.

Adda raised her stone high. "Initiate Devu."

Nasha's head snapped towards Adda, the fear of what was to come overtaken by the name. "Bahar's son?"

Nasha searched the Tivezzi's eyes, but they were blank, directed at Jabillo and the stone in her hand.

"We do not consider ties of blood, only bonds created by those proven deserving of the clan, Warden," Jabillo said.

Adda had nothing to add, and Nasha was left looking from one face to another while they all stared at the fire. Jabillo coated the bloody ancestor-stone with the thick powder from his pouch and threw it into the pit. The flames rose, but Nasha was dead-cold. Mansa was still looking at her, his eyes trying to say something, but words would not help her here.

Adda took a step back, the blood dripping off her hand.

"If there are no others." Jabillo beckoned to the Chief.

Tomu strode past him and pulled out a white-pulsing stone without looking down. There were runes on it—the name of a Sloper who'd requested to be proven.

"The Earth knows best," Tomu said, and handed the stone over to the Speaker, still without reading the rune.

Jabillo cleared his throat. "Initiate Zima."

The Speaker repeated the ritual with blood and earth, fed it to the fire, then beckoned to Nasha. She didn't move.

"Warden." Jabillo indicated the Cradle with an open palm.

Nasha's eyes darted around like trapped animals. Her heart thumped hard in her chest, and the burning, wooden taste of her fear returned to her tongue. Mansa was trying to stabilize her by projecting his own calm, but it would do little good.

"We do not have all night, Warden," Tomu said.

Nasha opened her mouth, and the words came without thinking. "I . . . I have an initiate."

Jabillo's face twisted, and he gave the slightest disapproving shake, but after a moment, he produced an unmarked stone and held his knife out to her.

Nasha moved slowly, as if she was about to put her hand into the flames. Jabillo slit her palm and pressed the ancestor-stone into it. She held her breath but felt nothing as Jabillo closed her fingers around the stone.

Then her hand began to burn.

The stone called to her, sending every kind of sensation through her fingers. There were no signs, no defense against it. All she could do was brace and struggle in the endless torrent. Rising, rising.

The emotions skittered along her skin, and Nasha's body came alive. The wind blew the heat from the pit, and the fire ran through her, scorching her arm, growing in her chest. Vengeance, fear, helplessness, excitement, anticipation, rage. The feelings mingled inside her like dancers capering to the steadily rising beat of the war drum that was her heart, pulling her apart in a thousand directions.

Nasha took a step forward, rage winning out over the others. Her muscles trembled with it, full of power, begging for release, begging for the taste of death. She turned burning eyes towards Adda—

Something cut her off, as if plunging her head in ice water, and Nasha fought back the gasp of someone taking a first breath after emerging. The Roots were staring at her, waiting for her to announce the name, but Adda had that curious look in her eye—the same as when Nasha had been dragged before the Chief, and a shred of a smile seemed to be trying to break through her lips.

"Shai," Nasha blurted out, and thrust the stone back into Jabillo's hand.

The girl wouldn't like it, but she was the only one Nasha knew could anchor her. Besides, living as a Sloper was no way to live. Ife had asked Nasha to protect his daughter, and the clan was the only path for that.

Jabillo scowled at her, took the stone, coated it in his powder, and threw it in the flames.

Nasha couldn't listen to the names that followed. She fought to control her breathing and keep herself contained. The effects of the ancestor-stone were lessening, but a thought remained. One Nasha could not batter down.

Something had stopped her, pulled away the emotion, and kept her under control. It wasn't her will or any of the rituals she used to fight the emotions, and she wasn't foolish enough to believe the Earth had lifted her curse. No. Adda's expression was enough to understand.

She's done something. She knows.

Nasha didn't know what the Tivezzi had done, but the thought that another Root knew about her curse sent a shiver through her. Still, Adda hadn't revealed it.

Could she be an ally? Like Mansa?

Nasha had her eyes on Adda as the Tivezzi stepped towards the hall, but before she reached it, the back door burst open, and a child ran towards her. Tomu grabbed the boy midway and lifted his grandson onto his shoulders, then held him upside-down. The boy giggled, and the emotion shot at Nasha in strong, almost directed streaks. It was better than the fear and anger she had just experienced, but she fought it back just the same. Her body felt the strain, and Nasha turned to rush away.

"Warden, a word? Go on, Razi." Tomu put the boy down, and he scampered after Adda. Nasha remained.

"You know what this Proving means for the clan?"

"Yes, Chief. The clan must grow. The initiates—"

"Not the initiates. There is more at stake than lives to be returned to the Earth." He put a hand on the Cradle. "I inspected the ancestor-stone that came back from the dig today. It was dull. No glow, not even the white."

Nasha remained silent.

"Our ancestor-stone protects us from Zala's fury. It is what keeps the village, the Ronar, safe. If what the Slopers bring us is dull, the stones that still retain power become even more important."

He ran a hand over the rim of the Cradle. "The Cradle still pulses. Losing it—and all the rest that was agreed upon—to the Yltigg would do more than splinter our pride. It would weaken us in the eyes of the other clans, the Earth, and the Domain. It would make us vulnerable. We cannot afford that." He stepped forward, holding her gaze in his own. "The initiates that have been given to you are a tool. The clan is more important than any single life. The Ronar come first. Always."

Something itched at the back of her mind. Had she been just a tool for Mansa during her own Proving? Did he still see her like that?

No. Mansa knows me. He knows I am more than that.

Nasha swallowed hard, fighting off Tomu's waves of anxiousness. It seemed like he meant the words, at least, or maybe she was just eager to get away. She could see why he'd chosen to share this with her, though. The Chief thought she'd meant what she said at her trial and would stand for the Slopers. It sent a prickle of irritation across her skin, but she was in no state to argue now.

She nodded. "The Ronar come first, Chief. Always."

CHAPTER TWELVE

Ruin-stone remains one of the most valuable and mysterious elements of our world. They were here well before us, and the stone is hard enough that there are no records as to what might have broken entire buildings into the ruins we know today.

— Records from the Royal Archaeological Academy of Vizcarra

They traveled on the main road for two weeks, sharing mostly meals and silence between them. Ferrin was still working through what happened at the temple and hadn't smiled since leaving Pyrran. Death might be the curse of the unworthy, but the living were the ones who struggled in its grasp.

Lynn looked up at the mark in the sky.

What are you looking for? Guidance? Dentos laughed. *The Seraph is not watching you.*

Lynn brought her eyes back down. The traffic was heavier than normal, with wary-looking people clogging the roads. It seemed Pyrran wasn't the only city fleeing the Madness. It had spread wider and more quickly than she'd expected. "Be patient," Elwin would have said. "There is a right time, a right way, to strike."

There was little else to go on, by the looks of things, but patience alone would not keep them alive, and the roads were becoming too exposed. Lynn gripped the reins tight, digging her fingers into her palms, and steered the cart onto a dirt path. There was comfort in the shade of the trees, but leaving the people on the roads to fend for themselves felt wrong.

How many of them will die? I am still a—

Was she still a Sentinel? She'd been repeating it, but she was still running, and all she'd done to preserve life had failed.

You know what you are, Alren said, but Lynn drowned his words out with Elwin's lessons of patience, looked forward, and flicked the reins.

The broken tower rising over the trees marked the edge of the Farkhul church grounds. A relic of another time, the priests at the House of Farkhul had found it shattered, but rebuilt what they could and polished the raw, blue-veined ruin-stone until it took on a silvery tinge and the veins turned white. What remained was stout and centuries-old and had a wide base used to welcome visitors. There'd always been priests in the tower—guards, too. It was a bastion on the path to the church itself.

Lynn's shoulders tensed as they neared the tower. Abbot Orwen would certainly recognize her, but he'd always been kind. Always tended to her bruises after sparring and was patient when she could not remember the words from the scriptures. Would he turn her in? Would Leardin even have alerted him that Lynn had run from the order? Probably not. Leardin was too proud a man for that.

The tower was nothing like she remembered. The stone was rough and overgrown with weeds, no silver shine or white glow. There were no sounds, no priests or guards coming to greet them. The chill she'd felt at the temple in Pyrran crept up her spine again. Lynn inhaled. No scent of blood, but the empty silence was still heavy.

"Watch the cart," she told Ferrin, then jumped off and crept inside.

The entry hall was empty, the guard rooms covered in dust. No sign the tower had been used in at least a week. Lynn closed her eyes to steady her racing heart and let out a cramped breath. Empty, but no bodies. She paced around, peering through patches of light with drifting motes of dust, memories of the last night she'd spent here trickling back: the last night before being anointed a Sentinel.

Elwin had taught her all he could. They'd sparred and gone through hours of reflection on the sacred scriptures until the words came as easily as a breath, but he could not help Lynn through the final night. A Sentinel was not a Sentinel without a mount, and forging a Bond was different with every griffin.

Lynn had stood in the room with the shard before her. Its syphoning effect put her in the same haze as when standing near a griffin. The shard—a sliver of a griffin's ruin-stone heart—was, after all, what she needed to establish the Bond. She pored over the pages, going through every lesson, every word, every form, searching for the right emotion that would allow her to latch onto the shard.

She went through every feeling in the histories Elwin had taught her. She wallowed in sadness, digging up the memory of her dead brothers, of what she'd seen her father forced to do. She let the guilt run through her, let herself project the love she still had for her father, for Elwin, who took her in—her awe of how he'd treated her, raised her, taught her more than she ever knew existed.

None of it worked.

The shard kept pulling away piece by piece, until Lynn could barely remember her name. But she did not forget death, and the thought of succumbing to the enemy filled her with an unquench-able fire. Death had taken her brothers, driven her away from her home, and followed her every step. The fire burned through her veins, and it was only then that the shard answered: when she was sure she would die, when she let the rage of the thought of it take over. The shard came to life, veins glowing white, taking even more out of Lynn. But it was not taking her memories or the conscious-ness that made her whole: it was taking her anger.

Lynn felt him then. Vedyr, feeding off her emotion, answered her anger with his own, consuming it as she channeled more and more towards him and was rewarded with the strength of his limbs, the speed of his wings, the fury of his claws.

Her body was strengthened, but she was still not whole, and Lynn knew what she had to do to regain what the shard had taken.

She plunged the thin slice of ruin-stone into her chest, melding a sliver of Vedyr's heart into her own. It would have killed a normal person, but Lynn felt no pain. She'd found her Bond: she'd found Vedyr. She'd become a Sentinel.

Lynn traced a finger across the thin line over her heart, then across her Sentinel coin, which was a chip that had broken off the shard, molded into the Sign of the Breath. She turned the circle of stacked crescent-moons in her hand and let her burning memories take her back to when hope was still untainted by her past, the future was a shining certainty, and Alren, Roki, Dentos, and Cara were her companions rather than accusing voices in her mind.

She looked towards the entrance and made her way back through the old, dusty tower. Those days would not return.

Lynn stepped out, squinting in the daylight. "Nothing here, Ferrin. We—"

Ferrin had his spear up, facing five men who were surrounding the cart. Four of them had crossbows pointed at him, one—the leader, it seemed—standing before them.

"You can shoot, but I'll take at least one of you bastards with me," Ferrin said.

"Now, now. There's no need for blood. All we want is gold and the horse," the leader said.

"Can't sell blood," another one said.

"You should step back," Lynn called out, a few steps out of the tower doors. "No gold here, and we need the horse."

"Do you, now?" The leader turned to her with a bemused stare.

"I won't say it again." Anger was already coursing through Lynn, and it felt like Vedyr was closer now.

The men turned their crossbows to Lynn.

"We can't sell blood, but we don't mind a little if you're going to be difficult," the leader said. "Be reasonab—"

An anguished scream cut his words short. A bloody claw pierced the chest of one of the bandits, a madman snarling behind him. The horse reared and stamped its legs, then bolted past Lynn, throwing her to the ground and pulling their cart into the trees.

The leader looked at Lynn like she was some kind of witch from the clanlands, but his companions were already shooting at the madman, who'd wrenched his claw out of the bandit's chest and was running towards them.

Lynn jumped to her feet, eyes darting from the attacker to the bandits. Were these lives that warranted saving, or would they threaten others on the road? Was this what the Seraph wanted?

She hesitated, and she watched as the madman ran through the arrows and ripped open the face of a bandit struggling to reload, then leaped onto another, hacked his claws into the man's chest and ravaged the body on the ground in pure rage.

The remaining bandit shot another arrow into the madman's back, then fumbled his weapon, seeming indecisive between fleeing or standing by his leader. The beast was there in two quick steps, but so was Lynn. She used the momentum of her charge to ram her shoulder into the madman and throw him away from the bandit, then pulled on her Bond and fell heavily onto her opponent's back. The man thrashed his arms and squirmed under Lynn's knee but could not break free. Lynn gripped her knife, arms frozen, reluctant to let death's hands guide her own, even if Elwin would have told her it was the right thing to do.

Lynn raised the knife, but a crossbow bolt flew past and into the madman's skull. He stopped moving. Lynn jumped to her feet, knife in hand, eyes on the bandit leader, who was holding up his crossbow. The man looked between Ferrin and Lynn, then towards his butchered crew, and started to inch away without giving his back to them. He held Lynn's gaze for a moment, then dashed away into the tree line with the remaining bandit close behind.

Lynn was still unsure if protecting the bandits had been the right choice, but she couldn't have let the Madness rage before her without action. She turned over the madman with her foot, and Ferrin stepped in beside her.

All the signs were clear—the way he moved, the sharpened claws and the black tinge around the eyes—but even so, the itch at the back of Lynn's mind grew. The girl had not displayed the signs at first. Had she been infected already? Had the Madness grown in the dark while Lynn was hiding in the shadows herself?

That's what you get for being a coward, Alren said, but both her questions and her voices were silenced when Lynn noticed the dead man's clothes. He wore the robes of a priest of the House of Farkhul.

"Shit," Lynn whispered beside Ferrin.

"This your abbot?"

"No, but he's from his church. If priests are being infected, this is spreading even faster than I thought. We need to hurry."

Roki laughed in her mind. *They're all dead.*

Ferrin narrowed his eyes, still locked on the dead priest. "I'll take down every one of these bastards. Don't care how mad they are."

"Only what's necessary, Ferrin. Nothing more. Revenge may smell sweet, but the taste of death is bitter."

He frowned at her again. "Maybe there was a good reason you were locked in Kerr's cells, after all."

Lynn looked away. "Get the horse back. Shouldn't have gone far."

Ferrin set off and was soon back with a still-whinnying horse, its eyes filled with fear at the smell of the corpses. Lynn picked up the madman's body and laid it in the back of the cart. She put a gentle hand on the horse's neck and stroked him until he had calmed down, then climbed onto the cart and held the reins in her sweating hands.

Lynn looked up at the mark in the sky again.

Help me protect Your people. Help me protect Your Domain.

She received only silence in return, but that was the way of the Seraph. Elwin had taught her as much. "Faith is silent," he always said. She let out a long breath; she could use Elwin right now, but Leardin would never allow Elwin to bring her back. Her days of working with her mentor were in the past, as dusty as the tower where she'd left her memories behind.

"Come on. Abbot Orwen will know what to do."

Ferrin got on beside her and Lynn flicked the reins, pulling away the cart with death in her wake once more.

The cart rattled along the dusty path, and Lynn's neck stiffened with every bump on the road. Travelers grew thicker as they approached the church: two, maybe three scores of faithful searching for the protection of the Seraph. Ferrin's eyes were straight ahead and riddled with pain. Maybe the bodies they'd left behind had reminded him of what had been taken from him. There was a time when she would have preached the Church's words and told him the Seraph's judgment was always true. But the dead voices were too loud in her mind for her to be sure. Maybe this was an enemy strong enough to challenge the Seraph's will, regardless of the Church's scriptures to the contrary. Those texts were glowing words in gloomy halls. They did not face the bloody reality that was ravaging through the Domain. Lynn kept an eye on Ferrin but left him to his pain. She was beyond judging the worthiness of the dead, especially that of a priestess.

He's lost everything because of you, Alren said.

Lynn gritted her teeth, pushing Alren's voice to the back of her mind and focusing on the approaching house of the Seraph.

Though it stood in Othonea, the church was modeled in typical Alterian fashion: square towers with vaulted, triangular roofs, tinted glass on all sides with the Signs of the Faith—Breath, Body, Blood, and Bone—and low-roofed housing at the back to shelter the monks and abbot.

Lynn had held rooms here for a long time, but from afar, the grounds were hardly as she remembered. The patch of earth where she'd sparred with Alren and Dentos was overgrown with weeds, and the rooms beyond were closed off, seemingly uninhabited for weeks at the very least.

The church itself was slightly more familiar. Half of the Sign of the Breath was still chiseled into each of the ruin-stone doors, though a lot more faded. Parts of the stone had broken off, and there were deep grooves on one side, as if someone had clawed lines over the symbol. Lynn frowned at it. It would take a special kind of madness to strike at a house of the Seraph, and she couldn't imagine it happening in Farkhul. This had been a place of safety, of hope, of staunchness and resolve to bring the Domain into the Promised Dawn. She struggled to pull up those feelings, but the chaos inside her made it impossible.

She stopped the cart at the doors, and Ferrin made to get off, but she extended a hand. "Pull the cart around, then meet me inside." Ferrin nodded, and Lynn jumped down.

She padded across the threshold, a familiar weight pressing at her chest, her breaths hard and shallow. The reflection hall was filled with silence and the old scriptures shining through the mural. People were heading straight to the chapel beyond, under the watchful eye of the Church guard.

Lynn followed the scores of faithful, stepping around the sunlit inscriptions projected on the floor but pausing at the Ever-Tree in the alcove to the left of the chapel doors. She found none of the comfort she usually had meditating here. Lynn knew she'd never find it again. Not without Roki holding down laughter as Cara made silent faces at the texts, trying to understand before Elwin drilled them with questions. Now all she had were their voices, and they were never silent.

Lynn moved her eyes down the bark of the Ever-Tree and felt a hard knot form in her gut at the sight of fallen petals. She still couldn't believe it. Fallen petals were as absurd and horrifying as if the clouds turned red and rained blood instead of water. Some even floated in the blood-red pool of sap, which should have been color-less. The knot in Lynn's gut twisted and grew cold. The Ever-Tree at Baywater Temple was not the only one tainted. Had the Madness gotten even to the trees?

Her heart beat faster, and Lynn squeezed her eyes shut.

I need to find Orwen.

He won't help you, Roki said, his sharp laughter echoing.

"A shame, is it not?"

Lynn jumped at the voice, eyes flying open. The hall was empty now but for her and a thin man with a bald pate and bushy eyebrows wearing priest's robes.

"We were shocked when it first began to shed its petals, but a few more drop every day. The times are truly testing," he said. "Only our faith can win the Seraph's favor and heal Her Domain."

"Where's Abbot Orwen?" Lynn asked.

The priest was wiping his hands on a ragged cloth, too stained and brown to show the color of what he'd wiped away.

"How long has it been since you last visited?"

"Long enough." Too long, it seemed. She used to know every priest in the church.

"Abbot Orwen is unavailable, I'm afraid. I am Priest Talbot."

"When will he return?"

"That, I cannot say." His voice had taken on a tone of impatience. "Have you come for the ceremony?"

"No." Ferrin's passionless voice came from the stone doors of the entrance, and Talbot turned towards him with mild amusement.

"There is little I can do for you, then. My faithful await."

"Priest." The coldness from Lynn's gut had crept into her voice. "We found one of your own. He was . . . taken by a frenzy."

Talbot turned back to her and tilted his head. "We have had no reports of missing clergy."

"He wore your robes," Ferrin said, drawing closer to them.

Talbot shrugged. "I do not know what more I can tell you." He broke them a thin smile. "You are welcome to the ceremony, but I really must go."

"I'll find my way to Orwen's chambers," Lynn said.

"I'm afraid that, too, will be impossible."

Ferrin frowned at him. "We pay our tithes. The church is open to all—"

"Tithes are a worthy show of faith, but as I said, Abbot Orwen is unavailable. Abbot Andral presides over the House of Farkhul, and he has little time for favors."

Talbot turned his back on them again and paced towards the chapel. Lynn closed her eyes and took a deep breath. She didn't want to do it. She'd be too exposed, but Ferrin was counting on her, and pulling him away from the anguish of his dead sister was as close a step towards redemption as she could find.

Some things just have to be done, no matter the wanting of them.

They should have put those words into the texts, Elwin had said them so often.

"It won't be a favor," Lynn said to Talbot's back.

The man turned with a mixture of curiosity and unbridled irritation twisting his face.

Lynn dug into her threadbare shirt, hands closing around the grooves of her Sentinel coin. She held it up between Ferrin and Talbot, and both of their eyes went wide.

"You will take me to him in the name of the Sentinels of the Breath. I invoke the right to sanctuary."

CHAPTER THIRTEEN

The expansion of Her Domain is what will spread the Faith. It is the only thing that can keep our world safe from the heathens whose ignorance would tear it down.

— The Book of the Blood

It had taken another week, but Ashford had recruited more men, and the Legion had grown to almost three thousand strong, with not a semblance of discipline among them. Derren had appointed captains—some already Legion men, others chosen by the militia to keep their confidence strong—and they'd been hard at work, shouting the men into shape. A pious man might have said the Seraph was looking out for Adrian, aiding Her champion, but he knew better. Faith had never been a trustworthy strategy.

The greater numbers had helped, though, and in little more than another week, they'd organized their search and isolated quarters with rising attacks while intensifying the patrols. There had been losses to the Legion, of course, but that was to be expected.

The men still weren't as well trained as Adrian would've liked, but Ashford's presence seemed to spur more conscriptions to round out their numbers again. The madmen had dwindled, and a sense of safety was returning to Alteria—enough that things seemed almost organized, in control. If you could overlook the squabbling of the men, that is.

Burnham hadn't seemed to mind the demotion from commander to captain, but having Ashford as a general had finally riled the man: that and the obligatory training Derren had implemented were proving too much for him and the original men of the Legion. They did as commanded, but it was never easy, never quiet, and Burnham had tried to outshine Ashford at every turn, like dogs jostling for a clean tree to piss on. Or maybe a dirty one.

Derren had done what he could to keep them in line, and he'd shown himself as dependable a general as he had been a leader of Father's guard, but the effort seemed to weigh on him, and he looked wearier by the day. The weight was mounting on Adrian's shoulders as well. Sleep had been hard to find, and restless when it came.

Adrian sat in the antechamber of his rooms in the Legion barracks, still wrestling with his thoughts, trying to find sleep. Windows on either side dominated the walls from floor to ceiling, one overlooking the courtyard where he oversaw drills, the other where he spent nights watching the torchlight of sentries moving through the buildings that housed the men.

Adrian turned Myrra's Sign of the Bone in his fingers, tracing the ridged ruin-stone edges that framed the bone-carved eye in the middle. The Pontiff would have probably told him to get rid of it, but the once-vivid memories of her had been fading into wisps of remembrance. Adrian would have to follow enough of the Pontiff's wishes. The amulet would remain.

I am not just another of the Pontiff's tools, Father.

He'd built this Legion on his own, and not even Jovu had pooled men together this fast without Father's aid. What would it take for Father to recognize his efforts? And how would the Pontiff see it? Would he take exception to Adrian recruiting the militia instead of ending them? Adrian sighed. Father and the Pontiff were just two more dogs doing their own jostling. Maybe Adrian was the tree.

A sharp knock broke his line of thought, and Derren's weathered face peeked through a moment later. Adrian tucked the amulet away.

"Any trouble?" Adrian asked. Even he could hear the lack of hope in his tone.

"The usual," Derren answered, stepping into the room.

Adrian sighed, forefinger and thumb rubbing at his temple. "How are we going to fight this enemy if we're already fighting ourselves?"

"Things will settle down. We'll make sure of it." Derren looked out the window up at the Seraph's mark shining in the sky. "Has She, . . . you know, . . . talked to you?"

"Ellana?"

Derren hesitated. "The Seraph, . . . Lord Light."

"Derren, that sounds ridiculous."

"Faith is never to be mocked." He couldn't keep the grimace off his face. "You of all people should know it."

"I meant the title," Adrian said. "And no, the Seraph has not put words into my head. None that I've been able to hear, at any rate."

Derren still seemed troubled. He looked back up, but Adrian was following one of the streaking lines of torchlight moving through the barracks.

"The world is full of things we don't understand, Derren. We should keep our focus on the ones we do."

There was a long silence while both men regarded the predawn sky slowly lighten.

"Do you think it's grown?" Derren asked.

Adrian eyed him flatly. Of all the things he could dedicate his attention to, some sort of mark in the sky was not one of them. "Haven't been checking—"

Another knock at the door, more urgent.

"Yes?" Adrian called.

A disheveled herald appeared, looking as if he'd fallen out of bed and rushed over. One of Father's, perhaps?

"Yes?" he repeated, quieter this time.

"Things have deteriorated in the north, Prince Adrian."

"The north?"

"Attacks, my lord. Numerous reports from the northern reaches of Khet. The beasts, they seem to have gathered. Lord Governor Garrick requests your aid."

Heat bloomed on Adrian's neck, prickling up the back of his head.

Myrra.

"Gathered?" Derren said. "How many of them?"

"Reports say around a thousand strong. They've overrun the ports, and their . . . disease seems to be spreading, pulling the people into their frenzy. Milsport's had the worst of it. Its people have fled, and most in Khyr and Theria have left as well. They are flocking to Ultenvell, my lord."

"And the Othonean troops?" Derren asked.

"Focused on the provinces closer to the capital, sir. As are all nations. Help was requested from them as well."

Adrian nodded. "The Pontiff will be informed, and the Legion will march as soon as it has authorization, herald. Thank you."

The man saluted before leaving, and Adrian turned to look out the window once more.

"The ones here haven't seemed conscious enough to gather," Derren said once they were alone. "This is dangerous, Adrian."

And too close to Myrra. Adrian had no words. He was trying to keep his breathing steady.

"Should we send word to your father?"

"No. The Legion was rebuilt to fight this threat. I can handle things myself. Tell Ashford to ready his men. Leave enough behind to protect Alteria, and a captain you trust to lead them. Five hundred should do. That's more than what the Legion had before. The rest march north to Khet."

"At once, Lord Light." Derren bowed his head and left, leaving Adrian alone with his thoughts once more.

Adrian did not attempt to sleep, and by the time he donned his commander's uniform, the torches were going out, the first rays of sun breaching the horizon. He gripped Myrra's amulet tight again and strode out to meet the Pontiff.

Adrian moved quickly out of the barracks and up to the cathedral. The halls inside were as empty as the streets of Alteria, but he knew the Pontiff would already be in his private reflection chamber by now. He passed the Ever-Tree, still shedding its petals, and paced towards the Pontiff's chapel. He marched up the aisle with steady feet but a wavering mind—his gut jumping at the echo of his every step. Would the Pontiff treat him like Father had, a mere servant to carry out his will? Or would Adrian finally be recognized for his efforts? He'd dressed for it, at least.

His white cloak rustled at his back, and the buttons on his vest and cuffs glinted in the beams of light that shone through the openings in the high-walled chapel, metal reflecting the silver and white of the polished ruin-stone.

Two of the Pontiff's own guard stood at the door to his private reflection chamber. One of them rapped on the door, and the Pontiff's voice ushered Adrian inside.

The room was dark, the only light coming from the sacred scriptures glowing softly across the stone floor. Adrian made to kneel but remembered himself and settled for an awkward bow.

"You have news, Lord Light?" The Pontiff did not move his eyes away from the texts.

"Yes, High Pontiff. The militia, they've been dealt with."

The Pontiff turned to him. "So I have heard. Making friends out of enemies, I see."

Adrian's back tensed. "The opportunity presented itself, High Pontiff. It seemed to be the most profitable course of action." Adrian held his breath, but the Pontiff broke him a smile.

"I am not your father, my boy. I put you in command of the Legion, and it is yours to command. I wished the problem resolved, and you have done that."

The tension in Adrian's back settled down a touch. The recognition was foreign, but he couldn't deny it felt good.

"Of course, High Pontiff." Adrian paused. "I've received a herald."

"Hm?"

"Attacks have been rising in Khet, worse than other nations have reported. The madmen there seem to have gathered. As the Light of the Legion, I believe it to be our duty to strike them down: show the people of the Domain the Seraph is watching. Yet to march north would be . . . expensive."

The Pontiff turned back and walked through the light of the scriptures. "The faithful have paid their tithes. It is only fair we use them for the protection of the Domain. I will provide you with the means to maintain this new Legion—and for your march to Khet. The Legion must have a high priest, though. I've appointed Lindamm, one of my closest. The Legion is the sword, but there must still be one to spread the Seraph's word. You will leave men behind?"

"Five hundred strong. We've cleansed the East Row with General Ashford's help, and the Bracken Quarter has had no new reports in days. The men we leave will keep Alteria safe."

"Excellent, my boy. You have proven yourself to be a loyal servant of the Domain." The Pontiff fixed his green eyes on Adrian. "I'm sure your father will see it too, soon enough."

"He is not my primary concern, High Pontiff." Adrian gritted his teeth and stepped closer. "There is yet another matter I would like to discuss, but it does not involve the living."

The Pontiff raised an eyebrow at him. "I think you have earned the chance to speak of whatever matter troubles you, my boy."

"Myrra. The Dakhran princess." Adrian's back stiffened again. He hadn't said her name out loud since she'd died.

"Ah, yes. Syvern and Alaya have made their thoughts clear on the matter. You disagree with me as well?"

"No, . . . High Pontiff. But should the true followers of the Seraph not have more time to be judged? Those truly faithful . . . like . . . my mother."

"Ah, there were none more devout than Queen Dalenna, and it still saddens my heart that we must wait until the Promised Dawn to bask in her glow again."

Adrian's heart was beating too fast to reminisce on Mother now. "I had Princess Myrra's body preserved in Khet."

The Pontiff frowned, but it was more amused than aggravated. "Without my word?"

"She brought much to the Faith, Your Grace. She was well loved and well known for her piety. She was on the path of the Bishops of the Bone and would have pledged herself to the Church if not for . . ."

"If not for pledging herself to you."

Adrian breathed deep. "Yes, High Pontiff."

The Pontiff walked with his head bowed in reflection, while Adrian flushed with heat and sweat beaded his skin.

"The Seraph is the only one who can judge us, my boy, but maybe there is room for further reflection on the matter. You have done well. I will use the time you have given her to consider, and let us pray I can understand the Seraph's will. We will talk again when you have cleansed the north and the Domain is rid of this spreading scourge."

Adrian bowed his head, hiding the effort to keep the smile off his face.

"I will bring them the Seraph's light, High Pontiff."

With the way his heart was leaping, he might even have meant the piety in his words this time.

CHAPTER FOURTEEN

The Domain invasion into the clanlands was halted only when Tedros challenged their champion. The Domain man brought four warriors with him, betraying the agreement, yet Tedros fought and defeated all five at once. He proved himself a true champion, and the clans have held Provings in his memory ever since.

— Tales of the Ronar

Nasha walked up the sloping path with embers in the pit of her stomach. Having to announce the names of the chosen before a crowd was bad enough, but the thought that Devu and Shai were among them made the embers roll around and claw up her throat. Devu would probably relish the opportunity, but Nasha knew Bahar would not, and she doubted Shai would even see it as an opportunity. She had her own reason for picking the girl: she needed an anchor to get through this. But this would benefit Shai as well. The clan was the only way to keep her safe, even if she refused to see it.

Nasha breathed in the cool night air, trying to smother the burning inside, and forced her legs forward. The path ahead was clouded by the fumes of the Great Mountain, but the shadow moving onto it was clear enough.

The figure was hooded, a woman, silhouette framed by moonlight and smoke. Instinct had Nasha waiting for the prickling to start on her skin, and she focused on the fumes, but nothing came. She frowned at the hooded figure. Was she suppressing her own emotions? No, only Nasha could do that. It came with the curse.

The figure removed the hood, and Adda, with her elaborate bun, sharp features, and thin lips, was staring back at her.

"Warden."

The word fanned the fires in Nasha's gut, and they came searing up her throat again.

"Tivezzi," she grated out.

"We must speak."

Nasha's heart leaped. It might have been foolish, but the hopes of seeing the First Tree still enticed her.

"Your stand was bold, and you struck a mark with the people of the Slopes," Adda said. "That is to be commended."

Nasha's heart beat faster. Maybe her worth had been recognized: maybe Adda had seen something beyond a Sloper in her.

The First Tree is not lost.

"Do not mistake me for a fool, though. Your words will have a price. The Roots are not tools for your manipulation."

Nasha's hopes came crashing down with the Tivezzi's words— each of them cold and dead as stone, no emotion, as if she was still holding it back somehow.

"Tivezzi, I . . . did not mean offense. They would have taken my life."

"And I have commended you for your strength in defending it, but you would not have risen without my help. You are indebted to me."

Nasha focused her thoughts. She needed the path to the First Tree, but submitting was weakness. She was a Root now.

"I did not force your words, Tivezzi. I owe you nothing. I am a Root and will not be—"

Adda's face twisted in stark contrast to her usual stony expression. She grasped Nasha's forearm, and the fingers dug deep as if melting into it. The smell of burning flesh filled her nostrils, and her arm became a searing blaze of pain.

Nasha's ears were filled with a high-pitched ringing, her curse threatening to take over, and whatever suppression she might have managed was engulfed in Adda's scorching grip.

A scalding howl rushed up her throat but was quieted by the confusion and surprise that took over her, entwined into helplessness that came out only as a gasp. Nasha struggled, but Adda's hands were like the obsidian around the Great Mountain. Unmovable and unrelenting.

"I know what you are," Adda whispered. "You will do as I tell you, or I will take far more than your life."

Adda pulled on her arm and put a hand over Nasha's mouth. Nasha gave a muffled cry, but the Tivezzi was already whispering in her ear. "You will kill the emissary. Better if it is done during the Proving. It is the price for your life." She held on for another moment, then removed her hand from Nasha's mouth. "Do you understand?"

"Bahar? W-Why?" Every word was agony, but Nasha could not hold them down.

"It is not your place to question this, only to obey."

Nasha gritted her teeth. She struggled again, but it only seemed to spread the fire.

"Do you understand?"

"Ach—yes. Yes!"

Adda released, and Nasha clawed at her arm, desperate to peel off the burning skin, but there was barely a mark, not even a bruise. A thousand questions fought their way through Nasha's mind.

"How . . . how did you . . . . Do you—"

"This will remain between us, Warden. The pain is the very least I can do. I have given you back your life, and I can take it away just as easily. Now. We have an announcement to make, I believe?"

187

Adda had her stony expression on again and walked along the path as if they had shared nothing besides pleasant words.

Does she have my curse? Is she an Earth-Breaker?

The Ronar Stone-Shaper had always been more of a symbolic figure. She molded and blessed the ancestor-stone wards around the village and had her shapers fashion weapons out of obsidian and the more common, less valuable flint for the clan, but Nasha had never heard mention of anything like her curse. Only stones, herbs, and smoke, like in the stories. What she'd demanded didn't seem possible, either. Kill Bahar? Taking Devu from him was bad enough . . .

I'm not the monster, and they will not make me into one.

People were filling the streets around her, heading towards Mansa's hall. Nasha followed in Adda's footsteps, the embers in her stomach flaring again.

She rushed past the growing pack of Slopers clustered at the bottom of the outer steps. The usual signs had begun to take hold: the prickling on the skin, the shallow breaths—and even if these warned of lesser danger, Nasha was still gripped by fear, unsure how what Adda had just done would change her curse's reaction to the crowd.

She did her best to not be taken by their eagerness, trying once more to breathe in the acrid fumes, and moved quickly until she stood halfway up the stairs between Adda and Mansa. Close enough to the crowd to be heard, but far enough to manage their emotions. The chills over her skin seemed to be rising, though, and her muscles were weighing her down. The crowd numbered in the hundreds now, and a swirl of their anxiousness buffeted Nasha like a tightening whirlwind. She searched for Shai's face among them but found nothing other than hopeful stares.

A mad part of her considered asking Adda for help. The Tivezzi had neutralized the effects of the ancestor-stone during the draft, Nasha was sure of it. But she would not ask more of Adda. Not now that she knew how steep the cost was.

She pressed her teeth tight, but as the gathering thickened, some of the emotion found its way into her. These were different. No anger to blur her vision, no accusing looks that made her ears ring like at the trial. Instead, Nasha was taken by a warmth that spread through her chest and settled her heart until she almost felt comfortable. She wasn't used to this and hardly knew how to keep it back. Their awe enveloped her, and it was bolstered by their hope, lifting Nasha's mind until she was no longer on the steps.

She was in a room, but it didn't seem like one of the houses in the village or the Slopes. Her small hands were held in the larger ones of a woman who stroked Nasha's hair, singing while her other hand rubbed Nasha's back. It spread the warmth through her, and it felt safe. So safe that Nasha never wanted to leave this woman's arms. She closed her eyes and let the sweet humming carry her away. The scent of freshly picked lavender helped lull Nasha into a soothing sleep that—

The woman shook her, shouting her name, and for a moment Nasha could smell the burning wood and blood again. Then it was gone, and she was back on the steps. Mansa had one hand around her shoulder and was raising her arm with the other, using more force than necessary, shaking her as best he could without alerting the Slopers.

"Snap out of it," he said through gritted teeth.

Nasha blinked hard a few times and balled her fists.

Damned Earth-curse creeps up on me even with the good ones.

She couldn't remember the last time she'd felt emotions like that, but they were as dangerous as the anger. She couldn't give in. She needed to stay alert.

Nasha took Mansa's lead and raised her other arm, breathing deep, trying to maybe catch a whiff of the citrus trees, but what caught her was a shooting anxiousness mingled with confusion and a lingering touch of anger. Not the easiest of emotions to latch onto, but familiar enough that Nasha could use them to pull her consciousness through the madness of the crowd. Her eyes found Shai in a hollow of one of the surrounding houses, looking up at her through hooded eyes.

"Five have been chosen." Nasha kept her voice as flat as she could. "The Slopes must prove their strength if there is to be hope for more in future Provings."

A few grumbles from the crowd and spikes of surprise. There was always the hope for more initiates, probably even more so now that she'd become Warden, but Nasha latched onto Shai's emotion and pushed on.

"Berg, son of Geffe. Verena, daughter of Joku. Zima, daughter of Cedri."

The murmurs rose and Nasha closed her eyes for a moment, preparing for what was about to crash into her. Nasha took a deep breath.

"Devu, son of Bahar, and Shai, daughter of Ife."

Shai's rage shot into Nasha. She tried to close herself off and fight it, but it was as if the girl was trying to break her down. Nasha's heart raced and her skin burned as she desperately tried to keep Shai's emotions back. The drain of it was heavy, though, and Nasha's knees went soft with the effort.

Mansa grabbed her arm and pulled her up a few steps. "You're doing fine. It's almost over."

They turned back to the Slopers. A few of them were congratulating the chosen, others complaining about the small number given a chance, but most of them were moving away.

The pressure eased on Nasha, and she blew out slowly, trying to regain control of herself. Her gaze jumped to where she'd seen Shai. The girl was gone, but a figure was moving up the stone steps towards her now—square features, shaggy hair, and slow steps. Bahar.

Would he know this was not her doing? She hadn't seen him since the trial. Would he even respect her as Warden? Or would he threaten her with the power of the Visslands if she took his son?

He paused and put a heavy hand on her shoulder. It was meant to be comforting, but Adda's presence a few steps below seemed to pull Nasha down under the weight of Bahar's hand.

"Some part of me always knew this day would come." He tried to look unrattled, but his tone was detached and cold.

Nasha nodded—her stomach was clenched too tight for words.

She forced herself to look at him, and he forced a smile, but it was empty.

"I trust you," he said. "I know you'll take good care of him. He'll do great things for the clan, Nasha. Great things."

Bahar's words were distant, as if underwater, and she couldn't really make sense of them. Words of a dead man, perhaps? Had her mind already decided while her heart struggled against it? Was she becoming the monster?

He pressed her shoulder, trying to be reassuring. "It's alright. I understand."

You don't. How could you?

Nasha could do little more than look and keep nodding at him. Bahar walked back down the steps, leaving only concern in his wake. Adda was standing a few steps below. She looked past Bahar and straight at Nasha with a look that needed no explanation.

It hit Nasha with a chill, and she scowled. Nasha wasn't the monster, but it seemed the Ronar had enough monsters hiding among them.

CHAPTER FIFTEEN

*After creating the Body, raising it with Bone, and warming it with the Blood,
the Seraph gave us the Breath, so that we may spread her word of a world
untainted by death.*

— *The Book of the Breath*

Lynn sat in one of her old rooms. The floorboards were cracked and creaking and the thin veneer of paint peeling off the walls. The room was covered in dust and smelled faintly of musty, damp stone. The smell of home.

There was a rap on the door, and Lynn looked up to find Ferrin standing with an awkward look on his face, as if he didn't know the proper way to talk to her anymore or was missing some show of respect. Lynn sighed and shook her head.

"Nothing's changed, Ferrin. I'm still me. I'd tell you to sit, but I'm afraid the dust would eat you up."

He shuffled in, looking away, and remained silent as he pulled a stool under himself, trailing dust across the floor. He looked around for a long moment, then at her.

"W-why didn't you tell me?" His voice trembled, and his eyes did not linger on her for long.

Because you're a coward, Lynn, Alren answered.

"You don't have to fear me, Ferrin."

"Would have helped my courage, knowing I had a Sentinel with me," he mumbled.

"I'm not a Sentinel anymore. Not in the way it matters." No use lying to herself.

"It sure looked like it mattered back there."

"Probably the last of the clout I can muster."

"Why were you locked up?"

Tell him!

"I was still doing the work of a Sentinel. Got some lives out until . . . well . . ."

Coward.

"And now we're here," Ferrin said.

"And now we're here."

"I wish I'd killed her," he said, his eyes hard. "That girl. That beast. You should have let me kill her before she . . . shriveled away."

"It wouldn't have helped you, Ferrin. You don't want that weight on your shoulders. Death is the enemy. You forget that, you're as mad as the girl."

Ferrin fell silent, inspecting the dust under their feet.

"Why?" he finally asked. He looked up at her, looking like he'd regained some of his bravery.

"Why what?"

"Why are we even here, doing all this? The Seraph made us, didn't she? Why do we feel this way about the dead? Why is it wrong to feel for Morna? If the Seraph hates death so much, why can't she just make us forget?"

"The Seraph won't make us do anything because we're the ones who drove her away with our constant warring, Ferrin. We brought wanton death into her Domain and gave it power. We are the ones who must prove ourselves to Her, not the other way around. Your questions have been asked time and again, but it always comes back to faith and the proof that She gives us with her blessings. The Pontiff has lived for hundreds of years by Her power. So have others who have proven their faith."

"Including the Sentinels."

"Yes, including the Sentinels." Lynn had lived almost one hundred and sixty years herself, and she'd half expected to start withering away after leaving the Sentinels, but it seemed the Seraph still had Her eye on Lynn, even if it had been too long since she'd received a proper blessing by a priest. "Still, that changes little. Faith is the same, no matter how long you've been alive. You may believe Morna was taken against the Seraph's will, but to dwell on the dead like this will eventually drive you away from the Faith. That's why the Sentinels are here. We kill so others won't have to live with the weight of it."

That's rich coming from you, Roki said. He had a point, but these were the words Ferrin needed to hear, no matter if death was constantly in Lynn's mind. She held Ferrin's gaze and breathed out slowly to push Roki's voice away.

"Ask your questions," she said, "but remember the answers lie with the Seraph alone."

"That's easy for a Sentinel to say. Don't lose many people, do you?"

I've lost more than you will ever know.

Lynn didn't voice the thought, but it was reflected in her stare. That seemed to remind the watcher of who he was talking to.

"I . . ."

There was little consolation in Ferrin's expression, pain and accusation still riddling his gaze. He looked ready for another question when Talbot appeared in the doorway. The priest wrinkled his nose and lowered his bushy eyebrows as he stepped in, faintly acknowledging them with a nod.

"If you'd follow me, Sentinel."

Lynn got up and Ferrin followed.

"Only the Sentinel."

Lynn frowned at him, but Talbot replied with a thin smile. "I do not believe the right to sanctuary extends to others."

"I'll be back soon. Stay here," Lynn said, then left him behind, still unsmiling.

Lynn walked the familiar church hallways towards Orwen's old office, where Andral had taken residence. She tried to keep the memories at bay, but Elwin's lessons were all around her, drifting up through the cracks of her past. Lynn drove them away, took a deep breath, and pushed Orwen's—Andral's—doors open.

The abbot stood at a pedestal before shelves by the side wall filled with tomes, leafing through a book of the collected scriptures. It had begun to rain, and the slowly darkening room seemed to make the veins in the fist-sized ruin-stone amulet with the Sign of the Breath hanging around his neck glow. He looked up at her with small, dark eyes, then walked around the book and towards the desk.

"Welcome, Sentinel." He bowed his head, then took a seat. "Talbot tells me you are quite intent on this meeting."

"There have been attacks, Abbot. In the cities and on the road. Madness spreads through the Domain, and I fear Farkhul might not escape it. There was a priest—"

"Not one of our own." He smiled briefly. "Talbot has inspected the body. The robes were stolen. I've had him review our supplies, and he will burn the corpse tomorrow to cleanse our grounds."

A tingle ran up at the back of Lynn's neck, but her anger would be of no use here. "Even so, Farkhul has a duty to the faithful. The broken tower was unguarded. Your borders and roads are unwatched. Where is Abbot Orwen? The priests who served under him? Even your Church guard is well below expected."

"Those matters are not for a Sentinel to resolve, I'm afraid. Unless you have companions to bring to our aid?"

Lynn fought down her glare.

"You claim to have been acquainted with Orwen," he said, "yet we do not even know your name. I mean no offense, but with this madness running amuck, as you say, how am I to believe you? How am I to believe you did not happen onto that Sentinel coin?"

Lynn's anger rose now. She looked straight at Andral, extended her heart towards Vedyr, and touched the Bond, letting the flash of silver burn in her eyes. "Is that proof enough?"

Another brief smile touched the corner of his mouth. "Of course. I apologize." He bowed his head again, but there was none of the expected awe or fear that usually followed the revelation of being a Sentinel.

"Orwen has been summoned to Alteria by the Bishops of the Bone. He has left me in his stead. Until he returns, there is little else I can give you."

Lynn narrowed her eyes at the man. "Your archives, then. Let me search the texts, see if I can reflect on something to fight this while I wait."

Andral gave a deep sigh. "I must apologize for that as well. The archives are in the catacombs, and those flooded a while ago. They were too close to the river: the walls gave out." He spread out his arms. "Orwen should return by the end of the week with more information. You are welcome to stay."

Lynn nodded. Andral would have fooled a Sentinel who did not know this place as well as she did, but she'd spent too much time in those catacombs. The walls were pure ruin-stone. The river could never break through them. She couldn't confront the man now, though. She'd get nothing that way.

"Thank you, Abbot." She was still struggling to keep the anger out of her tone.

"You are free to visit my chambers as you see fit, Sentinel."

Lynn closed the doors and rushed back to her rooms. Ferrin was still sitting among the dust, looking out the window.

"Get ready."

"What?"

"They're hiding something."

Ferrin tilted his head. "Who, the priests?"

"Keep your voice down! Yes, the priests. There's a cleansing tomorrow. Keep them occupied. I'm going to find out what it is."

The Seraph's mark was frowning down on her, brighter than the setting sun. It looked almost like a sun itself now, having far outgrown the size of a common star.

Abbot Andral stood on a raised dais behind the church. His eyes were placid and fixed on the corpse, the darkening sky lit up by the torch in his hand. Talbot was already starting the chant beside him: a low hum, rising and falling. It brought back memories, the wails of the battlefield still ringing in Lynn's mind. Death's own voice if ever there was one.

A score of people had gathered to watch the cleansing of the church grounds, and Lynn stood at the back, waiting for the shadows to become thick enough. The faithful joined Talbot's chant, Ferrin at the very front of them, close to the handful of Church guard that surrounded the dais.

More people were joining the congregation, and Lynn used one of the arriving groups as cover to step away. She slipped into the church, hurried past the tainted Ever-Tree, then bound down the curving stairwell that led to the archives, two at a time, footsteps echoing off the walls.

Lynn paused as something clinked in the distance, but the sound was quickly obscured by the rising beat of her racing heart. Did they see her leave?

Her leg muscles twitched but stopped as the sound came again. Louder this time. Metal clinking, like the rattling of chains. It was coming from the catacombs.

Definitely not flooded.

Lynn moved to the back of the chamber and tried the heavy oaken catacomb doors. Locked. The chains rattled again—no doubt they were chains now. Lynn gritted her teeth. Whatever the priests were hiding here, she'd bring it to light, and then they'd answer to her. The bubbling anger in her gut rose to her throat. She channeled it to Vedyr and fell into her Bond.

"Seraph, watch over me," she whispered, then slammed her fist into the wood. She tried to blunt the sound, but the door was heavy. There could be no half measures here.

She hit again and again until the complaining oak cracked and again until the crack became a hole large enough for her arm. She undid the latch on the inside and the door swung open towards her, which made her wonder how anyone would open it from her side, short of smashing it in. Maybe it wasn't meant to open. That made her heart race even faster. What if whatever was chained up here was supposed to be that way?

No turning back now. She stepped inside.

A thin slit at the top of the wall let in the last fingers of setting sunlight from outside, and lanterns hanging on the walls glowed dimly enough to show bodies slumped beneath them; all were in clergymen's robes, bound by the ankles or wrists, and none were moving.

A draft blowing in through the opening at the top of the wall brought back the clinking as a body swayed on chains attached to the ceiling. A table beside it held all manner of twisted instruments, each one promising more pain than the last. Lynn refocused on the swaying figure, trying to scan the face in the dark, but what caught her attention were the abbot's robes.

"Abbot Orwen!" Even as she cried out the abbot's name, she knew he would not stir. The blood on his face and robes was dry, the skin pale. He'd been dead for some time.

Lynn took in a breath and let the heat spread through her veins and move her legs in bounds as she rushed away from the cata-combs, grabbing a blunt, macelike length of metal from the torture table on her way out and up the steps.

She should have recognized the unusual silence, but the angry pounding of her heart drowned out the world. It took her a moment to see the man waiting beside the Ever-Tree. He stood beneath it, behind the curved benches around the Tree. It was dark in the reflection chamber, but there was enough lantern light to recognize the man wore abbot's robes. The light also showed the gruesome mask on his face: stitched skin in an amalgamation of dead faces with holes in the eyes, mouth, and nose, and black marks circling the eyes beneath the mask. His identity was no secret. Andral.

The abbot held a handful of fallen petals and was thoughtfully dropping them at the base of the tree.

"Terribly rude, leaving a ceremony before the words have been said." He set cold, dead eyes on Lynn. "But snooping around in the dark of a house of the Seraph—that is a grievous offense. Grievous indeed."

Lynn struggled to control hard breaths. She'd fought the Madness for years. It had always been a frenzy, and she'd always known no fault lay with the afflicted. Andral seemed to have control over it, though. Like he'd given in willingly. Lynn stepped forward, her anger going cold in a mixture of shock, horror, and renewed determination. She channeled her rage into the Bond, and her eyes flared. There would be no half measures with these betrayers.

Andral looked up at the Ever-Tree. "Even Her trees are being tainted by the corruption of this world. No matter. We have been shown a new path by the True. We will cleanse the Domain of years of lies. We will bring the True Dawn."

"The only cleansing will be your own," Lynn spat.

She stepped forward, gripping the makeshift mace, but a figure stepped out of a dark hallway close to Andral wearing a similar mask, with a knife to Ferrin's throat.

"That is enough posturing, Sentinel. You will drop your weapon now," Talbot said.

Lynn glared at him, fists clenched tight, silver eyes darting around the church. The doors were closed and barred. Had the Church guard sided with the madmen, or would they come if she called out?

Talbot caught her eye and slowly shook his head. "They will not come." He smiled through his gruesome mask.

Ferrin had a look riddled with apology and fear. Alren was screaming at her, and she did not fight the voice this time.

I will not sacrifice your brother, Alren. Maybe protecting Ferrin was part of overcoming her guilt, or maybe she was just doing it to quiet Alren's screams.

Her weapon was no more than a rod with a cluster of metal at the end. Not much, but enough in the hands of a Sentinel. She slowly lowered it to the floor and held her crouch. Talbot's eyes flicked to the discarded weapon, recognizing one of his tools, perhaps.

It was all she needed.

Lynn channeled all her anger and frustration towards Vedyr. Her muscles surged, and she moved in a blur. She pulled out the old, rusty dagger she'd taken off the man in Pyrran and threw it into Talbot's forearm, close to the elbow. The priest flinched and dropped his own knife but did not scream in pain.

Ferrin broke free, scrambling to the floor after it, but Andral lunged at him from beneath the Ever-Tree, hissing, arms outstretched. Lynn grabbed the mace and jumped forward, arcing a swing from the ground straight into Andral's dead-masked face. He flew into the wall behind teeth and ribbons of blood, forming a cracked indentation in the stone, then fell to the ground and remained still.

Ferrin had stuck the knife into Talbot's gut, and both men were grappling over it. Talbot still betrayed no sign of pain and was pulling Ferrin's arm in, as if he wanted to get close enough to bite him.

Lynn drove her shoulder into the priest, then flung him away through the circular benches laid around the Ever-Tree. Talbot crashed through three of them, breaking the benches in half and sending splinters flying. Ferrin rolled away, but Talbot got up and charged, hands outstretched, his white robes stained with red where Ferrin had stabbed his gut. These conscious madmen were new, and so was the speed. He moved as fast as her, even with her Bond: faster than the girl she'd fought back in Pyrran, too.

Lynn swung her fist at his jaw and heard it crack, then grabbed the front of his tunic and threw him to the ground. He landed with a crack but barely took a breath before getting back on his feet and charging again. Lynn drove a fist into his gut, but the madman seemed to absorb the impact of the blow. He kept coming and pressed bloody hands around her neck, then fell onto her, pushing her back onto the ground.

He smiled. A broken-toothed, lopsided half smile stretched his mask as he choked the life out of her. Lynn hit his bleeding gut once, twice, three times, but his hands only pressed tighter. This wasn't like the girl. Even Vedyr's strength could not get him off her.

"I would judge you," he hissed, almost unintelligible. "But your death will cleanse this land even without judgment."

He pressed tighter, and the world around Lynn's eyes blurred. She punched and kicked, but the man was like ruin-stone. Painless, unyielding.

He became heavier, his body shaking with what felt like laughter, and she thought she saw a smear of blood going from the top of his head to his face. She opened her mouth to gasp, but nothing passed by the iron hands clamping down on her neck. She gave one last furious struggle, tried to call to Ferrin, to Vedyr.

Neither answered.

The cold spread through her, and the world slowly faded into darkness.

CHAPTER SIXTEEN

Our alchemists and engineers are the nation's pride, but your own pride is not welcome here. If you are enticed by defection to other, more primitive nations, remember that we are always willing to remind you of home, most of the time by the effects of the very poisons you neglected to understand.

— Dakhran Academy instructor's opening speech to her most recent class

The two-week march towards the Khetish capital had been enough to sour General Ashford's mood. Adrian sat upon his mare, surveying Ultenvell from afar with Derren and High Priest Lindamm beside him while Ashford dispatched one of his heralds. The newest Legion general bore a crumpled brow and distant eyes, but he seemed to manage his tone better than his expression.

"The scouts have returned, Lord Light. No attacks. All seems quiet in the city," Ashford said without looking up at Adrian. It had been weeks and Adrian still hated the title.

"Nothing?" He looked at Ashford with sleepless, dry eyes. The dryness had taken control of his tone.

"All quiet." The man's mouth twisted, but he kept his eyes straight ahead.

Adrian tried to sigh away his frustration. How had Jovu done this? How had he gained the respect of his men so completely?

"Lindamm, head to the palace. Send word of our arrival."

"Yes, Lord Light." The priest left without looking back.

"Speak, General."

Ashford's eyes slid towards Derren, and he paused for a moment, mouth working under his dirty-blond beard, but he soon turned towards Adrian. "This is not what you promised."

Adrian tilted his head. "Are you not a general of the Legion?"

"You promised I would be taken before the Pontiff."

"And you will, once we are done taking care of what the Pontiff requested of us."

Ashford shook his head. "We have come to the edge of the Domain to fight your father's battles—"

"Do not presume to know me, Ashford." Adrian's voice was rising. He had no time for this. "I am giving you a chance, and that is more than you'd ever get in Alteria. You'd still be a shadow there. But make no mistake: the Light stands in no shadow. You answer to me, here. Do I make myself clear?"

Ashford's gaze flitted towards Derren, who held it steadily in his own, then back to Adrian. He bowed his head. "Of course, Lord Light. I meant no offense . . ."

"I need your focus, Ashford, not your doubt."

"Yes, Lord Light. I'll see to the men." He bowed his head once more, mounted his horse, and rode off.

"The Light stands in no shadow?" Derren asked with a chuckle.

"They need something to respect me by. Is he going to be a problem?"

Derren shook his head. "I've asked around. He's had experience enough to know better. Sacanthan noble, lost his son in the Revolt of Merenia in Vizcarra and then two nephews. Looks like they cracked after one of the Dakhran wars. His brother had to put them down himself so they wouldn't kill the daughter. Family fell out of grace after that."

Adrian frowned. Noble families had fallen from the Seraph's grace before, but he couldn't remember any story quite like this one.

"I know," Derren said. "Wouldn't wish it even on an enemy."

"Make sure he stays in line."

"Yes, Lord Light."

"Stop calling me that in private, will you?"

Derren smirked at him, then followed as Adrian steered his mare towards Ultenvell Palace.

Adrian wore the full armor fashioned for him in Alteria. It glittered in silver and white—a shining bastion of hope to melt away the shadow hanging over the city—and people slowly crept out of gloomy doorways and darkened alcoves to bask in his presence. Their awe was for the Light, and there had been enough lessons from Father that Adrian knew to separate himself from the position, but he could not help the swell in his chest as hopeless stares lit up when they fell on him, the rekindled fire almost visible in their eyes.

The city was still dark, though—even darker than the last time he'd been here. The sky was a gray cloak hanging over them, and the patches of earth that peeked through the cobbles were so dark they looked almost black, ashen.

Adrian rode ahead of a small retinue with Derren at his side. They reached the square in front of the palace, and the procession of Khetish citizens was held behind, but the square was already full of people. They were clearly refugees. Some looked hopefully towards Adrian, but most stayed close to their tents, which had been set up among the monuments of the Seraph. The statues mimicked the ones in Alteria on a much lesser scale and mingled with statues of the old kings of Khet, who frowned down on Adrian as he approached the lightly guarded palace gates. Lindamm was waiting there, and Ashford joined them, riding silently behind. The sourness had left his expression.

There were no guards ushering them to the throne room this time. It seemed Garrick had diverted all his forces north, but leaving the palace so lightly guarded sent a stab of irritation through Adrian. Myrra was too exposed. He cursed silently and pushed the doors to the throne room open.

A dozen guards surrounded the throne, but it was not Garrick sitting upon it. Addo looked down at him instead.

"Welcome back, my friend."

The chamber was unchanged, apart from a faint stain of dried blood on the stone steps leading to the governor's chair.

Raklin stood beside the throne, seeming to have gathered even more ruin-stone pendants around his neck, and his wisps of white hair were wilder. "My prince, . . . welcome. You have come at our time of greatest need!" His eyes still had dark bags under them. It seemed like Adrian was not the only one eluded by sleep.

"We received word of attacks in the north, the ports being abandoned," Derren said.

"My uncle left for Milsport as soon as word reached the palace. He intends to deal with it himself."

"He's the governor. He shouldn't be on the front lines," Lindamm said.

"Yet, in Khet, we still bow to his will," Raklin said—a colder tone reserved for the priest.

"And he left you in charge?" Adrian pointed a look towards Addo.

"A burden, my friend. One you undoubtedly know too well, but one that must be borne all the same. Past grievances have been resolved, however." Addo smiled. "I hope we can mend our bridges as well, Adrian. We are of one nation now."

"Perhaps, once this is dealt with." He turned to Raklin. "The Legion has grown, and we have brought aid to the Khetish people as promised, Abbot Raklin. We will end these attacks and march to the governor's aid." Adrian turned to Addo. "You have men to lead us north?"

"Of course," Addo said.

Raklin stepped forward, wringing his hands. "Your help is much appreciated, Lord Light. However, with Governor Garrick taking most of the men, tempers within the city have been"—he looked around at the twitchy guards—"unstable. If more men are to accompany you, I fear the city would be left too exposed."

Adrian eyed the abbot. Was he trying to tell him something or just leveraging Myrra?

"I will leave a unit behind."

"I can stay," Ashford said.

Adrian's gaze moved to the general. Trying to make up for his previous complaints, perhaps? Or did he think his deeds protecting Ultenvell had a better chance of reaching the Pontiff than marching even further north? It didn't matter. Adrian had to resolve this. Myrra was waiting.

"General Ashford will remain, then. Pick out three hundred, General. The rest come with me."

He looked to Raklin, the desire to check on Myrra burning within him, but he knew the abbot would concede little until the immediate threat was dealt with. The priest gave him a smile, but no other sign.

He offers me nothing but faith. It tasted sour, but Adrian swallowed it down and left with Derren in tow.

"Tell Ashford to keep an eye on Addo. I don't trust him with that chair."

Derren nodded but hesitated before leaving. "Can we spare the men?"

We'll have to. I can't afford to anger Raklin.

"We still have over two thousand, and Garrick has men of his own to add once we find him. Our numbers should be enough."

"I've never liked 'should.'"

"It'll have to do. Ready the troops. We march at once."

The northern weather seemed as intent as the Legion to purify the Domain, but it was doing so in the form of a torrential rain, preventing the slow-moving army from seeing further than a few strides.

Adrian tried to make out the column snaking its way across the steadily degrading roads. The dry earth had looked almost like ash at some points, gray-black and puffing up with the heavy footfalls of marching men. The rain had been appreciated when it arrived, but it quickly went from sodden inconvenience to relentless aggravation, and now the water was icy cold on Adrian's skin.

"How much further?" Adrian asked one of the Khetish captains. Emric, he thought his name was.

"Over five leagues 'til the first port town, my lord. Should take us a few more hours," the captain answered in a thick Khetish accent. "Longer in the rain."

Derren was shouting at a soldier who'd led a wagon into a rut that had been deepening for the past hour. It had become a hole large enough that one of the wagon's wheels was submerged, only part of the spokes above water.

The mighty Legion, defeated by rain and mud. Derren had warned him against the possibility of rain, but this was the more direct path, and the quicker he dealt with these madmen, the quicker he'd get back to Myrra. His decision was proving a costly one, however. Had Jovu struggled like this in his campaigns?

The wagon blocked the narrow section of traversable road, while the men ahead marched uncertainly away, leaving their comrades behind. No use pushing them in this deluge. Garrick would have to wait a little longer. So would Myrra.

"We camp here. Send word for the forerunners to return and start setting up wherever you can pitch the tents."

"Yes, Lord Light."

There it was: that title again. The moniker didn't sound as ridiculous as it had in the first days since marching away from Alteria, but maybe that was just how deep Adrian had fallen into it. Maybe the Seraph could show him the true meaning of the name, or . . . stop the rain, perhaps? He might have an inkling of faith in Her then.

The Khetish captains set the camps up efficiently. His own generals were too occupied having to deal with men grumbling about the weather and the lack of fighting. Men were always calling for battle until they'd been run through and their guts were spilling out onto the ground. How long would it take for them to regret their complaints? A dead comrade? A severed limb?

The Khetish captains were the first to step into Adrian's command tent. The one Adrian had been talking to earlier, Emric, seemed out of place at the table. He took a position at the back of the tent and watched while both of his companions pointed out lines and compared numbers.

"The southern approach will be better. The rain will stop. We shouldn't divert the path," Hart, one of the captains, argued to profuse protests from Nevin, the other.

"Even if this bloody rain stops," Nevin said, "it'll be even worse than what we've already come across. Thick with trees too, easy to ambush."

"What do you suggest then, Nevin? Cut down the trees, fly over? I don't see any Sentinels with us."

Emric stepped forward. "We should go through the mountains."

"The mountains?" Captain Hart said. "Are you ill, Emric? That'll be at least two more days."

"It'll be drier and give us a view over the land," Emric said. "Two more days might be what we need to dig ourselves out of the muck if—"

"Two days? In this weather?" Burnham had barged into the tent. He was followed by Derren and two other Legion captains: Gotzon and Iker. "Where is your Khetish general, soldier?" He gave a derisive look towards Emric. "Perhaps we could get a moderately less laughable plan of action out of him."

Emric looked calmly towards Derren. "Khet is a province of Othonea. My general is the same as yours."

Burnham shot a look towards Derren, then mumbled something under his breath with a glare back at Emric. The captain smiled politely, and Adrian found his own lips were mirroring the Khetish captain's.

"Have the forerunners returned?" High Priest Lindamm said.

"Not yet," Captain Nevin answered.

"Damn savages," Iker said. "I swear, Gotzon, if you ever mean to be taken seriously, you need to stop employing those blasted clanfolk."

"They're better scouts than most," Gotzon said.

Iker shook his head. "What do you know about——"

"We are not here to discuss scouting, captains," Adrian said, with a tinge of irritation coloring his tone. "Gotzon. You'd better start getting me information. Send out more scouts if you must, and find out why the others haven't returned yet."

"Yes, Lord Light."

Adrian turned to the Khetish captains, "Can we make the trek through——"

Men's screams cut through the tent, followed by the clashing of blades. The officers whirled around, most of them already drawing weapons.

"Go!" Adrian said.

He rushed out, and the wind brought a chill along with the smell of burning tents and yelling from his men.

"Invaders!"

Then, after a moment, "Fire! Fire! On the northern edge!"

Adrian almost laughed, but he settled for a shake of the head. The rain had stopped just in time for fire to spread effectively in the camp. That was what faith and prayer had brought them.

"Derren," Adrian commanded. "Get your men to the north edge. Deal with the fire. Burnham, push the invaders outwards. The tents will be a maze. Deny them the cover."

They left without salutes, the chaos of battle weighing on them. Adrian turned to Emric. The other two captains had already gone after Derren.

"You're with me."

Emric nodded and Adrian strode off. He made his way through the tents, carefully turning corners to avoid ambushes from the enemy or wayward blades from startled allies. The din of battle seemed to come from the western edge of the camp now, and men were running aimlessly in the dark.

A man tripped in front of Adrian and fell into a tent, setting it ablaze. He thrashed desperately to get out of the burning rags but seemed to only dig himself deeper. Another was stabbing every shadow around him, friend or foe a secondary consideration.

"Form up on your units! Follow your captains!" Adrian yelled.

The cries were meant to rally his men, but there was no shining armor: only darkness and screams much louder than his own.

He turned to Emric. "We must——"

The pommel of the captain's sword bludgeoned Adrian's skull, and the edges of his vision blurred. The second blow had him on the ground with the taste of earth and blood on his tongue. Adrian lifted his head just enough to see the muddled outline of the Khetish captain standing over him.

That's where faith gets you was the only thought running through his mind as it slowly faded into shadow.

CHAPTER SEVENTEEN

The Earth-Breakers consumed our ancestor-stone, believing it would bring them power, yet Tedros slew them all the same. The ancestor-stones that remain today are holy relics of Tedros's power and a symbol of his protection, but many still lie deep in the Earth.

— Tales of the Ronar

The pack of training gear rattled as Nasha trudged along the path.

Heading towards the arena reminded her of the trial, as if she was stepping towards her own execution again. She knew Shai wouldn't be happy, but she'd expected a confrontation, at least: the chance to have words before training to try to fix things.

There had been nothing, and Nasha could only hope the girl would show up. There were few things she could do without a haven, and fighting was definitely not among them.

The sun was rising over the bowl-like arena of the Ronar. Nasha paused at the edge of the circular stone steps that descended layer by layer into a wide beaten-earth ring. Her hopes melted away when she saw only four figures waiting at the center of the arena. She made her way down the steps, trying to push away the anxiousness pressing at her ribs, but what took her thoughts were the memories of her own Proving.

She'd been confident back then. Mansa had been Warden, not Oringo, and he'd drilled the initiates hard and had focused even harder on Nasha's training in private. No other initiate had gotten that, but the hope that she'd stepped into the arena with was a false one. She'd slaughtered all of them: the enemy initiates and her own companions. None of them had expected it, and neither had the Lothrak Warden. She was lucky it had been against the nomadic Lothrak clan. Their Provings had always been held in smaller, more private groups, their nomadic nature weighing heavier than their will to watch young ones killing each other, it seemed.

There hadn't been much of a crowd, and thankfully, the other Roots and Chief had stayed to attend to the village rather than taking the long trek towards the icy Lothrak mountains to the south. What happened in that Proving was new, though. No initiate had ever killed a Warden, but Nasha was not proud of it. She could barely remember how she'd done it, and she'd barely regained consciousness after. Even if life had to be returned to the Earth, it was the Earth-Breakers, the monsters, who'd betrayed their own, and Nasha would not let herself become that—not consciously, at least.

She breathed out as she paced over the final step into the dusty arena battleground. Things would have to be different this time.

Nasha eyed the four initiates: Berg, Zima, Verena, and Devu, all of them eager-eyed and flooding Nasha with their mixture of anxiousness, excitement, and fear. Her heart beat faster, and her muscles brimmed with anticipation. She couldn't name what came from who, but she was sure these feelings were not her own, and they'd only rise when the fighting began. Nasha stayed conscious of her curse's warning signs, leaving some distance between her and the initiates.

Get through this.

She dropped the sack of gear on the ground.

"How many of you have ever held a weapon?"

Nasha knew the answer. Slopers were not permitted blades: they had no training, no skill, and were too close to the Zaruni for the village to allow it. Zima seemed to stir, but Devu stepped forward before her, probably having held a blade with Bahar. The others remained still.

"Good. You'll be the Warden, then." Nasha pulled out a dull machete. "The rest of you, pick one." She nudged the pack with her foot. "Then try to get past Devu. Swap when one of you gets another weapon out of the bag."

"But . . ." Verena was frowning at her. "We know nothing of weapons."

"You won't learn by standing there. And that is not the focus. All you need is to get past the Warden and pick up the ancestor-stone. Only one of you needs to lift it—not touch, lift—but you will need to coordinate your attack. Never give your back to the Warden if he is not engaged, and do not try to kill him. If you do, you'll likely end up dead yourself."

Nasha's memories of her own Proving threatened to flood her mind again, but she pushed them down. She dug her nails into her palms, trying to use the pain to focus herself away from their ever-rising anxiousness. It was a strain, though, and her muscles were starting to ache. She strode towards the lowest of the circular steps and sat there, breathing out as the distance softened the pressure of their emotions. Just a little.

"Begin."

The initiates were worse than she'd guessed. Devu knew the basics, at least, but the rest stumbled around like dazed bats in sunlight. Still, Devu could not hold back three of them, and they all eventually swapped roles, gaining the bruises to prove it.

They were only four initiates, but their emotions were intensified by the fighting. Nasha felt each strike, her stamina whittling away as she fought her own battle. Her breaths had already quickened, even at a distance. She wasn't sure how she'd spend entire days with them.

"Warden?"

The voice came from behind her, and Nasha turned to find two figures, a man and a woman, standing a few steps above. She'd been so lost in her defenses that she had failed to recognize the new emotions approaching.

"I am Anaya," the woman said. She had short-cropped hair and a scar running down the right side of her face. The man beside her had hair that fell to his shoulders in woven braids. "This is Bedri. Mansa sent us."

Nasha jerked her head behind her. "They're greener than spring. You'll need to whip them into shape."

Bedri frowned at the initiates. "You're missing one."

Nasha nodded, already moving ponderously up the steps. "I know."

Nasha made her way up the familiar narrow lanes she'd always taken on the Slopes. Her muscles ached from fighting the emotions of the initiates, but there was one last path to brave. No use lying to herself: she couldn't do this without Shai. It was close to midday, and most of the Slopers would be at the ancestor-stone mines or trying to find a day's work in the farms. Shai certainly wouldn't be among them, though.

There was movement among the unevenly built housing. Men holding the familiar Zaruni clubs prowled the streets. More than usual. Maybe they were emboldened by her recent promotion.

Nasha gritted her teeth at the notion that they thought she represented them and stayed away, using shadows where she could, moving towards the house she'd been to so many times when Ife was alive. He'd been her closest friend on the Slopes, and the only one whose emotions had offered her a refuge. Maybe it was Shai's own curse that the pattern of her emotion—the way it shot through, then lingered with fragments of secondary feelings—was the same as her father's. They stood out like stone pillars rising from the sea of emotion Nasha was always wading through, and she needed them now to get through the deepest sea she'd ever been forced to brave.

Nasha turned another corner through the maze formed by the crooked housing to either side and almost tripped over two men standing in her path. They wore the Zaruni mark on their chest and showed no surprise—they knew the Slopes like no others, and these two seemed to have been waiting for her. Two more stepped out of the shadows behind her, and Nasha's skin reacted with the prickling sensation of being surrounded by foreign emotion. The first warning.

"Hello, Warden," one of the men said.

Nasha only frowned.

"Leku would like to speak to you."

Nasha's scowl deepened. "I'm busy."

"There aren't many who are brave enough to say that to me." The voice came from behind her. She turned around to see a man with short, tight coils of hair and a wide nose. Two other Zaruni were flanking him, and Nasha was suddenly surrounded. "But I understand your position can have a boldening effect."

Nasha was already feeling the graver effects of her curse as her vision blurred on the edges. She looked up to the mountain, trying to fight it back down to just quick breaths and tingling skin, but she was too tired. The fumes kept the curse from escalating to the final stages, but she knew she probably had little more than a score of slow breaths to deal with these men. It was more than at the trial, at least.

She took the first one, then blew out and started to count silently in her mind.

"I don't have much time," Nasha said.

"This will only take as long as you make it, Warden." Leku smiled at her. "You find yourself in a most . . . beneficial position. One that our cause would greatly appreciate being a part of. You stood for us—"

"I did not stand for you, and I am no one's puppet." Four breaths, the blurring still strong at the edges of her vision.

Leku took a long breath of his own that took up two more of

Nasha's counts. He was taking his time with this. "Even so. I must insist that you consider our proposal. The Zaruni stand for equality among the Ronar and the Slopes. You could be of great aid in bringing our people the protection they deserve."

And their ancestor-stone tribute to the Zaruni would certainly triple.

Eight counts. Nasha pulled in more of the fumes, desperately trying to focus away from the rising trepidation of the Zaruni. Her ears were ringing, though. Maybe twenty counts had been generous.

"What would you have of me?" She wasn't considering it, but it would be best to get this out of the way.

Leku broke her a wide smile. "Information, to begin with. Once we find something we like, all we need is for you to open a door or two, facilitate the path through which supplies could flow from the village to the Slopes. You'd be reducing the need for raids. Saving the lives of our brave people who risk their safety for the cause."

Nasha blew out. Twelve counts. "I'll consider. You'll have my answer after the Proving."

Leku held her gaze for a moment. Thirteen, fourteen, fifteen counts. The brightness in her vision was beginning. Nasha breathed in, trapped the fumes in her lungs, almost coughing on the acrid feeling. The muscles in her legs were trembling. She wasn't even sure she'd have the strength to run away, but that was what every instinct was telling her to do.

Leku gave her a slow nod. "After the Proving, then. I hope you understand the gift that is our trust, Warden. Do not squander it."

Nasha moved away from the man. "I won't."

None of them followed, and as Nasha distanced herself from them, the pressure on her senses waned. The ringing vanished, and her sight refocused on the path ahead. She took a few more quick breaths and regained a hold on herself, her curse dulling to the initial tingling on her skin. The path ahead was long enough for her to regain a touch of confidence, but she knew Shai would not be happy, and her heart seemed to feel it too—its beat was quickening as she paused before Ife's old home.

The door was made of uneven wood boards, with cracks where one curved away from the other. Nasha peeked through them. No movement. She knocked, and after a moment Shai's annoyed face was looking at her. Nasha focused on the fumes instead of Shai's emotions this time.

"What do you want?" Shai asked.

Her words flared through Nasha like angry sparks.

"I'm trying to help you, Shai."

"Don't think this was what my father had in mind when you made your promise to him."

"I promised I'd take care of you and your mother and Uvo. That's what I'm trying to do."

Shai scoffed. "By making me fight Yltigg to the death?"

"Ife taught you enough. You can hold your own, and I'll be in the arena too."

"They killed him, Nasha! Like an animal. Strung him up for all to see. All because he was trying to feed his family! And now you want me to crawl back to them? Join the clan? Maybe he didn't mean that much to you, but—"

"Ife was like a brother to me, Shai! You don't know what I've been through to make sure you don't share his fate. The clan is safe, untouched by Zala's hunger. You didn't see the state of the Earth around Chatta, the corruption in his veins. I'm trying to protect you! If only you'd understand, and stop being such a—" Nasha bit back the word.

"Say it! You've left us behind. You don't care. Call me a Sloper!"

A touch of grief now. Nasha couldn't spare the strength to keep it out. There was something else as well. Regret, perhaps? Maybe it was Nasha's own.

"Look, Shai, I know how this looks, and I'm sorry I didn't warn you, but there was no time. They almost killed me, too, but now we have a chance to make something for ourselves, be part of something."

"You were part of something. Looks like we weren't good enough for you."

"Don't fool yourself, Shai. There's no safety on the Slopes. They'd cut you up and eat you if they ran out of food, and the Zaruni would do worse." The memory of Leku sent an irritated prickle across Nasha's skin. "The Earth itself rages against them. There is too much life taken from it, too much of it wasted, and no ancestor-stone wards to keep the mountain's wrath at bay. The clan is the only safe haven."

Nasha's tone was rising, taken by Shai's anger. "I'm heading back to the arena. If you want to honor your father's memory with more than angry words and a scowl, you can meet me there. Or you can sit here and wait for the fellowship of your neighbors, but I wouldn't hold my breath."

Nasha turned but paused before leaving. "I could use someone I can trust."

She walked off. Maybe she'd have to do this without Shai, after all.

The trek back to the arena was quick, and Nasha almost veered towards her hut. She'd spent enough of herself for one day, but the training was as important to her as it was to the initiates. She had to control her curse—or consume less of her strength, at least. She kept walking towards the arena.

Anaya and Bedri were sparring with the initiates, and Nasha, still fatigued from fighting off their emotions, stayed to the side, interjecting when her strength permitted it.

"You're leaving yourself open!" she shouted, shaking her head.

Berg had used his size to his disadvantage again. He was using the correct style—holding a parry blade before him to block Anaya's strikes while keeping his striking hand back for the right moment— but he put all his weight behind his blows, leaving him open to counterattacks, and Anaya had shown him his mistake with a whack to the back.

Zima was coming at Anaya now, using a different style, dancing on the balls of her feet and striking with whirling kicks that went over Anaya's head, or sometimes at her legs. The kicks were not the primary attack, though. They'd hurt if they found their target, but the leg movements were more of a decoy for the stabbing, arrow-head-like knives in her hands. These ones had rounded edges, of course.

It was a common enough style on the Slopes, and, even without the blades, one that a parent could easily initiate a child in because of its dancelike nature. It seemed Zima hadn't been effectively instructed, though. Her whirling kicks were too low, and not fast enough to mask the movement of her arms. Anaya saw through it and struck the girl's back leg, sending Zima sprawling to the ground. Both initiates would be dead if this were the Proving.

Devu was slightly more serviceable. He had the machete Nasha had given to him in hand and was trying to show Verena the correct footwork before they charged Bedri again. She'd also be dead with footwork like that—always moving forward, never to the side.

Nasha worked her jaw as the initiates failed in their drills. She almost called it a day, but Mansa had never given up on her. The least she could do was keep at it herself.

The First Tree is not lost. Get through this. You'll find it and break the curse.

Nasha chuckled to herself. Her mind still tried to convince her she could be healed, but just like the initiates, she'd probably be dead by now in the Proving as well.

If I do get out alive, though . . .

There had to be a way.

"Berg! If you leave that left side open one more time, I'll hit you myself."

The large boy nodded—shy despite his size—and shame wrinkled through Nasha. Too much, and almost certainly his. It blurred Nasha's vision for a moment, and she needed no more warning than that.

"Enough!" Nasha stood.

The initiates gathered, emotions slowly drifting away. She nodded to Anaya and Bedri, who departed up the steps unceremoniously. Nasha gave it a moment, then stepped closer to the initiates.

"Warden?" Devu had moved away from the others and was pulling her aside. "How are we doing?"

Nasha looked him over. "You draw the short stick?"

"No, it's just . . ."

"Speak your mind, Devu."

The boy hesitated, looking up at her behind the same squared features she was used to seeing in Bahar. Nasha's neck stiffened, the memory of Adda's demand rippling through her muscles.

"It's just . . . you don't seem that . . . involved."

"I've been through this, Devu. I know how it's done. Nothing will be given to you. You can't let that thinking from the Slopes prevail. You have to fight for it, learn to walk on your own."

There was a twinge of irritation prickling at her now. Devu frowned. "You got out, but you're not better than us. We're not lazy. We just—"

"You're just making excuses."

None of you have my curse.

Devu looked away, and Nasha smelled burning wood even though nothing was burning.

"You afraid of the Earth, Devu?"

"I'm afraid of dying an initiate," he said with defiance in his eyes. "You're the Warden. You're supposed to take care of us and guide us into the clan."

"Am I, now? Who told you that? Your father?"

Devu glared at her, and a wave of fury hit Nasha that was not her own. Nasha tried to move her heart away from it, but there was nothing holding Devu's rage back. There were no warning signs this time, only a distant ringing and a blinding brightness as a fire rose in her stomach, surging through her muscles but clouding her mind, burning away all she knew of herself.

He pointed a finger at her. "This may be a joke to you, and our Sloper lives may mean nothing, but they—"

She backhanded the boy before she could even think, taken by the storm he'd hurled upon her. He was sent flying and fell, sliding on the dusty arena floor.

This boy, this *Sloper* thought he could talk to her like that? She would show him. She would—

Her dwindling senses were hit with a mixture of confusion and anxiousness that shot through the rage and pulled her back into herself. Nasha looked up. Shai was at the top of the steps with a puzzled expression. Nasha breathed hard. She'd lost herself for a moment, but she instinctively latched onto the girl's emotions. A chill still ran over her skin. If there had been a crowd, she wasn't sure she'd even have noticed Shai.

Her thoughts were re-forming now, and Nasha blinked down at Devu. *I hit him. Bahar's son. I hit him. Oh Earth, I hit him!*

Saying it in her mind still did nothing to help her accept it. She kneeled beside the boy and offered a hand. Her words had escaped her, and it was the best she could do in the way of apology, but it was not enough.

Devu got up without help and walked away. The other initiates slunk out behind him, but Nasha did not object. Safer to keep them away.

"Is that why you wanted me here?"

"It's been hard for all of us, Shai. It won't happen again."

Not if you help me.

Shai walked around the arena, silent for a long moment.

"You've decided to fight, then?" Nasha asked.

"No. I'm not sure I can trust you yet, but I'll practice. I need to do more than be angry that my father's gone. You're right about that, even if he wouldn't like seeing me here." Shai looked up the steps, then back at Nasha. "I'll talk to Devu and bring the initiates back tomorrow."

"Good. We'll get through this together."

Shai gave Nasha a nod, then turned and hurried out of the arena after the other initiates.

Nasha grimaced. Now that she was stabilizing, the ache in her muscles was returning. She sat in the center of the arena for a while, regaining her breath. The sun was setting, shadows growing longer. One of them moved at the top of the steps, a black shape cut out against the sky. Mansa. He made his way down, carrying a bundle wrapped in cloth.

"You tell them not to attack the Warden, or do you think any of them are as crazy as you are?"

Nasha laughed. "I doubt you'll ever meet anyone as mad as me, but you know what happened. It was the curse. I wasn't myself, didn't know what I was doing."

"Let's hope they do."

"I'm not sure I know what I'm doing now, either." Nasha's face tightened. "I hit Devu today. Not sparring—just hit him, lost control. Didn't even feel the thought coming. I hit him too hard." Her voice trembled slightly, and her chest was tight with the guilt of what she'd been asked to do with Bahar.

"We all have our days, Nasha. He'll get over it and come out better."

"What if he doesn't?"

"Can't live on questions. All we can really do is try to answer them."

"And if I can't?"

"You'll never know if you sit there feeling sorry for yourself."

Nasha frowned at him, but he was already digging into his bundle. "Here. I brought you something."

He pulled out a small bangle, wrapped in fabric painted with runes. "Hold out your arm."

"What's that?"

"A test."

Nasha didn't move. "I—"

Mansa gave a long sigh. "Are you really going to make me force it on you?"

"Fine." Nasha stretched out her arm, and he fastened the bangle. It burned. Cold.

The ice shot up her arm faster than her mind could react: no time even for fear to burn her tongue, only the instinctive widening of her eyes as she ripped the fabric and found the pulsing blue veins of ancestor-stone beneath.

Screams rang in Nasha's mind, a maddening vortex of emotion storming inside her, taking hold of her limbs, too strong for her to think, to breathe.

She flailed around the arena. Her ears were ringing, and her vision was uncomfortably bright, but a part of her still heard something far away—words, maybe. They meant nothing. Nasha let out a wild yell. No, not Nasha. Nasha was small, drowning in the back of her mind. She was—

Something hit her head, bringing her mind back for half a breath, long enough to see the man in front of her. What was his name?

"Your anchor!" he screamed, pointing.

She looked up towards the Mountain, and something else seeped in: a scent, cutting through the emotion just a little. The Mountain. The fumes. The scent that was too strong, too acrid for her to think about anything else. Strong enough to keep her grounded. A small part of her remembered.

The man had something else in his hand now. He broke it open, and the citrus flooded into her nostrils. Nasha. That was her name. She pressed her teeth together.

"Good," he said. "Breathe it in. Good."

Nasha breathed, but her memories fought her consciousness. She was running, not even knowing what from, blood and bodies all around. Had she done that? She screamed again, and this time, no scent was enough to pull her back. Blood was all she could see. Her ragged breath all she could hear, and fear, so much fear, all she could feel.

A sharp tug on her wrist, another slam to the head, and darkness engulfed her.

The sun had already set when she opened her eyes. Mansa was sitting beside her on the hard earth, but she didn't move. Every part of her felt like she'd been in a landslide.

"You're insane," she said.

"We have little time. I did what I had to."

She wanted to be angry at him, make him pay for treating her as if she was an initiate—as if she was a Sloper. But her strength was still trickling back, and even willing her anger into existence was exhausting.

"If I broke into the village . . ."

"I was prepared."

Nasha didn't doubt it. For what? was the real question. What was he willing to sacrifice? Her, maybe?

"You held on there for a moment."

"Wasn't enough."

"No. Here." He handed her a citrus peel. "Keep these with you. Try chewing on them. You've been around the trees even more than most hunters. Maybe the taste will help."

She got up slowly and placed the citrus peel between her teeth. It might even help her stop gritting them so much.

Nasha held out her arm. "Hope you really are prepared. Let's go again."

It had been three weeks, and the Proving loomed over her. Only a few days left, yet the initiates were still progressing slower than expected. Devu was constantly sour, but that was one of the few things that made her days easier. It was justified, at least, and a lot lighter than Bahar's trust. And if prevailing at the Proving wasn't hard enough, Nasha could not imagine how she'd deal with Adda.

I will not kill Bahar.

She repeated the thought, but something inside her seemed to insist she might not have a choice.

Nasha made her way down the arena's wide steps, jaw tight, hands wafting the scent of citrus. She rubbed them together and breathed in, then chewed on a fresh peel. It tasted bitter, but it brought a thin veil of hope to what she was about to try, and some hope is better than none.

They were all waiting for her in the arena: Devu, with his usual standoffish gaze; Shai, wordless, but dedicated to her motions; the others with fearful or confused expressions. None of Mansa's hunters, though. She wouldn't need them for this.

She stepped silently into the center of the ring, took out one of her obsidian hunter's knives, and stuck it in the ground.

"This is your prize." She indicated the knife behind her, then opened out her arms, blunt flint blade in one hand, weighted sling in the other.

"Begin."

They hesitated, unsure what was behind her involvement in the drill, but they soon edged uneasily around her. There was a spark in Devu's eyes. He directed a few of the initiates, too quiet for Nasha to hear, then squared his shoulders and charged at her.

His emotions preceded him, and something flashed inside Nasha, making her legs light. Devu raised his machete and let out a howl. Nasha knew the motion. All she needed was to step at the right angle to parry the blade, then strike back with the back end of her own to send his weapon flying away. The forms were clear in her mind, but something in Devu's angered cry worked its way into her, and there was only a brief tingling on her skin as a warning. The emotions were raw and powerful. They didn't take over her mind, but Nasha's feet moved too soon. She missed her parry, and the machete grazed her shoulder.

Shit. She'd been training with Mansa and the ancestor-stone, but this wasn't as simple as keeping hold of herself.

Just another reason I shouldn't be fighting.

Another flash of emotion threatened to pull her in, but Nasha bit down on the citrus peel and rebuilt her plan. Devu was distracted, maybe not expecting to have hit her. She smashed the back of his head with the pommel of her knife, sending him to his hands and knees, then retook her stance, knife ready to parry before her, sling held behind.

Hurried footsteps closed in on either side. Nasha whirled the sling round and flung a stone at Verena. She angled away from it but stumbled and fell face-first, tangling with Berg.

Movement on the other side now. Zima was a shadow moving towards the blade. Nasha let go of one of the sling handles and hurled it at Zima's legs. It wrapped around them, and she fell, sliding close to Nasha's feet. She kicked the girl away, and Zima lurched on the ground, reeling in pain.

Devu was still dazed, but Shai leaped over him, using the boy as a stepping-stone and pushing his breathless face into the ground.

She was wordless but had a smile on her lips. Another flash. Hotter this time—angry. It was either Devu with his face covered in dust or Nasha's for losing track of Shai.

Nasha's mind teetered. She was past the tingle on her skin. Her head pounded, and her vision was starting to blur. She turned too late. Shai wasn't even attacking. The jump was one of the dancelike movements Zima had employed in training, but it was not a decoy to strike at Nasha. Shai was flying straight at the knife.

The ringing filled her ears, the world bright, and a fire bloomed in Nasha's chest. It was the last warning her body would give her before she cracked. Her instinct took over then, reaching out to Shai, groping for something to hold on to. Nasha found the familiar shots of emotion from the girl, but something was different this time. Her vision grew brighter and brighter until she could see nothing but white—but there was something else. The contrast of emotions swirling around her was clear, like different colored lines, all fighting to weave their way into her. Her eyes followed them until they fell on a cluster of woven lines that seemed to shine brighter than the others.

Use it, something said at the back of her mind.

It was insane, and too much of a risk, but perhaps a necessary one. Nasha followed her instinct. She grabbed onto one of the lines, and the energy that filled Nasha was too much to hold inside.

Shai was a few handspans away from the blade, but Nasha bounded towards her, the energy she'd just absorbed making her incredibly fast. Faster than she'd ever see anyone move. The strength in her legs pushed her forward, and the wind rushed past her, howling louder just as she barreled into Shai before the initiate touched the obsidian.

Shai was sent careening away, and the thrill that was running through Nasha became a bitter taste shooting along her tongue, not like the burning wood and iron she'd become accustomed to. This was colder, more afraid. It dried out her throat, but it was smaller now, manageable, as if Nasha had consumed the emotion threatening to take over and turned it into something she couldn't explain.

Berg was paralyzed, weapons on the ground and eyes wide. Verena was on one knee beside him, also still.

"We're dead," Verena said. "We've been practicing that for days. Shai was supposed to get the knife. We're dead."

Nasha was breathing hard. No use lying to them now. "You're right. You'll have to do better."

"This was better," Berg said. "This was our best. It worked on Anaya! Devu was even practicing his greeting, clasping arms with us all like he was the Chief!"

"Didn't work on me," Nasha said. "Shouldn't practice what you haven't earned."

Even Devu's usually confident eyes were faded.

Nasha wiped sweat from her brow and put her knives away. Berg was right. Shai *should have* reached the blade, because no normal person, Warden or otherwise, would have had the speed to stop her. But Nasha had burned her emotions away, somehow using her curse to her advantage.

The cold resurfaced on her skin. She tried to ignore the tales, but she'd heard enough to know there were those who'd done things like this. Tedros had never been the one doing them, though.

I am not the monster.

Rotting Earth, she hated the tales.

Nasha gritted her teeth, looking at the initiates. If any of them were thinking about what they'd just seen, it didn't appear on their faces or in their emotions. Desperation was all Nasha got from them. They needed her and couldn't afford to think about Earth-Breakers, it seemed.

None seemed noticeably different, but she knew she'd used them, consuming their emotions. Maybe that was the path to surviving this, tales be damned.

"You're not dead," she said.

"Their Warden. They say he's brutal. He'll kill us all," Zima said.

"He won't," Nasha said. "I'll kill them faster."

Might as well try to build her own tale. None of them were real anyway.

Nasha left the initiates to their discussions and walked away. The fire that had burned in her chest had quieted now, flickering into something else. This was new, something she might have felt before, but never like this. Her curse, what she'd done with it, had given her a twisted sense of hope. Only a sliver. But some hope is better than none.

CHAPTER EIGHTEEN

Water always finds its way to a fall.

— *Popular saying in the Visslands*

Adrian's eyes fluttered open, then fell shut. His knees were being dragged across a smooth surface, and there were men talking, probably deciding how to kill him. Father's face drifted into his mind, but Adrian knew his death wouldn't hit the old man like Jovu's.

Doors crashed, and light flooded into Adrian's darkness, prying open his eyes. He blinked away the blinding white and found himself on his knees in the throne room of Ultenvell Palace. The massive windows to either side let in the light that shone on the stone, jade, and gold-woven throne, but it was not Addo sitting upon it. He was standing to the side, with Raklin occupying the chair, while Emric and the other Khetish captains stood at the bottom of the throne's steps. Raklin's hooked nose seemed sharper over his smile, and his thin neck and wisps of white hair framing his face gave him an almost skull-like appearance.

"Raklin? What is this?"

"This, my prince, is the time to reveal the true servants of the Seraph. For too long, the Domain has been befouled by false stewards leading us astray. The so-called Pontiff preaches the words but does not act accordingly. It is time for the True to rise and usher the Domain towards the True Dawn."

Adrian winced. "You're betraying the Domain?"

"Oh no! I am not the betrayer! Our journey to Alteria was enlightening. They are the ones who have forsaken the Seraph. But . . . fear not. There are still those of us willing to rekindle Her light."

Adrian struggled, but an immense brute of a man pressed down on Adrian's shoulder and squeezed. The wound from his fight in Alteria had healed, but echoes of pain still shot through his arm. He stopped moving, but his thoughts were racing. The True Dawn? Raklin had gone mad, surely.

"You . . . . I pulled you from the darkness. I made you!" Myrra flashed in his mind. "If you've done anything to her, I'll—"

"I would worry about your own well-being for now, my prince. But do not fret. The Seraph has a path laid out for us all."

Raklin eased forward, inspecting Adrian like a horse for sale. His eyes were surrounded by a grayish tinge and were even more sunken than when they had been in Alteria. His ruin-stone pendants remained the same, clattering as he moved, but the white veins through the stone seemed to glow a touch brighter now. "I'd expected a little more fight from the Light of the Legion. Shows how poorly the Pontiff has chosen."

"Ran off like a pup in heat," Addo said. "Poor Uncle's been lying cold in the dungeons, waiting for your aid."

I'll kill you, you fucking coward. I'll—

"The Light stands in no shadow but the one of his own pride, it would seem."

Adrian tried to look behind him. He recognized the voice, but it took him a moment to accept it. General Ashford was standing by the entrance with a grin on his face.

"You fucking rat!" Adrian growled. "I'll have your head for this."

"You'd need to keep your own first," Ashford said. "Don't take it personally. I simply chose the winning side."

Adrian ground the rage between his teeth. He'd trusted Ashford in his need to grow the Legion, and now Myrra was at risk because of it. "You. Fucking. Rat."

Raklin was shaking his head. "Do not fault a man for seeing the true light. It takes courage to find one's way back into it." He stood and took two slow steps towards Adrian. "It is a vicious game, is it not? The worthy have Her blessing for as long as they remain in the Seraph's grace, the unworthy doomed to be ravaged by time until their bodies wither away. But who should determine those who receive Her grace? Her *protection*? The Pontiff? He has his priests doling out blessings only to those who serve his purpose." Raklin scoffed. "Can you blame a man for seeking blessings when he has been denied by all else?"

"The worthy are not chosen by men or blessings. Blood is all that matters!" Adrian said.

"I imagine you would think that way, taking the blessings for granted, given how long your own life has been. Let me show you, then, the true power of blood." He snapped his fingers and the doors slammed open behind Adrian. It was followed by the sound of more prisoners being dragged in on their knees.

Ice crept up Adrian's spine like the breath of winter. Derren—who he'd hoped had escaped and was mounting an attack on the palace—was pushed down beside him, nose bloody and face swollen. High Priest Lindamm and the Legion captains—Burnham, Gotzon, and Iker—were brought in soon after.

Raklin smiled and beckoned. "Commander Addo."

It was a step down from governor, but Addo seemed comfortable in the new title. He handed the priest what looked like a ceremonial knife. Raklin took it, made a slight cut on his palm and closed it into a fist, then walked slowly towards Lindamm.

"The time for true cleansing is at hand."

Two guards stepped forward. One pulled back Lindamm's head,

while the other held his mouth open. The high priest tried to wriggle them off with desperate cries but barely moved. Raklin stopped before Lindamm without averting his eyes from Adrian.

"The attack in Alteria. I thought I was done. Too many had died in Khet, and I feared the Seraph had found me unworthy." Raklin held his fist above Lindamm's open mouth. "She has shown me the true path, though. Her true blessing runs through my blood now. I should thank you. You are the one who brought me there, close to Her grace."

He let a drop of blood fall onto the high priest's tongue. The guards pushed Lindamm's jaw shut and held it long enough for him to swallow.

The room grew quiet, all eyes focused on the struggling high priest of the Legion. All except for Raklin's, which were still fixed on Adrian.

After a moment, Lindamm began to writhe. The guards let go of him, and the man fell convulsing to the ground, body shaking. He let out an anguished wail, then jolted to a stop and snapped up his head, teeth bared, snarling like an animal. Raklin shook his head and walked back towards the throne.

"The Seraph reveals us all, no matter the masks we wear through life."

The ravenous high priest rushed towards Raklin, bloodshot eyes fixed on his back, but the massive guard who'd been behind Adrian stepped in front and held Lindamm by the neck, lifted him, and slammed him down. Lindamm fell face-first on the cold marble, blood from his mouth splattering the green and gold inlays. Adrian had seen men grow stronger and faster when taken by this frenzy, but its effects on Lindamm seemed like most of the madman they'd faced in Alteria: no physical benefits beyond the lack of pain. The guard stepped back, and Lindamm scrambled forward, stumbling, using his hands to keep moving across the threshold, but he soon faltered. All energy left him in a heartbeat, like a fire sputtering out after the coals had been consumed—nothing left but ash.

The high priest fell shaking again, frothing at the mouth, muscles fighting amongst themselves, twisting his body at unnatural angles. He gave a guttural howl that pierced Adrian's ears and chilled every bone in his body. Then he lay still.

Seeing the effects on the priest made it undeniable. This was the same frenzy he'd seen when leaving Ultenvell, the same that had possessed the man in Alteria and the madmen the Legion had fought. And now Raklin seemed to somehow have control over it.

If Adrian had any trace of resistance left, it was frozen and shattered. He looked sidelong at Derren; his hands were shaking, and Adrian knew it was out of fear.

Raklin sat with a sigh and stretched out his hand. One of his men rushed forward and wrapped a bandage around his bleeding palm.

"This is how we will truly cleanse Her Domain of the unworthy."

Adrian was still too rattled to answer.

"You have a choice now, Lord Light. I doubt anyone will be calling you by that title for too long, but you will still answer for your Legion." He looked Adrian up and down. "You may give up your life. Commander Addo will take control of the Legion, and your men will not suffer. Or . . ."—he indicated Lindamm's crumpled body, still twitching occasionally—"you may let the Seraph be your judge and decide who among them survives."

"And if I survive?"

"Then we will respect the choice the Seraph has made."

Adrian looked from the body to the priest. He did not believe the answer, or that there was any kind of divine judgment involved.

The abbot stood, arms open wide, ruin-stone pendants clattering.

"Let it not be said that the true servants of the Seraph are devoid of mercy. This is not a choice made lightly, and you will have the proper time to weigh your thoughts. Three days in the depths with your men should suffice. Then we will talk once more."

"Say hello to Uncle while you're down there," Addo said, an infuriating smile crossing his face.

Raklin flicked a finger, and the guards dragged Adrian and his men out.

"You can't do this, Raklin. The Pontiff will send—"

The huge guard hit Adrian on the back of the head, and his words fell out of him. Two more grabbed hold of Adrian's arms and dragged him away.

Adrian had lost track of time. His hunger gave him a vague idea, but they were given the same gruel only once a day. He hadn't slept and couldn't even if he tried.

The Ultenvell dungeons sat in complete darkness and seemed to sprawl underground as far as sound could travel. Ashford had turned a sizeable portion of the men to Raklin's cause, but close to a thousand remained, their lives hinging on Adrian's word. They crowded the surrounding cells, unseen voices rising and falling like the dissonant whispers in the mind of a madman.

He'd heard cursing, hopeless laughs, and even a word of encouragement or two. Nothing sincere, of course: more like desperate attempts at maneuvering his decision. There might have been prayers, but Adrian didn't listen to those.

He could give up his life and spare them.

Would they love me like they loved Jovu if I did? Does it even matter anymore?

Adrian leaned back against the cold stone wall and shook his head. It wasn't about his life. He'd be taking Myrra's chance away with it, and no matter how hard he tried, he could not bring himself to accept trading her life for theirs. Raklin had put him in a corner with only faith as an ally, and Adrian had seen well enough what happened to men who relied on faith.

"How long you reckon it's been, Lord Light?" Derren's voice was rough.

"No light in here, Derren. Won't be a Legion for much longer, either."

"The men's faith rests on your shoulders, Adrian. The Seraph will watch over her faithful. Over you."

"I doubt the Seraph can see us in here, and where has the

236

Legion's faith led them so far?" Adrian shook his head again. He'd had enough of good men—smart men like Derren—believing some invisible hand would be the savior from the harsh reality that had bound them. "The Seraph cares little for our affairs, Derren, and you would do well to place your trust in someone more deserving. I'm not Jovu. These men do not trust me, and whatever faith they have is in the Seraph convincing me to give up my life for theirs."

A light chuckle sounded in the dark.

"Are you . . . laughing?" Adrian asked. Derren had finally cracked, surely.

"The Seraph will look over us, whether you believe it or not."

"What makes you so sure?" Adrian couldn't keep the hard edge out of his voice.

"Jovu."

Adrian was silent. The sound of his brother's name was heavier in the dark. It battered at his chest.

"He had similar thoughts before he went. Almost let myself fall into them too when he was bleeding out . . ." Derren said.

What? He'd never heard anyone talk about the moment of his brother's death. It was blasphemous, to say the least—not that he cared. But it meant something coming from Derren.

"You can see something change in a man when he knows he's done," Derren said, "a hard set to the eyes when their faith finally leaves them. Jovu wasn't bitter, though. All he cared about was you. Made me promise to look out for his little brother."

Derren paused. "He was different in that way, too. We all preach the Faith, but it is rare to see people accept their unworthiness or the unworthiness of the ones they love. What was it your father always says about sacrifice? It always looks good when others are the ones paying the price, eh?"

He chuckled again. "But even in his final moments, Jovu could see the light you bear inside, my prince. He understood that when some lights go out, others must shine brighter."

"And I'm what? Some kind of chosen? The savior come to cleanse the Domain?" Adrian laughed a bitter laugh.

"You *have* been named Light of the Legion, my lord."

"You've let faith twist your sense, Derren. Jovu died bleeding on a foreign battlefield outside the Domain—outside even the view of the Seraph."

"Might be, but I kept faith in your brother—in the Seraph—and I will keep it in you. Faith is a choice, Adrian. Maybe the men deserve that much: to stay true to themselves instead of serving a madman, even if it can mean death."

Adrian did not have it in him to argue, but it seemed Derren was done. He shuffled off, leaving his words to be digested in the gloom. Adrian did not move from where he leaned against the cold stone. He still couldn't track how much time had gone by, but the doors eventually creaked open, and torchlight, even low as it was, almost blinded him after all this time in the dark.

"Time to choose." Raklin's smooth voice came from the shadows beyond the light.

Adrian sighed. He wasn't Jovu, and most of his men would probably protest, but maybe they deserved the choice. Maybe Adrian deserved it himself.

"We will be judged."

He looked up at a faint outline covered in shadows, but even then, he thought he could see the fire reflecting off the yellow-white sliver of Raklin's smile.

The sky was the color of a bloodless corpse, cold and covered in clouds that hid the sun, but the dull light was still enough to make the men avert their dark-acquainted eyes as they stepped into the square before the palace. They walked with manacles clinking and scraping on the rough stone, under the watchful eye of the monuments of the Seraph and the old kings of Khet. Adrian looked up, eyes slowly adjusting. The mark of the Seraph still shone bright through the gray pall hanging over them, but movement in the palace caught his eye.

Addo stood on the balcony overlooking the palace square. His thin lips were spread into a smirk, but even from here Adrian knew it was cowardice that held him up there. He'd always stayed away from the people, afraid they'd pick his pockets or mob him, and he showed little more spine before his enemies. Even with them in chains.

Adrian blew out an angry breath and looked back down. The people around them were silent, hundreds standing to watch Raklin usher in a new order, yet none dared speak louder than a whisper. No cheering, no roaring crowd. It was either fear or faith in Raklin, and neither helped untie the knot in Adrian's gut.

The men were put into a line in the center of the square and pushed onto their knees, with Adrian at the very end. Raklin wanted him to see every member of his Legion mad with rage, then still with death.

"Faithful!" Raklin's voice echoed around the square. "The Seraph sends us a message this day. She sends us a show of Her strength. She sends us men who have stumbled in darkness and have finally found Her light: men who are willing to be judged, to be cleansed for the future of Her Domain!"

The crowd muttered, with somber nods and heads bowed in reverence.

"Who among you would join them? Who among you would match the faith of these brave men? Who among you will be the first to be proven in Her new light?"

Adrian gritted his teeth. Portraying it as an act of faith was bad enough. Convincing people to do it willingly was infuriating. He wriggled against his chains, but a heavy hand fell on his shoulder. It was the same guard who had held him in the throne room. He towered over Adrian, silent, not looking down, but his firm grip spoke loudly enough.

Slowly, people trickled from the crowd. They joined the line behind Adrian, heads still bowed, some even smiling.

Adrian's rage festered in his stomach. Raklin was leading people to their deaths so he could strengthen the belief of those who remained. He was laying the foundation for his own faith by preaching life—but using the lives of trusting people as sacrifice.

Adrian had never been a religious man, but he didn't need religion to hate what he saw.

The first soldier was unshackled and led solemnly to the priest. He stared death in the eyes, trying to keep his courage. It vanished as the first drop of blood touched his tongue and he quickly lost all semblance of control over his mind, snarling, and frothing until he was struck down and discarded like a rotten apple.

"One of the weak ones," Raklin said, then ushered more forward.

Some soldiers held on longer, and Adrian kept a close eye on Raklin, trying to understand how he was doing it, but there was nothing obvious, and after the first four Legion men failed in their judgment, the rest seemed less certain of their faith. The fifth man was quailing in fear and had to be dragged, his mouth forced open.

He swallowed the blood. Nothing happened. The man looked around at the guards, confused, but eventually Raklin put his hands on the man's shoulder and raised one of his arms. There were appreciative murmurs from the crowd, and some of the men looked up wide-eyed. A clever maneuver, feeding some hope to the crowd. Adrian still wasn't sure how he was doing it, but he knew there was no judgment. Raklin was fully in control.

"This man has been deemed worthy by the Seraph! Let him join the ranks of the True!"

He was pulled aside by the guards and given clean robes. The man kneeled and wept away his fear, but Raklin did not loiter on him for long, turning to the next man. Cold stabbed at Adrian when he saw who it was.

Derren had made his way forward through the line, taken by some bout of faith. He'd fallen into the trap, certain of his worthiness and of the reward at the other end.

The foolishness of it lit a fire in Adrian, and part of him almost wanted to let the general die with his faith. But Derren had been part of Adrian's life for as long as he could remember. He was practically blood, and blood held ties. Maybe it was his own twisted sense of faith, or maybe he was too much of a coward to see the old captain killed brutally before him, but he found himself clambering to his feet, still under the watchful eye of the mountainous guard beside him.

"Stop."

Raklin tilted his head towards Adrian, needing no time to find him at the back of the line.

"I will be judged, and you will spare these men." *I'm sorry, Myrra.*

His words were enough to cause a stir in the men. The guard behind Adrian smiled and pushed him forward, and they made their way up the line.

"The leader who would pronounce himself the savior," Raklin said to the crowd. "Deemed worthiest amongst us by the fraud who calls himself the bridge between men and the Seraph. Let us test the truth in his statement. Let the Seraph's blood flow through him and reveal the true light within."

The guard unshackled Adrian and pushed him to his knees.

"All men shall be judged free," Raklin said.

The priest opened the arm that held his ceremonial knife towards the crowd, then raised his bleeding hand, and Adrian opened his mouth. He watched the drop as it slowly dribbled down, then dropped onto his tongue. He closed his eyes, taking a deep breath—his last breath.

Adrian reveled in the darkness, setting his mind free of worry. No harshness, no duty. The square was silent but for the sharp whistle of the wind. He waited for the fire to rise within him, the fevered rage to grip his empty mind.

But it didn't.

His eyes snapped open. The guards were staring at him, expectant.

Adrian rose slowly with deliberate movements, a single objective in his mind. He looked Raklin deep in the eye and saw his smile fade as he recognized Adrian's still-sane eyes. *That's the thing about faith. You can be so sure of it that you're never prepared when it fails you.*

Raklin stumbled, jaw working furiously, looking for the words to explain the Seraph's slight to his rising cause. The guards holding Adrian turned to the abbot, and that was all the distraction he needed. He took one swift step forward, grabbed the priest's hand that held the knife, turned it towards Raklin's heart, and pulled him into a deadly embrace with a scream too angered to produce words. Blood spilled out of Raklin, flowing down his clacking ruin-stone pendants, surprise still strangling him into silence.

Adrian let the man fall, lifeless, then pulled the knife out and whirled on his heel, expecting an eruption of chaos in the square.

The silence remained. Even the wind seemed to have stopped to gaze down on them. Adrian's muscles were numb, ready to spring into action. "Your false leader is dead!" he bellowed. "He has betrayed the Domain, betrayed the ancient blood of the rulers who have kept their people safe, and he has paid the price!"

"The Seraph shows Her true champion! The Light stands in no shadow!" Derren cried beside him.

Adrian pointed his knife at the guard who'd held him. "Come on, then!"

The large guard took a step forward, a few of his men behind him, weapons still raised. Adrian set his feet. Derren had grabbed Adrian's discarded manacles and was swinging them in a circle, wrists still bound.

The guard took another step and kneeled before him.

"All hail the Light of the Legion!"

Other men followed, and soon, the entire square was on its knees. A smile spread across Adrian's face, though he felt no relief. His relief remained in the dark arms of death. All that was left now was a surging confidence—the certainty of victory.

He looked at the Seraph's mark in the sky. A pious man might have said She was looking out for Adrian, aiding Her champion, but he knew better. Jovu had put his faith in the Seraph, and Adrian could still recall the scent of his brother's ashes.

This was not the Seraph's doing. She had not judged Adrian, and She had not saved him. Whatever trick Raklin had employed, he had not considered the power of the blood coursing through Adrian's veins.

Blood holds ties.

He had built the Legion, and now he'd shown he could defeat any enemy. Derren was right. His men's faith, Adrian's faith, should be placed in himself. He was the Light of the Legion, and he would stand in no shadow.

Derren drew close. "How will we trust them this time?"

"I have something in mind. Check the dungeons. Free any who were against Raklin and might join the Legion." Adrian pointed at the giant guard who'd been the first to kneel. "Keep that one close to me."

Derren nodded, and Adrian looked up towards the balcony. Addo was gone.

"And Derren." The general turned to him. "Find Addo."

CHAPTER NINETEEN

Her house watches over us, and so we must care for all that surrounds it.
Hallowed ground must be cleansed with fire, the ashes removed from her
Domain.

— *The Book of the Body*

Lynn's eyes fluttered open, then fell shut. Her face burned on one side, and shadowy lines swam in the blackness of her closed eyelids. The burning returned on the other side, sharp and cracking. So this was death, already venting its frustrations on her for avoiding it for so long. She took it quietly, knowing she deserved it. Her face stung. A voice was saying something, sounding a lot warmer than she would have expected death to sound.

"You will not die on me as well!"

A scream, really. It made her eyes open. Not death: only a disheveled Ferrin with a bruised face and wild eyes. They went wide when he realized Lynn was awake, then he blinked out streaks of tears and looked down, still on his knees, body jumping with his sobs. There was a smile on his face. Not the one Lynn was used to, but it was progress all the same.

Lynn sat up on her elbows, world still bleary but sharpening with every breath. Talbot lay in a pool of his own blood, no mask, with a rictus smile still plastered above his broken jaw. His white robes were soaked in crimson and shredded.

"How many times did you stab him?"

Ferrin looked up, composing himself. "Enough for him to stop breathing."

"Sounds about right. . . . Guess I owe you now," Lynn said. "Not many people can say they saved the life of a Sentinel."

"Makes us about even, I suppose." He shrugged. "Wouldn't have happened if I hadn't let myself get caught by them."

Wouldn't have happened if you'd told him the truth, Alren said.

The proximity of death was still uncomfortable, but Lynn reckoned she'd have to get used to it. The Madness had spread, and it would only bring more death. That madmen could stay in control was even more worrying, and these were the strongest she'd seen. Had she been blind to the changes brewing in the shadows for all these years? Her voices certainly seemed to think so.

You failed us, they said. *We died for nothing!*

Lynn looked around, trying to focus on the present. Andral's body was still lying motionless where he fell after she'd struck him.

"He's still alive," Ferrin said. "Don't know how long he'll be out, though."

Lynn stood and started ripping off strands of Talbot's robes, meaning to bind Andral, but she felt something in his robes, and it stopped her: something flat and round, with ridged edges, its weight and size familiar in her hand. A Sentinel coin.

Her breath caught. There was only one coin Lynn had ever seen broken. She would know: she'd chipped it off the first time she got through Elwin's guard—the first time he ever looked at her like a Sentinel instead of an apprentice. That Talbot had his coin meant either that Elwin was dead or that he'd left it here with Orwen. Lynn doubted the first option was true, and if Elwin was alive, Lynn knew exactly where to find him.

She closed her hand around the ruin-stone coin and tucked it away, then ripped a few more strands off Talbot's robes and bound Andral's hands and feet.

"What should we do with him?" Ferrin asked.

Lynn eyed the unconscious priest. He might have information, but she doubted they'd be able to get anything out of him.

"Chain him up in the catacombs. We'll find a priest we can trust to pass on the message to the Church to send more priests here."

Ferrin nodded. "What now?"

"I need to see someone. Alone."

"Guess I'll be watching the cart again, then." His mouth hinted at a smile. Progress.

Don't you dare leave him behind. Not now! Alren said.

Lynn sighed. Alren was right. She couldn't leave Ferrin behind. She had killed his brother and had almost let the watcher die himself. She owed it to both of them to watch over him.

Lynn nodded slowly. "Guess you'll be watching the cart."

Lynn pulled off the road and led the cart through the trees on a rocky path until they came to a pool jutting out of a crumbling cliff face. Boulders had fallen all along the base of the cliff, and the other sides were surrounded by the trees.

"You'll have to wait here," she told Ferrin. Nothing would intrude into her sanctuary.

She left him by the cart and walked up close to the edge of the fallen rocks, put one foot on the slippery stone and, with practiced movement—even after all these years—jumped onto a ledge behind one of the boulders and disappeared into a hidden tunnel.

She made her way through to the opening at the other side, then down rough-carved steps onto the circular stone platform shaped to resemble the Sign of the Breath. It sat in a much larger pool than the one outside, a moat-like body of water separating it from the treed slopes rising all around.

Elwin sat on a lump of rock beside the Ever-Tree. The sap in its well glinted, reflecting the moon and the Seraph's mark like two eyes staring out at Lynn. The liquid inside was still translucent, untainted.

Death has not yet found this place, at least.

She eased her way towards him, hand closed tight around his chipped coin. His head was tilted down and his brown hair was streaked with white and covered his face in shadow. Lynn's heart leapt. She hadn't realized how much she'd missed him, and how much she still needed his guidance.

We'll fight this together. We'll beat it together.

"I got your message," she said, holding up his amulet.

Elwin grunted and there was a flash as his eyes flit towards her, then back down. The coldness in it stomped out the hope that had risen in Lynn's chest. Something was off. Was he here to take her in, after all?

He shifted his body, revealing a package beside him.

"Got this back for you." He patted the bundle beside him. "Comes with a price, though. You'll have to talk to the commander."

Lynn squinted in the half-light, but even at this distance, her heart was already telling her what he held beside him. The shade of the cloak was unmistakable, as was the whitish gray of ruin-stone-infused fabric that could deflect any blade, her war scythe, mace, and armor protruding from under it: her Sentinel Mantle.

"Not sure I can," Lynn said, a little more tentatively.

"You'll probably have to."

"Does Leardin know you're here?"

Elwin coughed a hard laugh and shook his head. "If he did, I doubt we'd be breathing. True believer in the Breath, that one—always taking it away from people."

Lynn frowned. "We? Elwin, what's going—"

Elwin raised his head.

The whites of his eyes were like shining stones in deep pools of black, tainted skin spreading around them and towards the side of his face, almost reaching his neck. His irises were the silver color of the moon.

Every part of Lynn's skin went cold, numbing her body and mind. No thoughts, not even the voices. Her words were an entangled mass that barely made their way into cohesiveness. "Elwin . . . . No, you—"

"Looks bad, doesn't it?" The silver flashed in his eyes, like a flame was consuming everything inside him. "The Bond is all that keeps me under control." He gave a slight twist to his mouth. "You saw the bodies on the streets, in the temple in Pyrran?"

Lynn's eyes widened. "That was you?"

"Went looking for you. But it took me some time to figure out how to channel away enough of the Madness to keep myself sane—and keep Emida safe from it as well. Can't say I'm proud of what I left behind."

She could not hold back the tears. "How long have you been channeling?"

"Days, weeks . . . . Can barely count the time anymore. It's not like fighting. Don't need to use that much, and I'm lucky Emida doesn't ask for anger like Vedyr, but I can't stop it. I'll hollow out soon. I can feel it pulling me away already." He chuckled, but there was no mirth in it. "Not that it matters. End's the same. I'm still unworthy. But I'd rather go out on my own terms." He looked away. "It takes from you, you know? This Madness. Till all that's left is the rage of losing who you were. That's when you attack."

"No," she said with all the finality she could muster. Even through all that had happened, she'd kept death at bay. She wouldn't give in to it now. Not with Elwin.

"There's no other way, kid. Believe me, I've tried."

"We'll find a way! That's why you called me here, isn't it? We're stronger now than we were back then. We know what it is. We can fight it. You can fight it!"

"Wish that were true. I really do, Lynn, but you're here because I'm a coward. . . . Didn't want to die alone. And because I need you to warn the others."

Elwin got up, arms shaking, legs seeming to feel the weight of his hundreds of years. He picked up one of the halves of her weapon, the war scythe, an elongated blade curving only slightly at the tip, equally deadly for slashing or stabbing.

"Keep hold of it this time. It'll help you remember. You are a Sentinel of the Breath, and you are stronger than this Madness."

Lynn looked away, not wanting to show the tears, but as soon as they'd welled up, she'd known there was no saving him.

Did you struggle like this with us? Or was it easier then?

Lynn shook her head like a swarm of insects was stinging at her mind.

They were all there: Alren, Roki, Dentos, Cara. Even a few of the others she'd killed. Some laughing, some sad at what was about to come, but none stronger than the presence looking over her shoulder. That old familiar dread. Guilty, powerful, unrelenting.

"How? How am I stronger, El? It's taken even you!"

Elwin's hand fell on her shoulder. "It's what the Seraph has chosen." He gave her a resigned smile and placed the scythe in her hand. "There's a reason they call us Sentinels, Lynn. We are the ones who take on the burden of death so that others won't have to. We are the ones who have the faith to know the death we deal is for the good of the Domain. We are the ones strong enough to not dwell on it."

Lynn looked down. Even now, he was still doling out lessons. "Then I am truly broken." Her eyes moved to the scythe. "I am not worthy of this—not worthy of the Mantle."

"The Seraph would have already taken you if that were the case." Elwin inhaled, then blew out with an effort. "You need to make peace, Lynn, with the ones you killed. Their shadows will only lead you astray. Your faith must guide you."

He looked up at the Seraph's mark.

"You'll need Leardin. This is bigger than him, bigger than all of us. We've stopped it before. You can do it again."

"Did it need to be here?" The weapon was trembling in Lynn's hand.

"Rather do it somewhere I know She's watching. Make sure to burn me, eh? Keep the place clean."

Lynn tried taking a deep breath, but it gave her little relent from the tears.

Elwin closed his eyes. His body was shaking, almost gone.

"Thank you," he said, trembling, weak. "For being here—for always being here."

Elwin exhaled and smiled at her, frozen for a moment, then his expression faltered, and his body fell to the ground, shaking, convulsing, until he finally lay still.

Lynn screamed out the pain, heart so tight it felt like it would stop. She dove into her Bond, unable to take the pain, the anger, on her own.

Seraph, where are you? Why do you not look after your faithful—

Elwin's hand twitched, and a flicker rose in Lynn's chest. The Seraph had heard her.

The hope was quashed when Lynn saw his eyes. Empty. Nothing of what she'd known in them. Elwin looked at her, and his mouth changed into a snarl. He wasn't there: it was only the Madness.

Panic gripped Lynn's heart as he edged closer through slow, ponderous steps. He shambled across the stone like some starved animal, thirsty for her life, yet unable to gather enough strength to become a threat.

There was nothing left in him. He'd hollowed out and should have been dead, but the Madness had strung him up like some demented puppet. It was as if it was taunting her, flaunting her failure through the twisted facsimile of her mentor.

Elwin tripped, but kept crawling towards her on the ground. There was a trace of silver in his eyes, and for a moment, Lynn thought she could read the expression in them, like the last shred of sanity, begging for a release he was unable to attain himself.

Lynn didn't want it, couldn't imagine it, but it was unescapable now. It was all she had left to offer him. Death was heavy beside her, tainted steps trespassing on her holy ground, invited in by the very man who she thought would always keep her safe from its curse.

She tried another hard breath, then sighed it away. Once, twice, three times. Had the air become damp, or was it just her tears? It stuck on her skin, clung to her flared nostrils as she labored to keep herself under control.

Her blade rose, and so did the cold inside. The icy voice of death spread the numbness through her fingers and gripped her lungs, expectant, like a father waiting for another babe to be delivered into his arms.

Elwin crawled closer and Lynn held her breath, scythe raised, muscles quivering. Then she dug the blade deep into the back of his neck. His body stilled. His fingers relaxed. The blood flowed, pulling his life out into the ridged lines of the Sign of the Breath etched into the stone beneath.

Searing tears streaked down her face, and cold hands grasped her heart. They squeezed tighter with every beat, making it colder and colder, until it was nothing but a shard of burning ice stabbing at the inside of her chest.

Lynn stayed away from the body. For a long time, her only companions were the sound of moving water around the platform and the cold burning in her lungs.

She tried focusing on what Elwin had said—tried convincing herself that he'd have brought a lot more death than his own to the Domain. But it was a fragile defense against the harsh laughter in her mind. Not her voices this time. Even they were silent, hidden in dark corners, chased away by the undeniable voice of death.

I always knew you'd be back. Let us never be apart again.

Lynn got to her feet. Death would not leave her, but she could remove it from Elwin's stare. She shuffled towards the body, each leg weighing twice as much, then kneeled by it. She closed his eyes and stroked his hair, smearing the tawny brown with the blood on her hands. She'd need to burn the body. Seraph's blood, she hated tending to corpses.

She stepped into the trees and found a branch thick enough to use as a torch, then went back to the Ever-Tree and plucked a few of the petals. None had fallen here, and new ones sprouted almost instantly. Lynn dipped the branch into the pool of sap, then rolled it around in the petals and put it down. Now all she needed was a spark.

She touched her hand to the Ever-Tree and pulled on the Bond. She wasn't giving anger to Vedyr this time: she was taking it. It flooded into her, burning hotter and hotter, heightened by the Tree.

Lynn opened her other hand and a silver flame flickered into life, floating on her trembling palm. Its heat coursed through her veins, taking pieces of her away.

She let go of the Tree and quickly brought the flame to the torch. It lit up, and the fire in Lynn's hand sputtered out. Breathing hard, she waited a moment to let her body recover from the colossal effort of willing the flame—even small as it was—into existence.

She moved to Elwin's side and looked up at the Seraph's mark. It was larger and brighter than the moon now.

Why do you make it so hard to understand the path?

She looked down at the body. She had to do this. It was what was expected and what he told her to do. But her arm didn't move. It began to shake instead, and the tears returned.

I can't. I'm sorry, El. I can't do it.

She looked up at the mark again. *You'll have to judge him.*

Coward.

Lynn threw away the torch.

Their ground would be tainted, but she'd had enough. She'd been trying to escape death, afraid of it, but she couldn't avoid it. Not anymore. Maybe it was time to stop running. She hadn't been there for Elwin, hadn't been there for the Domain. The least she could do was give him a chance. He still saw her as a Sentinel. She'd have to honor that.

Lynn washed her hands in the ring of water around the platform, folded Elwin's arms, cleaned the blood off his hair and face, then brought him to lie beneath the Ever-Tree. She crouched down, then cupped her hands, and slowly scooped and covered him in the sap that would preserve his body.

She let it harden, then got up and carried him in her arms. Lynn couldn't judge him, but Leardin could keep the body preserved until the Promised Dawn. The commander would probably kill her on sight, but if that was what Elwin needed to survive, she'd gladly give up her life.

She'd been searching for redemption in the shadows for long enough. Maybe it was time she stepped out into the light.

CHAPTER TWENTY

Tedros made peace with the Domain, but once he was gone, his people broke apart into four clans: Ronar, Yltigg, Lothrak, and Hagun. They had their share of battles, but war can only last so long, and the chiefs eventually found the wisdom to settle their differences, ushering in the Era of the Long Peace.

— *Tales of the Ronar*

The trees thinned out as they approached the pass leading to the Yltigg peaks. It was nothing like the Ronar Great Mountain: no rich earth, no scents riding the wind, all hard rock and sharp edges. Their village sat atop it, on the highest of a cluster of shelves close to the summit, while the arena was positioned well below the Yltigg village, on a wide shelf of its own halfway up the mountain. It was better that way, Nasha supposed. She was closer to the base if she needed to escape. Not a concern they should have, but one that stuck to the back of her mind should she lose control.

She looked back at the initiates. Sullen faces, mostly. Bahar was whispering encouragement in Devu's ear, both of them with heads bowed, yet Bahar looked even more uncomfortable than his son. No Domain-born would ever be comfortable around what was about to happen, but life had to return to the Earth. It was a necessary sacrifice to keep it whole, keep Zala sleeping. It was what kept the clans strong, the people within them safe from the lawlessness of the Slopes or the wilds. Bahar's life shouldn't be part of it, though, and Nasha still struggled with how to avoid Adda's request. Her skin prickled, sweat beading on her forehead. She made herself look away.

The Ronar column was moving closer in the straightening pass, bodies and emotions pressing in together. Nasha kept her distance from the warriors surrounding Mansa and the Chief. Tomu still had them following the Oringo instead of the Warden, but Iallo's glares were always close. Whatever he'd been harboring seemed smaller now, as distant as her days of freedom in the wilds. Nasha avoided the looks and chewed down on her citrus peel, eyes on the path ahead.

They wound up the trail until the rough sides of the cliff gave way to a wide shelf of flat rock that extended the better part of twenty strides. The Yltigg arena sat at the edge, up against a sheer drop into the canyon below.

Is this where I die?

Tomu and Jabillo went ahead, but Mansa paused beside her. "We'll get through this."

He couldn't feel emotion like Nasha, but sometimes she was almost convinced he could read her thoughts. She nodded unsteadily, and he dug his heels into his horse, hunters and warriors cantering after him on theirs. All Nasha wanted was to turn back— but she needed the clan. She followed the others, and was soon engulfed by the shadow of the Yltigg arena.

It wasn't very different from their own, except this one was high above the ground instead of sunken into it. It was an ancient relic, most of its walls ancestor-stone, at least two hundred strides across in a large circle, with wood filling out what time had chipped away. Within the beaten-earth battleground, two circular pits descended into the earth at either side. Each held a small platform in its center, with four stone pathways connecting it to the rest of the arena.

She gathered the initiates in the shadow below the square arch of the entrance, took a deep breath, and bit down tighter on the citrus peel, which was almost gone under the pressure of her teeth. There must have been at least two thousand Yltigg, probably more.

Her training with Mansa's ancestor-stone had helped, but it was like every person in the stands was seeking to tear her down, and the familiar tingling on her skin warned Nasha of what she was about to step into. She began to sweat, strength being pulled away before she even moved into the arena. Nasha focused on Shai's familiar pattern to ground herself, then threw another citrus peel into her mouth.

The Yltigg chief waited a few steps inside, arms open. He was a small man, plump as a peach in summer, but his eyes were sharp and confident. His people quieted as Tomu, Mansa, and Jabillo stepped into the ring.

"Welcome, Ronar!" the Yltigg chief said. "Far too long, far too long." He shook his head and cracked a smile, taking Tomu's massive hand in two of his own. "Welcome to the heart of our peaks!" He gestured towards the crowd. "Our people are ready to plant the seeds of our future."

He took out a knife, and Tomu did the same. Each cut a thin line in their left palm, then clasped the other's forearm with their right. They made fists with their bleeding left hands and let the blood drip to the Earth, holding each other's gazes before letting go and striding towards the stands. The Ronar were vastly outnumbered, but the chiefs had made the vow with blood. Peace was ensured, and the blood to be spilled would be only that which was agreed upon: the blood of the initiates.

Nasha's gaze followed the Ronar, then flicked back towards the opposing initiates pacing towards them at the far edge of the arena with coordinated movements, positioning themselves in warm-up stances without the need to share looks, as if they knew each other's thoughts. Not at all resembling Nasha's own shambling crew. The flicker of hope she'd allowed herself a few days ago quickly faded, and she turned to her own initiates. The color had drained from their faces, their courage blown away by the screams of the crowd above.

"Don't look at them," she snapped. "Warm up. Focus on your-selves." They scrambled about, stretching, holding stances, and moving through forms to push out the fear through their warm-up exercises. "There's nothing different. It's only noise."

Shai had a confident look about her, but Nasha caught her swallowing more than once, trying to dampen her dry throat. Bahar was close behind, as frightened as if he were about to enter the arena himself. Nasha put a hand on his shoulder, but words failed her. What could she say?

Bahar sucked at his teeth, curling in his lips. He took a deep breath, then scratched his head and looked down. If he had something to say, it was stuck. He closed his eyes for a long moment, then turned away from her, heading towards Devu.

Nasha sighed. He was not the focus. She'd have to deal with him later. She made herself look away.

The heat was mounting, sweat rolling down her back and under her vest. Her heart beat faster, her breaths quickened. The next stages of warning from her curse had already begun. Nasha unstrapped the cradle from her horse—gloved hands avoiding the touch of the ancestor-stone—and led the way into her side of the arena, her initiates trailing behind.

"Don't look up," she said before stepping into the blazing sun.

She walked along one of the stone paths over the pit on her side of the arena and positioned the cradle over the ancestor-stone pedestal on the platform in the center, then paced towards the Ronar delegation in the stands. She saluted Tomu, then Jabillo, and stopped before Mansa and clasped his forearm. He had that strange look, trying to be reassuring without knowing how. It was something: just a little more for Nasha to hold on to. A little hope is better than none.

She looked away from Mansa, and her eyes lingered on Bahar one last time before coming back to the arena. Later.

She pulled out her obsidian knives—strike and parry—and

strode to stand before one of the walkways leading to the platform where she'd placed the Cradle. Every step was like wading through water. She stopped with the pit at her back and looked over at her opponents.

The Yltigg Warden was a tall man. His muscles rippled in the sunlight, and there were scars all across his chest and arms—he'd been at this for a while. He embraced his chief, then positioned the Yltigg peak-shaped ancestor-stone and turned towards the Ronar initiates. His own initiates prowled before Nasha, never holding one position for too long, their backs to their Warden and the Ronar initiates, who were gauging the Yltigg man standing before their ancestor-stone prize. The fight wasn't among the initiates. Nasha would have to deal with these five quickly if she wanted to help her own.

Silence had taken over, but Nasha was still fighting against the pressure surrounding her. She could push back, but that would take too much out of her. There was no count in her mind, no past experience she could pull up to give her even the slightest idea of how long she'd last that way. Her training with the ancestor-stone, with the initiates themselves, had taught her enough. She needed to trust her anchor and let the emotions wash over her. She searched for Shai again, bit hard on the citrus, and left her heart open to whatever would come her way.

A crack pierced the stillness, and the crowd roared, sending waves of fire over Nasha until she was burning all over. The corners of her vision blurred, and her thoughts clouded, unable to discern among the sensations raining down from the stands. She bit harder on the citrus and searched out Shai's familiar shooting emotion. It was just enough for her to look up and focus on the Yltigg initiates rushing towards her.

Three boys came from the right, two girls from the left, and Nasha shifted into a defensive stance. Her movements came instinctively but took twice the effort in the upheaval of emotion around her. She parried a hatchet from one of the girls on her knife, but her slow movements made it impossible to counterattack. She blocked a hatchet from the second girl with her striking knife instead, muscles shaking, and kicked one of the girls into the other, then turned to the three boys on her right.

One of them slashed with a long knife, but Nasha gave two steps back, half her foot over the ledge of the pit behind her. The other two closed in, pushing more than stabbing with their spears, aiming to throw her over. Nasha ducked the first, dropping her knives, then pulled the second one's arm towards the hole. He stumbled sideways with half his body over the pit, but one of the girls she'd kicked back had gotten back to her feet and grabbed him away from the edge.

Nasha picked up her knives and rolled to the side with an effort, the long drop of the pit to her left now. She jabbed at another boy, but he jumped back, and an invisible torrent crashed into Nasha in his wake, pulling her consciousness into a whirl.

She bit down on the citrus, but her curse was unrelenting. Her vision was becoming more unfocused, threatening to dissolve into the brightness that was just a step away from cracking. She reached out for Shai again and found the girl's fear and stressed alertness. It was intense enough to halt the curse's advance but not push it back. The strength of Shai's emotions was a threat in itself, though, and Nasha missed the next spear-thrust as she was taken momentarily by fear. An instinctive jerk of her shoulder avoided a direct stab, but she took a slash to the arm.

The effort was more than she'd imagined, even without pushing back, and she wasn't fighting only these five: she was fighting the entire arena. She gave another step back, the pit still looming to her left, the opposing initiates ahead of her.

One of the boys rushed at her and whirled wide-arcing kicks. Nasha avoided them, but he slashed her leg. He had overextended, though, and she elbowed his neck, then followed through, using the momentum to fling him backwards. He hit the ground and remained there, gasping.

Nasha paced away from the pit, gritting her teeth as the wound in her leg flared in pain. The other two boys broke to the right, then came at her from one side while the girls came from the other, closing in like hungry jaws. The boys stabbed with their spears, one short, one long, and even through the fog in her mind, Nasha knew she couldn't dodge both. She took a deep stab on her shoulder from the short spear—dropping her knives again—but grabbed the long one and used its forward movement to skewer one of the girls coming from the other side, then spun sideways over the back of the boy holding the long spear to avoid the second girl's hatchet. Nasha held the spear shaft, still in the boy's hands, and broke off half of it, then stabbed the splinter into the boy's back and pushed him over into the pit. Two more lives given to the Earth. Only three more to go.

The one who'd left the short spear in her shoulder was heading straight for the Cradle now, probably thinking she wouldn't be able to reach him on her slashed leg.

Never give your back to the Warden. Even her initiates knew that.

Nasha pulled the spear from her shoulder, blood spurting, and flung it at the boy with a yell, every muscle in her arm burning with the effort. The stone tip sank into the boy's neck, and he fell with hands out, almost touching the Cradle, face in a pool of his own blood.

Nasha rolled back to her knives and stood glowering at the two remaining initiates, crushing the citrus peel under her teeth. The taste was a thin strand that kept her tethered to her consciousness, but it was fraying. The ringing in her ears had begun, and the world was growing brighter again.

I need to end this. Now.

The boy she'd elbowed was up, knives in hand and standing beside the remaining girl with the hatchet, both studying the moment to strike. Or maybe just too afraid.

She tried falling into her stance again but was hit by unbidden flashes of emotion, then more, shooting at her from the far side of the arena. Was that Shai? Devu? Had they—

They'd found their moment and were on her. The boy struck low at Nasha's bleeding leg, but she directed it wide with her parry knife, then whirled away as an overhead hatchet came striking down from the girl.

They continued their dance, but Nasha was weakening with every step. The ringing grew louder, her heart beat so fast she could hardly breathe, and the fire was blooming in her chest. It was the last step: her body's final warning before breaking. She took another cut on the arm, then a blow to her head, and stumbled back. It shifted her focus unwittingly towards the far side of the arena again.

Desperation shot through her, then left a lingering sensation that made her throat go dry. Nasha knew this. Shai. Her sensation was rising, pleading. It pulled something out of Nasha's mind, as if her body remembered the emotion somehow, delving into some feeling from her past. And there they were again: the colored lines shining brighter even than the glare overwhelming her vision.

Use it.

She spat out the citrus and swallowed down the burning taste on her tongue. The Yltigg had grown bold with their landed blows and rushed in for the final strike, but Nasha pulled in the twisting lines around her. There was no more pain, no more fatigue. Their emotions, the emotions of the arena, seemed to fuel instead of threaten her, and the energy brimmed within her.

The girl with the hatchet brought it down hard, meaning to slice Nasha's leg clean off, but Nasha moved it as if there had been no wound. She stabbed the girl under the chin, then struck the boy in the throat again with the pommel of her parry knife, crushing the breath out of him this time. The first fell silent, and the second clawed at his neck, fighting for air with a horrible scraping sound before lying still.

Nasha breathed hard. The bodies were strewn around her. She didn't know how she'd done it, but she'd consumed her curse again, and, as with her initiates in the Ronar arena, the warning signs had rolled back to the dullness on the boundaries of her vision. Still, there was no strength left in her. Whatever she'd done, it was gone now, and her whole body flared with the wounds.

Nasha gritted her teeth and dug for another citrus peel, then looked to the far side of the arena.

The spectators had gone silent, looking down on Shai and Zima, both with hands on the Yltigg ancestor-stone, but their Warden had Devu in his grip with a knife at his throat, while Berg and Verena lay sprawled out on the ground with their lives gushing out of them. She understood the silence then. It was the held breath of a clan not wanting to accept defeat, hoping their Warden could somehow protect their honor and their ancestor-stone.

Something hit Nasha at the sight of the initiates—her initiates—bleeding out, threatening to take over from within. She needed to help them, but staying on her feet was all she could manage.

The Yltigg Warden was not without injury. He bled from a cut above his eye, making him half blind, but he was still locked in a battle of wills with the Ronar initiates. If the girls made a move, Devu would be killed. If the Warden struck first, they would lift the stone, and it would be the Ronar's to take.

A sudden river of dread crashed into Nasha. It was almost as strong as the pain, cold as winter, and urgent like a storm. She didn't need to turn to recognize the voice calling out to her.

"Nasha, . . . stop this! You can stop it!" Bahar's tone was cracked, mad, desperate.

Nasha gave a small step forward but caught Mansa looking straight at her. He barely shook his head.

Bahar's voice was rising now, closer. "Nasha! Please! He's my son!"

Nasha turned to look at him, tears in his eyes as he thrashed against Mansa's hunters. "Nasha, for all that is right, save him! Save him!"

Nasha's fingers twitched. She couldn't know if the desire to save him was hers or if she was being overpowered by Bahar. Shai and Zima looked at her, expectant, waiting for the command. Her breaths were heavy, air rasping in her throat. Nasha gripped her blade, searching for whatever it was in her curse that had allowed her to move faster—anything to save Devu. But she found nothing. Shai locked her gaze on Nasha, posing the question. Nasha hesitated. She could not choose the life of one Sloper over the need of the clan. The Ronar came first. Always. But she wasn't the monster, either. Did she need to become one?

Her hesitation was answer enough, and Shai lifted the Yltigg ancestor-stone off its pedestal. The Warden's intent hit Nasha even before the knife moved. He had a twisted smile on his lips, and was looking through her, back at Bahar.

"Nasha! Nasha!! Na—"

Devu's blood rolled down his neck onto his chest, a deep valley cut into his throat. The Warden turned towards the girls but did not raise his weapon. It was over.

Nasha drew herself in, sweating, trying to maintain control, trying to keep Bahar's rage, his desolation, from taking over. It grew hotter, stronger, closer. . .

He had broken free and was charging towards her. The Warden had his back to him, guard down, probably feeling his own wounds and trusting the long peace that had stood among the clans.

Bahar stooped down, still moving forward, grabbed the dead Yltigg's spear Nasha had thrown, and hurled it at the Warden with a rage-filled howl.

And in the space of a heartbeat, the peace that had reigned among the clans was pierced along with the Yltigg Warden's heart.

The crowd was still silent, but their emotions were barreling down at Nasha even before the quiet was broken by outraged cries and stomping feet. The Yltigg in the stands erupted. Some went for the Ronar delegation, who had already jumped into the ring and assumed defensive positions around the Chief, and others came for Nasha, Zima, and Shai. Many seemed too stunned or too lost in the chaos to consciously choose a direction.

Nasha couldn't move, couldn't stop the tide that pulled her down into a bottomless sea of emotion. It was too much to hold back.

She could find no anchor to stop the dreaded ringing in her ears or the brightness in her vision. Her breaths were useless, as if her lungs were filled with water, but her heart burned with the angry fire of thousands of Yltigg until she was rage itself. There was no holding back her curse.

She cracked.

CHAPTER TWENTY-ONE

S creams filled the arena, but they were no louder than a whisper in her ears. All she felt were the waves surging their way through her, impossible to tell apart. There was no arena, no Proving, no Nasha. Only the vision she'd been plunged into.

She was in a town. Her obsidian knives gleamed in her hands, reflecting the red light of the setting sun. People were screaming, charging towards her, few weapons except for their overwhelming hatred.

She embraced the hatred and started slashing.

They came out from behind doors, jumped at her through windows, but she was somehow familiar with the paths of this town and did not need to see them to know where they were coming from.

Her blades sliced at necks and stabbed through guts, shining red even in the shadows, blood dripping from them as she darted among her enemies, the flaming fury pulling screams from her chest.

Someone called to her. She could not make out the name, but she knew it. She whirled round. Two people—a man and a woman —hands outstretched towards her, standing over the bodies of another couple.

Her heart tightened at the sight of the bodies, but the voices were urgent. "Come! Quickly!" No hatred. Something different: uncommon to her, hard to name.

She stepped towards them, knives inching slightly downward. Another step, and the town broke away, replaced by the arena. Bodies were laid out, necks sliced, and guts stabbed. Her shoulder and her leg were burning, but the pain only fed the fire within her.

The couple who'd called to her were gone. There was only a man now, familiar somehow, standing over the dead bodies of two young ones, screaming at her. "Come! Quickly!" No hatred. Something different.

Another step forward. She wanted to heed his call, but a wave rose behind him, and the hatred was there again, taking hold. It was strong. So strong it felt good—made her forget her own weakness. She chewed down on it, and the town was back. She crouched in a crumbling home, peering at the dark town square through a child's gaze.

People stormed into the square, a wild fire in their eyes, some with black stains around them. Men and women in heavy armor followed, and winged shadows blocked out the red sun.

The shadows descended, their great beasts sinking claws into the square's invaders. She was taken by the anguish of dying screams, and the fear made her small body tremble in the burned rubble where she hid.

The crumbling home faded. She was no longer a child. She held dark blades in hand, and the wild-eyed people were all around her now, some still trying to find a way out of the square, most blocking her path. They had nowhere to escape, and the rage was swirling in their eyes.

They turned on her.

She fought them back, a throbbing in her shoulder almost as angry as the fiery waves inside. Warning. Blazing through. But she did not heed it. She was the warning.

She wielded her blades like dancing flames, searing through the screams all around the square. Blood sprayed onto her face, her knives slicing through desperate folk trying to kill her, trying to escape, trying to survive.

The screams were mixed with sobbing. A man was on his knees, holding something in his arms. A body? A corpse. Blood was flowing from it onto the cobblestones. Darkness seeped from the sobbing man, reaching towards her, tendrils grasping, pulling her down, stronger even than hate.

They took hold of her, a chilling touch that spurred the fire in her instead of quelling it, challenged her to do something, anything to get rid of its icy grip.

"He was worthy. . . . Please, please . . . . He was worthy." He whispered it over and over.

Two armored men cut through the mad crowd and ran towards her. They had an anger of their own. They hacked at her with axes in both hands, but they were too slow. She stepped away from the first slash, then quickly back into range, and drove her blade between the plates of armor.

The other struck at her back. She felt nothing. She only turned and sunk her blade into the side of his skull, then pulled it out with a gush of blood.

The taste of it was cold on her tongue, like iron. It burned some of the grief away, loosening the tendrils around her heart and bringing her crashing back into the arena. This arena seemed familiar, as did the town, but it did not matter where she was. What needed to be done was the same. She kept slashing.

Two girls were close by. They held onto a stone, looking around uneasily at the crowd closing in. The girls headed for her like cubs after a mother's protection. They'd find none here. She snarled at them, and they stepped back, lost in a roil of screaming bodies that moved into the path between them.

The man who'd been calling to her had vanished as well, buried under the weight of a dozen warriors. She did not react. Maybe she had known him, but he was nothing to her now. Fire burns all: fire has no one.

Something shot through her, fervent, begging. It pulled her back to where the girls stood, and she recognized something about the way it hit her—the shooting sensation—hard and fast at first, lingering after.

One of the girls had imploring eyes fixed on her as the battle pressed relentlessly forward.

She stepped towards the girl, but her mind flashed back to the town.

A woman stood where the girl had, the same look in her eyes.

"Nasha."

It came at her in the same way the emotion had: piercing shot breaking into her, a lingering warmth afterwards. There was something familiar about that warmth, a feeling of . . . hope? The woman's last hope.

The name awakened a small part of her mind. The name was hers.

Nasha cut her way through, tearing at the raging crowd, heading towards the woman. They flooded the town square, the skin around their eyes stained black like those who'd fled the armored guards. She reached the woman, and dregs of hope drained into her.

"We need to get out of here," the woman said, inching her way back towards the tall building at the edge of the square. "We need to climb over. Hurry."

A frantic stab ran through her, and another woman blasted past them, bolting towards the building on the edge. She was skewered by a spear through her back and out the front of her chest. She screamed, and the dark tendrils of grief tightened around Nasha's heart once more. She turned to see another of the armored guards in the distance already pulling out another spear, dirty-blond hair flying in the wind and cold eyes sharper than the steel tips of her weapons.

The woman that had called Nasha's name grasped her arm, and hope shot through her again as the woman pulled her back towards the edge of the square—towards the edge of the arena.

A girl lay dead. A spear through her, but the one who'd beckoned to Nasha was pulling her towards the stands. Nasha followed. The rage was dwindling, diluted by apprehension and fear, but all of them were too weak to overthrow the hope coming from the girl before her. They reached the rough-hewn steps with her leg barely able to hold her weight, her shoulder throbbing in pain as her strength drained away with the dying rage. She wouldn't make it to the top.

Another spear flew inches from her face, and two men drew in from behind, bringing another wave of anger surging towards her. Her instincts let it in, and if part of herself had resurfaced, it was consumed by the rekindled, furious flame.

Her eyes flared, and her arm jolted with a vicious strike at the chest of one of the men, breaking bone. He rolled down the steps, and the other had little time before her knee found its way into his stomach, the open wound in her leg smearing blood on him as he doubled over. She brought down her elbow to the back of his neck, and his face cracked on the stone beneath, blood burbling from his mouth, body limp.

She turned back towards the girl, screamed, and charged. She crashed into her and was consumed by a dryness in her throat as both of them went over the edge of the arena and into the gorge below.

The anger was blown away by the howling wind rushing past her—throat dry, tongue burning, the taste of iron in her mouth—falling for an eternity before she plunged into icy water and was taken by a long darkness.

She was back in the town again. Hidden in the shadows. Afraid. Too afraid to move, too afraid to breathe. She pressed her small, trembling hands to her chest. A child's hands. Footsteps creaked on the floorboards she lay under, and she held her breath, the scent of burning wood from the buildings so strong she could taste it.

The screams were gone: only a few voices now. A flash of dirty-blond hair appeared through the cracks. Some of the voices were begging, others accusing. Some language she might have known once, but one she could not make out now.

The voices were silenced. One by one, their protests were cut short by the sound of steel slicing into flesh and bone until there was quiet but for the patter of blood dripping through the floorboards. It dripped onto her face, onto her lips, and the taste of cold iron mingled with the burning wood. She lay in a pool of warm blood, almost comfortable against the icy grip of fear that held her.

She closed her eyes and did not open them for a long time. Even after the steps had receded, even after nothing but silent darkness remained.

CHAPTER TWENTY-TWO

Samples of ruin-stone have been broken down by Dakhran alchemists,
discussed by Othonean philosophers, and studied by our own academics, but
none can find an explanation for its natural glow or the shift from blue to white
after being polished from its raw state.

— *Records from the Royal Archaeological Academy of Vizcarra*

Adrian paced down the steps towards the chapel with sweat
beading on his brow. It had taken him enough of the afternoon to make sure officers were in place to quell any lingering
threat from Raklin's followers. All that was left now was the final
stroke that would prove he was the undeniable leader of the Legion,
but he would not move forward with it before seeing Myrra.

He closed the doors behind him. They would be alone. A
private reflection, each enjoying the other's company in silence. Just
like old times.

He shuffled up the aisle, fingers closed tight around her amulet
of the Bone, heart building courage with each step. He was so

caught up in the faded images of her that Adrian only realized there was a man standing under the Ever-Tree when the shadows shifted as though the tree itself was moving.

He had an unkempt beard that was thick and full, but the rest of him was slight as a knife, willowy fingers brushing through a tome, bones protruding from under his copper skin. Not a common color in Khet, or anywhere near it. His hair was a darker shade, frayed and balding, and there were scars on his arms.

The man smiled as Adrian stepped closer to him, a repulsive show of browning teeth that smelled even worse than it looked. Adrian took a step back and was unable to stop himself from bringing his hand to cover his mouth.

"I am sorry, my lord Light. They give us very little to clean ourselves with in the depths." The man had a thick accent. Definitely not Domain-born.

"You've been in the dungeons?"

"The shifting tides have landed me in a somewhat tenuous situation, yet your Light has shone even in the most unforeseen corners, it would seem."

"Who is the priest here?"

"Priest Nasir, at your pleasure, my lord," he said with a slight bow.

"You're a priest?" Adrian couldn't keep the surprise out of his tone. "Your accent . . . . It's . . ."

"Azuri, my lord Light, but I've been in the dark for so long, I'm surprised they left me even that."

Adrian raised an eyebrow. "An Azuri priest, claiming to be an emissary of the Seraph—"

"A Priest of the Blood, my lord. My accent is the only Azuri part of me that remains."

"And do all priests carry scars like your own?"

"Only the most faithful," Nasir responded with a glint in his eye.

Adrian studied the man for a moment. "Who freed you from the cells?"

"Why, you did. Your own general was very thorough in his questioning, but alas . . ." He raised his hands and looked around the chapel. "A house of the Seraph cannot remain devoid of faith. There must always be one to tend to it."

Enough of this. He needed to get to Myrra.

"I'll need some time in the cleansing room. I do not wish to be disturbed."

"Of course, my lord Light."

Adrian gathered his courage once more and went through the back door, trying to quiet his anxious thoughts.

He was greeted by a small, empty room. A copy of *The Book of the Blood* lay on the altar in its center, and the furnace that took up one of the side walls was cold and dark. No ashes. Three stone shelves were carved into the far wall, each large enough to hold a body. Two were vacant. One was not. A flame sprung to life in Adrian's chest, and he paced across the room with a quiver in his heart.

Myrra's body lay on the shelf, and Adrian felt a deep smile pulling at his lips as he drew closer. It twisted into a grimace when he saw her face. She was preserved in the sap of the Ever-Tree, but her face was pale, and her eyes sat in dark pools of blackened skin. Adrian's heart felt like it was beating deep into his chest, sinking. They were the same markings as on the frenzied madmen he'd fought in Alteria.

A renewed wave of guilt swept over him. Had these madmen been here even before Father invaded? How had they gotten to Myrra?

He closed his hand around her medallion of the Bone and let out the breath he'd been holding, still performing the ritual she'd taught him, even if it did nothing to dull the pain without her at his side. He sat there for a while, trying to recall their final moments.

They'd been in Khet, still hoping Father would consider his proposition for an alliance, when things became heated. Maybe Syvern had heard something through his spies, or maybe he had his own plans. Whatever it was, there was a constant influx of troops, and Othonea was forced to amass its own army at the Khetish borders. Father called Adrian back to Othonea, probably more out of fear for his image if he lost another son than for Adrian's well-being, he was sure.

Adrian hadn't expected a Dakhran attempt on his life—Khet was allied with Dakhra, and there'd been Dakhran troops around the palace for some time, with no threat—but he did not deny Father's request.

Myrra had stayed, though. She was still a Dakhran princess, and Othonea would be dangerous, given the political situation. Still, he left her with the Sentinel Father had offered—Elwin. She was supposed to be safe, protected.

He could still feel the tugging at his heart when they told him, the confusion. The Sentinels were the Seraph's elite, death wielders, untouchable to those outside their order. None dared question their judgment.

Things were falling into place now. Myrra had either snapped, or the Sentinel had gone mad himself. Maybe both. But how had this madness reached them? Had it started with them?

He looked at Myrra one last time. He could still feel the warmth of her breath in their parting kiss. Adrian's constant sparring had left him with a bloody lip he thought she'd balk at. But she'd kissed him all the same—fiercer, even, as if she'd known it could be their last.

It still tasted sweet: so sweet it set Adrian pacing around the room. No matter how she'd died, it was still Myrra. She was safe, and he'd bring her back. Now he had to make sure Khet would be safe for her.

Nasir was still reading through a tome when Adrian walked out of the cleansing chamber.

"The chapel is to be vacated. You may take up rooms in the palace while I tend to the security of Khet."

Nasir had a curious look, but his expression held no resistance. "Of course, Lord Light."

He closed the tome and walked out before Adrian.

Derren waited outside with two guards behind him. "I don't know what you've set up, but they're ready for you in the square."

Adrian nodded. "You left them in darkness? Same cells as ours?"

"Yes, Lord Light," Derren said.

"And Addo?"

"Nothing yet. Hasn't tried to leave the city, though. There's no way the men would miss him at the gates."

Adrian nodded, then pointed at the guards behind Derren. "This door is to be guarded with your lives. No one goes in. Am I clear?"

"Y-yes, Lord Light," one of the men answered.

"Good. Derren, get more men stationed here, then meet me back at the square. Let's get on with it."

The people of Ultenvell surrounded the square as they had done when Adrian and his men were bound, but this time, it was Ashford and the three Khetish captains on their knees. The sky was still covered in clouds, and the people around the square were silent, expressions wreathed in confusion, some shuffling away, others staying, probably in search of some kind of stability in what was about to transpire. After all Khet had been through, Adrian couldn't blame them. He'd give the people something to have faith in now, though.

The hooded prisoners were bound by metal collars at their necks attached to long wooden shafts held by Legion soldiers, while Hyrkil—the massive guard Adrian had made a captain in the Legion—loomed a few steps beside them. Adrian nodded, and Hyrkil motioned for the hoods to be pulled off, revealing squinting, downtrodden faces.

Ashford blinked in the light a few times, then words were sputtering from his mouth. "Lord Light, please! I had no choice. The——"

"People of Khet!" Adrian opened his arms wide. "These are the men who thought they could betray the Domain."

"Lord Light, ple——"

Hyrkil slammed the back of Ashford's head, and he fell silent.

"These are the men who thought they could cast a shadow over the Legion! But the Light stands in no shadow. I have gone through the ordeal of their judgment. Let us see if they can do the same."

Adrian nodded to Hyrkil once more, and the large man signaled behind him. A soldier stepped forward and handed each bound man a short sword, while a second followed with a chalice in hand. It was filled with what remained of Raklin's blood.

"The blood of the traitor cannot overrule the power of true blood," Adrian said, looking around the square.

The soldier lowered the chalice to Ashford's mouth and forced it down his throat, then did the same to the struggling Khetish captains. They were still for a moment, then began to thrash— slavering, struggling against their bonds. Ashford let out sharp growls, then a horrific, rage-filled scream that had the people around the square stepping back. The guards behind them tightened their grips on the wooden shafts, straining to keep the prisoners still while Adrian prepared himself. He paced calmly to the edge of the square, took his sword from one of the guards, and was met with a frowning Derren.

"Adrian . . ."

"I know, Derren. I know."

Adrian was sure Derren did not lack faith in him, but the general had always worried too much. Adrian was the Light, and he would not shine if he let Derren's caution hide him away. When Raklin was sacrificing his soldiers before the crowd, he'd seen madmen driven to a frenzy but strengthened by it, while others only lasted seconds. These four were weak, though, and Adrian knew he could take them. There were no guarantees, but the people would not have faith in him if he did not show faith in himself.

"Adrian, you're too important to put yourself at risk like this. The Legion needs a Light. Wear your armor, at least!"

"They aren't wearing armor, and the men won't follow a flickering candle flame, Derren. I am the Light. They must be reminded of that."

Nasir was standing beside Derren with a smile on his lips. "May the Seraph watch over you, Lord Light."

Derren scowled at the man, but Adrian had no more time for words. He gave his back to them and strode towards the soldier with the chalice. Adrian took it, displayed it around to the crowd once more, then drank. He closed his eyes with a smile on his bloodstained lips. So this was what it felt like to have faith. He couldn't blame the people who believed in the blessings—the feeling was intoxicating. Still, he knew where to put his faith. It was not the Seraph protecting him but his own blood. His own power. Adrian opened his eyes. Still no effect, still sane. He raised his sword.

"Release them."

The former Legion officers were gripped by a demented rage, but they seemed conscious enough to direct it at Adrian. The soldiers released them and stepped back, and the four prisoners rushed forward. Nevin and Emric were closer, shouldering each other to get to him first. They slashed with blades and nails, but Adrian was ready. He kept his distance and drove his sword through Nevin's mouth, twisted it, then heaved the man aside onto Emric and kicked Nevin off his sword, throwing both to the ground.

Hart had stumbled, but Ashford was on him now. He was larger than Adrian and swung his blade like it was a butcher's cleaver, eager to split Adrian in half. Adrian parried the first blow and dug his fist into Ashford's ribs, but the man barely flinched, and he cleaved at Adrian once more. Adrian blocked, gritting his teeth with the effort. He held his sword in both hands, focused on Ashford, and only realized Hart was on him when rabid teeth sunk into his shoulder just as another of Ashford's strikes came down. Adrian deflected Ashford's blade and whirled to the side, avoiding a stab from Emric now, but Hart was dragged along as Adrian moved, clinging tight.

Hart had no regard for his own defenses. He was exposed, and Adrian dug his blade into the man's skull, splattering blood across both of them. The limp body fell away, but Emric and Ashford had closed the gap again. Adrian stepped back, turning away another stab from Emric on his blade, and kept moving sideways to avoid Ashford's slash. Ashford came again, frothing at the mouth, but Adrian stepped sideways again and rammed his injured shoulder into Emric, putting the man in the way of Ashford's overhead strike.

Ashford's sword split Emric's head in two, showering Adrian in blood and bone. His sword was stuck in Emric's skull, and Adrian used the opportunity to draw near and slide his sword into Ashford's gut and up into his heart. There was a flicker in the man's mad eyes, as if death's grasp had brought him a scrap of sanity.

"I'm glad you chose the winning side," Adrian said.

He removed his sword and let the man fall to the ground.

Adrian looked around the square, chest heaving in and out. He was covered in blood, and wrecked bodies lay around him. Not the most inspiring of images, perhaps, but if he could not gain the men's love, their fear would do. He'd just fought and killed four men. If any were inclined to betray him, he'd made it clear that only madness and death awaited them. He was not Jovu, but maybe Myrra had been right: maybe he could be better.

The Light stands in no shadow.

Adrian looked over the gathering. The men who'd followed Ashford were at the edge of the square, surrounded by Legion soldiers and bearing uncertain looks. Adrian could have them branded as traitors and executed. But there was little to gain from that.

"Men. You have been led by the false words of a heretic. Those of you who wish to join the Legion are welcome to remain where you stand. Those who do not are free to go, as long as you remember that the Light of the Legion is choosing to return your lives to you. Those who forget will be reminded by the noose."

A few shifted their feet, still uncertain, but slowly stepped away and vanished in the crowd. Most remained.

Ellana would have been proud of the preservation of life, but Father would have truly understood. Show a man death, and he will quail in his boots; give him his life, and he will forever remember who holds it. Loyalty cannot be requested. He understood that now. Blood holds ties, and the spilled blood of traitors creates the greatest ties of all.

Adrian's shoulder pulsed in pain, but he'd gladly take it. It was the price for the men's faith. The Legion would number close to five thousand strong now, and all would follow his Light. A small warmth crept into Adrian's chest. Not knowing what Jovu had died for still gnawed at him, though. A lesser man might have forgotten and moved on. But Father was not one to squander his resources, and he certainly wouldn't squander Jovu's life on something unimportant. Father would have to recognize his worth now: Adrian was sure he'd earned some answers.

This is what "nothing" looks like, Father.

Adrian turned to Derren and frowned. A guard had broken through the crowd and was whispering in Derren's ear. Adrian saw the general's eyes go wide, and the warmth in his chest turned to cold dread.

"What?" Adrian asked.

Derren's eyes were still wild. "We need to go. It's the chapel."

Adrian burst into the chapel antechamber with Derren in step and Nasir close behind. The smell of blood and voided bowels hit him before anything else, and his stomach contorted and threatened to rise out of his throat. His heart thumped—not at the sight of the dead bodies, but at the thought of what might have happened to Myrra.

"Stay here," Adrian said, then rushed forward into the chapel.

Dead guards were twisted on benches and across the aisle, but Adrian paid them no mind, continuing past towards the cleansing room. He shoved open the door with a trembling hand and froze. Myrra was gone.

His whole body was trembling now, numb, and it took him a while to feel the pain, but it was there, cutting at his insides. He breathed shallow breaths, trying to regain control, but the pain kept slashing through him until it reached his heart. Adrian let out the sorrow in a furious yell, and what he breathed back in was a cold rage that burned his lungs.

He'd fought so hard for her—killed madmen to keep her safe—and now he'd let her be taken from him again. The guilt was rising in his heart, but the rage consumed it before Adrian could produce a remorseful thought.

They'll pay. Whoever took her will pay.

He stormed out of the cleansing room and threw the chapel

doors open. Derren was in the hall ordering soldiers in all directions. Adrian turned to him, but before he could speak, one of the side doors crashed open, and two guards dragged a man in.

"We found him into the depths, my lord, trying to tunnel his way out."

Adrian grabbed the front of the man's tunic and slammed him against the wall. "Where is she?"

The man did not change his expression. He stared at Adrian, unfazed, then turned and spat blood on the floor. "You can rot in the depths, you Othonean bastard."

Adrian slammed the man against the wall again, but the prisoner only responded with a laugh. Adrian narrowed his eyes, gripped by the cold fury inside him.

"Hold him," he said to the guards. There was no time. He needed to find Myrra.

They held the man with his back to the wall, and Adrian pulled out his dagger and drove it into the man's left thigh, then twisted. The man's laugh became a scream.

"Where is she?"

The man showed him bloodstained teeth and the beginning of a snarl, but it turned into another scream as Adrian stabbed the dagger into his right thigh and twisted. Slower, this time.

"Lord Light!" Derren said, but Adrian did not heed him. Every breath put Myrra further away. He couldn't lose her. He let the prisoner's cries rise, then slowly pulled the knife up his thigh.

"It—it won't matter," the man said.

Adrian stopped the knife.

"You thought we didn't know? She brought this frenzy onto us. She tainted our nation!" The man was laughing again. "Addo's long gone by now. Took her with him."

"Where?" Adrian grated out through clenched teeth.

"You won't find him. Won't—"

Adrian pulled the knife up further and received another howl of pain.

"S-Sacantha. That's all I know. He's taking her to Sacantha.

There's more of the True there. Raklin was in contact with them—ach, please, stop. No!"

Adrian had reached the man's crotch. He stopped the knife and started twisting again.

"No, that's all I know. Please—ach!"

"Adrian!" Derren said again.

Adrian pulled out his dagger and turned to Derren. "Throw him in the depths. Let him rot."

Derren had a somber look in his eyes that sent a wave of shame through Adrian. It was clear the general did not approve, but Adrian had no time for his approval.

"Ready the men."

Derren was shaking his head. "We can't march without a high priest, Adrian. The Pontiff said he'd send candidates—"

"Nasir!"

The Azuri priest stepped towards them, seemingly unrattled by what had just transpired.

"You are now High Priest of the Legion, anointed by the Light."

"It will be an honor, Lord Light." Nasir bowed his head.

Derren was looking between them, a frown furrowing his brow. He scowled at Nasir, but Adrian gave him no chance for an objection.

He turned and strode towards the steps. "We march at once."

CHAPTER TWENTY-THREE

Some men may measure their worth in gold, and others in blood, but our actions are all the Seraph sees, and our years Her answer to the question of our worthiness.

— The Book of the Bone

The city of Durnn rose slowly on the horizon. The first rays of an orange dawn hit the sleeping buildings, reflecting off windowpanes and whitewashed walls, coloring them in the ochre glow of the waking sun. The city was surrounded by high ruin-stone walls, seemingly intent on keeping the dawn's light within.

The circular fortress itself sat above the hues of reflected light, like a stony crown upon a burning head. The deep-gray ruin-stone held its prized jewel at the center: the Sentinel Tower of Durnn. The tower had been made to stand out in Dakhran yellowstone, and it reflected its own shades of red and pink.

Lynn pulled up the cart and regarded the open fields, which formed a sharp contrast to the images rising from the depths of her memory. The growls of men, clashes of steel, and moans of the dying had been replaced with small houses looking for safety in the shadow of the fortress and farmers threshing wheat that shone red in the rising sunlight. Seemed appropriate, given how many had spilled their blood here.

Dozens of songs had been written about the battles at the gates of Durnn and its unbreachable walls, but Lynn had never understood them. Strange thing, battle songs: always framed by glory and the exploits of the brave. They almost made you forget that fear is the true ruler of the battlefield. No one ever sings about the screams; no one tells you how they'll echo in your mind. Except for that one bard—Boutros, was it? He sang it straight, shocked a few people, amused others, but it didn't last. Truth is never popular. People are always asking for it, but it's never what they want. Not really.

The thought made her eyes slide towards Ferrin.

He was looking at her, seemingly unsure why they'd stopped and if he should speak. Lynn plodded the horse along, brow furrowing.

She closed her cloak over her Sentinel Mantle and raised her cowl. "We should keep our heads low."

Ferrin gave her a puzzled look. "Isn't this supposed to be your city?"

"Not sure anymore. Best be safe for now."

Ferrin obliged, and they passed the gate with little issue, yet it was impossible to push away the unsettled feeling in her gut as they rolled into the emptier-than-expected streets.

Durnn stood at the intersection of the borders of Othonea, Vizcarra, Sacantha, and Dakhra, but, like Alteria, was a sovereign city-state of its own. It had always been alive with movement, the safety of the unassailable fortress fueling the population's natural state of hubris. They were citizens of the safest place in the world and acted as though that made them the natural protectors of the Domain, even if most hadn't even seen a blade, let alone held one.

The main street had a little more movement, but the shouting that caught Lynn's attention was not from one of merchants peddling their goods.

A man stood pointing, wide-eyed, yelling for all around him. "He has it! He has it!"

The accused had his hands up, backing away while shaking his head, but a mob was already forming.

"He'll spread it—taint the city!"

More people now. Looked like the streets weren't all that empty, after all.

Don't go, the voices said. *They'll find you.*

They were right, but they were in the shadows of her mind. Lynn looked up. The Seraph's eye still shone bright, maybe even brighter. She sighed. *Guess this is what stepping into the light looks like.*

She pulled the cart to a stop, and Ferrin gave her yet another puzzled look. "We should keep going," he said.

"We should," Lynn said before jumping off.

She left Ferrin behind and went for the mounting crowd. The accuser was still screaming, and people seemed to be joining him. The supposed madman was getting nervous, his eyes darting around at the faces closing in. He was still trying to talk them down, still trying to convince men led by fear and numbers. Lynn knew where this would end.

It started with a stone. It was small, but it opened the man's temple, and blood rushed down his face. The crowd advanced on him, then, like starving dogs onto fresh meat.

Lynn threw off her cloak and scrambled forward, pushing people out of the way, hoping her Sentinel Mantle would be authority enough to keep their numbers at bay. She reached the front of the crowd and pulled the accused back to stand behind her.

The man wore rags, but that did not make him a madman. There were none of the telltale signs around his eyes, no frenzied lust for death. His hands were over his face, and he was whimpering, begging for mercy.

The mob paused, wary looks darting from the weapons on her back to her face to the two Signs of the Breath hanging around her neck and on her chest piece.

"A Sentinel!" The lead accuser was dressed in nobleman's clothes. He turned to the people amassed behind him, pointing towards the Seraph's eye. "The Seraph sends us Her aid!" The man's arrogance was clear. Like she had been sent exclusively to serve his purpose.

"You will not touch this man," Lynn said.

The nobleman was taken aback for a moment, and the crowd waited, a ripple of doubt seeming to wash over them. Good. Doubt would hold them back. Lynn kept her eyes locked on the leader, who studied her for a moment, calculating. Then he narrowed his eyes, and a shadow of a frown creased his forehead.

"Where's your mount?"

Lynn's heart tensed, and it was all she could do not to lunge at the man.

"I've seen your kind before. Think you can outsmart us, do you? Think this is a game? I don't know why someone would impersonate a Sentinel, risk their life like—" The man's eyes widened, and he gasped as he turned towards the crowd. "She has it as well, impersonating our most holy protectors in her madness!"

The people stirred once more, teeth and glares showing, doubt dissolved by the inciter's words. Lynn took a deep breath and looked up at the Seraph's mark once more.

"Is this the path you wish me to follow?" she whispered.

Her voices' laughs were the only answer, and Lynn's eyes snapped back down as one of the men broke from the crowd and dashed towards her. She received him with a mace to the ribs. Enough to crack and leave him squirming breathless on the ground: not enough to kill.

The others didn't hesitate. They came in numbers, feeling safe in the thought that another might take the blow meant for them. Lynn set her shoulders, still favoring her mace instead of her scythe. These people were taken by fear. They did not deserve death.

A shadow passed over them, blocking out the sun. It gave the charging men no pause, but a second later, a massive shape crashed between her and the men, cracking the stones and making the ground shudder under her feet. A cloud of blinding dust rose, followed by a piercing cry that Lynn knew all too well.

The winged shadow of a griffin slowly formed in the settling dust. It towered over her, as tall as three men, eagle head regally poised and eyeing the awestricken mob; claws glinting in the sun, daring them to take another step. The Sentinel riding it was lean, and he seemed even slighter on the back of the beast, but he dismounted with practiced litheness and was in front of her before she could even lower her weapons.

He eyed the crowd with the formal, bureaucratic stare expected by a member of the city's highest authority. The nobleman was on the ground, thrown back by the impact of the griffin's descent, and people were breaking away now, the fear plain on their faces. The Sentinel's gaze fell upon the nobleman and shifted slightly. Nothing perceptible to an untrained eye, but enough for Lynn to recognize him as a more recent addition to the ranks. He was still tied to the old notions of nobility—still keeping ties to his family, perhaps.

The nobleman pointed a shaky finger at Lynn. "Sh-she is mad. She bears false signs of the Sentinels."

The Sentinel eyed him coldly, and the nobleman slunk back, his arrogance fled in the face of true authority. He got uneasily to his feet and limped away with the breaking crowd, but his words had done their job. The Sentinel was eyeing Lynn, eyes narrowed as they flitted over her Mantle.

"The punishment for impersonating a Sentinel is death," he recited.

"So I've been told."

"Tell me where you got that, and I'll make it quick." He analyzed her armor, frowning.

"Same place you got yours, most likely. Or is Olem not working the metal and stone anymore?"

The man's frown deepened at the name, but his mind was still set on death. "A slow one, then."

Lynn gritted her teeth. The brashness with which the new ones doled out the threat of death had always been irritating, but this one seemed to carry the natural arrogance of the Durnnish in him.

The man signaled, and the griffin rounded on her, but Lynn looked at the beast without flinching and called to Vedyr. Her silver eyes met the silver in the beast's, and it froze.

The man was unmoved, but there were flames behind his own silver eyes. He blasted past his griffin, swinging his mace with a speed Lynn hadn't seen in a long time. It took her a moment to react, and the man struck her in the ribs. He followed up by cuffing her cheek with his free hand, sending Lynn sprawling to the ground.

Lynn coughed, then got slowly to her feet, the Mantle absorbing most of the shock to her ribs, her pride taking the brunt of the impact to her face. She spat blood and steadied herself, then beckoned. So much for making a quiet entrance.

Her opponent took a step forward, ready to charge.

"Well now, isn't this a sight?" A flowing voice carried as if it had been blown by the wind from no particular direction. It froze Lynn's opponent in place. "I've read some obscure texts telling of the rise of the dead, but to see one so closely is quite a sight."

A copper-skinned man with piercing blue eyes stood before her, arms crossed under a heavily tangled black beard. He had a look that was hard to place, as if there was nothing in the world that could surprise him.

"Hello Rel," Lynn said. "Didn't expect a welcoming party, but it *is* always nice to be appreciated."

Rel laughed his easy laugh. It seemed to come to him as naturally as breathing and left him just as smoothly, echoing away on the wind. It had been so long that Lynn had forgotten how infectious it could be, but she kept her guard up. She'd seen that laugh disarm too many enemies to be fooled by it.

"You know how this goes," he said.

"I've got information for the commander."

"Unless it's where Elwin's hiding, he won't want it."

"Guess he's in luck then."

Rel raised an eyebrow. "That's convenient."

"Not really. I'm the one who came here. I've got him with me." Lynn pointed at the cart. "He's dead."

Rel took her in for a moment, expression hardening for the first time. He gave a pointed look at the arrogant boy who'd been fighting Lynn, who strode to the cart and lifted the tarp covering the corpse. Ferrin sat frozen with a look between fear and confusion, but the Sentinel ignored him. He looked back at Rel and nodded slowly.

"Well then, looks like we're both in luck." He took out a pair of manacles and threw them at Lynn. "Still, you know how this goes."

Lynn caught them and looked up at the Seraph's eye once more. She would not run. There was no redemption hiding in the shadows. She gave a deep sigh and fastened the manacles around her wrists, then followed Rel towards the fortress.

They walked up the steps of the tower and into the Sentinel common hall that took up the bottom story. Nothing was as she remembered. Two new statues of the Seraph flanked her way in, each with three pairs of ruin-stone wings veined with white—one had all Her wings spread wide and a sword held high; the other's wings were wrapped around Her, sheltering the Sign of the Breath in Her hands. The walls were lined with windows, but they were dwarfed by the colossal Sign of the Breath dominating the back wall. Sun shone through the glass panes, painting the ground in the Sign, forming a circle of crescent moons. That hadn't changed, at least, but the tables that had always been on either side now formed a circle of their own around it. Lynn's eyes drifted around the room, lingering on the staircases leading up to the rookery she'd rushed up so many times with a thrill in her heart.

You know Vedyr isn't here. He's left you too, Roki whispered.

Lynn looked away and breathed in, trying to recognize the familiar, mossy smell of Dakhran yellowstone, but even that seemed to have changed.

Rel marched her through the common hall, and they were greeted by at least a dozen pairs of eyes, all focused on Lynn. Some were familiar, others not so much, but a set with a hard stare pulled Lynn's focus towards them. They were the last she'd seen before leaving. She opened her mouth—

"Don't," Ildred said. "You don't get to even look at me." He spat at her feet. "You're dead, and the dead have no place here." He pulled in close, his features even sharper than she remembered. "Lucky I wasn't the one who found you. I wouldn't even have spared you the chance."

"Alright, alright, we've all got scores. Commander gets first crack," Rel said, steering Lynn past.

"Ildred's changed," Lynn said quietly as they resumed their way through one of the cold corridors of the tower.

"We all have." He didn't look at her. His own disapproval was probably buried under his stony expression, but Lynn was sure it was there.

They paused at the steps that led to Leardin's office, and Lynn edged towards them, but Rel shook his head, pointing to steps that descended to the cells. Lynn frowned at him.

"I'm sorry, Lynn, but you know how this goes."

Lynn's mind was trying to work up an answer, but the voices were laughing, making it impossible to concentrate. Rel nudged her along, and Lynn stepped down with a numbness taking hold of her legs. She'd lived in a cell back in Dalhold, but that was by choice. The Sentinel cells were only for those already branded as traitors, already awaiting death.

He led her into a cell and closed the door. "Why did you come back?"

She shrugged. "I'm done running." It might have sounded good, but it wasn't looking like the best of choices now that she was behind bars again.

Rel nodded. "It's good to see you. Commander will be down soon."

He turned and left her alone in the gloom.

Lynn sat on the cold ruin-stone slab of the cell, chest tight, but she didn't have to wait long. Footfalls soon echoed down the steps, and Commander Leardin emerged from the shadows. There was an odd respite to the fact that the commander had not changed since she last saw him: same gold-white hair so bright it almost hurt to look at, a neatly trimmed beard and mustache framing his squared face, and a cold, almost detached expression in the eyes of a man who'd maybe seen too much throughout his over two hundred years.

"Commander," Lynn said.

Leardin stood sideways to her, looking through a barred window, with a slash of setting sunlight falling on half his face. "Have you come here to die?"

She'd considered it once, but that was no longer the case. "No, Commander."

"You should temper your expectations, then."

"The Domain is more important than any single life, Commander. All I ask is a moment, if—"

"You are in no position to ask."

Lynn fell silent.

Leardin was still looking through the beams of light filtering through the window, motes of dust floating before him. "You killed him?"

Lynn swallowed the bitter taste in her mouth. "I did."

"Why?"

"He . . . didn't tell you?"

The commander's eyes fell on her for the first time, and he frowned.

"He had it," she breathed. "The Madness. I thought we ended it. We dealt with all of them. . . . But it's back. Stronger."

Leardin let out a slow breath. "Thinking we could kill even the memory of it was a mistake. We should have told the rulers." He looked out the window again. "I've had my mistakes, but at least I've been here, ready to fight it. Where were you?"

Cold was spreading up Lynn's spine—the same she'd felt when she was looking her companions in the face, not wanting to believe it.

"I'm sorry, Commander. I . . . wouldn't have been any help in the state I was in. I couldn't stay."

"And the Domain has suffered for it." Leardin was shaking his head. "I don't like it, but I am the commander of the Sentinels, and there are hard choices I must make."

This was it, then. He'd already had his mind made up long before she got here. Lynn bowed her head. The cold that had spread up her spine now turned to icy hands—death's hands—resting on her shoulders.

Fool! You thought you could walk in here and be forgiven? Dentos screamed at her.

The voices had been right. She'd killed them for nothing, and now she would pay the price.

"I have betrayed the faith of the Sentinels. I was not strong enough in my faith to be called one of you, but Elwin did nothing wrong. Take my life. I deserve it. But keep him for the Seraph's judgment."

Leardin chuckled. "I doubt Princess Myrra's cold body would agree with that."

Lynn's eyes shot upward. "What?"

Leardin shrugged. "They haven't let anyone get close to the body back in Khet, it seems, but if he had it . . ."

"Could have gotten it from her," Lynn mumbled, still feeling the need to protect her mentor somehow.

"We are not here to discuss Elwin."

He stepped closer and opened her cell. Lynn looked down and raised her arms to be taken away, probably to be paraded and judged before her old companions. Ildred would probably be the one to place the noose around her neck.

You'll be joining us soon.

The commander paused before her, then there was the clink of keys, and he removed her manacles. Lynn turned confused eyes onto him, muscles frozen.

"Any sane man would have you swinging from the rookery, but these are insane times." The commander worked his jaw as though he had swallowed something sour. "I need you," he said, tone loaded with reluctance.

Lynn's confusion was plastered on her face now, but the commander pressed on.

"They're organized and outnumber us by far more than I'd like to admit. They want to seem incoherent, but no enemy survives this long on madness alone. You've fought it, seen how it's changed. No one else in the ranks has, . . . other than Rel and myself, and even with you, that is far too few.

"I will keep Elwin's body, but the price is not your life. It is your allegiance. Help us fight the Madness once more. Show you are still worthy of the Mantle you wear."

Lynn swallowed hard. "They won't like it."

"Neither do I, but here we are."

You don't deserve this. You shouldn't be here! You'll bring death upon them again. Alren's voice was furious, but it was telling her to run, and Lynn had promised. No more running, no more hiding.

A true Sentinel does not flee from death.

"Some are stronger. Some barely last for a breath. I don't know why," Lynn said.

"That's a start. You can find out more once you're standing with us again."

She breathed out and fixed her eyes on Leardin. "Then you have my allegiance, Commander."

CHAPTER TWENTY-FOUR

The Earth-Breakers are the monsters who would end us all. It is the duty of every clan to watch for remnants of them in our time and pull out the weeds before they may grow.

— *Tales of the Ronar*

D *rip, drip.*
The blood fell onto her face. Cold. Sliding down her cheeks.

Drip, drip.

The darkness was absolute, but she didn't want to leave it. There was nothing in the dark. No need to move, no need to think, no need to feel.

Drip, drip.

Her body stirred against her will. Mother carrying her to bed, perhaps?

Nasha fell hard on her back, and her eyes shot open. She was met with a blinding light, forcing her to close them, then squint as her vision slowly returned.

Shai's face was hovering over her, something between fear and relief clouding her expression, but it quickly twisted into a frown. "You tried to kill me."

Nasha was still blinking her mind into consciousness. The river they'd plunged into was babbling to her side, and the Yltigg peaks loomed large above it. She tried sitting up and something pulled at her shoulder, followed by a stab of pain lacing down her right arm. She groaned and fell back. Her wounds were stitched—she didn't know with what—but they weren't actually half bad.

"You stitched this?" Nasha asked.

Shai's frown grew deeper. "You tried to *kill* me!"

Nasha looked her over, a flicker of shame rising inside her. She'd lost herself, just like in her own Proving.

What would Ife say? Have I become the monster?

"I didn't try to kill you, Shai. I went over, too. It was the only way out." Not what she'd thought at the time, but, well . . . . She hadn't been thinking at the time.

Shai turned back to Nasha, a finger in her face. "You don't make that call! Same way you shouldn't have thrown me into this Earth-damned Proving!"

Nasha's throat dried up, but she knew it was not her reaction to fear: it was Shai's. "Are you that afraid of losing your life?"

Shai looked away, her voice wavering. "They'd die without me, Nasha. Uvo and my mother. I can't let that happen. I promised, just like you." Her voice took on a cold edge. "I try to keep mine."

Nasha breathed in deep. "There's no time to think on what should have been done. The Yltigg will be here soon. We need to move."

"You sure you want a Sloper with you? Maybe you do, so you can sacrifice me if things go bad."

"I came from there too, Shai. The difference is I don't cling to it like you do. You're the one trapping yourself there with thoughts like that."

Shai threw away a wet, bloody rag, frown going deeper still. She stood over Nasha for a moment, then stomped a few steps away. "What happens now?" she asked.

Nasha tried a shrug, but the pain shot through her again. She winced. "War."

"What? W-we can't! Bahar's the one who threw the spear!"

Nasha scoffed and sat up, finally winning out over the pain. "Don't be a fool. Wars are never started by reasonable minds thinking things out. Their Warden was their chief's son. All they'll care about is his pierced heart, not the hand who threw it."

The thought of Bahar sparked a fire in her heart, and the questions clawed at her again. He'd always told her he gave up a life of leadership in the Domain—could have been a councilmember himself—but he'd traded that for Devu when his wife died giving birth. Some twisted Domain notion that Devu would bring death, which forced Bahar to become an emissary, a friend, and take his son to Tomu. He'd trusted the clans, trusted Nasha. And now she'd let his son be killed before him. To him, she probably was the monster.

No. She'd done what was needed for the clan. Devu had not been Ronar; his death was part of the Proving, part of the life Bahar himself had chosen for his son.

Nasha shook the thought away and looked towards Shai. Realization was setting into her expression, her eyes going from wide to rapidly blinking as she tried to process what was happening.

"We need to get back to the village," Nasha said. "No telling who made it out. We have to assume we're the only ones who can warn them."

Shai looked unconvinced.

"Look, you can sulk here alone if you like, or you can show your true worth to the clan. We'll probably die either way, found by the Yltigg out here or cut down protecting our home. At least I'm giving you the choice of how to go. That's more than either of us have gotten till now. More than your father got as well."

Nasha got to her feet, ignoring the pain in her leg. She could walk. That was enough. She checked the river, then started making her way upstream.

Her visions from the arena still weighed her down. Were they memories? The burning town, people being massacred by their own soldiers. Was that her life before the Slopes? Where she'd been born?

She couldn't be sure. They were fragments that danced in and out of her consciousness like a flickering flame. Too many and too fickle to put together now, but she had remembered, and that was a step further than she'd ever taken.

Still, it had been too dangerous, and she wasn't even sure how she'd returned to herself. Nasha paused, looking sideways, eyes picking up Shai moving behind her. Nasha nodded, a piece of her memory becoming clear. She knew how she'd returned to herself. Shai might have been unaware, but the pattern of her emotions—the way they pierced Nasha unceremoniously, shooting through and lingering within her afterward—had pulled Nasha out of her delirium more than any scent or taste ever could.

Nasha took a breath. Shai's emotions were simple to spot, but there was something else, almost invisible, flowing under her consciousness. She focused on it.

The memories from the battle were still in pieces, but the emotional patterns were clear: not just Shai's but Devu's flashes, Berg's rolling waves, even the way Mansa's sensations seemed to bludgeon those around him. A smile crept its way onto her lips. She was still cursed, but it seemed she could understand parts of it now. Something had awakened in her. Something that might even allow her a tenuous grasp on her curse instead of being controlled by it. Something that could prove she wasn't the monster.

"They'll have men at the border," Shai said behind her, pulling Nasha back to the present.

She turned back to the girl. "They will. That's why we're heading through Hagun lands."

"Shit." Nasha whispered.

Tents were pitched among the houses of the small village in the mountain pass that lead into Hagun lands, though much smaller than the fortifications on the path to the Ronar village.

"Could be empty," Shai said.

Nasha shook her head, feeling the wafts of emotion coming towards her from the direction of the small village. "Borders are never empty."

"Can we go around? Through the mountains?"

"Not if we want to find the village still standing."

"What if there are more guards than we can deal with?"

Nasha didn't respond. She was already counting, eyes closed. It was a lot harder to separate these unknown sources, but there were subtle changes. One seemed heavier, another hesitant, a third more distant. Bored, perhaps?

Nasha opened her eyes. What was she doing? Trusting the curse just because of . . . what? Surviving after losing herself in it? She ran her tongue over her teeth. Maybe it was the hunger making her reckless, but there was little else to go on. They had to push through.

"Probably three or four," she told Shai. "Nothing we can't handle."

"How do you know that? Are you really some kind of witch like in the tales?"

There it was. The burning on her tongue again.

"No, just . . ." What was she going to say—"Trust me?" "I'm a hunter, Shai. I've seen camps like these. Never full, and the few who stay there are probably bored or weak and kept out of the way."

"What if the Hagun attack their borders?"

"Have you seen any Hagun lately?"

Shai paused at that. "Not since . . ." She grimaced.

"Yes, not since I was sent after them."

"Fine, let's say you're right. What's the plan?"

"Same as the Proving," Nasha said. "Get to the other side, kill whoever tries to stop you."

Shai held Nasha's gaze for a moment, and Nasha's throat went dry.

"There's no other way, Shai. No need to be afraid."

"I'm not afraid," she said, and started heading down.

Nasha went straight through towards the village, with Shai circling around. She made her way on the craggy path over dried bracken and dusty ground. The air was still, the sun bright in the sky, hot on Nasha's skin as she paced into the village and approached a smoking fire in what looked like an empty village square, surrounded by empty huts. A man prodded the fire, with another standing behind him, weapons sheathed. Nasha didn't find the third. He was hidden or, more likely, asleep, but she could sense he was there.

She approached them, hands close to her obsidian blades. She stepped close to the men, but a spike of emotion ran through her. She ducked, narrowly avoiding the quarrel streaking past. Hidden, then. Both men turned on her. Armored men. Not Yltigg.

"Well," the one that had been poking at the fire said in the tongue of the Visslands. "Thought everything around here was dead. Wasn't expecting . . . this." He looked Nasha up and down with hungry eyes that made her skin crawl. He had a large scar over his right brow, but the revolting look in his eyes was what stood out.

"I'd stop moving those hands if you don't want a bolt through them," the other one, bald and stocky, said. "Bryne there's got old eyes, but a bastard of an aim in them, don't you, Bryne?"

"Restless fingers, too," a voice shouted from one of the huts.

Nasha raised her palms to them. "Just heading through, not looking for trouble," she said in the Domain tongue. "You keep poking at your fire, I'll keep walking. Sound about right?"

The bald man raised his eyebrows and seemed to consider this, but the one with the scar stepped forward. "Been some time since we've had one like you. Bet you're a screamer, eh?"

"Oh, I can scream," Nasha said with a smile he'd probably interpret in a wholly different way than she intended.

He leered at her and gave another step forward.

"Don't think we'll be having any of that, Lorn."

"You don't tell me what to do," the leering man—Lorn, looked like—said. "What'd you reckon, Bryne?"

No answer. A tingle shot up and down Nasha's back, then lingered before fading. Nasha smiled.

"Bryne, you old—"

Her knife flew from her hand, cutting the man's words in his throat. She charged towards the bald man, strike blade already out. He half stepped back and almost tripped over the fire, managing only a dose of fear towards Nasha as he fumbled for his sword. The fear spiked in her side. Nothing like hers or Shai's, but she could see it in his eyes as well.

It was weak compared to the flood she'd experienced in the arena, and it brushed over her like a summer cloud. Nasha slashed through it and shoved the man to the ground.

"No please! We're just scouts! Hired! No choice!" He chuckled nervously, crawling away on his back. "I know everyone in the borderlands, desperate folk who'll fight anything for a meal and warm clothes." His chuckling was getting more frequent. "You clan folk always need somethin'. Just tell me what you need!"

"You expect me to believe I can trust you?" These Domain folk from the border were all the same. Always looking for an easy way to take advantage of the clans. No reason to keep him alive. She raised her knife.

"No, wait. Hemlicht! I know him! He's been among you! Cryptic bastard, long beard, rotten smile! Always in chains. Ask him about me—just ask!"

Nasha paused, the image of the man who'd been chained up beside her before the trial forming in her mind. It couldn't be.

"Ah, yes, you know him! Just tell me what you need. I'll get it from him."

Her eyes narrowed. Was a favor enough to buy this man's life? Might be worth more than killing him, at least. "What's your name?"

"Eg-Egren."

"Well, Egren, you know I can find you if you run?"

He breathed in, eyes fixed on hers. He saw something there that made his fear spike again. Nasha felt it rising, felt her gut clenching, and the same voice that had told her to use the emotion in the arena was in her mind again, directing her. Nasha took control of the fear like it was an invisible strand coiling in her gut. She projected it outward, eyes locked onto the man, as if she'd turned it around and whipped it back at him. It was probably just her imagination, but his eyes seemed to widen a touch. He nodded, spit dribbling down his chin. She jerked her head, and he scrambled away.

Nasha turned towards where the first quarrel had flown from. Shai was standing over Bryne's body, uncertain, bloody axe still up.

"Guess you didn't leave me to die, at least," Nasha said.

"Don't really know the way back." She edged closer, slowly lowering her axe. "How'd you know you wouldn't take a bolt in the back?"

Nasha shrugged her good shoulder, not ready to reveal any more than she already had. "I didn't."

"And that one? Why'd you let him live?"

"He owes me a favor now."

Shai smirked at her. "How d'you know he'll pay?" She narrowed her eyes. "Ah, right, you're a wit—"

"Enough with that, Shai."

The girl looked off, knowing not to test Nasha after what she'd seen in the arena. "Why'd you hate the tales so much?" she said after a long moment.

"You see any living heroes?"

Shai opened her mouth and frowned, but Nasha was already walking away.

They hurried across the border in silence, keeping a steady pace up the Hagun main road. There was no movement on it. No movement off it either. Nasha didn't bother with stealth; she could feel the nothingness around her, that same vacant feeling she'd felt around Chatta, and it only intensified as they neared the Hagun village.

They approached the village slowly, but it was empty. Not just empty, it was dead. Shai suppressed a gasp, regarding the decaying settlement with flustered eyes. A few dead trees and graying earth were one thing. The scene that greeted them was another.

The air was still, but tufts of ash blew up as they paced around the rotted wood of what had been the village wall. A gate hung on one hinge, blackened and creaking, and a scent more acrid than the fumes of the Great Mountain sliced its way through them. Shai coughed, one hand over her mouth, but Nasha fought through it and looked past the crumbling wall.

Trees were broken, leafless, and decaying, and the wood of the houses seemed to be headed the same way. The layer of ash that covered the ground was thick, and holes had opened up in the earth in places. The center of their village held a tall block of ancestor-stone, but it pulsed neither blue nor white. It was dull and as dead as everything around it.

Just like the stones Tomu said they found in the recent digs.

Nasha's heart raced, suddenly scared of what was moving under the Earth. If it had reached the Ronar dig sites, dulling their ancestor-stone, the village could be next. She could not imagine it in this state, but the fear rising inside her seemed to be dulled as well, as it had been around Chatta. Shai gave another step, but Nasha shot out her arm.

"Don't get any closer," she said, the image of a dying Chatta in her mind.

"I thought the Earth was supposed to protect the clans. What happened?"

Nasha pointed at the dull ancestor-stone. "Their ward is dead, but I can't imagine how that could have happened." She picked up some of the ash and packed it tightly. "We'll have to ask Jabillo. If he's still alive. Let's go."

They avoided the ash and dead trees, picking up their pace towards the Ronar village through the empty Hagun lands. The silence helped Nasha's mind put things into place, at least. The Hagun hadn't been invading: they'd been running from the wrath of the Earth itself.

War with the Yltigg was bad, but fighting the Silent Earth? No matter how favored Tomu thought the Ronar to be, that was not a war they could win. Nasha would know. She'd been fighting it for as long as she could remember.

CHAPTER TWENTY-FIVE

They rushed towards the battle's call,
With death awaiting upon the walls.
The fields were bloody, the wounds were deep,
And even the victors were prone to weep.

— Excerpt from the battle songs of Boutros the Bard

R el was waiting at the same spot as always, overlooking the waking city with the same knowing expression on his face.

"You're breathing well for a dead woman," he said.

Lynn walked to his side and took in the view. She used to love the scent of baking bread when they stood here in the mornings, the din of people waking under her diligent gaze. The sounds were hollow now—lost in the constant whispers of her mind—and imagining any of the people below could be afflicted with the Madness brought a coldness to her gut.

"Sometimes I feel like I'm the craziest of them all."

Rel chuckled. "Have to be, if you want to be one of us."

"Guess I made the right choice coming back, then." Lynn looked up to the sky. A few griffins circled the rookery, shadows hovering over the Seraph's eye. She could feel Vedyr was close, but the hope that one of those shadows might be him seemed foolish.

"No sign of him, I'm afraid," Rel said.

"Leave him be. Better that he stays away."

"Thought you were done running." Rel eyed her for a moment. "They wouldn't blame you, you know?"

"They do."

"They were mad, Lynn. Think they'd do any different if it were you or me?"

"Doesn't matter. I'm the one who did it." Lynn was still looking out over the city, trying to settle her gut. She knew Rel was trying to help, but he could never know the look in their eyes before she swung the blade. "Do you think we could have avoided it? Avoided Gheria?"

Rel shook his head. "The world's heavy enough as it is, Lynn. You need to let some of it off your back or every step will sink you till you're buried under the guilt. Doesn't matter whose hand it was doing the killing: that weight isn't yours alone to bear."

"I left, Rel. I forsook my oath, my faith, and for what? Death still walks at my side."

He turned and put a hand on her shoulder. "Faith may take a while. It might not always be strong, and you may struggle with it sometimes, but it's always there. It needs no face, just like the Seraph needs no voice to speak to us.

"We need you, Lynn. There's an army of them now, six thousand strong coming down from Pehd, the scouts say. You may have left, but you came back to us. Your faith isn't dead. What matters is what you do now. That is what makes us Sentinels."

"You sound like Elwin."

Rel grinned. "I'll take that as a compliment."

They remained there for a while, watching the city rise with the sun. Any other time, the warmth on her skin might have felt good, but right now, Lynn was still working around the sinking feeling in her gut.

"That's Alren's brother you brought, isn't it? That's how Elwin found you."

Lynn nodded. "Didn't seem right to leave him behind. Doesn't seem right to put him in danger, either."

Rel nodded back. "I'll see that he's taken care of."

Lynn smiled for the first time she could remember in a long time. "Alren would have liked that."

Rel smiled back but was already turning towards the steps that descended back into the tower. "We'd better get ready. You haven't forgotten how Leardin is with tardiness, I hope?"

"I'll be right down."

Rel started making his way to the stairs, and Lynn breathed in the scent of baking bread once more before turning away.

No matter what they say, I am a Sentinel.

Time to face her old companions.

Sub-Commander Olem pushed open the doors to the common hall, and the Sentinels filed in behind him. Ildred and Thain—the one who'd attacked Lynn when she arrived—walked side by side, both shooting pointed stares at her. She didn't entertain them: nothing that could be fixed with words.

The sub-commander was not a tall man, and he seemed to have gained some weight since Lynn last saw him. He fell into a wooden chair behind one of the tables encircling the sun-painted Sign of the Breath, while the others took their positions in the chairs to either side. Lynn stood for a moment; she had no assigned place, so she took the one she'd always taken beside Rel.

"The threat has spread past Pehd. They've come down from the mountains and overrun the city. They're heading towards us now. Six thousand was the last count. Durnn has never fallen. We'll keep it that way," Olem said. He seemed to be trying to inject as much command as he could into his voice, but the Sentinels were paying him little mind. Most were turning scowls or curious looks at Lynn.

"Most of you remember Lynn." Olem shot her a glance.

He didn't seem too thrilled with his own words, but Lynn knew he'd never stand against Leardin. The frowns deepened towards her, and Ildred stood.

"Olem, the Sentinels have always been the bastion of light in the Domain. Surely the commander cannot be considering accepting this heathen back into our ranks."

"Considering?" Olem said. "The commander orders. He does not consider."

"Respectfully, sub-commander, our lives and the lives of those we defend depend on who fights at our side. There is no victory without trust, and she has betrayed that once already."

Olem's look had turned sour, as if he agreed with Ildred but still would not argue against Leardin's orders. Thain seemed like he wanted to get up, but Olem iced him to his seat with a cold glare. Lynn shifted in her own seat. Ildred and the others who'd known her she could understand, but the anger of the new ones was as galling as prideful children poking at a prisoner with sharpened sticks.

"This is not a topic up for discussion," Olem said through hard lips.

Silence hung between them for a moment. Then a woman, one of the new ones, finally mustered enough courage to speak up.

"I second Ildred's concerns. I cannot trust one who has walked away from us."

"We're outnumbered enough as it is, Gwyn. Every body counts," Olem said, but Lynn's heart sank as soon as he did. He'd given them leeway for discussion. More were rising now, gathering strength in numbers, just like the mob when she'd arrived. It seemed like numbers were still stronger even than a Sentinel Mantle.

"She must be judged! Do our traditions mean nothing?" Thain was saying.

"We cannot trust her. We don't know where she's been, what she's done."

"Who does she think she is to play us all for fools, then walk in here like nothing ever happened?"

The complaints were almost like the voices in her mind, but those were clear enough as well.

They'll give you what you deserve now. You shouldn't fight it.

Run!

No. She could let them accuse her, think herself the prisoner, but that was just another way of running. The commander had spared her for a reason, and Rel was right. They needed her.

Lynn rose. "What do any of you know about this Madness? Have you ever killed these madmen?"

Silence.

"Seen them up close?"

"You do not get to ask those questions," Ildred said. "You chose to walk away. You chose to not stand by your brothers!"

The protests rose again at that, but Rel slowly got to his feet, and a mixture of respect and curiosity brought the room to silence. "How many of you think you'll come out of this alive if you keep acting like scared children, afraid of what you don't know?"

"Easy for you to say. You know her well enough," Thain said to a few chuckles around the table. Or maybe they were only in Lynn's mind.

"Aye, I do. I know she's killed these beasts—brought proof, too."

He pulled out the stitched mask Andral had worn and threw it on the table. Even Lynn felt her eyes widening in surprise. She'd kept it in the cart but hadn't mustered the courage to bring it to the commander.

"I know she's stronger than any of you here for doing what needs to be done. Or would any of you have killed Elwin if he'd needed it?"

He let the question hang, and Lynn's throat tightened at the mention of her mentor, but she kept her gaze steady on the Sentinels.

"She's the best shot we have at understanding this enemy," Rel said. "And that alone raises our chances. Now, you can all take this to the commander, or you can—"

"Take what to the commander?" a voice said from the entrance. No one spoke, their eyes moving towards the hallway Leardin was striding out of. He moved to the head of the table but didn't sit. "The Legion's marching our way. Asked for help."

Olem nodded. "We'll fortify the walls. Their men will be a good addition to—"

"They're not coming to Durnn," Leardin said. "They're moving straight for Pehd Valley to intercept."

"Commander, this Madness . . . . We shouldn't be fighting them in the open," Lynn said.

"Your confusion is understandable. You haven't been here," Ildred said. "But we're Sentinels. No enemy can stand against us. We do not hide behind walls."

There were murmurs of agreement, and even Leardin didn't argue. Had he been among them so long he couldn't see the threat?

"This isn't a common enemy, Ildred," Lynn said, but the commander raised a hand.

"He's the Light, and he's asked for our help. We can use their numbers, as Olem said. They have five thousand men. Should be enough with our help."

"And her?" Ildred said, pointing a look at Lynn, then Olem.

Leardin looked at him, amused. "This is Lynn. I think you've met."

"We can't trust her."

"Then you can't trust me. Is that the case? Would any of you like to challenge me for leadership?"

The silence in the room was so thick Lynn could taste it.

"Do we ride to meet them?" Rel asked.

"Not all the way. Griffins descending on the woods would give our position away, and I won't have it known we've abandoned our walls in a time like this. There may be other enemies hidden in wait. We can fly to where the trees are still sparse, then we go on foot."

None argued with the commander, but Lynn could see their discontent with leaving their mounts behind.

"The Legion is heading towards the valley, but we're not sure what lies in their way. We'll need to spread out and make sure they reach it. Olem, head through the southern road. I'll take the cliffs.

Whoever finds them can aid their path, maybe try to convince the Light to come to Durnn."

Leardin thumped the table twice with a fist, signaling the end of the conversation. The Sentinels poured out of the room, but Lynn's gaze lingered on her commander. He didn't look back, and she knew he was not doing this out of love for her, but it still felt good having him on her side, doing the Seraph's work once more. Even if Rel had thought her strong and Elwin had told her it was the right thing to do, killing her brothers still felt wrong.

A glimmer of hope was now blossoming inside her, though. One that spoke of finally being able to atone for what she'd done. Lynn had always quelled hope's attempts at beguiling her—none of it was ever real—but she let this one grow. Maybe it would eventually be enough for her mind to be silent, all her own once more.

Adrian sat in the command tent, grinding away at his teeth. They'd crossed into Sacantha, and the Legion was making good time, but Derren had insisted on resting the troops. They were getting close, and the Legion could not fight at half strength, he'd said, and Adrian had begrudgingly agreed. He still had his armor on, still unwilling to accept they'd be stationed here for long, and even if the noises in the camp outside had dwindled, Adrian knew his night would be anything but restful. He hadn't slept since losing her and wouldn't sleep till he found her again, he was sure.

I'll bring you back. I'll kill that coward.

Derren had also pressed Adrian to send word to the Sentinels. Adrian hadn't denied him that, but he'd made it clear he wouldn't wait. They'd meet the Legion in Pehd Valley, which the scouts had reported the enemy army was marching towards.

Adrian poured a cup of wine and gulped it down, knuckles tight around the cup. It helped numb his thoughts, but Addo's face seemed to have found a permanent home in them. He slammed the cup onto the table, turned to the tent entrance, and strode out.

The sun had set hours ago, and the night was dark as pitch, the moon covered by heavy clouds, no starlight shining through. A shadow approached Adrian, and his instincts had his hands moving to the sword at his belt—Emric's betrayal was still raw, and the bite marks Hart had left in Adrian's shoulder pulsed in the cold night.

Derren held a torch before him, Burnham at his side in his new general's uniform. Ashford had needed to be replaced—there were too many men for Derren to command alone—and Burnham always seemed too concerned about his next bottle to even consider betraying Adrian. The men paused before him, and Adrian's hand moved away from his sword.

"My lord Light." Burnham bowed his head with none of his usual careless, nonchalant manner. He might even have been sober.

"Yes, General?"

"The scouts have returned. They've found a camp. Two thousand men. They . . ." The man sighed, and Adrian was beginning to consider bringing him a drink.

"Out with it, Burnham!"

"They claim to have sighted Addo Brandt, my lord."

Adrian ground his teeth, as if the mention of the name itself was offense enough. "Two thousand?"

"They seem to have split their forces. The night is dark, but the scouts are sure of the numbers."

Adrian looked up. Even the Seraph's mark was weak in the cloudy night, a hooded lantern that would do little to guide them, but Myrra was waiting for him in the darkness. His own light would have to be enough.

"We march at once."

Burnham saluted and set off, but Derren lingered. "Running blind into the night like this, Adrian? The Sentinels—"

"We won't need the Sentinels for this. The enemy is split, Derren. If we march on, they'll attack us from behind, crush us against the rest who probably wait ahead."

Derren sighed. "I want that bastard dead as much as you do, but we do not know what hides in the darkness. We could wait and check the camp in the morning."

"And wait until Addo's scouts find our camp and that coward

pulls back? No. I won't give him the chance. The night will give us cover, and I am the Light. No darkness will stop the Legion. You're the one who told me to have faith in myself. Now is the time to show it." Adrian turned back towards his tent. "Steel your men. We'll end this soon."

"Yes, Lord Light."

He did not see Derren's expression, but caution was not the way. Adrian had formed a legion, risen over betrayal, and showed the power in his blood. Jovu might have been favored by Father, but Adrian had shown all those around him who he was. He was the Light, and the Light stands in no shadow, even on a night as dark as this.

The sounds that had been dwindling in the camp soon picked up again as men prepared for the assault on the enemy camp. Adrian found his gut twisting in anticipation. He breathed deep and grabbed Myrra's pendant again—he'd been doing that more and more lately—so tight his palm hurt around the ruin-stone edges that formed the eye of the Sign of the Bone.

I will not lose you.

Adrian mounted his mare, rode towards where the Legion was gathering, and waited wordlessly beside Derren and Nasir for the army to form. There seemed to be a rift between the two men, but it didn't matter. They needed only to have faith in him.

The Legion assembled, and Adrian signaled the march through the gloomy night, anger and hope still mingled in his every breath as they moved off the road and into thickening woods. No lanterns were lit, and the men marched quietly, their silence broken only by the occasional curse of someone tripping in the dark. The spot the scouts had found was not far, and the Legion paused far enough not to alert the enemy of their presence: a slightly raised position, veiled in the shadows of the boundless forest that surrounded the enemy camp.

The camp was enormous, taking up almost the entirety of the vast clearing it stood in. The remains of fires smoldered before pitched tents, their smoke barely visible in the night. Some had men roasting meat or cooking stew over them. The night sentries, most likely, and Adrian caught a few glints moving among the surrounding trees: probably more lookouts, ready to rouse the camp in case of an attack. He had a sense of unease about the whole thing. Raklin had been in control of whatever afflicted him, but he seemed an exception. These men were too conscious and organized to be afflicted by the same frenzy he'd seen consume his men.

No matter. I'll crush them and have that weasel pay.

Nasir and the generals waited beside Adrian, most eyes on the camp, but Adrian's unease seemed to have seeped into Derren. It was too dark to see anything among the trees, but Derren's head was swiveling round at every sound all the same.

"Burnham, send Captain Iker round," Adrian said. "Have men take out the sentries in the trees. Put Gotzon on their flank. Derren, send your men up the middle. Pull the enemy towards us for Gotzon and Iker to fall on them from behind."

The generals nodded and ordered their units into position. Adrian waited, breath held in his lungs like Myrra had taught him, but still found no relent.

Lights flickered in the darkness as Iker's men took out the sentries at the tree line, then Derren raised a closed fist, held it for a while and opened his hand with his fingers pointing forward in a slicing motion. The officers closest to him relayed the orders and his men began to move. They charged down the wooded incline, breaking the sound of dying flames and murmuring men with screams and stomping hooves. Captains urged their footmen forward into the camp, but the uneven gaps between tents made it impossible to form a line. They clustered between them, slashing down the enemy sentries and setting the surrounding tents ablaze, lighting up the night and bringing a cloying scent of burned flesh back to Adrian.

The enemy had been roused into battle now, and men flooded from the tents and clashed with Derren's advancing unit.

"Contain them within the camp. Have the cavalry close off their flanks," Derren yelled, and commands were relayed until his horsemen had encircled the edges of the camp, but the enemy did not back down.

They used what cover they could among the tents that had not been burned and positioned spearmen to push back the Legion cavalry on their flank. The screams of battle were joined by the panicked neighing of horses and raw-throated, rasp-like snarls, but Adrian saw their moment. The enemy was fully engaged, with their rear lines exposed. It was time for Gotzon to strike. Adrian issued the command, and Gotzon charged from behind, pushing the enemy forward against Derren's men.

A thrill shot through Adrian, the taste of victory sweet on his tongue. His plan was working. They'd caught them by surprise in the night.

I'm coming, Myrra.

He looked to the far side where Iker was supposed to join the battle, but there was only stillness.

"Where's Iker?" Adrian asked.

He was answered only by his men repeating the question along the line, so he peered at the trees until he finally saw the light of Iker's lantern-men glinting like ships in a sea of shadow.

Then the shadows began to move.

The lights vanished, snuffed out one by one as the darkness closed in on Iker and his men. More screams joined those from the camp, going from confused to agonizing. They carried on the wind, seeming to spread, then turned into growls that were close. Too close. Adrian's mare whickered, and he whirled her around to find the shadows moving behind him. They were drawing closer: hundreds, maybe thousands, all howling towards the Legion commanders from behind.

"Forward!" Derren yelled.

Adrian spurred his mare forward, galloping down from his vantage point and into the camp, but the madmen were not just behind them. They flooded into the camp from the darkness on all sides and soon surrounded Adrian and his officers. He drove his sword through the skull of one on his left, slashed at another on his right, then reared his mare and had her trample through the camp to reach the bulk of the Legion, which had gathered in the center. But what once had been a unit was now scattered. Men headed desperately after flitting shadows, and more of the madmen were rushing in through newly sprouted fires, their faces covered in gruesome masks of stitched, dead flesh. Adrian wheeled his mount around, trying to find a position to direct his army towards. He looked to the edge of the woods—

There was a sharp pain at the back of his head, and a high-pitched buzzing filled his ears as he fell to the ground. Adrian blinked and put his hand to the back of his head, then brought it back covered in slick red. Hands were pulling him up, and he moved his groggy gaze onto Derren, who was dragging him away from the enemy and into the darkness of the trees. Adrian blinked a few more times, and his breath came back to him in a rush. It brought Myrra's and Addo's faces back, sending a jolt through him.

Adrian jumped to his feet, sword in hand, and strode through the trees towards a cluster of light that seemed like it was trying to push back the darkness. Some Legion standards were aflame, but Adrian could still spot his men and lantern bearers gathering around the unburnt standards among the trees, fighting hard to keep the enemy back.

"Form up on the standards!" he shouted at a lantern bearer.

The man sent flashes of light into the darkness, relaying Adrian's message. Adrian dashed towards a standard among the trees beyond the camp. There were no more tactics or positions to defend, only their lives. By the time the rampaging mass of enemies fell on them from the shadows, Adrian had not reached the line. But he was close enough to see a lancer thrust a spear into a charging madman, only to have the opponent run through with no show of pain and slash the soldier's neck with bleeding, claw-like hands. The madman broke the lance at the haft and continued his attack, but Adrian had reached his flank, and he swung his sword in a wide arc to cut off the madman's head before he reached the next Legion man scrambling to hold the line. The head rolled off cleanly, the dead man's hands twitching as he fell to the ground.

"Cut off their heads!" Derren was screaming as he slashed at one of his own attackers. "Slash, don't stab!"

"Cut off their legs!" another scream came from the darkness.

The line pushed back, empowered by Adrian's display.

"Form on the standards!" he shouted once more, and men all around flocked towards him.

"The Light!"

"The Light will burn the shadows away!"

"The Light stands in no shadow!" Derren yelled as he cut another madman down.

The flames had crept into the woods, showing the enemy clearly now, but even surrounded by flames, Adrian was cold to his bones. Their stitched faces of dead skin were pulled close, with holes for eyes, mouth, and nose. The sight spread the cold in his bones in a mixture of fury and fear.

I will not let that happen to you, Myrra.

He cut down two more twisted faces and raised his sword, letting out a wordless cry to rally his men. They'd cut down the enemy and were now pushing towards another standard among the trees. The men beneath it had formed a wide circle and were frantically holding off their maddened attackers. Burnham was leading the force, a cluster of lantern bearers behind him. The previous wave of enemies lay at their feet, but another was already charging.

Adrian bellowed into the darkness and rushed at the charging enemy's flank. They did not turn or manage any kind of defense as Adrian and his men crashed into them, slashing at heads and legs from the side, tearing straight through the enemy unit to break their line. Burnham's soldiers cheered as Adrian's unit joined them, but the fight was far from over. Steel rang in the distance, and heavy footfalls reached them soon after.

"Brace!" Burnham shouted, and the unit formed a line to take the attack.

The enemy slammed into them, and soon the men before Adrian were pressed up against the weapons and snarls of the madmen, each side desperately trying to tear the other down. A spear poked through a gap between the two men in the line before Adrian. He grabbed hold of it and pulled, bringing one of the dead-stitched faces into view, then stabbed it through the eye. The body fell limp, but others took its place. The press seemed to grow, pressuring the soldiers before him back.

Adrian pulled one of the men into his place and pushed back, out of the line, Derren and Nasir behind him. He'd rallied these men, but most were still lost in chaos. He darted behind the line towards the edge of the trees, using the light of the burning camp to search for more men needing guidance, but a figure on horseback at the far edge of the camp caught his eye. He wore a cloak of Khetish moss-green, and the horse was draped in emerald, gray, and gold. The colors of Khet. Adrian's body reacted before his mind made up the thought, but even from here, Addo was easily recognizable.

Adrian burst out sprinting from the woods, charging across the burning camp, screaming the rage and frustration he'd been gathering throughout the march. A handful of shouts joined his own, following him through the camp, Derren's and Nasir's probably among them.

Addo locked eyes on Adrian, but he did not move. A smile spread across his face instead, and dead-masked soldiers rushed out from the trees behind him. Two stood in Adrian's way while others went for his men. There were cries and the scraping of steel, but Adrian did not slow his charge. The first was weaponless, and Adrian did not give him a chance to react. He thrust his sword through his opponent's neck, and the man made a sound that could have been a scream, but it lasted for only an instant before he fell off the blade. Adrian turned towards the other. A woman. Her twisted mask was a single face, not an amalgamation of dead skin like the others, and the fire left him when he lay eyes on it.

The dead skin was stitched so close the face seemed real: Myrra was staring back at him with a savage smile and a wicked-looking blade in hand. Her blade did not move, but the sight of her sent stabs through Adrian's heart all the same. They'd . . . they'd killed her. They'd cut off her head, ripped the skin of her face from her bones, . . . defiled it into . . .

It couldn't be her. It couldn't—

They'll pay. They'll pay!

The thought came out in a furious howl, but Adrian's moment

of hesitation was enough for Myrra to drive forth in a smear of shadow, knife aimed at his heart.

Adrian's rage moved him. He was unable to avoid the stab, but he shifted so that the blade missed his heart. It found a gap in his armor, embedding itself in his chest, just below the shoulder.

The pain snapped him fully into awareness. Adrian made a fist and drove it into Myrra's ribs, and the woman reeled to the side but caught her balance on one knee. It hurt him almost as much as it must have hurt her—even more than the throbbing in his chest where she'd stabbed him. He could have followed up then, ended it, but some instinct stopped him: some primal part of his mind still hoping this could somehow be her. He hesitated. She did not.

Myrra rose with a madness in her eyes and a fearsome scream. She clawed at Adrian's neck with knifelike nails, but Adrian raised an arm to block, and it was raked from elbow to hand in a blistering tear of flesh. The force of it pushed him back, and Adrian's mind reacted then. Like a cornered animal, he fought back without thinking. He slashed at the dead woman, who jumped back, then crouched and leaped high overhead. She came down on Adrian with claws gleaming red with his blood, but Adrian held his blade with both hands and drove it up with a growl, falling to one knee and swerving his head out of the path of the hungry claws. The blade impaled Myrra from gut to heart. She slid on it, stopping close enough that Adrian could feel her final breath on his face before her body went limp.

Part of his mind was still screaming, but it was distant, and it grew quiet as Adrian looked into Myrra's dead face—wrecked and stretched over another, black stains around the eyes.

"I'm sorry," he whispered. "I'm sorry."

The tears came then, and they were furious. Adrian looked up, but Addo was gone again. His legs were moving him through the woods with little care about his destination. He let his screams pave the way. "Addo! Addo! I'll kill you, you bastard! I'll kill you!"

All Adrian could hear was the roar of his aching heart. Enemies were drawn to him, but he tore them down. One, then another.

Stab, slash, stab, slash. Each of them was felled without a second glance. They meant nothing. He needed to get to Addo.

Someone was yelling behind him. Derren, maybe Nasir. He didn't care.

"Addo!"

Only madmen answered—a dozen claws scraping against his armor, teeth trying to bite out his throat—but all they found were his sword and his anger. Adrian opened a path, sprinting forward until he broke into a moonlit patch of sparse trees where hundreds of enemies were charging at less than half their number in Legion soldiers.

Just more to cut down.

"Addo!" he bellowed again, and he rushed forward, stabbing wildly, pressing up against the enemy line. Derren had fallen in beside him, and the surrounding Legion men were sparked by his drive, but he was not doing this for them. All that was clear in his mind was the thirst for retribution for what Addo had done to her.

Even the enemy seemed taken aback by Adrian's ferocity, and the Legion formed a ragged line around him, trying to hold back the madmen. Adrian pushed hard against them. He needed to get to Addo, needed to break through—

Something slammed into Adrian's chest, sending him flying back onto the ground. Could have been a shield or a body—no way to tell—but it gave him a measure of consciousness. Men had plugged the gap he'd fallen back from, but the enemy's ranks seemed endless, and the Legion was being pushed back. Men were falling, their replacements taking longer and longer to fill their spots and failing to regain lost ground. Adrian's rage was still hot, but it was clear his men would not hold.

Derren was there again, pulling him to his feet behind the Legion line. Adrian took his hand, then stepped back, still searching for Addo or for a hole in the line where he could break through. Another step back and his heel hit something soft. Too tall for a corpse.

He spun around and found Nasir kneeling beside a body, hands covered in blood, mouth working furiously, speaking words Adrian did not understand. There were cuts on his arms, exactly like the scars he already had.

The priest looked up at him. "Stay close." He returned to his foreign words, hands working over the body.

The men were buckling under the pressure of the enemy bearing down on them.

Adrian looked down at the priest still performing the ritual. "Nasir, whatever you're doing, it—"

The priest jumped to his feet, blood coating his arm up to his elbows.

"Come," he said, as if there were no battle at all. His movements were not as calm, though, and he hurried away from the men, pulling Adrian with him.

Derren rushed after them, screaming at the men, "Retr—"

Flames roared over Derren's words as a fire spouted from where Nasir had been working on the body, leaping taller than the trees and at least ten paces wide. The cone of flame expanded into a burning wave that rolled through the night, illuminating the woods like a risen sun. It was aimed at the madmen but didn't discern between them and Legion soldiers. It crashed over the next enemy wave, pulling out seared cries and sending burning men to the ground.

Adrian turned to Nasir, eyes wide. "What did you—"

"There is no time, Lord Light. They are all around us."

Adrian could finally see their numbers, and his throat tightened —there was hardly a space among the trees where Legion men were not being preyed upon. Adrian's head jerked from side to side as he looked for an opening to turn the tide. He couldn't lose. He needed his Legion to find Addo and kill the bastard.

I am their beacon! I am their Light! I've proven myself. The Light stands in no shadow!

Yet this was more than mere shadow. It was the night itself come to devour them, and there was little he could do to chase it away.

Nasir was tugging on his arm. "We must leave. It's over."

Derren twisted his face, but even he could see they would not beat this enemy. "Retreat!" he yelled.

His cries were echoed, and what was left of the Legion fought to disengage and move away. Nasir stayed back, speaking his foreign tongue, arms still bloody. He waited until the enemy was on him. Then he raised his arms, and another wall of flame cut off the enemy from the fleeing Legion.

The moonless night had Lynn watching every step, but she preferred it to the accusing stares piercing her through the darkness. She'd caught Deria and Cedd eyeing her at times as if they were about to knife her in the back. Wyman had even walked up when he thought she was alone, but Leardin's frown had turned him away. Wyman's glare was a promise that things wouldn't end there, though.

Lynn had no time for them. She kept walking until the trees thinned out and they came to a ledge of rock that jutted out of the sloping path, forming a shelf that looked over the forest below. The night was too dark for them to see anything but the treetops. No sign of Olem and the others. Leardin paused, and a chill wind grasped at them, as if trying to tear them off the cliff.

The rest of the Sentinels stepped onto the stone ledge, but Lynn lingered in the shadow of the trees, trying to make out something in the canopy cover spread out beneath them. It went as far as she could see, almost indistinguishable from the dark horizon, no movement or sound beyond the soughing of the wind. The commander had his back to her, also looking below, but there was no moon, and even the Seraph's eye was shrouded in clouds.

She doesn't care. She wants you dead, Cara said.

"You are not fit for that Mantle."

Lynn paused at the voice. She knew this one well from her past, but it was not in her mind. Brehnna had slipped in beside her.

"I have nothing to say to you, Brehnna."

"Oh, but we have much to say to you, traitor."

Shady outlines gathered around Lynn, and cold steel kissed the skin on her neck from behind.

"You think you're safe? Think he'll protect you?" Brehnna said.

There was a sting as the blade nicked her skin, pulling a drop of blood from her neck that soon chilled in the cold night.

"Something to remember us by. We'll always be here. Watching."

"Quiet!" Leardin hissed.

The pressure of the blade released, but the commander was not heading towards them. He was signaling in the dark, creeping towards the trees.

Lynn was still trying to make out the signs when she heard it: footfalls coming through the night, trampling the underbrush with abandon. The sounds were signal enough for the Sentinels to take up quiet positions among the trees, and it did not take long for outlines to form on the ledge. One stopped close to Lynn. Too close. Her heart was pummeling her chest, her muscles light, slightly numb in anticipation. Lynn placed her hands on her weapons, waiting silently and still.

"They're here. I can smell 'em," one of them said.

Lynn frowned. She'd never heard the madmen communicate with more than snarls and claws. How many of them had control over it?

A giant of a man drifted through the tree line behind what seemed to be a small enough company, probably no more than fifty soldiers. Odds any Sentinel would take, even if they numbered less than a dozen.

"Spread out. If you don't find them, put fire to the trees and carry on." His voice was deep as the pit in Lynn's stomach.

The men obeyed. They had odd faces, parts protruding at uncommon angles as if they had been broken and put together again, but as they came closer, Lynn saw they wore masks of dead skin, just like Andral and Talbot had.

There was a man drawing close, a little more than a stride off. He put something to his lips and took a long gulp, then threw it to the ground, and the glass shattered. He took two more careful steps towards her, and the face on his dead mask came fully into view.

Rel had shuffled up beside Lynn. He pulled out a small shard of ruin-stone and placed it into her hand. Should be a short battle, then, if he thought she only needed one shard. Still, it was better than burning her own anger. She'd been using her Bond too often and had been too far from Vedyr for too long. Lynn took it, and the anger rose inside her, syphoned from the stone.

Death was approaching again, but she would not run from it. These madmen were enemies of the Seraph and her Domain, and death was her tool to protect it. That was what Elwin had taught her. That was what it meant to be a Sentinel.

I hope you're right about faith, Rel.

She let the anger flow away from her, let Vedyr's strength filter in until her eyes burned and the usual calming clarity replaced the rage, and emptied her mind. There was a roar from the far end as Leardin signaled the attack with his own strike. Lynn drew on her griffin's speed, fixed her mace and war-scythe into a polearm, and thrust it straight through the gut of the man standing before her, then pulled it back and swiped off the man's head.

If the enemy were surprised, they didn't show it. A man behind the one Lynn had felled jumped forward—mouth twisted behind his mask—and lunged, scratching at Lynn with bleeding hands, long, razor-sharp nails scrabbling to find purchase in her flesh. Lynn pulled on Vedyr's speed and sidestepped, but the madmen were crowding the ledge, and another rammed into her chest and sent her staggering back, breathless.

Lynn bared her teeth and spat, then charged behind her scythe. Her new opponent ran straight at it, uncaring, probably expecting to be stabbed and planning to run through it at her. Lynn knew from Talbot the stab wouldn't work, though, and she rotated the shaft of her weapon, splitting it into mace and scythe at the last moment, one in each hand. The madman was carried by his momentum through where the tip of Lynn's scythe had been, leaving himself open as Lynn spun out of the way and met the back of his head with her mace, Vedyr's strength sending the man ripping through trees into the darkened wood.

Death was still bitter in Lynn's mouth, but there was little time to taste it. The narrow ledge was a cacophony of screams, snarls, and urgent cries. The Sentinels were engaged, and enemies were still coming out from the trees. She fixed her weapon into a double-sided polearm again and darted forward.

Cedd fought off one of the madmen, but a frenzied woman clawed at his face, then bit down on his neck, bringing him to the ground like some mad animal. There was no time to think if he'd do the same for her: Lynn held the mace side low, then swung it upward into the mad woman's chest, throwing her off Cedd. She followed up with a stab to the woman's neck while she was still on the ground.

Cedd didn't get up. Blood gushed out of his neck and the long scratch marks over his face, but Rel was there in an instant, eyes silver and hands crimson, working furiously to pressure the wound. He grabbed another ruin-stone shard from his pouch and muttered words under his breath. Lynn's body weakened, as if the wind was blowing her strength away. Her vision blurred, and she took a deep breath, but no sooner had she let it out than the world came back into sharp focus. Rel handed her another shard before darting off towards the next cry, leaving Cedd blinking up at the dark sky, the healing just enough to stop the bleeding, the pink gashes still burning angry in the night.

Lynn looked away, setting her sight on the large man leading the crew. The ledge was filled with entangled madmen and Sentinels, while their leader fought Leardin on the edge of it. He had an empty vessel in his hand like the first man she'd attacked. He crushed it before roaring forward at Leardin, who had six madmen laid out in awkward positions at his feet. There were more coming from the trees, crowding the path towards the commander.

Lynn dashed towards Leardin, but a man and a woman stood in her path. There was fighting to both sides, no easy way past them. Lynn didn't hesitate. She split her weapon once more and slammed the mace side into the man's knee. He was slower than the others, and his bones crunched under the blunt steel. This one screamed as he went to the ground, and Lynn paused, stunned by the sudden admittance of pain, but the woman was already slashing at her. Lynn gasped as the nails missed her face by a hair's breadth and tore into the front of her Mantle. She stepped back and kicked the woman to the ground before she could strike again, but a sharp pain in Lynn's side and the familiar burning of pierced skin stopped her finishing blow.

She looked down and found a throwing knife in her ribs. Fear laced through her with the pain, threatening to take her strength away: if the knife was tainted, it could infect her with the Madness. Her Bond wavered, but there was no stopping now. She gripped Rel's ruin-stone shard and bit down on the pain. Anger seared through her once more and Lynn dove deeper into the Bond, feeding Vedyr her anger, taking his speed. It was enough to avoid the woman's next slash and duck another knife flying towards her, then thrust her scythe through the woman's heart. She fell lifeless to the ground, and Lynn refocused on the commander.

Leardin was clashing with the enemy leader on the narrow ledge, moving with perfect knowledge of the ground beneath him, but his opponent was enormous and moved with speed a man of his size should not possess. Leardin swung his hammer in powerful, directed blows, but it was deflected once at the shoulder, a second time at the knee. The third strike hit the man in the side, but his opponent barely moved.

The commander brought his heavy hammer back and slammed at the same spot, swinging it with both hands and what looked like all of his strength. There was a cracking sound and a grunt from Leardin's foe. The blow would have crushed a normal man, but his opponent held the hammer beneath his arm, then pulled Leardin into a crushing bear hug with a smile spread on his face.

Lynn was mere strides away, rushing at them with her weapon fastened into a polearm again, but not close enough to stop what was happening.

Leardin looked up, defiant but defenseless, and was received with a vicious blow, forehead to forehead. The commander staggered, still in the man's embrace. Lynn jumped, polearm raised overhead, the knife wound in her ribs burning—but in the time it took Lynn's body to fall, Leardin's foe delivered two more blows with his head, and the commander's body sagged. The man released him, and Leardin stumbled back, feet teetering on the edge, body swaying unsteadily.

Lynn aimed at the opponent's head, but he moved it out of the way, and her scythe sliced through his shoulder with all the weight of her fall, opening the man from clavicle halfway through his chest. It felt like cutting through stone, and Lynn's weapon was left lodged in the man, but she twisted the mace and pulled it free of the polearm.

The bulk of the man obscured Leardin, and Lynn couldn't see if the commander still stood on the ledge.

"Rel!" Lynn howled, but a shadow was already darting past her.

The enemy leader was gushing blood but moved unencumbered. He stretched out an arm to grab at Rel, turning his uninjured side towards Lynn. She slipped around his back and brought the mace down onto her scythe, driving it deeper and sending him to one knee, then bashed her mace into the man's skull with both hands. It took three blows until he finally fell unmoving to the ground.

Lynn whirled round, chest heaving. The battle was winding down, madmen either fleeing at the sight of their dead leader or being finished by the remaining Sentinels. The sounds drifted away, but they did not give chase. Most were flocking towards the edge where Leardin had fallen.

Lynn looked their way, but Rel caught her gaze and shook his head, answering the question that did not need to be asked.

A shocked silence hung over them. Some seemed to look down at the sheer drop with nothing but hope, while others seemed adrift, dazed. No enemy had been powerful enough to fight a Sentinel in hundreds of years, and Lynn could not have imagined one strong enough to best the commander. It was clearer than ever that this was not the same Madness she knew. The ones she'd slain in the past were never this resistant, nor large as the man who'd defeated Leardin, and she still could not understand how some could control it. Could there have been hope for Alren and the others? Had she misused death? She looked to Rel for guidance, but he returned her gaze, expectant. They had no leader with Leardin gone and Olem away.

Cedd was making his way towards them, step after uneasy step. The Sentinels turned towards the sound, but his strength abandoned him midway as he lost his grip on his Bond and fell to his knees, eyes full of fear, sunken in the black patches already forming around them.

They were all looking at her, all of them knowing what she'd done to Elwin and unwilling to do it themselves. Lynn drew the knife from her ribs, sending streaks of pain pulsing through her. It hurt, but there did not seem to be anything lacing the blade, and Rel was beside her in two quick steps, one hand closed around a ruinstone shard, another on her wound.

Her strength returned, but the anger was still hot, the air rushing noisily through her nose. Whether Leardin was alive did not matter—what they thought of her did not matter. She didn't need their love. They were looking to her to make the hard choice so that they didn't need to. Cowards.

Maybe Rel was right, maybe this was not her weight to bear alone, but no one else would, and she could not let the Domain be taken by the Madness, no matter how much her mind recoiled at the thought of leading Sentinels again. Lynn stepped forward, eyeing her brethren.

"Now you have seen it. Now you know the danger we face."

They were silent, gazing at Lynn from a distance, Brehnna still with a blade in hand. Lynn walked up, grabbed Brehnna's hand, and placed her neck on the edge of her blade.

"We do not have time to fight amongst ourselves. If you wish me gone, do it now. Otherwise, it is time you listened. The commander is gone. I'm the best you have left."

Brehnna eyed her for a while, but her rage seemed to have been overtaken by her disbelief at their situation. She opened her fist, and her blade clattered to the ground.

There was shuffling behind her, a few of the Sentinels heading towards the edge. For a moment, Lynn expected Leardin to climb up and curse them all for fools for thinking he'd been beaten, but what she saw was smoke rising from the forest below, and then flames clawed up the trees in what looked like a wave of fire.

The fire illuminated what they could not see before. Men were running aimlessly in what looked to be a battle, presumably the Legion—and it looked like they were being torn apart. The screams of the burning drifted on the wind, and the outlines of madmen clinging to soldier's backs and driving vicious claws through flesh were clear even from up here.

"Head to the fire. We'll gather what remains of the Legion. Let's hope Olem finds them in time," Lynn said.

They looked at Lynn for a moment, still unsure.

"Move!" Rel bellowed.

That sparked them to life, and they started helping up the wounded.

Rel pointed at Brehnna, the fastest runner they had. "Head to Durnn and sound the bells. Send what aid you can."

She dashed off.

A group had formed around Cedd, still waiting for Lynn. She walked past them and kneeled at his side, holding the knife that had been in her ribs out with the pommel towards him. Rel might have been right, but the hand would not be hers this time.

"You know what this is. You can end it now, or you can wait until you are a shade of yourself, and we'll strike you down then."

Lynn closed the man's trembling hand around the knife, and a sliver of light shone as the moon finally broke out of the clouds— only a flash before it was covered again, but it was enough to show the strewn-out bodies of their enemies and the expression on Cedd's face as he saw them.

That's the thing about light. All you need is a touch to see the horrors lurking in the dark.

He died quietly, heavy breaths followed by his body falling onto the stone and the knife rattling out of his hands, but even in death, the fear still lingered in his eyes.

Lynn looked up at the Seraph's mark again, then headed towards the fire, the Sentinels following in her wake.

They'd left the fire behind, but Adrian's face was still burning. His light had not been enough to drive the shadow away—had not been enough to save Myrra. He'd run, like the scared boy his father had always said he was. Seraph take the old man. He had a habit of seizing Adrian's thoughts in situations like this.

They'd retreated to their camp and set up a perimeter in case the madmen followed, but the enemy did not give chase, Nasir's fire probably creating enough doubt. Adrian paced around the empty command tent at the back of the camp. The moans of the wounded could be heard, and the reports coming were stating they had lost half their numbers, maybe more. Adrian's mind was set on a single loss, though.

They'd taken Myrra's body, stitched her face into a mask, and likely discarded the rest. There'd be no Promised Dawn for her, no chance of the Seraph bringing Myrra back without her preserved body. The image of his blade piercing her burned at him like the steel had gone through his own chest, and he almost regretted not taking the mask. Her face was defiled, misused, nothing like she had been in life, but some mad part of him insisted it was all that was left of her. All he had left. His hand moved to her ruin-stone pendant, still around his neck, and hot, angry tears streaked down his face.

There was a soft rustling at the entrance of the command tent. Adrian snapped his head towards it and found Derren standing there with an uneasy look in his eyes. He knew Adrian's pain, but the man would never mention the dead.

"Any leads?"

"Not yet, Adrian, but we'll find the bastard."

Nasir had entered beside Derren. "The night has cleared, my lord. The Seraph watches over us once more."

"The Seraph does not care, Nasir. Her Legion burns in the darkness." Adrian didn't want to have this conversation, but the words were already out before he could stop himself.

Nasir raised an eyebrow at him. "If the Seraph and those who served her lived solely on victory, the Domain would have conquered all of Avarin long ago. Our faith in Her is strong, but the truth is that the Seraph has enemies in this world that hold great power. That is why She has chosen us to face them. Not for our victories, but for our ability to resist defeat."

Adrian moved his face within inches of Nasir's. "Enough of your preaching! All we had is lost. Words won't bring them back!"

Nothing will bring her back.

"As you wish, my lord Light. If we are to fight this enemy, however, we need a Legion. Their numbers are great, and our own have dwindled. We have barely over two thousand left."

Adrian balled his hands into fists and slammed the table. She was gone. She couldn't be gone. He shot a cold glare at Nasir, but the man was right. He'd need more men if he wanted to get his revenge.

What else do I have left?

"How do the Domain armies stand? Can they send men?"

Derren shook his head. "We've sent runners to call a reserve up from Durnn, but the madmen have spread throughout Sacantha and Vizcarra, and the Visslands have as many men at their northern borders as they have patrolling the southern borderlands with the clans. They've shut down—no one in or out. That leaves Dakhra."

"We can't trust Syvern," Adrian said. He might have if Myrra were alive and could help him come up with a plan. But he'd seen how Syvern and Alaya treated him before the Pontiff. Even if he did trust them, there was no telling if they'd send help.

"We represent the Church, Lord Light," Nasir said.

"My father's blood still runs in my veins, priest."

Derren was silent, and Adrian pressed his jaw hard, but it did nothing to dull his anger.

"There is one other option, Lord Light," Nasir said. "We get help from outside."

Adrian looked at the priest. "I won't leave that weasel running about, Nasir. We need to end him. Now."

"There is no way to end him now, Lord Light. We have stumbled, but without more men, we will surely fall."

Adrian narrowed his eyes—Father's plan of making him Xakhar rising in his mind. He balked at it, but he raked his mind for an alternative and could find none.

Damn the old man.

He hated doing it, but he needed the men. The old words echoed in his mind: "Yes, Father." Adrian stabbed at them, but they resisted, like the madmen, refusing to die.

He turned to Derren. "Leave Burnham in charge. Tell him to gather what remains. Hold this position for a few days if there are men still lost in the woods, then try to find the Sentinels."

"And you?"

"Assemble a guard. We're marching north." He pointed a look at Nasir. "You get me a ship."

CHAPTER TWENTY-SIX

When Tedros became chief, he had a thousand warriors guard the First Tree so that the Earth-Breakers would not threaten our world.

— Tales of the Ronar

The world slowly regained its color as they made their way out of Hagun land. The ash receded from the ground, leaves returned to the trees, and the scent of citrus trees accompanied by the trill of birdsong rode the air. Almost peaceful.

"Think they made it?" Shai asked with a hopeful look in her eyes.

"Better to assume they didn't. Come on. We need to find Adda."

The guards at the Root Gate stared at Nasha as if a corpse had risen from the earth. "W-Warden! Where's the Chief? The others?"

Nasha didn't answer them. She flew through the village like an arrow, steering clear of the gathering mass of people beginning to crowd the streets, eager for word on what had happened. Her instinct was to grab onto Shai's emotions to brace for the impact of what came from the crowd, but the wave that crashed into her did not threaten to pull her away. She knew who she was, knew what was flowing around her.

It seemed as if the arena had extended her resistance, unlocking some part of her mind that could now understand and navigate what was coming her way instead of simply push back on it. Old Kolg was recognizable, but so were many others now. Most of them were foreign, but she knew herself, and that was all she needed to press on.

The Root side of the village was emptier than the rest, but people still clamored for news around her. Nasha pushed them to the side and stepped past the guards at the entrance to the Chief's Hall. Hope fluttered deep in her chest that somehow the others would be here, but it was a cold hope, and it quickly vanished as Nasha found only Adda and her son sitting around the hearth. Adda whispered a few words to Razi, and the boy left quietly before Adda rushed towards Nasha, sending waves of emotion before her.

Nasha halted. This was new. The Tivezzi had always been shut off, but even her stony expression seemed to have finally cracked to show the apprehension beneath. Adda flashed a look towards Shai that said more than any words, and the girl did not dare step further than the door. There was still a prodding in Nasha's ribs, though, same as when her own irritation was rising.

"I'll find you later," Nasha said. "We'll make things right."

Shai gave her a long look, and Nasha thought she could feel the slightest warmth coming from the girl. Her gaze reminded Nasha of Ife.

I've kept my promise. I'm not the monster.

It lasted just for a moment before Shai turned and strode out and Adda was in Nasha's face. "Where are they? What happened?" There was a slight threat in her tone.

"Things got out of hand."

"Where are they, Nasha?" Her voice rose almost to a yell.

"I don't know. Bahar killed their Warden. Things fell apart from there."

Better to leave out the part about remembering only the flashes of her past and nothing of what really happened.

"That rotting little Domain fuck. I told them he shouldn't be allowed to go, but my father has always been too soft." She worked her jaw almost as expertly as Nasha. "You killed him?"

"The Yltigg probably will, if they haven't already."

"I need to be sure, Warden."

"We don't have time for this! The Yltigg are coming, Adda. We need to prepare for war."

"Without the Roots? Without the Chief?"

"Don't be a fool. We'll all die if we wait."

She lowered her voice, but it pierced through sharper than before. "Call me that again and I will end you where you stand. Or have you forgotten? You're mine. You will do as I say."

Nasha's pride was rising to her mouth, ready to deliver the retort, but the burning sensation in her arm was still clearer than any memory from the arena.

She swallowed it down, only frowning and softening her words. "What if they didn't make it out? Do we leave the village to die?"

Adda paused. "Fine. Get the warriors to gather the Slopers. Have them attempt to prove themselves in real battle. They've been asking for a chance, haven't they?" She gave Nasha a derisive look. "You can even lead them if you like."

Something stirred inside, and the fire rose to Nasha's throat again. She wasn't sure why she felt the need to defend the Slopers, but she could not stand idle while Adda sent them to their deaths.

"This isn't a chance, Adda. This is war. The Slopers are untrained. We can't—"

Cries rang from the village outside.

They're here, she thought, though she couldn't tell if she expected the Roots or the Yltigg. Adda was already halfway towards the door when Tomu's vast frame appeared out of the crowd, Mansa, Jabillo, and a handful of Ronar trailing behind. Iallo was nowhere to be seen. A small comfort, at least.

Adda launched herself into her father, apparently still uncaring about the stony reputation she'd crafted. Tomu was more like stone, though. He hugged her briefly with one arm and pushed his long, wiry hair out of his face, then strode into the hall, past the ancestor-stone tree engraved in the entry hall and up to the table at the back.

"Good to see you alive, Warden, but we have little time."

He threw down his tattered cloak, and Mansa walked in behind him with a cautiously guarded expression. He was trying to hide his frustration, and Nasha might have missed it a few days ago, but it was clear now. The frown she'd been nursing from her conversation with Adda deepened.

"How did you get out?" Nasha asked, more towards Mansa than the Chief.

"They weren't all warriors, and you're not the only one who can fight, Warden," Tomu said. "Once Bahar broke free, Mansa and his men were already moving. Only had to cut a few down before we got out of the arena."

"Then we ran," Mansa said without a smile.

Jabillo still seemed too shaken to speak, and Nasha found she rather enjoyed a more silent version of the Speaker.

"They were still on our tail, though, but they were spread too thin to attack the village," Tomu said. "They'll fall back, regroup. Should give us a couple of days. Mansa will prepare his warriors."

An irritated spike pierced the frustration. Mansa narrowed his eyes at Tomu, nodded, then looked back to the fire. "Jabillo, send out word to the Slopers. I want your speakers promising all they've ever dreamed of. We'll send them to the border. I want skirmishes only: hit and run to slow down the Yltigg advance while we prepare a defense on the walls."

"Chief, we can't throw untrained . . . children at Yltigg warriors! They'll never stop the attack," Nasha said.

Tomu had a deep glare set on her. "Our warriors will lead them, and I don't expect them to stop the Yltigg, only to give us more time. All life that is wasted must be taken, Warden."

"You'd kill them all?" Nasha knew the Ronar way, but not all Sloper lives were a waste. She'd climbed out, for one, and Shai had done her part as well.

"They are doing their share for the clan. Those who survive will be considered for acceptance."

Nasha clenched her jaw. She'd become so used to her body's warning signs when subjected to other people's emotions that the lack of them almost felt like some part of her was missing. She could sense Tomu's irritation and was sure it was his, but it posed her no risk. She was still in control.

It took an effort to keep her own anxiousness over her next question under control, though. "And my initiate who survived? I can induct her. She has proven herself an able fighter."

Tomu looked around the hall. "I do not see the Yltigg ancestor-stone in our hall, Warden. Do you?"

"Ch—"

The doors slammed open, and an outline of a man dragged in what looked like a struggling body with a bag over the head. Iallo had a smirk on his lips, and Mansa's frustration seemed to flare for an instant, but it slowly receded, changing into something more comfortable.

"Chief Tomu, I found him!" Iallo said, dumping the body before them.

Mansa's emotion might have subsided, but Nasha's irritation only flared at the sight of the warrior.

"Is this supposed to mean something?" Tomu grumbled in the unamused, low tone only he was capable of.

"This . . ." Iallo said uncertainly. "This man is the noble the Domain has been looking for. The Carswell boy." Saying it seemed to bring him some confidence. He stood proud, expecting immediate recognition, and slowly, Tomu's face changed.

"The Yltigg had him?" Jabillo gasped.

"Stumbled across him trying to come over the border."

Tomu walked to the whimpering man and removed the hood. He pulled him up, put both his massive hands on the boy's shoulders, and spoke to him in the Domain tongue. Nasha caught "how," "escape," "safe," and "home" before the boy broke into tears.

"We will keep him in the upper rooms. My personal guard will keep watch," Tomu said. If he had found out how the boy escaped, he didn't seem inclined to share it. "Mansa, you knew Bahar well enough. Can you get someone in the Visslands who'll trust your word?"

Mansa gave his answer little thought, but a triumphant spike hit Nasha just as he said, "Aye, Chief."

"Good. Get a runner there, then. They'll have received word about Bahar by now. Tell them the Yltigg have the boy. If we can get the Domain to march on the Yltigg to get him . . ."

"They'll pull back, give us time, if not force the Yltigg into a full retreat," Mansa said.

Tomu gave a satisfied nod.

"And if the Domain decides not to march?" Jabillo asked.

"They'll march," Mansa said.

A smile broke on his lips, but Nasha knew smiles and could feel the emotions shifting. She could almost see the thought forming behind Mansa's eyes. There was something else being birthed in his mind.

"None are to know we have him here. Once the Domain has invaded the Yltigg peaks, we'll cross the border and return him." Tomu regarded the Roots, settling his gaze on them one by one. "No one else hears of this. Tell me when you've received an answer, Mansa."

Iallo was still standing to attention, eyes moving from face to face, waiting to be acknowledged.

Tomu turned to him. "You'll be in the room with the boy. Keep him safe. This is the most important task any Ronar can have."

Iallo's face lit up with a flash of a smile that was quickly suppressed into proper sobriety. "Yes, Chief. You can trust me, Chief."

"I better, or it will be all our heads." He turned towards Mansa and Jabillo again. "You'll need to motivate the Slopers. Promise induction, but remind them they're protecting their own homes, same as we are."

Nasha gritted her teeth, but further discussion would bring her nowhere. She pulled out the tightly packed Hagun ash instead. "There's more." She chucked the packet towards Jabillo. "We came through Hagun. Their village is dead, taken by rotting Earth, just like Chatta." She turned to the Chief. "Their wards were dull. No pulse."

Tomu watched her for a moment, probably making the connection with the pulseless stones at the Ronar dig, but his mind seemed set on the coming threat at their borders.

"We'll deal with this when the Yltigg are off our backs," he said.

Jabillo's eyes were wide, staring down at the ash, but what pulled Nasha's attention was Mansa. Something bludgeoned her when he saw the ash. Recognition, perhaps. A rough kind of pattern, but one she could now easily distinguish as his own. It was gone now, along with the rest of his emotions, hidden behind a veil of emptiness.

Nasha studied him, but his eyes were as empty as his heart. He was still playing some game—Nasha just wasn't sure which one. Whatever it was, she had to find out.

Mansa sat on one of the upper steps above the arena, sharpening his knives with the ritualistic aspect to his movements that Nasha had grown accustomed to during their evening sessions before the Proving. She opened herself but still couldn't sense his emotions. Strange how she'd started using her curse almost naturally, like sight or smell, but it was still a curse, and she could never trust something that had taken so much from her.

Mansa continued his scraping as Nasha walked up to him and sat on the lip of the circular step, jaw working under his neatly trimmed beard.

"Got through it, then," he said without looking up.

"Not sure you could call it that."

"You're alive."

"And Bahar?"

"Not of the Ronar. A necessary sacrifice."

Nasha frowned at him. "You don't really believe that."

"It doesn't matter what I believe. All that matters is what I do."

Nasha kept her eyes on the wide, circular steps, the memory of

Bahar's grief tugging at her heart. Had she killed him, after all? Was she the monster?

"How much did Tomu and Jabillo see?" she asked.

"You're safe. It was all madness. They were fighting their own battle, and if they suspected anything, you'd probably be sleeping with Zala by now."

A touch of solace, perhaps, but the larger question was still looming above them. She'd had time to think on Mansa's emotions in the hall, and the conclusion was clear.

"You lied."

"You'll have to be more specific."

"You lied to me."

Mansa stopped his sharpening. He looked more amused than offended. "You read me?" He couldn't keep the smile off his face. "Looks like you've learned a new trick or two."

"You planned all this, didn't you? With the Carswell boy. You had him. That's why you were frustrated when you got back. You'd lost him."

Mansa shrugged and went back to his sharpening stone, emotions still behind a wall.

"Mansa!"

"What?"

I need to trust someone. I need to trust you! Don't take away what little I have!

He sighed, and for a moment Nasha almost thought she'd said her thoughts out loud. "I'm only doing what's best for the Ronar."

"How do you know what's best?"

"How does Tomu? As I said, it doesn't matter. What matters is I'm doing something about it."

"He'd kill you if he found out."

"We're already dead if we keep living like this, under the boot of the Domain. You just can't see it because Tomu's blinded you with power like he blinds everyone else with the promise of it. At least you've gotten a taste. I'd be careful, though. It sours quickly."

Nasha pressed her teeth together. Always treating her like a child. "Tell me, then. I'm a Root! I—"

"Stop lying to yourself, Nasha. The title means less than you think."

Nasha scowled at him. The title might not mean much to him, but she'd earned it, survived more than anyone else would with her curse. She wouldn't be treated like a child.

Mansa ignored her expression, got to his feet, and gave a slight jerk of his head for Nasha to follow.

They made their way out of the village and down into the valley and walked away from the roads through patches covered with trees, far enough from prying eyes that may have followed. Mansa paused before a clearing. There were voices coming from it.

"I never wanted any of this," Nasha said. "All I wanted was for Adda to take me to the First Tree."

"I know, but you need to open your eyes—or be willing to see the truth, at least." He stepped towards the edge of the clearing but turned back to her before going in. "You step in here, the only way you turn back is in the Earth."

Nasha's teeth hurt from the constant pressing. She eased the pressure on her jaw, nodded, and stepped after him.

The clearing was death itself: earth rotting, trees fallen, all in tinges of gray and black. Two of Mansa's men turned to her as she entered, guarded expressions and emotions held back somehow, but something else wafted towards her. A pungent smell coming in sharp, fleeting waves. Maybe it came from the Earth, or maybe it was the scent of fear coming from the bound man in the center of the glade. The urge to bolt away slammed into her, but the emotions vanished just as fast, just as they had at the patch of dying Earth where she'd found Chatta.

Nasha kneeled on the blackened ground and ran her fingers along the Earth. The emotion flowed out of her and faded like water draining away. She looked towards Mansa, then to his hunters. They weren't holding back. The Earth was affecting them. Was this what had happened to Chatta? Had the Earth syphoned his life away?

The hunters pushed the prisoner onto his knees. He was Domain-born, and his face was familiar.

341

"This man has lived for one hundred and thirty-two years, if he is to be believed. Enough to drain more life from the Earth than any man ever should," Mansa said.

"Is he doing this?" Nasha asked, gesturing at the surrounding blackness.

"No. But he'll undo it." He drew the knife he'd been sharpening. "The Silent Earth will take you back now," he whispered in the Ronar tongue.

The prisoner did not move, only whimpered and pleaded weakly in the Domain tongue, but his words fell on deaf ears; Mansa took a quick step back, then drove the blade smoothly through the man's heart. The rotting scent that had consumed Nasha when she entered the clearing spiked as the knife pierced skin and sinew, then slowly dwindled as the man's life drained away.

Nasha looked around at the glade. There was nothing for a while. Then color started bleeding back into the Earth. The gray became brown, and the sieve of emotion slowly faded. The effect did not spread far, and the glade did not bloom back to life, but it was enough for Mansa to make his point.

"The Earth does not thirst for the blood of the clans." Mansa turned to her. "It thirsts for the blood of the Domain."

Nasha gave a step back from the glade, and Mansa moved after her. "What is this, Mansa?"

"This is the true message of the Earth, Warden. And we're going to give it exactly what it wants."

"War? With the Domain? There's a reason we've avoided that for so long."

"That's what they want us to think. They make us want this mockery of a life, killing our own, going to war between ourselves for scraps. They've twisted even our tales, made us believe we should kill anyone with gifts like yours so that we don't become a threat." He jerked his head back. "Do you know who that was?"

Nasha gave him a blank look, all of it a little too much to swallow. What did the Domain have to do with her curse?

"He was the general they sent here with Bahar. Misher. He's the one who told the Chief we needed a Proving, and Tomu went along with it. Always does. Thinks bowing down to them is the only way to keep us safe." Mansa scoffed. "The Earth doesn't demand our lives, Nasha. The Domain does. They're all for life, as long as it's their own."

Nasha was shaking her head faintly. "You can't know that. You can't provoke a war on the assumption—"

"I assume less than you think. They've been snooping around the northern reaches for months. That Othonean prince who attacked the Hagun? That's when it started. The Domain hasn't attacked us in years. I knew there was something wrong. He was after some old text. Easy to find once the Hagun abandoned everything. Mostly nonsense, but there was one interesting bit. Did you know the first clansmen were exiles from the Domain? They've always seen us as lesser folk, and they keep their boots on our throats to make sure it stays that way."

He smiled at her. "You were right. I knew about the boy who vanished, but I never had him. The Yltigg I enlisted to take him betrayed me. Thought they could use him to gain favor with their clan and throw the Domain against us, the fools." He looked back at the body, then at Nasha. "But I knew the Proving would allow us to head into Yltigg lands, get the boy back, and spark this war. Chatta didn't like it too much when he found out, though. Another necessary sacrifice."

Nasha's head snapped towards him. "You did that?"

"He threatened me, so I had my people grab him, take him away from the village. Seemed cleaner to do it far from the other Roots. Still, I lost him too, I'm ashamed to say. He killed a few of my own and ran. I didn't know about the corruption, though. That was the Earth's doing, not mine."

"I thought . . ."

"We all feel the effect of the Earth, even if we don't have your . . . sensibility. You stand on the decay for long enough, it'll do more than suck all your feelings out.

"Still, Chatta must have known he'd never get back to the village without my people finding him. Probably fled to the Hagun lands. . . . And then the reports of Hagun breaching our borders came."

Nasha was silent, emotions working their way through her just for a moment before being pulled away. "You never sent me to find Hagun. You wanted me to kill him all along." *Should have known. The wounds . . .*

"Didn't expect that mess. Thought I'd taught you better."

"You could have stopped it! The trial! Stopped me becoming . . ." She paused. "Warden," she said through clenched teeth.

He looked at her deep, as though he was reading her emotions again. "I couldn't tell you, Nasha. I needed to be sure. There is no space for error here."

"And Iallo, Embe. Why did you send them? If they'd found Chatta, you think they would've killed him?" Nasha's voice was rising.

"I already had hunters after him, but Tomu isn't stupid. He didn't know I wanted Chatta dead, but not sending warriors when the Hagun crossed our borders would raise questions. Especially after they found Chatta was gone. As I said, I needed to be sure. I sent you because I trust you." Mansa put a hand on her shoulder. "You did your part, and I'm proud of you for it. The clan is better for it."

Part of her broke then. It was whatever part was responsible for keeping her faith in Mansa: the part that knew he'd always be there, the part that knew he was the only one she could trust. The pieces fell away, sucked into the Earth. It didn't matter if she'd done her part or if he was proud. She was just another necessary sacrifice. Just another tool. He'd risked her life like a common Sloper, willing to have her face her end for his plans, his vision of the clan. Even if that future might not have included her. He'd let Bahar pay the price as well, all based on some fevered notion taken from obscure texts.

Her skin tingled, then her entire body went numb. If she hadn't been standing in a clearing of emotion-syphoning death, she wasn't sure she'd be able to hold on, but instead a cold clarity ran through her. She frowned, straining to not let her expression betray her thoughts. She nodded to him, and Mansa opened a smile.

"I'll need you to be better this time," Mansa said. "We're taking that noble and pushing the Domain off our backs."

Nasha nodded again, empty inside, almost as if the Earth had taken hold of her already. Mansa had raised her to believe in him, believe in the clan, but he'd said it himself: it didn't matter what she believed, only what she did, and the emptiness sharpening her mind told her exactly what needed to be done. She smiled back at him, and his emotions finally hit her, filling her chest with warmth, but it was not enough to overcome the cold that had taken hold.

"I'm with you," she said. "But Tomu? He'll never accept war with the Domain."

"No," Mansa said. "I don't expect he will."

———

Nasha walked slowly up the side of the Great Mountain, Mansa's words still ringing in her mind. She shouldn't have let them take root. But there was no stopping them, not when they reached that deep inside. There was little doubt about it, though. Mansa might even be right about the Domain, but she could follow him no longer.

The Slopes were alive with preparations for the coming war, old disputes between Ronar and Slopers temporarily buried by the coming Yltigg threat. People ran about, and the Zaruni seemed intent on making the most out of the opportunity as well. Some gazes lingered on her as she walked by, but most were focused on their own affairs, preparing for the Yltigg and the coming war.

Her mind wandered to Leku. Did he still see her as an asset? Or had war provided him other opportunities? She kept away from the Zaruni all the same, and if any of his men had spotted her, they did not engage.

Shai was sitting outside her family's hut, eyeing the movement of the Slopes. Her gaze narrowed at Nasha's approach, but Nasha brushed off the projected anxiousness. The girl would have questions, but now was not the time to answer them.

Nasha stopped a few paces away. "We need to talk."

CHAPTER TWENTY-SEVEN

The Skygate was Othonea's answer to Dakhran engineering. The airships were a feat, but they did not have enough power to fly higher than the mountains that encircled Dakhra. The gate was constructed from ground to peak in the single pass that gave access to the other nations and always kept under close watch.

— Histories of the Domain

W hat was left of the Legion was in disarray. They'd entrenched themselves in a spot that looked safe enough, but calling it a camp would be optimistic, to say the least.

There were men running on every side, each on a seemingly fruitless task as messengers were sent between captains and tents were being raised. The smell permeating every corner of the makeshift encampment would probably send any sane mind running for the shadows, but Lynn held her breath and plowed through the chaos towards a large, lopsided pavilion at the back of the settlement—as close to a command tent as she could find. She flung aside the flap, leading the way for Rel, Wyman, Gwyndel, Deria, and the other surviving Sentinels.

Olem stood before a table, figures representing armies laid out upon it. Ildred and Thain stood beside him, surrounded by a handful of what looked to be Legion officers. The Legion men stirred, and some even shot fearful gazes as the Sentinels entered, clearly uncomfortable around so many.

The sub-commander surveyed them, eyes searching. "Where's Leardin?"

Silence. Seemed like the Sentinels still had not gotten over the shock of defeat, let alone losing their commander.

"Gone." Lynn almost spat to get the taste of the word out of her mouth.

"What do you mean, gone? Gone where?"

"Gone, Olem. Fallen," Rel said.

This gave the old Sentinel pause. He sighed and smoothed out his hair. "I see . . ." He looked around at them. "It is my duty as his second to assume the post, then. Until a choosing is held." A brusque change of subject, but Leardin was dead, and the living do not dwell on those taken by the enemy.

Ildred stepped forward. "Looks like having you didn't change much, after all."

Lynn stepped up to Ildred, letting the rage rise within her. This had to stop. Now. She didn't reach out to Vedyr, instead injecting the anger into her words. "How strong do you think your faith is, Ildred? You sure the Seraph favors you?"

Her fists were balled, eyes steady. Rel had stepped in beside Lynn with a silent glare, but Olem was already raising his voice and moving between them. "The commander brought Lynn into our ranks. If you wish to challenge that, Ildred, do so by casting your name for the choosing. Right now, you answer to me."

Ildred eyed her for another moment, then stepped back, but the anger was still hot in his stare.

Lynn kept her gaze on Ildred for another moment, then moved away. She knew that his rage stemmed from the feeling of betrayal in his heart and that there was little she could do to change it if he would not allow her the chance. It felt odd seeing the boy who once ran bright-eyed after Elwin and his apprentices, hoping to join them, taken by this unforgiving hatred, but maybe that was just another of the changes she had failed to foresee.

Lynn moved her gaze towards the Legion officer standing beside Olem. "Is this the Light?"

The man shook his head. "The Light has left to rebuild our ranks." He had a goblet beside him and eyed it briefly before looking back at Olem.

"We will fight with what we have," Olem said. "Now." He stepped forward towards a map of their surroundings the Legion general had laid out. "General Burnham's men have brought news about the enemy movement. General?"

"The force that ambushed us has met with the larger one coming through the valley. They've stopped before the pass to the Skygate . . ." Burnham took a sip out of the goblet, seemingly gathering his courage. "They have six thousand men with what seem like ladders to besiege the walls, and . . . siege weapons."

"And how many men do you have left?" Deria asked.

"Little over two thousand," Burnham said. "We were hoping you Sentinels would even the odds." He gave them a drooping smile, either the wine or the weight of their recent defeat weighing on him.

"We would have if you had waited," Thain said. "As it stands, our best chance is Durnn."

"How long do you think your walls will stand?" a hulking captain said beside Burnham. This one did not seem to share the awe of being around Sentinels.

"Hyrkil's right," Burnham said. "Their numbers alone would be enough of a threat, but your walls will not stand against these numbers with siege engines."

"You obviously haven't been to Durnn," Thain said.

"Pride has already taken enough of our men, Sentinel," Hyrkil said. "We should retreat, burn everything behind us until we can get help."

"You're insane! What would the rulers think? Will you tell King

Iridan or Queen Niria we'll be stopping by with our torches to burn their palaces down as well?" Ildred said.

Voices clamored in agreement and outrage on both sides, and not even Olem could silence them this time, but Lynn was furiously scanning the map as a plan of her own began to form. Her eyes were on the one nation that would be close enough to help. She slammed her palm on the table over Dakhra, and all eyes moved towards her.

"We shouldn't have left Durnn, but returning now and hoping to hold isn't an option either. Durnn has never fallen, but its walls have also never faced these odds."

"What then? No army can march here fast enough to lend their aid," Olem said.

"They won't be marching." Lynn unfurled one finger, pointing to the map. "We get Dakhra and their airships."

Ildred shook his head. But he would have probably done that no matter her plan.

"We asked for men to build the Legion and they had none to give. What makes you think they'll send aid now?" Burnham asked.

"They won't be joining the Legion: they'll be answering a call to battle from the Sentinels in the name of the Church. They won't need to conscript men for us, only send aid so we can push this attack back. Once the opposing army is broken, we should be able to clean things up across the Domain, starting with Dakhra if they need it. They'd be helping themselves." There was silence and a few nods of agreement throughout the pavilion. "They won't be able to fly over the mountains. We'll need to open the Skygate. It's the only path through the pass."

"King Iridan won't like this. He's made a point of keeping King Syvern's airships on Dakhra's side of the mountains for years," Deria said.

"And we've made a point of fighting these madmen," Lynn said.

She looked at Rel. His gaze was drifting over the pieces laid out on the map. He paused before the pass, and his brow furrowed into deep lines. "The Skygate. They're guarding it."

Lynn found what Rel had seen and nodded. "They see it too.

They don't want Dakhra moving in behind their ranks. They might be mad, but whoever heads them knows what they're doing." Leardin had said as much. "We'll have to move them to open the gate."

"And how do you propose we do that?" Burnham asked.

Lynn had the room's full attention now, and a flush ran up her neck. "We charge."

"What?" Ildred said.

"Not the traditional way. Only enough to pull them towards us. Then we fall back." Lynn traced her finger across the valley below the Skygate, showing the false charge. "Then we come from here." She traced her finger on the other side. "Once enough are engaged, we'll sneak a small force through, then fall back to the fortress. Durnn should be able to hold off the attack until the Dakhran airships arrive, but we'll need a Sentinel to go through the gap. King Iridan and Queen Niria have soldiers at the Skygate. There's no time to send word to the rulers—we'll need a Sentinel's authority to convince the soldiers to open it, to convince King Syvern to send the airships as well."

There was silence as the soldiers chewed on what Lynn had just fed them. Their eyes moved from the map to the faces surrounding the table and back.

Olem shifted behind the table, then slowly gained enough confidence to nod. "General Burnham, gather the cavalry. You can have the first charge."

"What? Olem!" Ildred said.

"Do you have a better plan, Ildred?"

"I'll take the gate," Thain said before Ildred could answer. "I'm the fastest you've got."

Ildred's glare turned towards him, but Thain was looking at Lynn, something different in his eyes than the contempt he showed when they'd first met in Durnn. Maybe even a seed of respect. Ildred was still looking around at the Sentinels, but the argument was done. Men moved out, throwing shadows all over the tent in the wavering candlelight.

It had been a while since Lynn had felt it, but the sensation of men following her brought a flutter to her gut. She hated the responsibility, and they were still resistant—most lacking Thain's foresight to swallow their pride—but Lynn could not let the Domain fall to death. She'd take up the role even through their discontent. She'd sworn her allegiance to Leardin, and, no matter where he was, she would keep her word. Besides, she'd promised herself. No more running.

CHAPTER TWENTY-EIGHT

There are many dangers across the sea, but none greater than distancing oneself from the Seraph's reach.

— *Unnamed text. Not catalogued.*

Adrian scrubbed his chapped lips, trying to get rid of the roughness that had plagued him for the last hour. If that damned deckhand had mixed up the drinking water and seawater again, he'd have the boy drowned.

It had been four days since he'd left Myrra's defiled face on the battlefield. Hardly enough to forget, but enough for the rage to fester within him and burn whatever patience he'd had.

"Oy!" he yelled at the boy loitering beside the water barrel.

Adrian opened his mouth, but something caught in his throat, and he began to cough, prompting the deckhand to rush over with a water-filled bowl. Adrian grabbed it, giving him nothing more than a scowl in the way of thanks, and the boy scampered off before Adrian could scold him. Adrian looked suspiciously down for a moment, then took a quick sip as his throat threatened another bout of coughing. His lips were cool against the edge of the bowl. No salt.

He raised his head, eyes falling on the horizon and the source of his discomfort. The wind had picked up and was blowing hard against his face, carrying the reddish sand from the Azuri banks drawing near.

The capital city of Dar Drezji shone like a jewel on the edge of the Ulean Sea. Copper glimmered against the brownish-red desert sands, draped in the uncountable colors of the banners representing the ruling guilds.

Adrian noticed the Rhiall and Erhul flags first, billowing in the sand-filled wind. The two merchant families had been a favorite topic of one of Adrian's old tutors. The purple and blue of Rhiall fought the red of Erhul, the latter sometimes accompanied by the orange of the Taraff spicers. Probably an alliance to take on the larger and more ancient Rhiall.

Adrian had heard endless lectures about the changing alliances among the families, but what stuck with Adrian was the betrayal. There seemed to be few alliances that lasted longer than a decade or so, and they always ended in death—or imprisonment, . . . followed by death most of the time.

Adrian's stomach clenched at the symbols waving proudly in the sea breeze. There were too many more he did not know. And having only Nasir to guide him through this heathen country seemed hardly enough to convince the Xakhar to give up men for the Legion. The tutors had taught him the language, at least, and Adrian took that as the slightest of comforts.

He recognized one final banner as they approached the dock. The proud military symbol of the Khorfa covered the land and sea —an upright blade with knotted rope swirling around it, laid out on a field of gray with light accents of green. They extended all around the bay on sails and lined the quay.

"They're probably our best path into the palace." Derren pointed to one of the Khorfa banners. "Hard to tell the state of the alliances, but the Khorfa rarely associate themselves. That's only one interest to deal with, at least. Only one debt."

"That will not be necessary, General." Nasir had appeared beside them, and Derren's irritation was displayed on his face like a family symbol of his own.

"You may have been born here, priest, but I've fought these people for longer than you've been alive."

"Then you have undoubtedly recognized the symbol of the Xakhar."

Derren scanned the horizon, and his eyes fell on something that made them go wide. Nasir nodded.

"You may have the past, General, but I keep information on the present." Nasir pointed at a massive copper building with a sky-blue dome in the center that could only be the palace.

A tower rose from it with a banner hanging on either side. One showed crossed scimitars with a star in the middle, displayed over wavy lines that reminded Adrian of the sandy wind scraping against his cheeks. The other seemed to have the same symbol but was rolled open only halfway.

"The symbol of the Xakhar, my lord Light," Nasir said.

"Why is it not fully displayed?"

"Mourning," Derren said.

"Of what?" Adrian asked, sincere confusion riding his tone.

"The dead, my lord Light," Nasir replied.

Adrian looked at the priest with a mixed expression. "For all to see?"

"The Azuri believe the dead must be remembered. They have a different kind of judgment here," Nasir said.

Adrian grunted. He could understand the allure. Might have made things easier for him with Myrra. But what use was it to remember the dead if there was no Seraph to bring them back? It would bring only the pain that had found a permanent home in Adrian's chest. It was a fool's notion, and the idea of recruiting foreigners to the Legion seemed suddenly foolish as well. Still, he needed the men.

"And what does that have to do with the Khorfa? How will we

get men from the Xakhar?" Adrian asked.

"The palace is open for all those who wish to mourn the prince, my lord Light. It will be for seven days. All those who can contribute to his memory do so to the Xakhar himself. Then Prince Niilar's actions will be weighed and judgment on how he will be remembered shall be passed."

"Judged by who?"

"The Council of Consuls, leaders of the ten families."

"And when the Xakhar finds we have nothing to add about his dead son?" Derren asked.

"Then the Light of the Legion must shine," Nasir said.

"Faith again?" Adrian looked wearily at the priest.

"Only in yourself, my lord Light."

Adrian set his eyes on Derren now. The old guard shrugged in what looked like a rare moment of concurrence with the priest.

A thousand more questions still spun in Adrian's mind. He was reluctant to shy away from them, but he doubted he'd be satisfied with the answers, same as when he'd asked Nazir about summoning the fire. The priest had only recited Father's old words, adding a few of his own: "Blood holds ties, but not all ties are equal." The answer only made Adrian angrier, and after that he left the priest to his own affairs on the ship.

He kept the questions in the back of his mind, sighed, and drank deep from the water bowl once more, then flung it to the side —the ship was already pulling up to a quay. Adrian followed Derren, Nasir and a handful of guards off the ship into the sun-bathed Azuri capital.

The streets of Dar Drezji were a mess. The copper-tinted stones of the buildings gave the city a monotone background that would have blended into the red desert sands were it not for the vines sprouting from cracks and spreading across the rounded constructions. They were complemented by the vivid colors of family banners and tinted silks, all contributing to the confusion, yet fitting together in a way that made the city as striking as any Adrian had ever laid eyes upon. Adrian's white cloak was stained almost black. It stood out from the livery of the city, but less so as they drew closer to the palace, where mourners wore black—either in flowing silk or threadbare linen—from head to toe.

The palace itself was a singular work of art. Sunlight shone off copper plates interweaved with silver lines coiling their way around pillars and tracing patterns onto arches, windows, and doors. The windows had greenery growing around them and were covered in blue-tinted glass, but they did not compare to the great dome in the center, shining a deep sapphire, as smooth as a cloudless sky. It made no sense. Why the display if there was no Seraph to appease, no higher power to convince of their worthiness?

Adrian caught glimpses of black-hooded people looking more curious than mournful who made their way towards a side entrance, while a few headed towards the main doors. This was where Nasir led them.

Guards with the crossed scimitars of the Xakhar's crest on their chests were vetting all who came through, but they did not seem to be particularly thorough, and Adrian's group was ushered inside after Nasir spoke a few words of fluent Azuri. They stepped into a vast room supported by azure pillars in the same sky-blue as the dome. The floor was polished yellow marble, and there was a coolness that immediately embraced them as they moved out of the sunbaked streets.

People in black cloaks stood talking in hushed tones here and there, scattered throughout the throne room's expanse in private groups, each waiting their turn. Adrian's eyes were pulled to the back, where a woman in white robes draped with gray and black silks sat atop a dozen steps in a chair colored in the same signature blue of the palace. He threw off his cloak and strode towards her.

Nasir might have said something, but Adrian paid him no mind. He blew past a man in black who was retreating from the bottom of the steps, stopped, and looked up with all the regality he could muster. Several other men and women sat in their own chairs on a lower level than the throne, each decorated in colors Adrian assumed represented their families: the ten guilds of Azur, consuls under the Xakhar.

Now that Adrian was closer, he could see the woman better. The princess had dark-green eyes, and the lines of her jaw, nose, and mouth were smooth, as if someone had drawn them over and over until each part of her was placed exactly where it should be. Her beauty was like the city's: unfamiliar but striking to behold.

"I would speak to the Xakhar," he said in the rough Azuri he remembered.

The woman on the throne cocked an eyebrow at him. "An Immerian. We rarely get *your* kind here," she answered in the same language. "I do not recall my brother visiting your continent. Have you anything to add to his memory?"

"I am sorry, Princess Kahlia, I am afraid the Lord Light is unaware of the customs," Nasir's voice came from beside Adrian, speaking Azuri. A tinge of fear in it, perhaps?

"I am Nasir, Your Grace, high priest of the Legion. And this is the Light of the Legion, Lord Adrian Pell, son of King Iridan, an old friend to the Xakhar."

"Light of the Legion. That is a title I am not familiar with," she said.

"It is an old one, Princess. The highest of titles," Nasir said.

It was her turn to look Adrian over. "You must be the very highest of champions, then."

A few of the consuls held back laughter or chuckled behind their hands.

"I have been judged worthy enough."

"Ah, yes, your Seraph. I've always found the Immerian beliefs amusing, but I never did quite understand your fondness for this invisible woman who judges us all."

She'd have been killed for that in the Domain. Here, Adrian smiled as best he could. If he was to rebuild the Legion, some sacrifices would have to be made, and his taste for revenge was still burning hotter than his wounded pride.

"We have nothing to add about the dead," Adrian said. "A darkness rises throughout Avarin, and a sea as narrow as the Ulean will not stop it from reaching your shores."

"You Immerians are always going on about death and darkness rising," said an old man in a chair of yellow and blue adorned with a crest Adrian did not recognize. "Yet the sun still rises after every night."

There were smiles and an actual laugh from one of the consuls now, and Adrian had to take a deep breath to keep the irritation off his face.

"This is a night that will last a great deal longer, I'm afraid, my lord Attar," Nasir said. "It is not a threat of men but of the mind."

The old man looked unconvinced, but a younger woman bearing the crest of a black hood on midnight-blue was staring at them intently. "And how would this darkness affect us?"

"It is an invisible enemy, Lady Zarath—a madness." Nasir bowed his head. "I myself am Azuri born, trained in the great house of the Afterdark, and have never seen anything like it."

"Madness?" Lady Zarath asked.

"A beastly ferocity and savage taste for death. They remove the faces of the dead and wear them as masks."

A murmur rose in the throne room, some actions seemingly brutal enough to offend even the heathens.

Adrian caught the princess's eyes at Nasir's comment, and something seemed to shift behind them. She held up a hand for silence.

"And what do you expect of us?" she said.

"We have fought them, and we need more men. If Azur would add enough soldiers to the Legion of the Seraph, we would end this blight."

And I would get my revenge on the worm who took Myrra from me.

Kahlia considered him for a moment. "You have reached us in a time of great turmoil, Lord Adrian. The Domain must offer more if we are to consider this."

Adrian narrowed his eyes and ran his tongue along his teeth, gauging the princess, but her stare remained locked on his own, unwavering.

"The shipping routes," he said. "We can open them again. A token of the Domain's appreciation for your help. You would be allowed to trade with all of Avarin. Our ships would block the Ulean no longer." He'd have to talk to the Pontiff about that, but she didn't have to know that.

There was a stir from the consul with the Khorfa symbol, and Lord Rhiall seemed to be intrigued as well. Adrian's gaze flitted over them, then back to Princess Kahlia.

"I will bring this matter to my father when the time is appropriate." She stood. "In the meantime, the Lord Light will be our guest in the palace."

The princess exited through a backdoor, leaving the consuls to argue about the decision while Adrian and his men were excused.

Adrian looked sourly at Nasir as they left the chamber. "What now?"

"We wait, my lord. The princess favors you."

"Didn't sound that way."

"The Azuri are known to take their time, but offering to house you as a guest in the palace shows true favor. Especially in a time like this. None of the consul families are allowed inside."

Adrian did not look at the priest. His thoughts were wandering the back paths of his mind, trying to find a faster way. "The dead will overrun Othonea in the time it takes for these"—he bit off the word *heathens*—". . . before they make up their mind."

"We must be patient. Pushing them will only delay the response." Nasir looked up at the merciless sun, then back down at Adrian. "I will find our escort, and we may talk further in the shade of the palace, yes?"

Nasir stepped away, and Adrian was left to his thoughts and the sour taste rolling around on his tongue.

"I don't like it," Derren said.

"Neither do I. We can't depend on their whims." Adrian lowered his voice. "You still have people here?"

"I can dig them up."

"Find some, then. If the stories of backstabbing and betrayal are true, there is bound to be at least one seat on the council that'll lend us a friendly ear."

Derren nodded just as the palace guard approached them with Nasir in tow. Adrian gave the general a meaningful look, then followed them into the palace.

CHAPTER TWENTY-NINE

You will never turn on your fellow Ronar. You will do what is required by your station without complaint, and above all else, you will work towards enhancing the strength of the clan. Weakness is a corruption of its own.

— Words of induction into the Ronar clan

Half of the village was scared and locked inside, the other half scared and preparing to head towards the forests that extended from the foot of the Great Mountain. The hope was to have the Slopers adapt their knowledge of the twisting paths of the Slopes to the shadows of the boughs in the Ronar forest. Nasha could feel the excitement brimming off them. It might have been veiled in opportunity, and most had gone willingly, but she wasn't sure how long it would last when they started to fall. The trees were not the Slopes, and, as usual, the Slopers would pay the price.

Anaya and Bedri had been sent to accompany Nasha once more, and they sat in her old hut, silent but for the scraping of obsidian blades on sharpening stones, waiting for the Ronar and Slopers to march so that Mansa's plan could be carried out.

He'd made it simple. Nasha would enter the Chief's Hall, then let the hunters in to help her deal with Iallo and whoever else was inside—obviously counting on her newfound control of her curse. They'd fashioned hoods to cover their faces and not give Mansa or themselves away. Simple enough, yet Nasha found herself working her jaw. The simplest plans were always the ones that found the most complicated ways of going awry.

The sun was already vanishing behind the horizon once the flow of people exiting the village had subsided enough for Nasha and the hunters to step out of the hut. Bedri and Anaya circled around as they neared the hall, leaving Nasha standing alone before it. There were no guards at the door—none could be spared with the Yltigg coming—but there'd be enough guarding the prisoner. Nasha pushed open the doors and paused in the common room. Fruit and meat were displayed and available as always, but the ancestor-stone relief of the First Tree in the wall was a touch darker than she remembered, the mahogany around it not as warm. Nasha chuckled to herself. She'd been awed by the hall the first time she was marched through here, but she couldn't tell if what had dulled was the ancestor-stone itself or her opinion of the Roots whose power the surrounding grandeur represented.

Iallo sat before the carved ancestor-stone with pieces of meat and fruit on a plate as if he were a Root himself. He glared at her. "Hope you're enjoying your time here, Sloper. Won't last long."

Nasha gave an angry step towards him. She'd earned her place here, and that meant something, even if Mansa had said otherwise. "You get back to guarding your prisoner like a good little dog, Iallo. This isn't for you."

Nasha swiped her hand, sending his plate flying to the ground. He jumped to his feet, hands darting to his spear, but Nasha opened out both arms. "You going to strike a Root, Iallo?"

"You are weak. I'd be doing the clan a service."

Nasha gave him a grin. "What was it Embe said to me after I

killed Chatta? 'That's not your choice to make.' Not where a Root is concerned, at least."

She turned her back to him and made her way towards the stairs. He wouldn't strike at her. She could sense his rage like a burning gust around her, but there was nothing pushing him to action. She headed upstairs to her room, stepped in, and halted, blinking at the figure sitting on her bed. Adda was looking out the window, her back turned.

"Mansa told me what happened in the Proving. You did what was needed for the Ronar, it seems."

Nasha frowned, caught off guard not only by the lack of aggressiveness in Adda's tone but by the radiating emotion. She could identify the nuances now. Focused, projected towards her, almost . . . intentional? Was that fear?

"Why did you want him dead?" Nasha asked, stepping into the room and around the bed to stand before Adda.

The Tivezzi kept her gaze on the window. "What we want is of little importance, Warden. Our actions are all that ring true."

Nasha's frown deepened at the words. Mansa had said something similar.

Probably some foolish saying from the tales. She couldn't linger.

"The debt is paid, then," Nasha said.

Adda's gaze slid towards Nasha, slow and hard. "You will soon find that debt for people like us is hardly ever paid." She looked out the window once more, hands folded on her lap. "I might have need for you still. You may have paid the price for your life, but it would be wise to consider what else I can give you."

Adda rose to her feet. "A Root is always in need of friends, Warden. Choose them carefully." She strode towards the door.

"What are you afraid of?" Nasha asked.

Adda paused, turning her head only slightly, but not looking back. "It is wise to be afraid in times like these. Fear keeps those like us safe."

"Those like us?"

"You should know what that means by now, Warden."

She left, closing the door behind her. Nasha gave it a moment, waiting for the footsteps and emotions to slide down the stairs and out of the hall, but her own emotion crept up on her. She drove a frustrated fist into the wall, feeling the wood crack under her knuckles. She'd had enough of the cryptic conversations that kept pulling her deeper into their schemes.

Nasha breathed out and refocused on what she had to do. She lowered the rope out the window, held it tight in both hands, and braced her feet against the wall beneath the opening. There was a tug, then a heavy pull, and soon Anaya's closely shaved head appeared in the window, followed by Bedri and his long braids. They were inside in a few quick breaths.

"Thought you'd given up on us," Bedri said, smirking at her and pushing his hair back out of his face.

"Room was occupied." Nasha returned only a slight frown.

"Shh. Let's go," Anaya said. They put on their hoods and made their way out through the narrow corridor towards where the Domain noble was being kept, pausing at the corner. Anaya was trying to peek around, but Nasha had already identified the different shades of emotion that told her two men stood guard outside. There were more patterns coming from within. Five, maybe six. Each of them manifested differently: a tingle on the skin, a tightness in the chest, or a heavy weight on the shoulders. Nasha was not taken over by them, though. They were like whispers spoken in her mind.

There was one other, as well. Unstable, likely the prisoner. Nasha closed her eyes, and she could almost see them: the Domain boy a core of fear and anxiety, the others a few steps away, emotions much more subdued, but alert.

She readied her weapon, a small wooden club rather than the sharp knives she was used to. Those were sheathed behind her back. These guards were Ronar, doing their duty for the clan. There was nothing to gain from killing them.

Nasha nodded to Anaya, and they both darted around the corner. Nasha went for the guard furthest from them. She rushed at him and bashed her club upward into the man's chin. A flash of surprise was his only reaction before he was out cold, and Nasha caught him to avoid alerting those inside.

Anaya had knocked out the woman on her side as well, and Bedri now stood behind them, ready to charge in. Nasha raised a hand and opened herself up to the emotions again. She sensed the patterns coming from inside the room, all of them stable, still unaware. She nodded once more, and Bedri kicked the door open.

The six warriors to the left, who seemed to have been throwing stones, looked up wide-eyed. Their bewilderment hit Nasha like a weapon of its own, but after the arena, these sensations were like droplets in a breeze. They scrambled, jumping off chairs, hands searching for weapons, but the hunters were already on them. Nasha crashed her club into a rising woman's jaw, knocking her unconscious, then swung it sideways into the temple of a man who was groping for his weapon.

Anaya and Bedri had knocked out two each themselves and were moving towards the prisoner now. He was crawling backwards, talking too fast for Nasha to understand. Anaya hit him on the back of the head, and he fell silent. They threw a hood over his head, gagged him, and tied his wrists, then tied rope all around the boy's body. Bedri fastened a rope of his own to a table, then threw it out the window and climbed out. Nasha and Anaya lowered the prisoner after him. Once they were down, Anaya followed with nothing but a parting nod to Nasha.

Nasha walked over to Bedri's rope but froze as a wave of incoming emotion rushed towards her. She turned towards the door. Iallo stepped through, and his eyes bulged at the sight. He gripped his spear, threatening a charge.

"Where is he?!"

Nasha removed her hood, and his eyes went even wider. The surprise lasted only a moment, but it felt good. There was no need to hide from him. She'd finish what she started now. He dropped his spear and produced two knives like Nasha's own: one for parrying, the other for striking—weapons better suited for close quarters.

He assumed the familiar stance with parry knife before him, the other held back. "They should have killed you long ago. I'll make sure you die this time."

Nasha pulled out her hunter's knives, assuming the same position. "I'd like to see you try."

Iallo paused as if he were about to call for help, but Nasha wasn't fooled. He knew as well as her that the village was too empty for anyone to come. They circled, studying each other's movements, gazes locked.

Iallo's back arm twitched, but his emotions betrayed him. It was too stable for an attack, and Nasha recognized the feint, which lasted only a split second before the thrill of his true strike rushed at her. He darted forward, stabbing with the parry knife instead of the back arm, still fast, despite the lack of surprise. Nasha turned away from the stab, but it scraped her arm, and Iallo used the opening to kick at her leg that had been injured at the Proving. Her leg pulsed and weakened, sending her to one knee.

Bastard.

Iallo lost no time and drove the striking knife towards her head. He put all of his body into the move, pulling back the parry knife and twisting his torso forward with more power and even more speed than his first attempt. She'd have been done if this were a few days ago, but her curse sent a warning thrill up her spine before he moved, and she caught his strike on the ridges of her parry blade, then twisted the attack to the side. She countered with a stab at his gut, but Iallo had kept his own parry knife close and batted Nasha's stab away, then jumped back and circled her again.

"They'll make me Warden when I kill you," he said with a smile, but Nasha was done talking.

She gritted her teeth and pushed forward, slashing instead of stabbing now. Iallo blocked the slash, then went for her injured leg again. He was fast, but he didn't have her curse.

Iallo's rage was strong enough to be almost visible—a shade of the lines that she'd seen in the arena—but it was easy enough for Nasha to grab onto it and pull with her mind. It surged through her, and she moved her leg out of the way of his lunge, then rammed her head into Iallo's nose.

The rage was hot, but she was in control. Nasha charged him again, but Iallo barely moved, as if she'd pulled more than just rage out of him. She crashed her forehead into his nose again, and his head lolled back, eyes rolling up into their sockets. He dropped his knives, and Nasha grabbed him by the front of his vest. His eyes rolled back down, but he was still groggy, weak.

Nasha threw him to the ground, pulled his hair back and placed her knife on his neck. "Go ahead. Call out. See if any of your friends hear you," she whispered.

Iallo struggled with another spike of rage, but Nasha did not let it last long. She slid the knife across his throat and let his blood pour out.

Nasha dropped the body and strained her senses, searching for approaching emotion more than approaching sound. Nothing but her heart, roaring in her ears. She looked at Iallo's dead body one more time, regaining her breath. The plan didn't involve dead Ronar, but she had plans of her own.

Weakness is a corruption of its own.

She spat onto Iallo's body. One more life returned to the Earth. She took a few moments to still her heart and quell the rage she'd taken from him—the last strands of what was left of his life—then crept out of the room and down the corridor towards her chamber. She changed into clothes that were not bloodstained and discarded the old set into a bag, then slung it on her back, sheathed her knives, and went down to find the hunters.

The common hall was still empty, the village outside silent. Nasha made her way to the edge of the trees where the hunters waited with the prisoner.

"Trouble?" Anaya asked.

"Not anymore," Nasha said, and stepped into the trees.

CHAPTER THIRTY

A close councillor will bring you wisdom. Too many will bring you a knife in the back.

— *Azuri saying*

The view of the palace gardens was trying hard to convince Adrian they were not in a desert. The stifling heat, hanging heavy all around the room, didn't let him forget. There'd been no sleep, even in his underclothes.

It was his third night in Dar Drezji, and there had been no shortage of courteous servants and questionable food choices, yet still no word from the princess or the Xakhar.

Adrian slid his hand over the velvet-covered arm of the chair, but the heat had transformed the normally comfortable smoothness into a cloying embrace, and he eventually found himself pacing in front of the window again, fingers wandering along Myrra's amulet while he looked down into the gardens. The pools reflected the full moon, but the Seraph's mark was nowhere to be seen.

He let his gaze wander over the surface of the pools, but his ears picked up shuffling outside his door, and he turned towards it with a frown. Perhaps that was the true reason they'd offered him to stay at the palace. His guards had not been given quarters inside the palace, and he doubted Derren would share his lack of sleep to stand at his door all night. Being murdered in his own rooms suddenly seemed like a surprisingly straightforward proposition. Was this the way the Xakhar would deny his request?

Adrian's eyes flicked towards his sword. There was no time for armor, barely even time for a proper shirt. Adrian grabbed the sword and slid into one of the shadows beside it, gripping the hilt tight, ready to strike down the intruder.

A dry knock and Adrian froze.

Derren sending a runner, maybe? No, he wouldn't likely be able to find a reliable runner at this hour. Maybe the general himself. Another knock. Louder, impatient. Adrian placed his sword back and slowly opened the door.

A short man with a well-pruned beard was looking up at him. He wore no crest, and his eyes flitted only briefly over Adrian's disheveled state, then fell on a small piece of parchment he was thrusting out. Adrian took the message, but the man did not leave. He waited with a restless look in his eyes. Maybe expecting compensation? None was coming. Adrian opened the folded parchment where he stood.

King's courtyard. Now.
Gashkin will direct you.

There was no signature, no sign of who would summon him at this hour, but by the curtness of it, this was clearly not one of his staff. Maybe Derren had already found an ally. Adrian weighed the chances of a trap, yet the opportunity was too great to ignore.

"You're Gashkin, I presume?" he said in the Domain tongue.

The short man looked up at his name but did not seem to understand the other words. That was answer enough, though. Adrian went back into his rooms and put on a shirt and the lightest trousers he could find. He was buckling up his sword when he realized Gashkin was in his rooms and shaking his head. He pointed calmly at the sword, then at the chair where it had lain, as if there was no doubt Adrian would follow his command immediately. Adrian held the man's eye, but the orderly did not waver, looking at him with a penetrating stare of his own. Adrian frowned and threw the sword belt back on the chair.

"Fine."

Gashkin did not react. He simply turned and made his way along the shadow-wreathed halls, stepping across the moonlight shining in through the arched windows.

The man left him at a cloister that looked down on the open courtyard. It was empty, and Adrian reconsidered the possibility of murder. Maybe they didn't want to soil the room with his blood. He imagined himself lying pale and lifeless in the heat, dead outside of the Domain, outside of the Seraph's reach, just like Jovu. Would they bring him back to burn and scatter over the sea? Probably not.

Footsteps rustled beside him, and Adrian turned to find a hooded figure standing not five feet away, also looking down at the courtyard.

"I've always enjoyed the smell of this place," Princess Kahlia said in Othonean, with a barely perceptible accent. "The wind always brings just the right amount of nightshade blossom so that you never tire of it."

Adrian looked around them. "Not much of a breeze."

"Not tonight." She took a deep breath. "But the scent is still sweet."

It was faint, but there was a smell trailing up from the flowers in the gardens below, and a few of them grew on vines along the balustrade. Adrian plucked one, and the scent filled his senses— sweet but stronger now, almost biting.

"Is that why you sent your charming manservant to fetch me in the middle of the night?"

Kahlia regarded him with a delicate smile. "Is it not reason enough?"

Adrian looked at her coolly, but even his stare seemed to thaw in the heat, and that sweetness from the flower was still there, flowing through him, growing stronger.

"You must certainly be desperate to come to us," she said. "You Immerians rarely leave your so-called Domain."

"The threat we face does not limit itself to our borders, Princess. What do you think will happen if we fall?" His throat was dry. Too sweet. The smell was cutting through him. More than uncomfortable now, it was starting to hurt.

"Most of you call us mad. Should we be slaughtered, then? Return to the war between our continents after years of peace?"

Adrian coughed, trying to get the sweetness out of his lungs. "The only war I propose is an . . ." He coughed again. "An inevitable one. We would eradicate this plague before it has even touched your lands."

Kahlia's smile had turned to a frown below her hood. "We have our own problems here. There is dissent among the consuls. And while the Xakhar is never safe, I fear my father has more enemies posing as friends than he would care to admit." She paused, took in the smell once more, then sighed. "There are too many sweet smells that will bring you in, only to poison you at the barest touch."

Adrian's eyes shot down to the flower he'd plucked. It had turned from midnight-blue to coppery red, almost like the color of Kahlia's skin. He tried to take a step towards the princess, but his legs were as heavy as the doubts that had weighed upon him throughout the night. He tried to gasp but could not pull in air.

"How unrelenting our world is. A slight misstep and our life is dangling by a thread." She stepped closer. "You might be finding the scent a little much right now. Understandable. You are a foreigner, and so many of our wonders can be an acquired taste. Don't worry, though. It'll take a while to kill you."

Adrian was coughing again, unable to respond.

"You will tell me the truth now."

He doubled over, unable to even cough appropriately.

"I am sad to say that word has spread of the weakening of the Xakhar. A lie, of course, but a good lie with an enticing promise is more than enough for most men. You can see how the death of my brother complicates things, yes?"

Adrian didn't look up.

"Yes?"

He nodded as best he could.

"Your arrival has been conveniently timed if one of our enemies was trying to make a move on the throne. Which of the consuls sent you?"

Adrian shook his head in a frantic motion. "None . . ." he wheezed. "I . . . I barely know their crests." More coughing. His body had gone cold.

The princess's fierce green eyes were fixed on him. He probably made a pathetic figure, but breathing took precedence over image at the moment. His lungs burned, but his body was ice, and every attempted breath was like being stabbed a thousand times.

She scoffed at him. "You really are that desperate, then."

Adrian was on his knees now, gripping the balustrade tight.

"You will get your men, but we cannot leave Dar Drezji to the mercy of the vipers, ready to strike at my family from the shadows. There have been talks, whispers in the dark. One of the consuls is planning to move against my father, trying to bring others into their attempt. I'll need you to find who that is."

Adrian had one hand on the ground, but the princess lowered her face to him. "You understand what is requested of you, yes? Just play along for now. Undoubtedly, many will have seen the same opportunities I did when you walked into the palace. You are in a . . . unique position, close to the royal family. Some will approach you. All you must do is report to me. Once the threat has been handled, we will find you a suitable marriage. One that will give you means to rally your Legion."

Adrian's gut clenched. His instinct to deny the proposition. But there was no time. His body was as cold as the bottom of the Ulean Sea, and he needed to breathe.

Adrian nodded to her once more, neck growing stiffer.

"Excellent."

She snapped her fingers, and Gashkin moved forward with a vial of clear liquid. The servant tilted Adrian's head back and emptied the vial down his throat.

Adrian collapsed, shaking, uncaring about the humiliation. There was no strength left to stand.

"You know your way back." Her voice drifted away, and her footsteps receded into the palace while Adrian slowly regained his breath with new appreciation for the warm air around him.

A breeze finally broke the stifling air, but it brought him the poisonous scent of the treacherous flower. Adrian lay there, no strength to escape it, the thought of Myrra in his mind, the sour taste of what had been proposed clawing at his throat.

After what seemed like hours, he found the strength to get to his feet and stumbled back towards his rooms. Kahlia had struck at his pride, but she'd accepted his terms, given him a path towards rebuilding the Legion and getting his revenge. There were still a few steps he'd have to go through, but it would have to do.

His body gave out when he finally reached his rooms, and he didn't know for how long he drifted in and out of consciousness, but it couldn't have been long: the sun still wasn't up. He tried to move, but his body ached all over. He couldn't tell if it was an aftereffect of the poison or his muscles reacting to the unslept hours of the past few weeks.

Adrian's gaze drifted across the room as his senses sharpened, and he thought he saw a shadow of movement beneath the door again. The insolent manservant coming to check on him, perhaps? The knock was soft, almost a whisper. Adrian struggled to get up and, after a long moment, fixed his sword belt tightly, determined not to remove it this time, then shambled towards the door.

He opened it with one hand on his sword, but it was Derren's face peering through the crack. Adrian pulled the door open and scuffled back into his chamber. He let himself down in one of the velvet chairs, eyes dry, velvet still uncomfortable in the heat.

"Have you slept?" Derren asked.

Adrian looked away, clenching his jaw.

"I've contacted my people. We'll get an answer soon," Derren said.

Adrian shook his head. "We'll need them for something else."

Derren gave him a look as if the heat had gotten to his head. Maybe it had.

"There are families moving against the Xakhar," Adrian said. "We need to find out who it is. Kahlia will give us an army then." Adrian was still working out how he'd avoid the part about marriage and couldn't bring himself to raise the matter.

Derren studied Adrian. "And if I can get someone else? Faster?"

"Who?"

"I . . . don't know yet . . ."

"An unknown ally is as good as an enemy, Derren."

"Like our priest?"

Adrian narrowed his eyes at the general, but Derren did not give him time to respond. "I think you'll find soon enough that a prospect is the best you can hope for in this city." Derren sighed as he sat in the chair opposite Adrian. "We shouldn't have come here, Adrian."

"Yet, here we are." Adrian opened his arms and gazed through his open window. The wind seemed to have picked up. It brought back the sweet scent of the flowers and the cutting chill of the poison. "I'll take the prospect I know, for now. Get me something on the families. They don't have access to the palace. I'll try to negotiate something with them on my side."

Adrian thought he saw Derren's mouth pull up a fraction. "You try to deny it, but you remind me of your father too often. I suppose blood really does hold ties."

"I'm my own man, Derren. You'd do well to remember it. The Light—"

"Yes, yes, the Light stands in no shadow. I meant it as a compliment." Derren stood and made his way towards the door.

"Derren?"

He turned to Adrian.

"Whatever feud you've got going on with Nasir, end it. We're surrounded by enough enemies as it is."

"I will . . ." Derren paused in the open door, face held in a beam of moonlight. "As soon as I'm sure he isn't one of them." He closed the door, leaving Adrian's frowning face in darkness once more.

Damn the old guard. He'd been too close to Father for too long. He'd never have talked like that to Jovu. Then again, Adrian couldn't imagine Jovu running off to Azur to beg for an army. He shook his head and paced the room again until he ended up in his usual spot, standing by the window to wait for the dawn, while his hopes of sleep dissolved with the night.

CHAPTER THIRTY-ONE

Never forget. The enemy's true weapon is not one made from steel, but one that weaves itself into the mind. Fear and doubt are more dangerous than any blade.

— Sentinel battle-instruction from the Book of the Blade. Restricted.

Lynn shifted in her horse's saddle, every trot sending a jolt through her. How could people ride for miles on these things? Her heart ached at the thought of Vedyr, ached for the days she wasn't strapped to the ground. But nostalgia was the byproduct of sacrifice, it seemed, and she knew the griffin, like mostly everyone else, was better off far from her and the eyes of death ever looking over her shoulder.

To wield the enemy's weapon is to diminish its power over us, but what do I do when I am buried in it, Elwin?

No answer. At least his voice had not joined the others in her mind. Lynn heeled her horse along, trying not to take out her feelings on the undeserving animal. She made her way towards Rel,

377

who was waiting for her on a ridge at the edge of the trees that over-looked Pehd Valley.

"You sure about this?" he asked.

"Of course not," Lynn said. "But what else do we have?"

Rel nodded and might have even grinned in the darkness, but Lynn kept her eyes trained straight ahead.

"You did good. Stepping up," he said.

"Should have been you."

"I'm too soft."

"Leardin was hard enough. . . . Look where that got him."

"We don't know he's gone." Rel's tone shifted slightly. "He's been in command for over a hundred years. Hard has got him through."

"Olem's in charge now. Probably for the best."

"Hah! There's a reason Olem's been second for so long. He hasn't got that . . . flare you have, the one people look to follow. It may be Olem now, but he'd only lead us on a short path to all our deaths if the future of the Sentinels were in his hands."

Lynn grunted. "Perhaps I'll take you the long way then." She turned her horse around and offered her arm. Rel clasped it. "Whatever the path, . . . thank you. You believe in me far too much for your own good." Her mouth pulled up slightly in an attempted smile. It felt odd on her lips.

"Not my place to judge." Rel flashed a wide grin of his own, and his gaze moved up towards the Seraph's eye. "See you on the other side."

Lynn nodded and dug her heels into her mount, clamping her jaw as it set into a jostling trot once more.

Burnham's unit was surprisingly well organized. Not much could be done about the mud-splattered uniforms or the bottle seemingly attached to his hand, but the line was in place, with only a few soldiers still bearing fearful faces. Either faith or a more immi-nent threat of death was putting some steel into them.

Lynn spurred her mount towards the general but was stopped by someone stumbling into her path, and she pulled up her horse, almost rearing. A wide-eyed man crouched before her, and another was pulling him out of the way.

"Ferrin?"

Ferrin urged the man out of Lynn's path, then looked up, and his face was taken by a smile of recognition. "Lynn, you're alive!"

"I thought I told you to stay in Durnn, out of trouble."

"No escaping it, is there?" he said. "Not in times like these."

"So you joined the Legion?"

"Oh, haven't joined it as much as tagged along. The guard was taking volunteers from the city, said the Legion might need us. I'm only in the reserve." His smiled widened. "Looks like we're needed now, though."

"Ferrin, this isn't a game."

"You think I don't know that? I've had enough death in my life. Figured I'd take a page out of your book, fight it. Seems to have worked for you well enough."

Great. How many other fools had followed her hopeless path?

You're going to kill him, too, Cara said.

This was your plan. His life is on you. All of their lives are on you, Alren said.

Lynn pulled in the cold air around her and trapped it in her lungs for a moment before letting it out. Hearing Alren's voice was never comfortable; she couldn't let Ferrin throw himself into this.

"Please don't make this harder than it already is," she said.

"I'm here to help. We all are. Fighting's gonna reach us sooner or later."

"You're not joining the charge," Lynn said.

"Already did. Got my horse rig—"

"Stay here." She rode forward, hardly feeling the discomfort in the canter this time.

Burnham was gesturing everywhere, making sure his men had saddles tight and arrows stocked. He fell silent when Lynn came into view and made his way towards her, still pressing shoulders and shaking hands to keep the motivation above breaking point.

"Come to oversee my work, Sentinel?"

"Only to make sure your men aren't feeling more heroic than necessary, General."

"No heroes here. Those are all mad or burning in the trees where we left them."

He took a swig from the bottle while Lynn looked over the men. Burnham seemed to have the truth of it; they looked a lot closer to deserters than heroes.

"Keep them in line then, General. Hit and run, yes?"

Burnham eyed her and gave the slightest movement of acknowledgement.

"I'm taking some of the reserve with me," she said. "We'll be ready if things go awry."

Burnham nodded. "Glad you have our backs."

He probably shouldn't be. But Lynn only nodded back and made her way towards where she'd left Ferrin. He was standing with a ramshackle band of men and women who could hardly be called soldiers. Most of them had their own gear, and most of it was in such disrepair—chipped and rusted—that it was more likely to betray than protect them in battle.

Lynn dismounted. Her horse seemed to have noticed her feelings and tried to bite her as she gathered the reins in her hand. She didn't hold it against him, but she tugged at the reins firmly enough to show who was in command.

"You're with me. Leave your horses."

"What?" Ferrin said. "How are we supposed to—"

"You're the reserve. We won't have need of them if all goes well. Take them to one of the captains. Gotzon looked like he needed them." Lynn looked them over. "If any of you wish to leave, it will not be held against you." Ferrin had been right in that, at least. The fighting would reach them soon enough.

A murmur rippled through the reserve. There were maybe two hundred of them, but none with a look as angry as Ferrin's—like that of a child stripped of a prized toy. But it was just another glare, and glares had been in ample supply since she arrived. He'd have to do better. He slowly led his horse to where some others were picketed, bound it there, and made his way back to stand beside Lynn.

Some of the reserve turned their horses towards the two-day path that led to Durnn, but most followed Ferrin.

Lynn looked over at him. "When did you become a leader?" she whispered.

He shrugged. "Dunno. When did you?"

Lynn had no answer to that, but Alren was already giving it to her.

They have no one else.

He did not seem as angry this time.

The madmen had begun to move in the night. They marched down Pehd Valley like a slow-moving beast, slithering with patient hunger but sure of where its quarry lay. The Legion had marched for the better part of a day to reach this position, and Durnn was now a two-day march to the south. Even if an enemy force this large might move slower than that, especially with the siege engines, their numbers did nothing for Lynn's confidence in the fortress's defense.

We'll need Dakhra. This plan has to work.

Lynn stood with her force of barely two hundred on the ridge that surrounded the valley. A few strides after the tree line ended, the terrain sloped down; it was smooth enough to employ their plan with the cavalry. Her force was between the mouth of the valley and the western edge of the ridge, the Skygate—still under guard—at the far end. The other units had been positioned at opposite sides: west a little further down from Lynn and east and close to the mouth itself, all ready to pull the enemy force away and give Thain an opening to move through the Skygate. She tilted her head towards the sky and took a deep breath, using the cold to sharpen her thoughts and push away the voices trying to instill doubt into her heart.

This is the only way.

A light in the distance caught Lynn's eye. Olem's lantern bearer was signaling the charge. In a blink, two more lit up, and the sound of hoof beats reverberated under her like a steady drum. The ground shook beneath her as the shadows spilled out from the tree line and ten score horsemen charged from the east, their screams and brandished weapons paving the way.

The enemy army scrambled in disarray, tripping desperately over each other to meet the charge. The surprise had worked, but it was strange to see the surprise among the madmen. Were they even more conscious than Lynn had thought?

A weak line formed, and, for a moment, Lynn thought the cavalry would crash into it. Spears were raised in anticipation, and the men that had lined up on the flank let out a garish howl of their own. The cavalry pulled away at the last moment. They spun their horses in a motion that would have been almost graceful if not for the mud and shouting. Steel tips glimmered in the moonlight, and the enemy line was peppered with arrows. There weren't many screams of pain, but Lynn could see them falling.

The madmen's own archers were forming now, their focus on their east flank where the charge had come from, but the Legion horses were already retreating. Madmen gave chase up the slope, and archers hidden in the trees let loose, sending the enemy rolling back down.

There was another signal from amongst the trees on their side, and another ten score horsemen charged from the west flank. These were faster, galloping frantically down the slope with bows already drawn, looking to take advantage of the enemy's backs being turned towards them. Enough of the opposing archers fell for a glimmer of hope to threaten the darkness swirling inside Lynn.

No. No hope, especially not now.

These were only shallow cuts on a thick-skinned beast, and the enemy troops flowed like blood through the valley, rushing to plug the wounds that the Legion had created.

The second charge took out more men than the first, but they didn't pull back as fast. The engagement was unavoidable, and soon the night was filled with the desperate neighing of horses and yelling of men as they spun their mounts, slashing at the madmen swarming around them. Most had the clarity of mind to urge their horses away, but too many were caught in the wave rolling over them and soon disappeared in the sea of hands, spears, and snarls.

Lynn's hands were balled into angry fists, and Ferrin had his glare on her.

"We just sit here watching them die?" he asked.

"Unless you want to spill your guts down there, we wait for the right time."

We waited. You told us to wait as well. And here we are, Roki said.

A third charge began, this time Olem leading the Sentinels from the south, Rel beside him along with the bulk of what remained of the Legion foot soldiers. The horses came first, but surprise was lost. The enemy raised shields instead of spears, waiting for the horsemen to pull back, but Olem crashed into them, opening holes for the Legion footmen to spill through. The enemy rushed forward to meet them, and many were still charging up the slopes after the retreating cavalry with little care for the arrows shooting at them from the trees. The madmen were spreading, forcing the enemy army to pull up the rear ranks and creating a large enough gap between the army pursuing the Legion and the two or three hundred men guarding the pass. If Thain was going to make for the Skygate, this was the time.

Lynn caught movement along the edges of the battle. Thain had seen the moment as well. He and his men moved down the slope under the cover of shadows with cloaks made from leaves. It wasn't much of a disguise, but it should be enough for them to get the jump on the force still holding the pass, which was small enough that if she helped pull them away, he might actually make it.

"Get ready," she told Ferrin.

Lynn checked the pouch of ruin-stone Rel had given her. Two shards. Not much, but it would have to be enough to keep her from hollowing out. She looked down on the valley, and a thrill ran through her that came out as a yell. She raised her weapons and charged down the hill towards the men guarding the pass. Lynn howled as if she was charging at death itself, ready to take command of its power to serve the Seraph and Her Domain. Her force reacted with a wordless cry of their own and followed her down.

Screams of dying men filled the air, but Lynn's attention was on the masked, dead faces charging to meet her. She gripped one of Rel's shards, and the anger flooded into her, mixing with her own. Her thoughts went to Vedyr, and the anger was drained away with them. She fell into her Bond, his strength pushing her forward.

Lynn clashed into the enemy, tearing through them in a whirl of slashes and stabs. Body after body fell before her, death holding her hand in the dance of steel and blood once more.

They're already dead. They're already dead.

A cheer went up from somewhere behind her.

"They're running! They're running!" an incredulous voice was screaming.

Lynn turned her burning eyes to where the men were pointing. The enemy wasn't running. She'd pulled a sizeable force of them away, but they'd seen Thain and his men now and were rallying back to stop him. He was close, fighting his way up to the Skygate, but there was no way he'd make it if the enemy reinforcements arrived.

"With me!" she yelled, not knowing who would follow.

She pushed more anger towards Vedyr, her muscles surging, but her mind was falling into a haze, warning her of the risks of the Bond. Lynn gritted her teeth and pushed through. Her strengthened muscles gave her enough speed that she overtook the enemies bearing down on Thain's troops and stood between them and the pass, with Thain still fighting his way towards it at her back. She held her weapons out to either side, panting, eyes ablaze, head light.

They regarded her for a moment, then realized she was alone and dashed forward. They were not as fast as the ones she had fought on the ledge with Leardin. Most of them hardly even seemed mad, and there might have even been a flash of fear in an eye or two. That did not incline her towards mercy, though.

Lynn slashed open the first one's neck with her scythe, and in the same swing buried it in the chest of the one beside him. A woman tried to get behind her, but Lynn brought her mace down over her skull with a crack, and she fell face-first into the mud. All of them screamed as they fell, but Lynn barely heard them. A faster one barreled towards her. This one was crazed, with cuts on his hands and claws stretched out. Lynn threw her scythe at him, and it cut through the air and sunk into his forehead. He toppled over mid-charge, skidding towards her feet. Lynn retrieved the scythe and glowered at the madmen.

They hesitated enough at the sight of their fallen companions for Lynn's own troop to catch up and for her to pull out the second and final ruin-stone shard. Lynn clenched her fingers around it and felt the surge that sharpened her mind and renewed her strength.

Her troops stood beside her in rusted armor and gripping chipped blades, faces awed. Ferrin raised his spear and howled at the dead-faced men, then rushed towards them almost as insanely as the man who'd just been split by Lynn's scythe.

"Ferrin, no!" she yelled, but there was no stopping him.

He bound off, charging with his spear, stabbing wildly at the first enemy, but failing to recognize others coming in behind his fallen foe. He ran down the first man and was left completely unprotected as he dashed further into enemy lines.

The world froze. The Legion had engaged enough of the enemy, but there were still a score heading for Thain, with Lynn and her unit the only ones standing between them. Ferrin had gone in too deep. He wouldn't survive alone, but she doubted her force would hold without her. There was the plan, and there was Ferrin. She wasn't sure if the screaming was coming from the battle within her mind or the one without. She glanced back for a split second. It was impossible to tell if Thain had gotten through the pass.

Shit.

Lynn abandoned her post and charged towards Ferrin, picked up a fallen spear and hurled it past him. It plunged deep into the chest of an enemy with a raised sword, but there was still another rounding on Ferrin, who was thrusting his spear at a new enemy, still lost in his own madness. Lynn got to him just as the enemy blade fell and tried to parry, but she couldn't get her footing on the muddy valley floor and settled for pushing Ferrin out of the way and taking the slash on her shoulder instead. He sprawled to the ground with a scream more shock than pain.

Lynn's shoulder throbbed, hot blood streaking down her arm, but she gripped her mace as if it were the pain and strangled it away, using Vedyr to strengthen herself.

Alren, Cara, Dentos, . . . Roki.

Her head pulsed, and the names were coming slower. She couldn't push much further without risking hollowing out.

Part of her instinctively wanted to search for Rel to get more ruin-stone, but the madman's blade slashed down at her again. Lynn focused the strength she'd pulled from Vedyr and shattered it with a swing that went through the descending steel and into the man's chin, taking off the lower part of his jaw.

Ferrin had gotten up beside her, half his face caked in mud, the other half in the enemy's blood. Her men were pointing, screaming something, but Lynn couldn't hear them. She followed the fingers and saw the signs of lanterns being waved.

Retreat.

Lynn bashed a chest plate out of her way and sliced off an arm that held an axe meant for her neck, all while moving towards the slope leading back into the tree line. Ferrin was breathing hard, laboring beside her, and she could sense her own breath getting heavier.

Alren, . . . Ro . . . ki . . .

The Bond was changing from boon to curse, pulling parts of her mind away. Lynn released it, and her anger dwindled like coals sputtering their last warmth into a cold wind.

She gave one last look towards the pass. No sign of Thain. No use hoping, but maybe a little faith? She ran, pulling Ferrin towards the shadow of the trees.

They'd been running too long to remember when they started. She kept moving through the thick underbrush, pushing between the trees in the darkness. Her unit had retreated before them, lost to the trees now. No way to tell who had survived.

The enemy had broken their march after the battle and taken back to the trees to hunt for stragglers. Screams rang in the night—sounds of mad hunters and dying men, impossible to tell apart—but they kept Lynn moving.

By the Blood, she'd give anything for a horse right now. Didn't even have to be a good one, just had to know its way back to Durnn so she could close her eyes for half a breath. The weight in her legs had turned to pain, and her head was pounding with the aftereffects of the Bond. She'd gone too deep and used it too often, and she was dangerously close to the edge. If she hollowed out now . . .

Lynn plowed on, but the burning in her legs persisted until it matched the throbbing in her shoulder. She breathed in and out, in and out, trying to exhale the pain away. It didn't help.

Ferrin didn't look any better. He wasn't bleeding, but his twisted expression was a wound in itself. His eyes flashed towards every rustling leaf and moving shadow, and it was getting to Lynn. The fear almost as infectious as the Madness. Nothing but the wind, she'd told him, but wasn't sure even she was convinced of it.

They'd stopped for maybe an hour in a ditch during the second day, but there was no stopping at night, and Lynn was still keeping hope far away. One less thing to lose in the darkness. Still, they had to be close—

There was a snap, her foot caught in the underbrush, and Lynn crashed down into the roots at her feet. There were no leaves to soften the blow or the sound, and nothing to mask the taste of wet earth. She tried to get up but was frozen on her hands and knees. Her legs were not responding, and her shoulder was threatening to give out. All she could do was spit away the mud and let out a wavering gasp, waiting for her muscles to thaw.

Ferrin offered a hand, and she used it to lift herself to one knee.

"We can't stop," Lynn said before he even suggested it.

"Looks like you can't walk anymore, either. Won't do any good, stumbling along. Take a moment."

Lynn stayed there, trying to breathe.

"I lost a brother to these woods, you know? Never even knew what he was fighting for." He chuckled, mirthless, almost as cold as the night. "He'd probably have liked you, though."

Lynn's muscles stiffened again, but it had nothing to do with the fatigue this time. Alren had never told his family he'd become a Sentinel. Most of the order didn't: it made it easier to cut ties.

"Never talked about him much. He was dead, and Morna had gone off to join the Church. Not right to dwell on the unworthy, eh? Still miss him, though."

She didn't look up.

"Seems pointless now, don't it? With all this death running around, good men dying everywhere. Makes you wonder if the Seraph ever chose any of us at all."

She did, but your brother was not Her choice: he was mine.

Tell him, coward, Alren spat.

"Ferrin, I—"

Another snap. Lynn's head spun round. A shadow moved. Not the wind: there was none.

"Run!" Lynn screamed.

What remained of her sanity was crying out against it, but a mad instinct was already gathering what it could. She was out of ruin-stone, so she grasped at the pieces of her broken mind and infused it with the smoldering anger of the fresh memories of Alren, channeling all of it towards Vedyr.

It sparked just enough of a flame in her for her muscles to respond. Her mind burning along with her eyes, a desperate warning, but Lynn could not heed it. There was no enhanced strength or speed. All the Bond did was allow her to move. To run.

The snarls had already caught up with them, the earth rumbling with hungry footfalls.

Lynn ran among the unchanging trees, not looking back. The Bond kept her standing, but it coursed through her like a poison. It strained her muscles, pushing her close to the hollow state from which she would not come back. Her legs were slowing.

Al . . . ren, . . . Ro . . . I'm sorry, she told them. *I gave it all I have.*

Her eyes blurred, but at the edges of her vision, something

cleared. She followed the soft glow until the trees ended abruptly and the moon shone down on open ground. Lynn stumbled out of the woods and tumbled down a slope, sticking her hands out to steady herself.

Lynn skidded onto her bad shoulder with an anguished cry but didn't stop to think as she reached the bottom. She surged the last of her anger away, and it was enough to propel her up, but hardly forward. Her mind seemed to break, pieces scattering to the wind, and her muscles seared with pain as she tried to keep shuffling ahead.

Ferrin was bolting up the road. Lynn couldn't keep up, mind dazed, more pieces of her breaking away.

Al . . . . What was the name?

She stole a glance up into the night sky. Nothing. Not even a cloud. Her head shot back to the forest, and there they were: madmen breaking out of the treeline, rushing down the slope, barely slowing.

Something dark streaked past her face, pulling the wind behind it in a whistle. An arrow, finding a home in one of the pursuers. The man fell, but there were still too many. The fortress came into view, and Lynn tried another surge, but there was nothing more to channel away. She gave a few more steps, then collapsed.

Take me, then. Purge Your Domain.

The world was dark and hollow, screams and snarls filling her ears, the thump of approaching feet filling her chest. She thought she heard the air being battered above her and felt something grasp her around the ribs. The Seraph, no doubt, come to pull her away from this world. Seemed only fair.

CHAPTER THIRTY-TWO

When Warden Ikke's son threatened war with the Domain, she did what was necessary to protect the Ronar. She killed the boy and brought his body to her Chief. It was no simple task, and her heart was shattered, but she did not regret her actions, because she knew the Ronar come first. Always.

— Tales of the Ronar

Anaya and Bedri checked the ground for markings, an increasingly difficult task in the waning light of the early hours of night. Nasha followed their lead, finding broken twigs, scattered branches, and unsettled grass that pointed in different directions.

"More movement than normal," Anaya said.

"Yltigg?" Bedri asked.

"No reason for them to be here," Anaya said. "Could be the Domain."

"We should stay away from the tracks. Circle round, then. Can't risk losing the boy," Bedri said.

"No," Nasha said.

Both of them turned, Bedri's irritation slamming into her hard, constricting her ribs.

"We can't—"

"We won't lose him, Bedri. We can't afford the time it'll take, and we don't know who else is lurking in these woods. We follow our path, follow the plan."

Anaya studied Nasha while Bedri frowned at her, but they knew better than to argue with a Root, it seemed. It felt strange to be leading hunters, but it would all be over soon. Nasha continued on the path, and the hunters followed, tugging the Domain captive along.

They walked for hours. The terrain was uneven, the going hard, but there was no time to look back. The Great Mountain was getting smaller and smaller behind them, and the trees were growing sparser but were still thick enough for cover. Nasha felt the occasional wrinkle of doubt, strong enough that she knew she could give them no opening for questions, only drive forward at a harder pace.

The trail led them to a ledge looking down on a camp. The land had flattened out here, and trees grew thick around them again, their leaves blocking out the light and casting a lattice of shade and sunset on the ground. The scent of citrus wafted in the air, and Nasha breathed it in deep—not that she needed it to ground herself anymore, but it was a comfort all the same. They crouched behind one of the citrus trees, searching for movement.

"What do you think?" Anaya asked.

There were two soldiers around a cookpot in the center, sitting between pitched tents. No way of knowing how many were inside. The ground around the cookpot was black, as if a stain had spread from the coals, but the decay was recognizable enough by now. A sentry stood a little further, his eyes carelessly wandering among the boughs above him.

"Domain born," Bedri said. "Hunting party."

He had barely finished the word when there was movement behind them, and three Domain men stumbled onto where they were crouched. The leader was short and stocky and was pulling a hooded girl bound by manacles and a chain. Anaya and Bedri were on their feet, weapons out. Nasha drew her knives as well and lingered behind them.

"Easy now," the man with the chain said. "Not lookin' for no trouble. Just passing through."

"Is she Ronar?" Anaya asked.

"What, this?" He jerked his head back at the girl. "No. Found her wanderin' the wilds. No markings, just a straggler."

The men behind the one with the chains had their hands on half-drawn swords and eyed the Ronar hunters warily.

"Take off her hood," Bedri said.

"Now, I can't be doin' that. This here's mine by right, you see."

"You are on Ronar land. You will do as we say." Anaya stepped forward, raising her knife, the stubble on her head almost bristling.

"Remove her hood! Now," Bedri said.

The man lifted his palms towards them. "Alright, alright. But this is our livelihood, mind you. We're the ones keep your land clean of the wanderin' folk."

He removed the hood, and the tension in the hunters hit Nasha even before she saw their muscles tightening. Shai was easily recognizable: they'd trained her.

"That's—"

Bedri's words turned into a gasp as Nasha slid the knife from behind into his lung and his heart. Anaya's head snapped towards Bedri, and Shai took the opening, throwing off the false chains and stabbing a knife of her own into Anaya's throat. There was a spike in their emotions that tugged at Nasha's heart. Surprise and betrayal mingled in the confusion of their lives draining away into the Silent Earth. It made her skin tingle, but Nasha saw the shape of it, saw their emotions rushing towards her, and steered them away.

The Domain man—Egren, the mercenary she'd let go at the pass—looked inquisitively at her, half expecting Nasha to turn on him perhaps, but she sheathed her knives and shot him a steady look. He held her gaze for a moment, then whistled, and more men appeared from the trees, followed by Uvo and Landi—Shai's family.

Even now, Landi still kept the elegant posture she'd always had—shoulders wide, chest out—while Uvo bore the same frown below his thick eyebrows that Nasha had so often seen coloring Ife's expression.

Mansa might have his plans, but Nasha had been close enough to the Roots to see the truth now. The clan would never be safe for Shai or her family, and Nasha had promised Ife she would take care of them. She wouldn't use them like Mansa had used her. The Ronar would not come first this time.

Nasha could sense the urgency rushing from Landi. Her heart beat faster and her chest tightened. She breathed out Landi's emotion and embraced her, but Uvo stayed behind, lingering beside his sister, eyes wide at the dead bodies, emanating ripples of fear and disgust. He was unaccustomed to death like most Slopers, yet eager to participate in the Proving all his life. He wouldn't need to anymore.

"Thank you," Landi said. "For everything. Ife would be proud."

Nasha smiled at her. "We'll get through this soon."

"Happy you kept me alive, then?" Egren said.

Nasha's eyes moved towards the Domain man. "As long as you keep your end of the deal."

"Don't worry. Got you this far, didn't I?" He chuckled, but there was something different in it. Some kind of anxiousness, perhaps—a lingering nervousness. She was still trying to understand Egren when Shai stepped forward with an impossible jumble of emotion coming from her. No, not her. Nasha's gaze shot to the bag the girl was carrying.

"You have it?"

She opened a bag, and the blue pulse of ancestor-stone hit her. Nasha still didn't touch them, but it was clear these were some of the stones from the Cradle of the Ronar.

"Enough to buy the ship papers?" Shai asked with a grin.

Nasha nodded with a grin of her own. "We should move. Tomu's men will be on the trail soon. They don't suspect us. We need to keep it that way." She turned back to Egren. "Where's Hemlicht's contact?"

"Waiting for us in the borderlands."

"Alright, head down to the camp. I'll take care of the bodies."

Egren trundled away with his men, but Shai lingered for a moment. "You need help?"

Nasha shook her head. "Go be with your family, Shai."

Shai smiled at her again, then led Landi and Uvo after the Domain mercenaries.

Nasha grabbed Anaya's legs and dragged her towards Bedri so she could burn them. She wouldn't follow Mansa's plan, but there was no reason to expose him to Tomu. Not now, at least. She put Anaya down beside Bedri, but something hit her senses through the trees. Nasha turned, frowning, hands on her knives. She scanned her surroundings for emotion. Seemed like only one source, but it was focused, directed at her. Nasha turned her head towards the spot, and Adda walked out of the shadows.

"Warden."

Nasha tightened the grip on her knives and stepped forward, pressing her jaw hard, but Adda raised a hand.

"No need for that. It wouldn't do you any good."

"It might."

Adda's expression was not as hard as it had been in the village. Either she didn't need her stony mask outside of it or that anxiety— the same Nasha had sensed when she got back from the Proving— meant something larger than she had thought.

"They'll be on your trail soon, my father's men, and I doubt you'll be able to escape trial a second time after . . ." She looked at the bodies still bleeding on the ground. "This."

Nasha didn't lower her knives. She stepped closer, and Adda's eyes narrowed. "Do you need a reminder?"

Nasha pressed her jaw even tighter, the memory of her burned arm strong but not enough to deter her rising anger. She would not be manipulated by the Roots. Not ever again.

"Seems like you're in need of a friend," Adda said, "since you've killed all the ones you had."

"And you're that?"

"At the moment, yes."

Nasha shook her head. They were almost out. She wasn't about to fall into Adda's grasp again. "We'll be gone before they arrive. I don't need you."

"You can tell yourself that. You can try to kill me too, but are you sure you'll be able to know who to kill?"

Adda's mouth split into a smile, and the emotion that she'd been shooting towards Nasha intensified, stronger even than in the Yltigg arena. Nasha's mind slipped. That awakened part of it was suddenly closed off. She was drowning again but couldn't tell what she was drowning in. The rage was hotter than ever, pulling her consciousness away.

It stopped, and Nasha lowered her knives, breathing hard.

"You're lucky you've made yourself useful, Warden, but there are so many things you do not know." Adda's smile vanished. "I offer you friendship in return for a small favor. Not much of a choice, really, if you want to live."

Nasha only glared at Adda, unable to put herself consciously in her service again.

"You've played your hand well, smart, getting the Slopers to help you, steal the prisoner. Even Mansa didn't see it. I bet he'd be proud." She paused, and Nasha sensed the anxiety returning. Adda might be able to influence Nasha, but she was not half as comfortable with her level of control over the situation. "You're trading him over to the Domain, stopping this foolish war Mansa wants with them. Commendable. The true sign of a Root, standing up for your clan instead of your friends."

No. She was doing this for Shai, not the clan. "Spit it out!"

Adda nodded slowly. "Razi!"

The boy sprang from the trees. Nasha hadn't recognized the second presence, but how could she? Adda's son felt like a syphon. He gave out nothing and drew in all around him.

Realization set into Nasha then. "He's like you."

"Like *us*, Warden, and not even my position as Root could protect us if the clan found out."

"You seem comfortable enough with your curse."

Could I ever be that comfortable with mine?

"My gift did not manifest as a child. I have learned to control it —hide it from the clan and the Domain. Razi has not been so fortunate."

"Hide it from the Domain?"

"There is much that is hidden even from the Roots. Much you will yet learn. That is why you need my friendship." She stepped closer. "You're shipping them off to where? Dakhra?"

"Azur."

"Then you're sending us with them."

Nasha eyed the Tivezzi, a deep frown over her eyes.

"I understand the hesitation, but we'd all be getting what we want. You'd be rid of me, and I'd be free to raise my son in peace."

Nasha did not answer for a long moment. She didn't want to accept this. Still, there was little reason to complicate things; the taste of it was bitter, but Adda's logic was clear. Nasha shook her head and lowered her knives.

"Let's go."

CHAPTER THIRTY-THREE

There is a reason their sand is red. They're bloodthirsty, traitorous bastards.

— *Boutros the Bard. In private.*

A drian followed Derren and Nasir into the dimly lit chamber, squinting through the thin veil of smoke that hung in the air. He moved slowly around the rectangular walkway surrounding the pitlike opening in the center, where linen was draped over a body that rested on a red-brown slab of sandstone. Nasir touched his arm and quietly indicated the platform rising from the haze at the far end. A tall man with sunken eyes in robes of dark copper and black stood there. He did not look particularly intimidating, but there was only one man in Azur Princess Kahlia would hold such a posture of deference toward. The Xakhar. Adrian covered his mouth, stifling a cough and drawing a chastising look from Nasir.

There were men and women dressed in colors of the ten consul families—all of them interspersed with black—holding solemn gazes around the room. The consuls themselves soon filed in, occupying the space around the chamber, all of them eyeing the body in the center.

"Has the council come to a decision?" Kahlia said in Azuri. The way she spoke the language was like honey being woven into words; they poured sweetly off her tongue, but Adrian knew now not to be fooled by the sweetness of Azuri wonders.

"It has," an old woman with a crest in the form of a red drop said, her words nowhere near as graceful as Kahlia's. "It is the belief of the ten guilds of Azur that Prince Niilar should be remembered for his valor and contributions to our nation, his memory held in a place of high honor and his body set upon the river to rest beneath the waves of the Ulean."

The Xakhar bowed his head. No words, but there was an evident release in his stance. He gave a slight nod, and men in sky-blue silks made their way down steps on either side of the central opening, lifted the Azuri prince's body on their shoulders, then carried him towards large copper double doors. The doors were flung open and sunlight flooded the chamber along with the mumbling of an awaiting crowd. The men carried the body out and cleared a wide swath before them, then the leader of the procession pulled out an unlit torch and put a fire to the tip. There was silence, and, for a moment, nothing happened. Then it burst into blue flame, and the crowd erupted into a cheer.

"Seems like too much cheering for a dead man," Adrian said quietly to Nasir, but the priest did not answer.

After a suitable moment of applause, the body was brought back, and the men in silks began preparations for the next step of the ritual. They stepped around the body, checking his hands and feet, then removed the linen from his face. Every muscle in Adrian tensed at the sight. Even Nasir paused. The prince had a blackish-gray tint around his eyes. Just like Myrra. Just like the madmen.

"This can't be a coincidence," Adrian said, but Nasir only shook his head again and exited the chamber.

The Azuri were following the Xakhar and consuls towards the banquet hall to celebrate the memory of the dead prince, but Adrian and Derren lingered for a while. Derren had a wary look about him, maybe wanting to discuss what they had just seen, but the hall was not the place to do it. They kept their silence and followed Nasir outside.

"There are certain steps that must be taken, Lord Light. Pushing them now will not end well," Nasir said.

"This is a strike in our favor, Nasir. Only a fool would not use this opportunity," Derren said.

"He's right, Nasir. We can use this."

"Not today. Today is a day for celebration, a holy day. It will not do to discuss ill omens. It will only push them away."

"I understand, Nasir, but there are madmen rampaging through the Domain. We must rebuild the Legion to aid them." *And I must kill that bastard.* "Their prince had it. Derren is right. It is the time to use this to our advantage."

"I would still advise caution, Lord Light."

Adrian paused. Derren had advised caution, and Adrian had followed the faith in himself that Derren had sparked in him in the first place. Maybe the priest was right. He'd need to approach this more carefully this time. He turned to Derren and Nasir.

"Talk to the consul families, try to understand if they knew about this. I will have a . . . cautious word with Kahlia."

Nasir bowed his head with expressionless eyes and was silent the rest of the way.

The banquet hall was crowded. It was located on one of the lower floors of the palace, with multiple thin but tall blue-tinted windows lining the walls to either side, dark now with the night. To the right of the room, the windows were interspersed with glass-paned doors that led to a wide balcony. People and servants swarmed around tables filled with enough food for a lifetime, all of which Adrian could hardly recognize. He focused on the wine and tried to catch Kahlia's eye, but the princess seemed to make a point of not looking his way.

Adrian lingered close to the high table where Kahlia sat beside her father, standing before one of the balcony doors. He gave her another glance and thought he saw a flicker of her gaze darting towards him, then away. It was enough. He stepped out.

The balcony was not high—a short jump away from the pools it overlooked. Flowered vines grew on the balustrade, and Adrian stayed well away from those, even if they did not look like the ones he'd been poisoned by.

It was only a moment before Kahlia stepped out after him. She kept her back to the glass and her side pressed against one of the columns that held up a stone overhang above the glass-paned doors.

"You have something to report?" she asked in Othonean.

"Not yet, but there is something I must bring to your attention."

"Today is not a day for ill omens."

"So I've been told, yet they plague us just the same, I'm afraid."

Kahlia's eyes flashed.

"What do you know about the circumstances of your brother's death?" Adrian asked.

Kahlia's lip curled almost into a snarl. Yet somehow, she was still graceful. "The moment of his death does not matter. What does is the memory that remains, and our leaders have decided it should be honored."

"Your customs are strangely similar to our own. And I respect the meaning of this day, but—"

She swiveled on her heels, ready to go.

"He had it," Adrian said. "The Madness. That is why you stopped me in the throne room. That is why you've kept me in the palace. The Madness isn't threatening to cross the Ulean. It's already here."

Kahlia stopped with her back turned.

"A poison flower is the very least of what I can do."

"I don't doubt it, Princess. And I do not wish to taint his memory. As I said when I arrived, I have come in search of allies, not enemies. I—"

There was a glint of movement reflected on the glass. Kahlia saw it too and jumped to the side moments before a dagger sliced through the air, whispering past Adrian's face and shattering the window. Adrian snapped his head around and found a figure—an assassin—already darting away through the garden.

His heart leaped to his throat, and his legs were already rushing towards the edge of the balcony, his eyes locked on the fleeing shadow. This was his chance to take care of Kahlia's demands and get his army. Adrian jumped over and splashed into one of the shallow pools but quickly burst into a sprint after his target.

"Adrian!" Derren shouted at him from the balcony.

Adrian did not turn, but he soon heard splashing and heavy footfalls trying to keep up. The assassin was lithe, skittering across the garden path, then up the palace walls and out into the streets. Adrian followed. He rushed past the gates, paying no heed to the men standing guard, and paused outside, head moving from side to side.

He found the assassin on a rooftop, looking at Adrian under a beam of moonlight. A woman, Adrian could see now. There was a glint in her left eye, something reflecting off it. It lasted for only a moment, then she was scrambling across the roofs towards the market. Adrian tried to keep pace through the thickening mass of people, pushing some out of the way, almost crashing into others while his gaze was aimed at the roofs to avoid losing the woman.

They approached the market, and the woman jumped down, disappearing into the teeming streets. The people made it impossible for Adrian to keep running. The market was even more crowded than Adrian remembered it being during the day. Louder, too. Adrian kept pushing through, searching frantically for the woman, but the press was too thick to keep up the chase, and eventually Derren caught up to him, panting.

"Woman. All in black. Glass eye," Adrian said, then pressed on through hanging silks and the stretched cloths that covered the market. He didn't run now. There was too much movement, too many places that would be easy to hide in if he just sprinted past.

Torches illuminated the stalls, but along most of the pathways, they had to make do with the moon. The colors were muted by the night, but the smell of cinnamon, clove, oil, and fresh saffron was intoxicating. Adrian twisted through paths of people and merchants clamoring for attention and haggling over goods, the hope of finding the would-be assassin sinking in his gut. The scents shifted from the sweet spices to peppers, then roasting meat as they reached the back of the market, and Adrian paused before an open space leading off into a web of dark streets and alleyways.

A mirror merchant was waving flaming torches, trying to direct attention towards his goods. The light reflected from them, and there was a flash in one of the narrow streets. Adrian's head lurched towards it, and he caught movement. He dashed after it, heart beating so strong his head pulsed. There was a crash and the creaking of wood, and Adrian came to a dead end. A crumbling building stood to his right, its bricks more sand than stone, with rubble scattered before a creaky door still moving on noisy hinges.

"Adrian, hold on!" Derren said, but Adrian was already heading down dark steps. The memory of Myrra's defiled face fanned the fire inside him. It burned his tongue with the taste of revenge, each step bringing him closer to it.

The steps opened into a small, gloomy chamber with the same brownish-red sandstone walls, but in a much finer state of repair than those above. A bearded man sat in an alcove at the far end with his hands resting over each other on his lap, cloth covering his face and a turban covering his head. There were two low wooden stools before him, and the assassin stood by his side.

"So glad you could join us, Lord Light." The man spoke with a rasp, and his Othonean carried a heavy accent.

Adrian had his sword in hand, still taken by the fire. He drove forward, ready to cut them down, but three hooded figures stepped out of the surrounding alcoves with long daggers in hand, blocking his path. Derren crashed into the room and took only a moment to draw his blade and stand beside Adrian.

"I must apologize for my methods. It was the only way I could get you here safely, but there is no need for violence."

Adrian was panting, his mind cooling from the chase. He lowered his blade, and so did the men before him before they stepped back into the shadows. "What do you want?"

"To talk. I've heard you are in search of men, and there is something I too am in search of. It is the time of the night market. Let us negotiate."

"It is a foolish man who spouts words without knowing to whom he is delivering them," Adrian answered.

"In that you are correct, but a measure of foolishness will be required." The rasp in the man's voice continued, making his words sound almost broken. "Please sit."

Adrian gritted his teeth, but he stepped forward and took one of the stools. Derren remained standing behind him. "What do you need?" Adrian said.

"Prince Niilar's memory may have been honored, but as things stand, my employer would have much to benefit from the removal of a few more pieces from the board."

"The Xakhar?"

"And his daughter."

That gave Adrian pause. "You'd end the entire royal line?"

"Only to create another. Isn't that the thing about royalty? The blood is only as noble as those beneath it make it out to be."

Adrian was silent. What did this man know about blood? He pressed his teeth tighter, and Jovu's image intruded into his thoughts. Dead in some heathen land. Adrian would not allow that to be his own fate.

"What assurances do I have?"

"Assurances can be arranged. We have . . . connections that will aid you when the time is adequate."

"That will not be enough," Derren said.

Adrian nodded. "We need more."

The man moved his eyes to one of the hooded men, and Adrian's hand jerked towards his sword pommel, but the man walked calmly before Adrian and removed the cloth covering his face.

"This is Amal Ban Khorfa, a son to one of the most powerful military families in Azur." Amal nodded towards them. "There are others before him in the line of family succession, but he is a man of vision, and he has a clear vision for not only his own future, but that of Dar Drezji and all of Azur. When you take care of the Xakhar, we will ensure the line is considerably shortened for Amal, and once he has control of his house, you would have the military force of the Khorfa at your disposal. At least ten thousand men, and that is only the beginning."

Adrian considered the numbers. It would be enough to double what he'd gathered for the Legion, but what would the Pontiff think of an army of heathens inside the Domain? And how would he even kill Kahlia?

"I'm no assassin," Adrian said. "You seemed to have no problem getting someone inside. Why not do that again with one who has better aim?" Adrian's eyes flitted towards the woman but there was no movement apart from the firelight dancing off her glass eye.

"We made our attempt, but this was a unique opportunity where the palace gates were open to the families, Lord Light. One that will not repeat itself, especially after what has transpired." The man looked at the woman, then back at Adrian. "Knives will not be required. The poison we wish you to administer requires little skill, but your position by the princess is . . . irreplaceable."

Adrian's brow was tight in thought, gaze darting from the bearded man to Amal Ban Khorfa. Even if he delivered this boy's name to Kahlia, there was no assurance that he'd be able to lead her to the bearded man. The man seemed . . . cautious, prepared. What if she decided that was not enough? He'd need more proof.

"We will consider your offer." Adrian stood. "And the price that must be paid."

The man bowed his head deferentially but did not rise. "Do not take too long. The fruit is sweetest when ripe, but it is soon taken by rot."

Adrian took one last look at the man's eyes, trying to commit any detail he could to memory. Wrinkled, brownish skin surrounded dark eyes looking back at him. Little to go on. He turned and made his way up the steps, followed by Derren.

Adrian walked among the market for a long while, eyes down, barely even noticing the sights and sounds around them. People haggled and screamed, each trying to get the better of their counterpart. They thrived on the madness, and his thoughts echoed their yells, arguing like hagglers themselves, fighting to convince him of the correct path.

They made their way out of the market, but his mind was still at it. This man was too great a risk. Adrian knew nothing about him. Still, Kahlia was probably as dangerous as any consul, and there was no telling how long she'd take or even if she'd get him his army. He had to pick a path. He had to reclaim his faith in himself.

The thought gave Adrian pause. He'd forgotten himself, saying the words but not acting accordingly. He'd let himself fall into the shadow of the princess, of these consuls, *and the Light stands in no shadow, no matter how tall.*

"Derren, find their contact in the palace and follow through."

"How should we go about it?"

"We'll plan for the hardest first."

"The Xakhar?"

"No," Adrian said. "The princess."

———

"We should go over it again."

"I think the plan is clear enough, Adrian."

Adrian looked at the two vials in his hand, then back up at Derren. "You're sure they'll work?"

"As sure as you can be in this city. Our new friends would have little to gain with our deaths." Unless he'd been sent by Kahlia to test Adrian's loyalty. "Still, I should take them," Derren said.

"No." Of this Adrian was sure. "This poison, a brush of the skin will do?"

"That is all it should take. It will take two days to manifest in her, enough for the suspicion not to fall on us, but ingesting it will be a lot faster. Don't linger. All you need is to touch her skin, then leave." Derren rubbed at the back of his neck. "Still, if things go awry . . ." He handed Adrian a dagger.

Adrian raised an eyebrow. "Quite the show of faith."

"We are far from the Domain. Best be sure."

"You used to have more of it."

Derren laughed. "What, faith? It's always been here, but most of it has always been placed in you, Lord Light. If I lost you—"

"You won't," Adrian said. "Blood holds ties, and you are as good as my own. We will soon get our men and return home."

He squeezed his old friend's shoulder, and Derren's weary eyes showed a lack of strength for argument. They'd been awake all night, and even if this was time better spent than Adrian's usual pacing and wrangling of his thoughts, the older man was showing signs of the hours of lost sleep.

Adrian held up the vials, one a deep night-blue, the other clear. A third one, black, sat in a shallow bowl of ice water.

"Blue is poison. The other will hold off the effect until you can return and take the antidote." Derren pointed at the bowl. "That one won't survive the heat, even at night. You'll need to leave it here."

"I've always hated Dakhran poisons," Adrian said. "But I guess they're all we have."

"That is one area where the Dakhrans cannot be faulted. Don't care to assume it myself, but . . . best be sure," Derren said. Adrian looked at the slowly brightening sky. It was the pale blue that preceded the birth of the dawn. "When will you meet her?"

"The hour before sunrise. You need the hour of sleep?"

Derren shook his head. "It'll only get my thoughts in a haze."

"Good, then let's go over it again."

———

Adrian knew his way to the concealed courtyard this time. It looked different in the early hour of dawn, and the scent of nightshade hadn't become overwhelming yet, at least.

He paused in one of the shadows of the hallway and rolled both vials around in his hand.

No time for caution.

He downed the night-blue vial.

The poison was sweet, and Adrian almost retched. Desperation gripped him instinctively as the memory of his slowing heart washed over his tingling skin. He downed the clear vial—bitter, but better than the sweetness of the poison—but his heart was still beating slower and slower. His throat tightened, and he wavered for a moment, expecting his muscles to tense and his legs to give out. Then his heart picked up with a jolt and Adrian gasped, but he soon regained control of his breathing.

A few deep breaths and he was as normal as he would ever be with the poison coursing through his veins. He stepped forward just as Nasir was turning a corner through the dark hallways.

The priest smiled at him. "We have come a long way, my lord Light."

Too long . . . . And it ends now.

"Your work with the consuls is still unfruitful, I assume?"

"Oh, far from it," Nasir said. "In fact, I have faith the sweetest fruit will come to bear very soon." His brown smile was as repulsive as ever.

"Let us hope so." Adrian stepped into the cloister surrounding the Xakhar's courtyard. The light was changing, night's last stand against the approaching sun shrouding the courtyard in twilight.

Kahlia stood overlooking the twisting paths between the poisonous garden below, a hood over her head once more, wrapped in a light shawl, only the skin of her hands showing. Two of her guards stood behind her, and one stepped close as Adrian approached.

"It is good to see you well, Princess," Adrian said.

Kahlia scoffed at him. "Please. Flattery is the weapon of a desperate man. Have you fallen so low?"

"Every passing moment is a heavy burden for the Domain."

"Time matures all things, Lord Light. I'd expect one with a faith claiming immortality would know how to deal with the passing of it."

"All too well, Princess. Enough to know that time only allows our enemies to grow stronger."

Kahlia shook her head. "The strength of your enemy should be of little consequence in the face of your faith. At least if your high priest here is to be believed."

"I would rather not sacrifice my people. As you would keep the lives of your own." Adrian stepped closer to her. All he needed was a brush of skin. Then he'd have his Legion.

"My people appreciate the sacrifice, as we appreciate your show of faith in us," she said.

He moved to place a hand close to her own, but she recoiled almost instinctively, and her guard gave another step forward. She didn't look at him, instead gazing at one of the paths in the courtyard. Adrian's muscles cramped. Maybe it was the effects of the poison taking hold. Or, more likely, it was the tension of recognizing Derren striding through the garden with a guard of his own—the raspy-voiced man's contact, no doubt.

Adrian shot a look at Nasir, who smiled placidly and nodded his head, which pulled a frown from Adrian. He never should have trusted the priest. Kahlia had turned him and learned of Adrian's plan.

His mind raced, overloaded with questions and half-baked plans of escaping with his life. He moved his hand towards the dagger in his cloak and gauged the positioning of the guards. Adrian's fingers tightened around the hilt. Slow movements—ready, but not yet showing his hand.

Kahlia and Nasir did not look at him. They were focused on the courtyard below, giving him the perfect moment to strike. Adrian stepped forward, but movement in the garden drew his attention.

Men rose from the shadows of the bushes, their clothes wreathed in leaves and nightshade flowers. Derren and the guard jerked to a halt, and Nasir smiled at Adrian again. It wasn't him he'd betrayed. He was making his own move, sacrificing Derren.

No, no, no. He couldn't. Not Derren.

Before the gasp could escape Adrian's throat, the men darted around the stupefied pair. They did not need weapons, only a brush of the skin.

Derren and the guard went to their knees, coughing violently, clutching at their chests. Derren tried to crawl away, but even if he could have walked, there was nowhere to go. They were trapped in a heathen land, far from the Seraph's gaze. The garden was filled with the sweet scent of nightshade and the sound of Adrian's most loyal companion struggling for his final breath. Then it fell into silence.

Adrian gripped the parapet to stop his hands from shaking. Kahlia was eyeing him with a blazing sun in her eyes.

"You have done well, Lord Light. The Khorfa boy has been taken into custody and will be questioned extensively. He will soon regret his ambitions." She took another step back, and her guards flanked her, ready to leave. "This is a great service you have done our family. It was only fair I should return it. I am happy to see we can work together, removing disloyalty from our ranks."

Adrian looked away. He could sense the irony—the threat—in Kahlia's tone. Derren hadn't failed. He'd been nothing but a dedicated servant, a trusted advisor. He'd given Adrian hope when none would look his way. And this was all Adrian had managed to give him in return. His hand balled into a fist, but the rest of his body did not seem to respond. He faltered, muscles weakening: the poison was taking hold.

"Faith always lights the path," Nasir said with his head bowed.

"Rest assured, the Xakhar is not without faith of his own," she said. "Especially in those who can prove it is well placed."

She gave him a smile then, a knowing smile that told him she'd always been a step ahead. It was as sweet and dangerous as the scent of nightshade, and it threw a cold veil of fury over Adrian. Kahlia turned and parted without another word, leaving Adrian to stare at the body of his oldest friend laid out below. Dead in a heathen land, just like Jovu.

"The fruit comes to bear," Nasir said.

Adrian scowled, but his head was a fog. The poison was still working through him. He would collapse soon.

"This has been a show of faith, my lord Light. Let this be a lesson before you follow any other misguided attempts in the shadows. It was not easy convincing her to spare your life."

"You . . . you betrayed Derren?" Adrian rasped.

Nasir held Adrian's eyes. "It was not a betrayal, Lord Light. I acted for the benefit of the Legion and the Domain. It was an act of loyalty to the Light, to you. I am sure you will see it in time."

"Fu . . . cking . . . Azuri . . . hea . . . then!" Adrian's hand went for the dagger in his cloak, but his fingers were unresponsive, the poison making them stiff and slow.

Nasir placed a hand on Adrian's shoulder, careful not to touch bare skin. "I know the signs of amanthium when I see them, my lord. You should return to your rooms. What you will soon go through will be unpleasant, to say the least."

The priest removed his hand and walked away. Adrian held for a second, nothing but rage and shock keeping him upright. Derren had been the barking dog, but Nasir was the snake striking from the underbrush. Slithering in the shadows while they chased after empty promises.

Adrian stumbled away from the courtyard, heading towards his rooms, swaying under the weight of his reeling mind and the pain that had started to spread. He barely made it to his door before his vision began to swim.

He slammed the door behind him and collapsed onto the ground of his chamber. His eyes slowly closed, forming his last image of Derren: body sprawled out, hands clawing at the ground for breath. Adrian's whole body shuddered. He needed the last vial, or he'd soon be joining his friend.

He gripped the rug beneath him as his stomach cramped and burned his insides, bringing up a howl of pain. Derren had said it would be faster, but it seemed Adrian had underestimated the speed the poison would work through him. He needed to get to the antidote. Adrian clawed his way towards the other room, where he'd kept the third vial. His arms were like lead, and every movement sent pain lancing through him.

Jovu, Myrra . . . I can't join them. Can't let Derren's death mean nothing as well.

Adrian set his jaw and crawled towards the table beside his bed. He raised one shaking hand, groping around for the vial. The bowl of icy water fell onto him, but he barely felt the cold. Adrian grabbed the antidote, placed it in his mouth, and bit as hard as he could. The glass shattered. He spit out the cork and drank, tasting blood and the sourness of the antidote.

He lay there, shaking, not knowing if his blood had finally failed him and his life was at its end. His whole body racked with the sharp, burning stabs of the poison ripping its way through him. Adrian did not have the breath to scream, but the room was filled with his groans and gasps for long moments before the antidote took effect.

It took all his strength to get to his knees and clamber onto the bed. The pain was receding, but he was still colder than death, his body hanging by a thread, weaker even than when Kahlia had poisoned him. He crawled under the covers, shivering violently, and his eyes fell shut. His mind was swallowed by darkness, and Adrian was taken into the depths of a restless sleep.

CHAPTER THIRTY-FOUR

The city of Durnn has always been a bastion of the power of the Sentinels and the Church. Its placement at the converging borders of four Domain nations is a subtle reminder that the Sentinels are always watching.

— *Histories of the Domain*

Lynn's eyes drifted open, and the world was a blur, her vision covered in mist. Had she hollowed out? Was this what it looked like? Her eyes closed. Her head was resting on something soft, and something else was brushing against her face. Something hard. Not brushing—nuzzling her.

Her eyes shot open, and there he was. Vedyr. Three times her size, with a massive eagle's head and feathers going down his neck, changing into fur along his feline body and leading to a long tail with a mace-like cluster at the end—just like her own mace, and hard as ruin-stone.

Lynn blinked a few times, trying to sharpen the world. The rookery was a circular room atop the tallest of the fortress's towers.

It was lined with huge stalls for the griffins going all the way around, broken only by the opening in the wall for the creatures to take flight. The room was wide, but the walls could accommodate only six stalls, which meant the chamber extended upwards—ten stories high.

Lynn was in one of the stalls on the ground floor. She kept her gaze on Vedyr, unable to keep back the smile creeping onto her face. A true smile, as she hadn't had in a long time. She tried lifting her arms, but there was no strength in them. Vedyr felt it and brushed his head against her hands instead. She closed her eyes, and his warmth seeped into her, melted away the voices and the presence of death, even if just for a few moments.

"You shouldn't have come back," she whispered.

"You really going to tell him what he should do?" Rel was coming into the rookery with a fresh set of bandages, dwarfed by the size of the stalls around him. "Hadn't seen him since you left, but they always find their way back, I've learned."

Vedyr's silver eyes were fixed on her while Rel kneeled to look at her shoulder. "You were lucky he was close by. Would've hollowed out if he wasn't."

Lynn nodded. "Lucky."

"We scooped up your friend, too."

"Ferrin? Is he . . ." She looked at Rel.

"He's fine, Lynn. You can rest easy."

"And Thain?"

"Either dead or on his way to Syvern. We can't be sure. . . . Still, bastard of a stand you made there. They'd have overrun him if it weren't for you. Felt like old times, like you never left."

Too many things felt like old times, and not in a good way.

"Where's my Mantle?" Lynn asked.

"Being patched up. You'll have it before the battle."

Lynn got up with tentative steps, supporting herself on Vedyr with one hand, but Rel had an uncertain look in his eye.

"What?" she asked.

"Olem's gotten comfortable in the commander's chair. . . . There . . . was a vote."

"For what?" Lynn said, more forcefully this time.

"You. Remaining in the order . . ." Rel let out a heavy breath. "Seems like you convinced enough of them in the valley, and Olem wants to respect the commander's wishes . . ."

"But?"

"They want you on the ground for now, as a general. Say they can't trust you to fly with us." His eyes searched hers for a reaction. "Burnham's happy to have you in the Legion, though."

Lynn blinked, words too far to reach. She'd stepped up then, but she wasn't a leader, and she couldn't be away from Vedyr. "Rel . . ."

"It's only temporary, Lynn." He gave her an apologetic look. "The Legion could use at least one good general. Wouldn't hurt for her to be a Sentinel, either."

"I'm not sure how much of the Bond I can take, and Vedyr . . . . I can't . . ."

"He'll be free to join the fight if he wishes, as always, and I'll get you enough ruin-stone to get through it."

Lynn looked down, shaking her head. "Don't suppose I get a vote?"

"We all have our sacrifices to make, Lynn."

Lynn knew that all too well, but the only question she could ask herself was when her sacrifices would end.

She looked again at Vedyr, mustering all the apology in her gaze as she could. "You shouldn't have come back," she whispered. Then she turned to Rel. "Watch out for him?"

Rel nodded. "Always."

The Stand of Pehd Valley, they were calling it. The story had spread quicker than the fire that had crippled the Legion, yet all they could remember was how Lynn held back the dead-faced army to allow Thain a chance through the pass—and survived. Not a bad thing, perhaps, focusing on life.

The retellings had already changed in little more than a day, though. Apparently, Lynn was a master tactician who had hidden

Vedyr until the final moment, her delayed retreat from the valley part of the plan just so that she could take out a few more of them. The near hollowing was downplayed as well. Lynn didn't hear a single tale in which she'd actually passed out, and definitely none in which she thought herself unworthy of remaining alive. She wondered how Boutros the Bard would have told it and how popular he'd be in the ranks afterward.

Maybe in the past she'd have told herself this was a good thing. She'd faced death, survived, brought back lives with her. . . . But she knew better. She was about to risk those very same lives once more.

They'd given her Mantle back in better condition than she'd received it in from Elwin. It was perfect, save for the four Signs of the Seraph on her spaulders and emblazoned over her chest—the sign of a general of the Legion. Lynn pushed against the overwhelming need to hide it away somewhere. Men shouldn't be following her; it was a madness of their own to put her in command. But there is little that is ever sane in war.

Lynn donned her Mantle and made her way down the stairs of the fortress. She paused in the main hall, regarding the light of the moon shining in through the Sign of the Breath that dominated the back wall. This was it, then. All she'd struggled against all these years, every companion she'd lost—she'd killed—was embodied by the Madness waiting at the gates. She'd tried saving lives, but it seemed like she was closer to finding her path to redemption by taking them.

They are unworthy. They threaten the Seraph and all that we've fought to protect.

She ignored the voices laughing in her mind and strode out of the doors of the Sentinel Tower, out of the fortress, and towards the Legion army waiting atop the city walls. They rose ten strides high and encircled the city in unyielding, dark-gray, white-veined ruin-stone—standing defiantly before the madmen sprawled out before them.

The battle in the valley had maybe taken a thousand out of the enemy ranks, but their numbers were still reported to be close to five thousand, all amassed before Durnn in an endless sea, ready to run over the walls.

Lynn made her way up the back steps of the wall and into one of the high turrets close to the main gate. Elwin had always told her moments like these would come, when she'd have to accept death and wield it to protect life, but it was still bitter to swallow. She looked up to the Seraph's eye, hoping her faith had led her down the right path, then down at her troops.

The walls jutted out to either side for miles, filled with soldiers receiving instructions from their captains, lighting torches, and making sure bows were strung and weapons were ready. Some gazed up towards Lynn with what looked like hope, but most had their eyes fixed on the enemy beyond, surveying the army of death stretching out towards the trees and into the forest.

There were banners displaying the four signs of the Seraph on each of their corners and, in the center, a white hand on a field of black, red lines snaking though it like the bleeding hands of the madmen who'd attacked her. Lynn frowned at the banners. They were truly mad if they thought the Seraph was on their side. Commands were shouted, and wood creaked as rams were pushed forward and enemy soldiers formed up in preparation for a charge at the wall.

"General," Ferrin said. He looked fully recovered from their escape.

"Don't call me that," Lynn said. "This is temporary. I won't be responsible for you out there. Pull what you did last time and I'll leave you to die." She knew it was a lie, but she couldn't afford to have him run off again.

"Inspiring," he said, breaking a smile. "Wouldn't use that partic-ular speech with the troops, though."

"There'll be no speech. And stop treating this like a game. A life is a price too high to gamble away."

"Probably right about no speech. The stories will speak for themselves. And don't worry, General, there is no gambling when you are certain in your faith."

"Blind faith in the Seraph has killed better men, Ferrin."

"Oh, no. Not in the Seraph." The smile touched his eyes. "In you."

He walked away towards his unit, Lynn already regretting her decision to make him a captain. Still, the familiarity would help, and he'd shown enough ability to lead at the battle in the valley, even if he'd let battle-rage take over.

You're in the perfect place to fail again, Dentos said.

"That I am," she said to the open air. "That I am."

There was a loud cracking sound, and the madmen began to move. They dashed forward, shadows accelerating until it was a full charge. They cried to the sky as they rushed towards the walls, too many to count, a wave of darkness, as if death itself was bearing upon them with the thunder of thousands of bloodthirsty foes shattering the ground. Some had flaming torches in hand, ready to burn down the city beyond the gates; others bore only insane howls.

Lynn glanced at the houses below. Those close to the wall had been evacuated, but the hubris of the Durnnish still stood stronger than any foe knocking at their gates. They'd been offered refuge in Alteria, and other nearby cities had offered to harbor them as well, but most had refused to be led out of the city, and many still waited in their homes, sure of the safety of their walls and the Legion defending them.

"Archers!" Lynn yelled to the lantern bearer beside her.

Ferrin and the other captains echoed the cry, and soon hundreds of flame-tipped arrows were flying over the wall, burning the sky in smoldering lines. The arrows pierced the front line, setting the fields alight. The Sentinels followed, some swooping down onto the enemy archers to preempt a counterattack, while others flew for the rear to break the enemy lines. The shriek of the griffins pierced the clouds as they bore down like great rocks from above, crashing into the enemy ranks, sending some flying, ripping others with beaks, spears, and claws. They couldn't stay on the ground for long, or they'd be swarmed. Instead, the griffins launched into the air again to crash into different spots.

The enemy army was engaged, but the front lines didn't stop. A few fell to more arrows, but the charge raged on as soldiers approached under tall shields, covering dozens bearing long ladders between them. The shielders blocked most of the next wave of arrows and reached the foot of the wall, then made way for the men behind to throw the ladders up against the wall.

"Aim at the ladders!" Lynn yelled.

In seconds, the ladder-men were riddled with arrows, but it did not stop them. They were even more frenzied than Lynn had seen in the valley, and their snarls became louder as they rushed up the rungs.

Lynn kept shouting commands from the top of her turret, directing the men towards the more crowded spots. Her men knocked away what ladders they could and slammed their weapons into skulls as they appeared over the wall, but more were coming, too fast to turn away.

"Signal the Sentinels," Lynn told her lantern bearer.

He did, and in moments, griffins were plunging down, snatching ladders and madmen off the walls, others crashing into the enemy at the base of the walls, Sentinels jumping off and whirling their weapons in deadly storms of steel. A triumphant cry rose from the Legion, but there was still an uncountable mass of enemies bearing down on the walls.

The rams had reached the gates and were battering at the sturdy wood. The wall trembled, but Lynn had little time to look towards the gates. An enormous shadow moving amongst the trees had caught her eye, and a flash of torchlight revealed the siege weapon: a ramp-like contraption aimed steadily at the walls. There was another loud crack, and a score of huge, flaming boulders arced from among the trees. Some hit the walls, sending pieces of ruin-stone raining down and making the floor shudder beneath Lynn's feet. Others tore through the men on top, sending flaming bodies screaming as they fell off the walls.

"Siege engine!" Gotzon, one of the Legion captains, shouted. The walls were strong, but it wasn't clear how long they'd stand a barrage like this.

Lynn's eyes searched for Rel, but she could not find him in the chaos of the field. Olem seemed to have heard the captain's cries, though, and the Sentinels who'd been protecting the walls to the right of her turret flew off into the trees.

"Ferrin! Take command of the signals. Keep the charge back. Don't overextend. I'll hold the wall," Lynn yelled down.

Ferrin rushed up to stand beside the lantern bearer, and Lynn darted to the right edge of the turret, eyes locked on a cluster of enemy ladders being thrown against the walls.

She dug her hand into the pouch of ruin-stone Rel had left her. It was more than enough this time, and as long as she had them, she wouldn't hollow out. She grabbed one and channeled its anger towards Vedyr. Her muscles tightened with power, her mind cleared as if the battle had slowed, and she sprang off the turret, landing with a thunderous boom onto the wall, but the ruin-stone did not crack. Her limbs pulsed, and she screamed as she dashed at the madmen coming over the ladders.

The first barely got his weapon up before Lynn sliced him in half with her scythe. She inverted her grip on the polearm and brought the mace around to smash the helmet of the one standing next to him. He flew sideways, taking another man off the top of the wall. A hand crept over on the battlement, but Lynn stuck her scythe in the mouth of the crazed woman who tried to pull herself up after, then pushed the ladder away with a backswing of her mace. It fell away, crashing into enemies below.

Lynn cut away, feeding off the anger in the ruin-stone shards and urging her men onward with wordless battle cries. The ground was slick with blood beneath her feet, but the Legion soldiers stood with her, pushing back more and more of the enemy.

We can do this. Durnn has never fallen.

Fewer boulders were crashing into the walls now, but the ruin-stone trembled under her.

"Fight on! Durnn will stand!" she screamed.

Men around her rallied and pushed more enemies and ladders away until the madmen started to withdraw and regroup. The battle was far from over, but they seemed to have repelled the first wave. A cheer went up across the wall, and Lynn added her voice to it. She looked over her men. They were not without their own losses, but if they held strong and Thain came through, they might actually have a chance.

She scanned the horizon. There were flames rising in the woods, illuminating the crumbling carcasses of the siege machines, but no sign of Dakhran airships, only unrelenting griffins crashing down onto the enemy. A few more flames went up among the trees as more siege engines were destroyed, and another cheer went up from the men.

"Keep steady!" Lynn cried. "The battle is not won yet. Get the wounded down from the walls. Archers, stay alert! Ferrin, with me!"

She strode into the turret to get a better view of the enemy ranks standing beyond the wall to the left side of the turret. Ferrin came down the steps and stood behind Lynn while she searched for weak spots. A glint caught her eye. What looked like a round glass vessel filled with liquid was sailing up above the walls. It gleamed with the light of the moon for a moment, then scores of enemy arrows shot at it.

The glass exploded, hurling a thick red liquid onto the men. More followed, bursting over them, their contents hailing down. Some of the men tried to avoid it, but most were showered, the liquid streaming into their helms, mixing with their sweat. They looked confused at first, eyes searching for meaning among their companions. Then the afflicted dropped their weapons and began to snarl, spittle flying from their mouths with crazed screams. Some seemed faster, and others seemed to have grown claws. They turned on the men beside them and tore through.

Lynn's eyes widened, and her gut opened into a cold pit. Tainted blood. The blood of the madmen. The Sentinels were still in the woods, hunting for siege engines, pulled away by a lesser threat while the true weapon rained down on the defenders of Durnn. Lynn turned to Ferrin, muscles quivering, knowing the only command she could give was to cut her losses.

"Pull away who you can and get off the walls. Form a defense in the fortress. I'll open a path."

The Legion men were caught between raising their shields to protect themselves from the tainted rain and protecting themselves from their maddened companions. They were gripped by desperation, attacking their own, mad or not, desperately fighting for their lives without knowing friend or foe.

The barrage lessened, then halted; the newly infected Legion troops were enough to spread the Madness faster than the raining blood of the madmen. Lynn darted out of the turret, weapon fastened into a long polearm before her, scythe on one side, mace on the other.

"Shields up! Off the walls!" she shouted at her soldiers.

Madmen crowded the path, and she swung her weapon in a wide circle around her, cutting them down, heading for the steps that descended into Durnn, but more were being turned, and the ladders crashed onto the walls again.

She ducked an attack and used her mace to shatter her opponent's knee. He cried in pain and folded over, but Lynn continued her motion, spinning the scythe up into another man charging rabidly at her. The scythe went into his chin and through his skull, lifting him off the ground. Lynn flung him at the remaining madman in her path, sending both bodies flying off the wall.

She rushed forward, screaming, "Get off the walls!"

"Retreat!" Ferrin echoed behind, and the cries spread along the wall.

Lynn crushed another shard and crashed ahead, barreling into more enemies standing between her allies and the path of retreat, and they rolled down the stairs in a jumble of arms, legs, and sharp edges. She fell onto them like a boulder, crushing one man's ribcage and falling on another's leg. His howl of anguish was silenced by her mace cracking into his head.

Something itched at the back of her mind at the screams of pain, but she buried it beyond her consciousness, held her position, and waved her men along past her.

"Retreat! Head for the fortress."

A few men fell, and more jumped off the walls, joining the panicked stampede of citizens and soldiers towards the fortress in the center of the city, while others made for Durnn's rear gates, likely reconsidering the offers of shelter from surrounding cities.

Some of the houses on the east side were already aflame, and the gates were rocking behind her. The thumping added to the maddening concoction of screams, clashing steel, and the scent of Durnn and its protectors burning.

More lives that you have failed to protect, Roki said.

Ferrin was the last one down and paused beside Lynn, waiting for a command. People were running desperately towards the safety of the fortress, but more and more Legion soldiers were descending into frenzy on the walls and turning their maddened gaze on the fleeing citizens.

"Help them get to the fortress!" she yelled at Ferrin, then turned back towards the gate. They needed more time.

Death had taken the wall, and it was rushing forward, spreading through the burning buildings with howls and battle cries. The gates crashed open and more flooded through. There was only one chance left. Not even the fortress would hold this many now.

A few hundred men still stood beside Lynn, trusting the woman who'd stood in the valley. She steeled herself before the incoming wave, but her breath caught as a shadow moved on the horizon. It could have been one of the many Sentinels flying back to protect the tower, but it persisted, like a cloud moving towards them. More eyes around her looked up, and the rising fires in the city lit up the sky, outlining the rounded hull and flat-topped deck of a Dakhran airship. It was dropping barrels. They smashed open on the ground and set fire to fields and enemies alike.

They lit a fire in Lynn as well, and her heart pumped the triumph of victory through her veins. It had been at the last moment, but her faith had paid off. The plan—her plan—had worked. The Seraph was watching over her, after all.

CHAPTER THIRTY-FIVE

The dangers of the Slopes may be many, but they are known and can be dealt with together. To wander the wilds is the true mark of desperation, for we do not know what threats Zala still keeps in the shadows of the world.

— Zaruni cautionary tale

They'd reached the borderlands, but the trek had done nothing for Shai's mood, it seemed. She had her eyes fixed on Adda all the way, alternating between frowns and head shakes. The dirt roads were lined on either side with shacks, no two of which were alike, seemingly constructed with whatever was available. It tended towards what the Slopers had built on the side of the Great Mountain: an amalgamation of people looking for shelter between the Visslands and the clans, scrounging up and building what they could. There were the same dangers, too—dark corners and hungry eyes veiled by the shadows—and people rarely lingered, rushing from one spot to another along the streets or gathering close to buildings. Nasha kept the Ronar nearby and heeling Egren's hasty steps.

The Domain man's nervous anxiousness had wheedled at Nasha all the way, and it was growing stronger. Nothing she couldn't handle, but that and the mounting crowd sent cautious shivers across her skin. She could have opened herself to the emotions instead of keeping them back, but this was the first time she'd encountered a crowd that rivaled the one in the Yltigg arena, and this land was foreign enough that the risk of losing control seemed like a prideful, foolish idea.

It is still a curse.

She looked at Adda, considering if she could still find the path to the First Tree, but shook her head and looked away. It was still a curse, but she'd wrangled pieces of it away from the Earth and had some semblance of command over it, at least. She'd been trusting her fate to others for too long. It was time to trust herself.

I can control this. I am not the monster.

They were moving to a less crowded part of the makeshift town now. The sun was almost touching the horizon, and the alleyways gained an ominous air as darkness fell heavier over them. They paused in an empty alleyway, Egren's emotions as anxious as ever.

"What's wrong?" Nasha asked.

The mercenary's head snapped towards her. "Nothin'. Just don't quite enjoy this part o' town, is all."

Nasha frowned at him, trying to delve deeper into the man's emotions, but he was already pointing at another alley entrance on the other side of the dirt strip that passed for a street. "Head down there, make your way around. Best stay out of sight."

Nasha grunted, but she kept her focus on the man. She led Shai, Landi, and Uvo across, pushing the bound Carswell boy before her, while Adda and her son followed.

She didn't trust Egren, but he'd followed through, and they were past the hard part already.

I'm close, Ife. They'll be safe.

They paced through the darkening crack between low-roofed

housing and came out in woods that marked the edge of the borderlands.

One tree grew taller than the others. It was thick bodied and blooming, its deep-blue flowers pumping a sweet scent into the evening. Nasha frowned. Bahar had told her about Lashki trees, but they were supposed to grow far to the north, in Azur and beyond. There were no accounts of them this far south.

Something sour rode her tongue at the thought of Bahar—no telling where he was now, if he was even alive—but Nasha's attention was pulled away by Uvo approaching the tree.

"Don't touch them," Nasha told the boy, who was looking at a flower up close—a few of them lay on the ground, like traps laid out for unsuspecting prey. "Your throat would tighten up before you could blink. You'd stop breathing soon after."

Uvo took several steps back, as if what he'd been looking at was the maw of some beast instead of a sweet-scented flower. Its color rippled in the setting sun, blue flowing into purple into a darker blue, like midnight. Some on the ground were a deep copper red.

"Poetic," Adda mumbled. "They're supposed to have scores of these in Azur. Nightshade, they call them." Her expression was bitter, as if she'd chewed on one of the flowers and just found out they were poisonous. "Looks like these Domain folk aren't without their sense of humor."

If this was supposed to be humorous, Nasha wasn't laughing. She looked around the base of the tree. No blackened Earth here, at least.

"Stay alert," Nasha said. "Let's hope this is the only surprise they have for us."

A shot of emotion brought Nasha's eyes up. Shai was standing beside her, pulling her away from the others. "You shouldn't have brought her," she whispered, shooting a sharp look at Adda.

"Wasn't much of a choice, Shai."

"We can't trust her."

"Shai." Nasha put a hand on the girl's shoulder. "We've won. I don't trust her either, but there is nothing for her to gain by threatening you or your family."

Nasha tightened her grip on the girl's shoulder and held her gaze. Shai frowned back, working her jaw—a habit she seemed to have picked up from Nasha—then sighed.

"Never simple, is it?" Shai said.

"No, it isn't."

Nasha's head jerked up as a wave of emotion came rolling through the trees. "It's time."

Shai pushed the hooded prisoner onto his knees and held the bag of stolen Ronar ancestor-stone tight in one hand. Her family stood a few strides back, as did Adda, holding Razi in a protective embrace before her. Men stepped out from the back of the house and drew near them through the trees, black outlines against the burning red sky, a sense of alertness running before them. Nasha kept her blades sheathed but let the sensation run through her, dancing up her arm and on her fingertips.

There were five in the approaching party from one of the houses at the edge of the town. A woman led Egren and two rough-looking men with scars, ripped clothing, and hard eyes, all displayed proudly, as though they'd fought hard to acquire them. The last man moved with an effort and a slight limp—older, perhaps. He used a staff and was looking down, his face obscured in the shadow of his cowl. He put his back against a tree and waited behind the other four.

The woman leading them stopped a few steps away from the Lashki tree that loomed to Nasha's right, keeping a distance between them.

"You have the papers?" Nasha asked.

The woman nodded and pulled out a bound leather packet. Nasha gave Shai a look, and the girl raised the heavy bag of ancestor-stone, displaying its contents to the mercenaries.

"We'll need two more," Nasha said. "There should be enough in here to cover more than that."

The woman narrowed her eyes, then looked back at the old man. Nasha extended her senses towards him but could garner little else than an underlying thrum coming from his emotions, as if he was struggling to keep something painful down. The pain in his legs, perhaps?

Adda pulled out a pouch of her own. Not ancestor-stone, but the clink of gold pulled Nasha back into herself.

"We can pay our way," Adda said.

The woman was still looking towards the old man, and eventually, he gave a slow nod.

"You got a problem showing your face, old man?" Nasha asked.

"The borderlands are never safe," the woman answered. "We show only what we must around here." She stretched out a hand with the leather-bound papers and jerked her head towards the Carswell boy, who'd started to whimper softly through his gag. "He in one piece?"

"Seems to be," Nasha said. "But you're free to check."

Something odd was clawing at her, something she couldn't quite make out, like a voice too far away to be heard.

Shai brought the prisoner to his feet and pushed him forward. One of the men in the back stepped up and put an arm around the boy's shoulder, then pulled him away, speaking some dialect Nasha could not understand.

"We done?" the woman asked.

Nasha looked over to Adda, and the Tivezzi stepped slowly towards the mercenaries, arms still around Razi.

"We're done," Nasha said, gaze locked on the Stone-Shaper.

"Egren told you what would happen if we don't receive word they've reached Azur?" Shai said.

The woman broke a crooked smile and spat on the ground. "Don't worry. Got a reputation to uphold."

She threw Nasha the papers. Nasha checked them. All seemed to be in order.

"You'll get two more as soon as you've handed that over." The woman pointed at the bag in Shai's hand.

Shai stepped forward with the bag of ancestor-stone, Adda beside her, both holding out their payments. But there was still something odd about the old man, empty.

Nasha went deeper into the flow of sensation and finally picked something up from him. The voice at the back of her mind crept closer, almost to where she could hear it now. It reminded her of something that seemed to be lost to a previous age, a past where she did not know even herself. Something like . . . . No, she was trusting her curse too much again. They'd won. It was over. She breathed out, but the feeling did not leave her. Insistent, something familiar in it—too familiar. Enough for her to—

"Stop," she said.

Adda turned to her, pulling back the pouch of gold. Shai, only a few steps beside her, did the same. Egren narrowed his eyes at them, and the man beside him let off the thrill that was becoming easier for Nasha to recognize: the thrill of impending battle.

Their hands flew to their blades, and they lunged forward. Shai tried to react but was buried under the weight of one of the men, while Egren had taken advantage of Adda's turned back to restrain her and put a blade to her neck.

"Looks like we all have our secrets," the old man by the tree said. "But I never took you for a betrayer." The feeling that had been clawing at the back of her mind took form when she heard the old man's voice, but she still struggled to accept it. Surely it was the curse playing some trick on her.

He pulled his hood down.

Bahar's face was nothing like the one she'd known. Twisted, with half-healed wounds starting to scar. The worst one was on his right side, a burning line of red that ran from the end of his lip up to his cheek, still partly scabbed.

Nasha stepped forward, gaze moving between Adda and Shai, both held with blades at their necks now.

"That's far enough," Egren said.

"Bahar, whatever they've done to you—"

"To me?" He laughed, dry and cold. "They've done nothing to me. They did take my son, though. And that is on Tomu and all of you who stood by and watched them do it. I'd have settled for you, but when they told me the Stone-Shaper herself was with you, I could hardly believe it. Seems like the Seraph watches over her people even in this faithless land.

"Devu gave his life for your clan . . ." He flashed a grin that was mangled and dark like the grief that had assaulted Nasha in the arena. "Seems only fair I return the favor."

"Warden!" Adda croaked. Her eyes were filled with pain and fear, and it was bleeding out in her emotions. They moved from Nasha to Razi, who'd been thrown and was scrambling towards Nasha on his elbows, back on the ground. "The Ronar come first. The Roots must survive."

Nasha was still frozen, unable to decide what to do. She looked between Adda and Shai, and something hit her then, hot and focused—the Tivezzi trying to overpower her. Nasha tried to push back, but Adda's assault was already draining away. It wasn't being pulled by the Earth: there was no dead Earth around them. Instead it seemed to be going into Adda's son, whose eyes were darting wildly from face to face. Razi lacked his own control, probably latching onto the familiar feel of his mother's emotions and unconsciously sucking it all in.

"Nasha. I can teach you. There is so much you don't know. Think of Razi, Nasha, please!" She struggled against her captor but was held fast.

Bahar's smile was widening at every pleading word, but Nasha was pulled by a numbness shooting through her. It was calm, cold, and collected. It was Shai's. Her gaze was on Nasha, eyes telling her they'd come further than most Slopers ever would, but it was over now. Don't save me, they said. The boy needs her. Her lips were almost a smile, accepting. She'd probably been expecting it to end like this her whole life, end up killed like Ife.

The emotion passed through Nasha, and what lingered was warm only for a moment. Hope, snuffed out. They'd been so close. They'd won, hadn't they? But it seemed there was still another necessary sacrifice, just as Mansa had been willing to sacrifice her.

No. It ended here. The Slopes had paid more than enough, and she wasn't like Mansa. She wasn't the monster.

Bahar signaled the men, but Nasha burned through Shai's emotion before the blade started moving and was standing in front of her in a breath, her knives moving too fast to be seen. Nasha slashed away the mercenary's knife hand, then stabbed the side of his chest four times in the space of a breath.

She turned to Adda before the man's body fell to the ground, but all she saw was the blade cutting deep into the Tivezzi's neck. Egren took his time, going slow enough for her to feel the pain, to scream with desperation, eyes locked on her child. He kicked her to the ground, and the mercenaries burst into action.

Whatever speed her curse had given her was gone now, burned away, but Nasha was fast enough to stand between Razi and the woman rushing towards him. She stabbed at Nasha, but it was a poor strike, slow enough for Nasha to sidestep and let the woman's arm sail past her, then grab her wrist and pull so that she stumbled forward. Nasha buried her knife into the woman's back, sending her to the ground face-first, then stabbed the back of her skull, and she stopped moving.

Uvo was struggling with Egren, while Shai had engaged the final mercenary. She cut him down with a furious scream but didn't notice the Domain boy creeping up on her with a trembling knife in hand. Nasha threw her striking blade, piercing the back of his knee. He fell on it with an agonized cry, and Shai turned, already slashing, with nothing Nasha could do to stop it. He fell, blood pooling around him and draining into the Earth.

The river of sensations that had flowed around her slowed as the enemies fell. Egren was backing off towards the trees, eyes locked on Uvo, but Nasha wouldn't repeat her mistake. She darted forward, headbutting the man to the ground, and the anger rose in her, almost as much at herself as at the man's betrayal.

He had a hand before his face, trying to crawl away. "No, please, I can still—"

Nasha stabbed her parry knife through the man's hand and into his eye. He yelled, the back of his hand pinned to his face. Nasha twisted, channeling her rage through her movement, then pulled the knife up through his head, screaming. She jolted up and looked beyond him, eyes searching desperately among the trees, but there was no movement. Bahar was gone.

"Shit!"

She closed her eyes and extended her awareness. Risks be damned. She dove deep: she couldn't lose him. Nasha pressed her eyes harder, bit down on her teeth, but there was nothing around them—only the flow of emotions coming from the town beyond. Too many to single out Bahar.

Nasha let out a frustrated howl. Her mind was slipping, heading into the same darkness that had consumed her during the Proving. It rose, closing off her awakened mind, forcing itself through her.

Then it was taken away. Syphoned out.

Nasha looked towards where it was being pulled and found Razi on the ground, shaking his mother's dead body. Faint lines swirled around him: the darkness, her darkness, drawn out of her and into the boy. Landi was wrestling him away. He struggled, resisted wordlessly, but eventually turned his tear-streaked face to Shai's mother and let her pull him close. Nasha stepped towards them, but the boy recoiled deeper into Landi, and Nasha moved back again. The fear in the boy's eyes sent a ripple of shame through her, and it took a long moment for Nasha to stabilize herself.

Shai was a mess of sensations, and Nasha did not dare latch onto the girl, instead settling for deep breaths, trying to exhale her frustration away. Shai was looking at her, though.

She stepped close and pulled Nasha away from the others, something working behind her eyes. "Your speed . . . . No one could have saved me before the man cut my throat—or stopped me like you did in training before the Proving either. No one moves that fast. You're . . . you're one of them, aren't you? A witch, like in the tales."

Nasha clenched her jaw and felt her fingers tightening around her blades. "I'm not a monster, Shai!"

Shai's eyes were wide, but she raised her hands before her and gave Nasha a timid nod. "I know. . . . Your secret's safe with me. I'm just glad I'm on your side."

Nasha let out the breath held in her chest, then looked at Razi.

"What now?" Shai asked.

"You go with your family. I'll see what I can do with the boy. He's like Adda, like me. We'll need to check the house, see if we can get him passage on the ship. We'll forge it if we need to, but he can't stay. Tomu would kill him if he found out."

It was hard for Nasha to let go. The boy was the closest link she had to her curse, but she would not risk him, not for herself or any misguided notion that it would help the clan. She wasn't the monster.

Shai's gaze shifted towards her mother and the trembling child in her arms, and a deep sadness shot into Nasha, as if there was something pressing at her heart and pulling it down into her stomach. Shai looked back at her.

"Forging papers won't work," Shai said. "It'll put all of us at risk."

"There's no other way. He can't—"

"I'll stay."

Nasha's throat tightened as if she were holding down tears, but the emotion wasn't her own. It was Shai, invading her senses.

"No, Shai."

"You said it yourself. There's no other way. Besides, I can't have gone through the Proving for nothing. Still need to convince the Chief to take me in."

She gave Nasha a grin, then walked to Uvo, then Landi. She approached carefully, gave her mother a long hug, then began to explain. Tears rolled from her mother's eyes, but she nodded and embraced Shai again, longer than the first time. Shai gave her mother the papers, then turned to her brother. She put her axe in Uvo's fist and spoke a few more words in his ear. Her brother nodded as well, and he strode ahead of Landi, who was pulling Razi by the hand. They paced away through the trees, and Shai strode back to Nasha.

"Still think we've won?" she asked.

Nasha looked down, twisting her mouth. "Seems like it's not over yet."

The words tasted like ash, clinging sourly to her tongue. She breathed in the sweet scent of the Lashki tree flowers. It had been a simple plan. Too simple, perhaps, or maybe things had just been too complicated from the start. There was no running from it now, though. Bahar had escaped with a heart full of rage and a mind set on revenge, and he was sure to tell his superiors in the Visslands what had happened to the Carswell boy. Mansa was getting his war, and she had to pick a side.

"War's coming," Nasha said. "We should head back and warn the clan. Tomu's men didn't see us. We'll burn the bodies, make up our own tale."

"You sure it's safe?"

"Nothing's safe now, Shai. No one is prepared for what's coming. . . . But we've faced worse odds, I think. We'll have to go through it like last time. Together."

Nasha grinned at Shai and reached out her arm.

Shai stood frozen, even her emotions silenced. She narrowed her eyes for a moment, and a few shots of uncertainty hit Nasha, but eventually she stepped forward and clasped Nasha's arm in her own.

"Welcome to the Ronar."

CHAPTER THIRTY-SIX

Those who fear death have never truly had faith in themselves.

— *The Book of the Bone*

The enemy's back lines were broken, but those within the city were enough of a threat. Men and women ran in every direction, some towards the rear city gates, others to hide among the houses. Those who had kept their senses ran anywhere but the path of the airship raining down fire on the enemy. Some did not run. They were fewer in number, every one of them in a frenzy as wild as the flames devouring the city, and they attacked all in their path, forcing painful screams even out of the enemy. Lynn frowned at the madmen's screams. They rarely felt pain, but maybe that was just another change she didn't recognize.

Some men of the Legion remained, most still battling their own companions who'd been taken by the Madness. More were coming through the gate, fleeing the fire-barrels being dropped by the airship. Lynn rushed towards the main gates, ready to plug the gap that would let the madmen through.

"Hold the gate! The airship will thin them out. More will be here soon!" Lynn shouted, and more soldiers rallied towards her. There was still fighting on the walls, but what caught Lynn's eye was movement beyond the broken gate, an outline rising from the flames and heading towards them.

A man with a familiar gait was opening a path around him. He swung a heavy hammer left and right, sending men flying away, while others, lacking the courage to bar his path, broke and ran back towards the fortress. Lynn stood alone before him. The Sentinels were still beyond the walls, slaying as many as they could to keep the enemy from flooding the city, while others flew overhead to prepare the defenses of the fortress. She was the only one here to stop this madman.

He paused before her, and fire erupted from one of the burning houses, illuminating the man's weapon. It was Leardin's hammer. Her eyes jumped to the face, expecting a dead mask, but it was no mask. Leardin stood snarling before her, eyes bloodshot and skin stained black around them.

Lynn opened her mouth. She had to say something, anything. . . . But there was nothing left of the Leardin she'd known. This was a twisted mockery, a weapon sent by the enemy to shake them, just like Elwin had become in his final moments. Whoever was commanding this army was clearly no madman.

Lynn gave him an unwavering stare; she knew what needed to be done. She held her polearm in one hand and dug into her ruin-stone pouch with the other. She had an anger of her own burning in her gut, but the ruin-stone would keep her stable, whole. Her fingers pressed tight around the shard. She pulled the anger from it, and it burned through her and straight to Vedyr. Her eyes ignited and her mind sharpened, cutting away the fatigued haze of battle.

Leardin lunged at her, hammer raised high and a mad scream raw in his throat. The hammer came down fast, but Lynn jumped back, and the hammer shattered the cobbles where she'd stood a heartbeat before. Leardin's eyes were not silver, but the madness had given him everything he needed. He was stronger and moving faster than she'd ever seen.

He pulled his hammer free of the broken stones, but Lynn was already leaping towards him, weapons split. She slammed her mace into his hunched shoulder and stabbed at his exposed back. The commander only glared at her and jerked his back away, pulling the scythe embedded in it from her grip.

Leardin swung the hammer in a wide arc, forcing Lynn to pull harder on Vedyr's speed. She went low to evade the blow, then bashed his chin with an upswing of her mace. He flew off his feet and through the wall of a burning house.

Lynn held her breath.

Don't get up, don't get up.

But he did. He walked out of the smoking house with blood flowing from the wound where he'd landed on the scythe that now pierced out of his chest, his right side covered in slick red. He charged, both hands on his hammer. Lynn whirled sideways to move away from the descending blow, but at the last moment, he twisted and swung it sideways at an impossible angle. It hit Lynn in the side, sending her crashing into the wall of another burning house, then onto the cobbles, scattering the ruin-stone out of the pouch that had kept her safe from hollowing out.

She clawed her way breathlessly to her knees and gulped in air. Her ribs were like daggers piercing her insides, but she couldn't stop, couldn't give up. Not now. She stumbled to her feet, pain shooting through her with every breath, but the hammer was already veering towards her head. Lynn surged her speed and moved her head but took the hit on her shoulder—the one that'd taken the cut for Ferrin in the valley. The throbbing bloomed, and her left arm went numb. She rolled away, but the mace clattered from her hand, and the scythe was still in Leardin's back. She was weaponless and almost falling out of her Bond.

The mad commander paced around her with a beastly growl. Smoke filled the air, blurring the battlefield that the city had become. Her eyes watered, and her throat was dry. Not long now. Her mind was slipping away, barely enough to keep her standing.

Her mind raced, desperate for a solution, straining to keep the panic at bay.

This is it. You'll be joining us soon, Dentos whispered.

You can't beat him, Alren said.

I hate you, she told the voices. *I regret nothing. I'd kill you again. All of you.*

It was her anger talking, her exhaustion. She'd had enough. The flame in her mixed with the pain and flowed freely. She kept it this time, focusing for one last burst towards Vedyr. Lynn backed away, but her path was blocked by a crumbled wall.

Leardin rushed her again, and Lynn gritted her teeth. Her body was weak, but her mind was still sharp, and Leardin had become predictable in his madness. His hammer was raised, but Lynn recognized the movement this time. He twisted again midswing.

Lynn gathered the last of the anger and pain and stepped onto the crumbled slab of wall behind her, then took all she could from Vedyr and channeled the last of her strength into a leap. She vaulted over Leardin, and the hammer hit only smoke. Lynn pulled the scythe from his back as she fell, and stabbed him through the other side, piercing his heart. Leardin was pushed forward with the force of Lynn's strike and stumbled a few more steps before falling to his knees, hammer still clutched in both hands.

Lynn approached, heart pounding, almost pierced by her broken ribs. He looked up at her, and silver flashed in his eyes. Lynn's muscles tensed, ready to spring at the slightest movement. But he did not move. Their gazes remained locked, and his expression seemed to soften a touch. There was something dancing in the silver of his eyes. Sanity, perhaps? Was he fighting it like Elwin?

One hand let go of the hammer and went to his belt. The commander grabbed something and brought it up towards her. A glint of firelight reflected off the glass vial he was holding. Lynn took it, giving him a final look before she released her Bond, and his head bowed once more.

The fire was casting shadows onto his face, but Lynn thought she could make out the hint of a smile. A final defiance in the face of death. He remained on both knees, one hand limp, the other clutching his hammer, expression frozen as his chest stopped moving.

The vial was filled with the same reddish liquid that looked thick as blood, but it was not blood. Slowly, the screams of pain from the enemy, the bleeding hands, the sudden madness in some that others had seemed unaffected by, all fell into place.

They're not all mad.

Murderer! Roki screamed at her. *Death bringer!* Cara yelled.

An icy hand gripped her, and for a moment she had trouble breathing.

This was not some divine judgment sent to purify the Domain. She was holding the source of it. The Madness was manufactured. And there was only one nation that had the alchemists to produce such a thing.

Anger boiled within Lynn's gut, but she didn't direct it to Vedyr this time. It came out in a frustrated howl that tightened her chest with shame. She looked up towards the Dakhran vessel flying over the walls. The fire barrels did not stop, and all around her, the triumphant cheers of the Legion were turning to surprised dismay as the fire consumed them and the madmen alike. Syvern had played both ends, and Lynn had delivered him all he needed to turn against the Domain. She'd convinced the Legion to open the Skygate, paved the path for Syvern's airships to invade.

Did you think you'd find redemption? They laughed.

It's over. We told you.

You shouldn't have tried.

Lynn was still close to the gate and men were rushing past, some desperately looking at her for guidance, the same pleading in their eyes that she'd seen in the prison, that her companions—her voices —had shown before they died, but Lynn could not guide them. She was paralyzed, looking up at the death falling towards them in a fiery embrace.

"What do we do?" a man screamed. "General, what do we do?"

The voice echoed around her. Would it be the next one to join the collection in her mind? Lynn looked at Leardin. He'd led, and he'd failed, but his expression was clear. Nothing like Cedd's. Not

443

blank like Elwin's. She'd been measuring her life by her failures, keeping them all in her mind. She'd been afraid, but Leardin was still leading her, even in death. He had no fear, and death is nothing without fear at its side.

Maybe she'd finally cracked, or maybe it was her faith.

"Get as many as you can to safety and evacuate the city."

Lynn breathed in and pushed through the pain of her wounds, finding strength to pick up her weapons and dash towards the tower.

Ferrin had managed to get people to shelter in the fortress, but many were still pouring in, a desperate crowd stealing glances at what they now saw was an enemy airship. She waded past them and into the fortress, ribs and shoulder throbbing, but she was not looking for safety. She rushed into the tower, fastened her weapons into one, and sprinted up the stairs to the rookery two, three at a time, her heart leaping almost as high as her feet up the steps, her last dregs of strength reaching out to the griffin whose heart beat as one with her own.

The rookery door was in sight, and she could feel Vedyr in there through the Bond. Lynn dashed towards it but was thrown back as the wall of the tower burst open beside her, shattered by a heavy ballista bolt shot by the airship, now blocking her path along with the crumbled wall. There was a rope attached to the end of the bolt that was already recoiling, being pulled back by the airship crew for another shot.

Wind howled through the gaping hole. There was no way past the rubble other than through the air. Lynn looked out the opening, every muscle balking, but her mind was already set on a plan. She wrapped the rope around her good hand and slashed it off the heavy anchor, holding fast before she was pulled into the night, flying towards the airship. She held on with all her strength, arm twisting in the coiled rope, but it was slipping; her grip wouldn't last long, and there was no way she'd reach the airship. She tried to pull herself up the rope, but her arm slid another fraction.

Lynn breathed deep. Maybe she'd cracked, or maybe it was her faith.

She let go.

The smell of the burning city invaded her nostrils, making her eyes water as she fell through the sky with her gaze locked on the Seraph's mark.

Falling.

Falling.

The mark vanished for a fleeting moment, and then Vedyr's cry filled her ears. Lynn landed on his back, and it was like she had become whole again. Her exhaustion vanished; her strength surged. They were Bonded, and nothing could pull them apart. She echoed the cry, holding on to the familiar feathered muscle beneath her, already steering him towards the enemy.

They were lightning, furious, streaking through the black sky. She guided Vedyr towards the airship, and the tip of her scythe caught the moonlight moments before it ripped through the side of the vessel, cutting a deep gash in the wood that sent out alarmed cries from the crew. Arrows and ballista bolts flew, but Vedyr was too fast. They were one, and their Bond burned stronger than ever in their rage. They rolled and angled down, flying below the ship. Vedyr did not slow. He flew close to the hull and Lynn raised her scythe, digging into the wood and opening the ship's midsection as if she was cutting out its guts. It creaked and groaned as if in pain, and the cries of alarm turned to desperation.

The crew aimed at them again, but Lynn flew higher than any arrow or bolt could reach. She flew up and up and then turned . . . and let go of Vedyr.

She fell straight towards the airship, mace side aimed at the deck, her limp arm using Vedyr's strength so she could grip the polearm with both hands, while the griffin streaked past her in a blur. She fell like a star out of the sky, muscles still strengthened by the Bond. Lynn gripped her weapon tighter moments before she smashed into the deck. Her mace opened a hole in it, and her body followed. She ripped through the wood, broken pieces cutting at her arms, the pain of the impact coursing through her but not slowing her down. She shot all the way through, splitting the great wooden beast in half where she'd sliced its underside.

It groaned and fractured and fell out of the sky.

Lynn fell, eyes closing, giving herself into the arms of the night. She was slipping—close to her limit, even with Vedyr by her side. Her eyes faltered, but a cloud dashed under her and Vedyr was there, catching her aching body as the ruined ship fell towards the city in a rain of splinters and enemy cries.

Lynn held on. It was good to have him back.

More wings unsettled the air around her, Sentinels approaching. Olem and Rel were the first to come into blurry view.

"What now?" Olem asked, as if he wasn't the one in command. She couldn't blame him. It had been her plan.

She forced herself to look around. The outlines of more airships had formed on the horizon. There was no winning this battle.

"Ev . . ." she tried, but the words sputtered.

Rel put his hands on her, and she felt a rush of life, as if she'd taken a long breath, and it came with the strength to keep her awake.

"Save all you can and evacuate the city," she said. "We need to get word to the Pontiff. Dakhra has betrayed the Domain."

The soldiers were leading citizens away from the city. Lines of people flooded out of the back of the Sentinel Tower, with Legion men and griffin riders steering them towards Dryss, Ratha, or maybe another of the Othonean cities. Durnn had fallen.

CHAPTER THIRTY-SEVEN

Blood holds ties.

— Othonean royal family saying

There was a shadow sitting beside his bed when Adrian opened his eyes. What was Derren doing here at this hour? Had their plan worked?

Adrian blinked once. Twice. The memories flooded back. Couldn't be Derren. Derren was dead. The realization made him press his eyes shut again, but no matter how hard he pressed, nothing would change the reality he had awakened to. He still refused to believe it. They'd had a plan and discussed it all night. They were going to get their army, sail back, and defend the Domain. Adrian took in a deep breath. He did not fight the tears. Seraph be damned—she wasn't watching. His throat was burning and raw, and he tried to swallow it down, but that only made it flare in pain.

He coughed, slowly straightening himself, but something moved in the gloom of his bedchamber. A man, standing by the window. Adrian squinted in the half light, heart racing, eyes searching but barely making out the man's features. They were mostly shadow but for the piercing green eyes. Almost like Kahlia's . . .

Adrian sat up as he recognized the Xakhar. Had he come to finish his daughter's work?

"Your eminence. I . . ." He looked down at his clothes, then around at his room and the tiny fragments of shattered glass. He could still taste blood on his tongue.

"There is no need for formality." The Xakhar's voice was oddly common, and he spoke perfect Othonean. "You have proven yourself serviceable enough."

Serviceable? For what?

"I did not expect . . ." There was so much Adrian had not expected, he could barely put it into words.

The Xakhar turned away from him. "No time is more important than our own time to grieve, Prince Adrian, yet I am told we have little of it where this matter of yours is concerned."

Adrian's chest tightened. The Xakhar surely meant his son, not Derren, but the thought of the old guard stabbed at him just the same. "Yes, Your Eminence."

"Then there is not a moment to spare. I have decided to take up your father's offer, and so has my daughter."

"Offer?"

The Xakhar waved a piece of parchment in Adrian's direction. "Humility is too often mistaken for ignorance, young prince. There is no need for it now."

Adrian took the parchment, frowning down at the words. It bore the royal Othonean seal and an elaborate signature at the bottom in his father's own hand.

"The ceremony is being prepared, yet it is still a royal marriage. In this, there will have to be patience on your part."

Adrian looked back to the Xakhar, then down at the message, trying to make sense of the written words as well as the ones spoken by the Azuri ruler. Kahlia had talked about joining bloodlines, but never theirs. Maybe he was still asleep—some nightmarish aftereffect of the poison, surely. Why would she marry him after knowing what he'd tried? Did she think she was so in control that he would not be a threat? Whatever it was, she did not seem to have told her father about Adrian's attempted betrayal.

"I understand this is sudden," the Xakhar said, "but we've agreed time is of the essence, have we not?"

"Ahm . . . . Yes, Your Eminence."

"Your father believes blood holds ties. Let us tie ourselves in an alliance the likes of which this world has never seen. You will have my army at your back, and when you've dealt with these rampaging madmen, both continents will quake at our feet. You will find we can be hard to convince but are fierce allies once all the haggling is done. In Azur, the bonded are true family. You may address me as *Father*. You will be considered my family, my blood."

Adrian had a vacant stare, and for once he was thankful for the shadows. His thoughts were still stumbling out of sleep, and Myrra was still too present in his heart to even consider the offer. For a moment he almost wished he'd known more about the Azuri customs and understood what it would feel like to preserve her memory. But the mask of her dead face flashed in Adrian's mind, and he was reminded that even the memories had been tainted. He tightened his grip on the bedsheets. It felt like a betrayal to accept marriage, especially one arranged by Father, but how else would he avenge what had been done to her?

It was the path he had laid out. The path Derren had died for. This marriage would not be out of love, only necessity. And there was still the matter of what Jovu and Father had been after in the clanlands. That seemed so distant now it hardly mattered. But Adrian knew better than to forget something Father had been so intent on uncovering. Maybe this marriage was just another of Father's requests he could not deny. He looked up to the Xakhar, and the answer that came to his tongue was the same it had always been.

"Yes, Father."

Adrian had been moved to more suitable rooms, overlooking the courtyard where Derren's life had been taken. He kept the curtains closed and was thankful he hardly had any time to even consider looking out of them. Attendants of every kind labored over him, measuring, questioning, arguing amongst themselves on sizes, colors, and styles for the event. It helped keep his mind off Derren, and the tightness in his chest slowly gave way as his thoughts were occupied by a thousand unimportant decisions that were made to sound as if every life around him hinged on Adrian's correct reply.

He eventually settled on the white and silver of the Church, as was proper of his title. Word would reach the Pontiff. Best to have some show of consideration. He let them include a hint of Othonean red, though, as word would certainly also reach Father.

The Othonean delegation arrived on the sixth day of preparation. It was nothing more than a formality on his father's behalf, and absent the king and even Ellana, but that was to be expected. They would never set foot on heathen soil. The Xakhar did not seem to view it as a slight, refusing to consider the Othonean king a necessity and belittling him in his own right by doing so. The game continued, and Adrian was just a pawn they were grappling over once more, but he would not serve them. He'd lost too much to bow to their will.

The morning of the ninth day came, the day of the marriage. Adrian had requested his clothes to be light, but it seemed the tailor had overruled him. His garments were as heavy as armor, and Adrian was already sweating before his aides were halfway through helping him into the outfit. They were still peppering him with questions, but he didn't answer. Talking had become a painful endeavor after shredding his mouth with the glass vial, and the discussions throughout the preparations had not allowed it to fully heal.

Adrian eventually pushed them away. He'd held on enough. His Legion was waiting.

"You won't have died for nothing," he whispered, holding Myrra's amulet and thinking on Derren, then made his way down and stepped through the courtyard towards the rounded Azuri temple where the marriage would be held.

The scent of nightshade filled the air, and Adrian had to hold his breath while crossing the courtyard. His own poisoning had been bad enough, but now the smell brought back the memory of Derren's pained face as life left him, and that pain was too much to bear.

Adrian looked up. Only the searing sun—no mark, no Seraph watching over him. Not that he'd ever cared, but it would be nice to have someone. He scoffed. The Seraph was not that, and he should know better than to let his thoughts be taken by the tools of the Pontiff. All that mattered was his blood. It was what had gotten him this far. It was all he could put his faith in. He squared his shoulders and plowed on, puffing out his breath to get rid of the scent, yet his stomach was still in a tight knot.

He paused before the temple doors, copper shining so bright against the white walls that Adrian could hardly keep his eyes open. He ran his tongue along the back of his teeth. No reason to be nervous. It would all be over soon.

I'm sorry, Myrra.

The doors were flung open, and countless heads turned his way. A priest was chanting in Azuri, almost screaming. Adrian caught a few of the words—"over the sea," "foreign," and "alliance"—but they faded away when his gaze found Kahlia.

Her dress was close cut, highlighting her back and neck, colored like the sea, shifting from green to blue as she turned towards him. It paled in comparison to her glimmering eyes, eager to display the streaks of honey dancing among the shifting shades of green that caught the light all around her. She gave him that smile then. The same one from the courtyard. It might have fooled a weaker man, but it only brought a sourness to the bloody taste on Adrian's tongue. No measure of heathen beauty would ever make his heart beat like it had for Myrra. She was all that had ever mattered, all that ever would. He pressed his teeth hard, and a few more of the wounds in his mouth reopened.

Adrian swallowed it down and paced towards the raised dais

where Kahlia and the Xakhar waited beside the chanting priest. Kahlia stretched out her hand and set eager eyes on him, waiting for his lips to touch her skin. He kissed her hand with tight, dry lips, then looked at the priest, who had fallen silent.

Nasir was at Adrian's side, serving as the main representative of the Church of the Seraph, while a line of unknown Othoneans stood behind him. He'd claimed to have acted out of loyalty, but it was all Adrian could do not to throttle the man. Still, he had run out of allies, and Nasir was a necessary compromise if Adrian was to navigate this land.

I'm sorry, old friend.

"And now, we bond the blood. All that comes after will be as one. Othonea and Azur, united as a single family. Drink and show your consent before the ten consuls and the Xakhar." The Azuri priest raised a cup filled with the thick red liquid they called blood wine, reserved especially for the occasion.

He offered the cup to Adrian, who took it and drank deeply, eyes still on Kahlia, some instinct keeping him alert after being poisoned and betrayed. She was next, also keeping her eyes on him, maybe for different reasons, maybe the same. Finally, the Xakhar gulped down what remained, then returned the cup with a red smile.

"The families are bonded." The priest began his chanting again.

Kahlia still had her eyes on Adrian, but her forehead was creasing. She seemed to have grown nervous, her breaths ragged. Something was wrong. Her smile was lost. Her hand flew to her chest, and she staggered back on the steps. The Xakhar was there to hold her, but he, too, was fighting for balance. He held Kahlia, both with hopeless looks and reddening eyes locked onto Adrian. His heart was pounding, and his mind whirled as he tried to make sense of it. It couldn't be the amanthium. He'd taken the antidote, and it wouldn't have held for this long. Adrian turned a frown at Nasir, but the priest looked as surprised as any.

Guards surrounded them, facing the crowd, and Adrian's hand dashed to his belt, groping for a nonexistent sword. He took a step closer to Nasir, gaze jumping around the room. Consuls were on their feet, screaming in outrage, others quietly making their way away from the commotion. The Xakhar's hands moved aimlessly, and Kahlia was on the ground, back arched, desperate for air, gasping as she fought for breath. Her eyes were so red now they were bleeding. Her father's were the same.

One of the old consuls, Lord Attar, rushed forward and pressed at her chest. "Get a physicker!" he yelled in Azuri. "A healer! Anything! Now!"

The blood spread around Kahlia's eyes and blackened, pooling on the surrounding skin. Adrian could only watch, wide-eyed, as Kahlia regained her breath for a moment. Her eyes flashed with rage, and she clambered to her feet, taken by the frenzy Adrian had seen too many times now. She darted forward and clawed at Adrian, tearing a gash on the side of his face, but that was all the strength she had left.

Her hand fell limp, and she lay beside her father, both trembling on the ground, bodies writhing, faces growing pale while the blackness around their eyes grew deeper.

The Azuri were still desperately trying to find a savior, but Adrian was too stunned by the wave of cold understanding to move. This was no poison. This was no coup. A healer would do nothing: they'd be dead before any arrived.

Nasir stepped close to Adrian, alert but unrattled.

"Looks like your blood does hold ties, Lord Light. Only not the ones we imagined, it would seem."

A NOTE TO THE READER

Dear Reader,

Thank you so much for reading *A Touch of Light*!

I truly hope you enjoyed your first dive into Avarin. I can't wait to show you more. Having readers not only read my book, but also review it means the world to me. Reviews are an author's life's blood. They make sure more people get to know my book exists! If you wouldn't mind writing a review either on Amazon or Goodreads that would be amazing! I'd love to know your thoughts, good or bad.

Muito obrigado! (*Thank you very much!* in Portuguese)

Thiago

ACKNOWLEDGMENTS

The first person I would like to thank is you. Thank you for reading, and I truly hope you enjoyed the ride.

The following people are the reason this story has been put into words. I would like to extend my deepest gratitude to:

Julian Delfino, my editor at The Editorial Department, for his unwavering dedication and belief in this story. He captured the soul of what I had imagined for Avarin and made it better in every way. This story truly would not have been possible without him.

Ross Browne, Jacqueline Sinclair, and John Robert Marlow at The Editorial Department for incredible support and help with the prologue, as well as enlightening me on the self-publishing path.

A very special thank you to Pedro 'Ped' Khouzam who supported me from the start, and tirelessly read through rough drafts.

All of my friends and family who believed in this story and were kind enough to read something that was not in their native language. I deeply appreciate the time you dedicated to me.

And, of course, Erica, my incredible wife, who dived into this journey with me, and kept me afloat through it all.

ABOUT THE AUTHOR

 Thiago was born in Brazil but grew up in the fantasy worlds from the stories he kept in his mind. He has inhabited everywhere from Middle-Earth and Azeroth to the planes of Dominaria, Ravnica and Tarkir. No matter the medium, what kept him coming back was always his love for story.

He could never wait for the next world to dive into, so, after being (indirectly) urged on by the (printed) words of Joe Abercrombie, Mark Lawrence, Patrick Rothfuss, N. K. Jemisin and many, many others, decided to create his own.

Printed in the USA
CPSIA information can be obtained
at www.ICGtesting.com
LVHW091612241023
761966LV00006B/770